PANAMA
And the Canal

IN PICTURE AND PROSE

A complete story of Panama, as well as the history, purpose
and promise of its world-famous canal—the most
gigantic engineering undertaking since
the dawn of time

Approved by leading officials connected with the great enterprise

By WILLIS J. ABBOT
Author of The Story of Our Navy, American Merchant Ships and Sailors, Etc.

Water-colors by
E. J. READ and GORDON GRANT

Profusely illustrated by over 600 unique and attractive photographs taken
expressly for this book by our special staff

Published in English and Spanish by

SYNDICATE PUBLISHING COMPANY

LONDON   NEW YORK   TORONTO
HAVANA   BUENOS AIRES

1913

CONTENTS

LIST OF COLORED ILLUSTRATIONS

LIST OF BLACK AND WHITE ILLUSTRATIONS

3

INTRODUCTION

PANAMA. They say the word means "a place of many fishes," but there is some dissension about the exact derivation of the name of the now severed Isthmus. Indeed dissension, quarrels, wars and massacres have been the prime characteristics of Panama for four hundred years. "A place of many battles" would be a more fitting significance for the name of this tiny spot where man has been doing ceaseless battle with man since history rose to record the conflicts. As deadly as the wars between men of hostile races, has been the unceasing struggle between man and nature.

You will get some faint idea of the toll of life taken in this conflict if from Cristobal you will drive out to the picturesque cemetery at Mount Hope and look upon the almost interminable vista of little white headstones. Each marks the last resting place of some poor fellow fallen in the war with fever, malaria and all of tropic nature's fierce and fatal allies against all conquering man. That war is never ended. The English and the Spaniards have laid down their arms. Cimmaroon and conquistadore, pirate and buccaneer no longer steal stealthily along the narrow jungle trails. But let man forget for a while his vigilance and the rank, lush growth of the jungle creeps over his clearings, his roads, his machinery, enveloping all in morphic arms

of vivid green, delicate and beautiful to look upon, but tough, stubborn and fiercely resistant when attacked. Poisoned spines guard the slender tendrils that cling so tenaciously to every vantage point. Insects innumerable are sheltered by the vegetable chevaux-de-frise and in turn protect it from the assaults of any human enemy. Given a few months to reëstablish itself and the jungle, once subdued, presents to man again a defiant and an almost impenetrable front. We boast that we have conquered nature on the Isthmus, but we have merely won a truce along a comparatively narrow strip between the oceans. Eternal vigilance will be the price of safety even there.

If that country alone is happy whose history is uninteresting, then sorrow must have been the ordained lot of Panama. Visited first by Columbus in 1502, at which time the great navigator put forth every effort to find a strait leading through to the East Indies, it has figured largely in the pages of history ever since. Considerable cities of Spanish foundation rose there while our own Jamestown and Plymouth were still unimagined. The Spaniards were building massive walls, erecting masonry churches, and paving royal roads down there in the jungle long before the

Photo by H. Pittier.   Courtesy American Geographic Magazine, Washington.
THE SENTINEL TREE

5

palisades and log huts of Plymouth rose on the sandy shores of Cape Cod bay. If the ruins of the first city of Panama, draped with tropical vines, are all that remain of that once royal city, its successor founded in 1673 still stands with parts of the original walls sturdily resisting the onslaught of time.

It appears there are certain advantages about geographical littleness. If Panama had been big the eyes of the world would never have been fastened upon it. Instinctively Columbus sought in each of its bays, opening from the Caribbean that strait which should lead to far Cathay. Seeking the same mythical passage Balboa there climbed a hill where

"— with eagle eyes,
He star'd at the Pacific—and all his men
Look'd at each other with a wild surmise
Silent upon a peak in Darien."

Hope of a natural strait abandoned, the narrowness of the Isthmus made it the shortest route for Cortez, Pizarro and other famous Spanish robbers and murderers to follow in their quest for the gold of the Incas. As the Spaniards spoiled Peru, so the buccaneers and other international pirates, mostly English, robbed and murdered the Spaniards. The gold fever filled the narrow Isthmus full of graves, and of moldering bodies for which there was not even hasty sepulture. In time the Peruvian hoards were exhausted, Spaniards and Englishmen, buccaneers and pirates vanished. Then came a new invasion—this time by a nation unknown in the days of the Great Trade and the Royal Road. Gold had been discovered in California, and now troops of Americans fought their way through the jungle, and breasted the rapids of the Chagres River. They sought gold as had Pizarro and Cortez, but they sought it with spade and pan, not with sword and musket. In their wake came the Panama Railroad, a true pioneer of international trade. Then sprung up once more the demand for the waterway across the neck which Columbus had sought in vain.

The story of the inception and completion of the canal is the truly great chapter in the history of Panama. Not all the gold from poor Peru that Pizarro sent across the Isthmus to fatten the coffers of kings or to awaken the cupidity and cunning of the buccaneers equals what the United States alone has expended to give to the trade of the world the highway so long and so fruitlessly sought. An act of unselfish bounty, freely given to all the peoples of the earth, comes to obliterate at last the long record of international perfidy, piracy and plunder which is the history of Panama.

This book is being written in the last days of constructive work on the Panama Canal. The tens of thousands of workmen, the hundreds of officers are preparing to scatter to their homes in all parts of the world. The pleasant and hospitable society of the Zone of which I have written is breaking up. Vil-

SCENE ON OTOQUE ISLAND, PANAMA BAY

THE RANK, LUSH GROWTH OF THE JUNGLE

lages are being abandoned, and the water of Gatun Lake is silently creeping up and the green advance guard of the jungle swiftly stealing over the forsaken ground. While this book is yet new much that I have written of as part of the program of the future will indeed have become part of the record of the past.

I think that anyone who visited the Canal Zone during the latter years of construction work will have carried away with him a very pleasant and lively recollection of a social life and hospitality that was quite ideal. The official centers at Culebra and Ancon, the quarters of the army at Camp Otis and the navy and marine corps at Camp Elliott were ever ready to entertain the visitor from the states and his enjoyment was necessarily tinged with regret that the charming homes thrown open to him were but ephemeral, and that the passage of the

first ship through the canal would mark the beginning of their dismantling and abandonment. The practiced traveler in every clime will find this eagerness of those who hold national outposts, whether ours in the Philippines, or the British in India and Hong Kong, to extend the glad hand of welcome to one from home, but nowhere have I found it so thoroughly the custom as on the Canal Zone. No American need fear loneliness who goes there.

In the chapter on "Social Life on the Canal Zone" I have tried to depict this colonial existence, so different from the life of the same people when in "the states" and yet so full of a certain "hominess" after all. It does not seem to me that we Americans cling to our home customs when on foreign stations quite so tenaciously as do the British—though I observed that the Americans on the Zone played baseball quite as religiously as the

British played cricket. Perhaps we are less tenacious of afternoon tea than they, but women's clubs flourish on the Zone as they do in Kansas, while as for bridge it proceeds as uninterruptedly as the flow of the dirt out of the Culebra Cut.

Nobody could return from the Zone without a desire to express thanks for the hospitalities shown him and the author is fortunate in possessing the opportunity to do so publicly. Particularly do I wish to acknowledge indebtedness or aid in the preparation of this book to Col. George W. Goethals, Chairman and Engineer in Chief, and to Col. W. C. Gorgas, Commissioner and Chief Sanitary Officer. It goes without saying that without the friendly aid and coöperation of Col. Goethals no adequate description of the canal work and the life of the workers could ever be written. To the then Secretary of War, Hon. Henry L. Stimson, under whose able administration of the Department of War much of the canal progress noted in this book was made, the author is indebted for personal and official introductions, and to Hon. John Barrett, one time United States Minister to Colombia and now Director General of the Pan American Union, much is owed for advice and suggestion from a mind richly stored with Latin-American facts.

On the Canal Zone Hon. Joseph B. Bishop, Secretary of the Isthmian Canal Commission, Hon. Maurice H. Thatcher, Civil Governor, and Mr. H. H. Rousseau, the naval member of the Commission, were particularly helpful. Thanks are cordially extended to Prof. F. A. Gause, the superintendent of schools, who has built up on the Canal Zone an educational system that cannot fail to affect favorably the schools of the surrounding Republic of Panama; to Mr. Walter J. Beyer, the engineer in charge of lighthouse construction, and to Mr. A. B. Dickson who, by his active and devoted work in the development of the Y. M. C. A. clubs on the Zone, has created a feature of its social life which is absolutely indispensable.

The illustration of a book of this nature would be far from complete were the work of professional photographers alone relied upon. Of the army of amateurs who have kindly contributed to its pages I wish to thank Prof. H. Pittier of the Department of Agriculture, Prof. Otto Lutz, Department of Natural Science, Panama National Institute; Mr. W. Ryall Burtis, of Freehold, N. J.; Mr. Stewart Hancock Elliott, of Norwalk, Conn.; Mr. A. W. French, and Dr. A. J. Orenstein of the Department of Sanitation.

The opening of the Panama Canal does not merely portend a new era in trade, or the end of the epoch of trial and struggle on the Isthmus. It has a finality such as have few of the great works of man. Nowhere on this globe are there left two continents to be severed; two oceans to be united. Canals are yet to be dug, arms of the sea brought together. We may yet see inland channels from Boston to Galveston, and from Chicago to New York navigable by large steamships. But the union of the Mediterranean and the Red Sea at Suez, and the Atlantic and Pacific at Panama stand as man's crowning achievements in remodeling God's world. As Ambassador James Bryce, speaking of the Panama Canal, put it, "It is the greatest liberty Man has ever taken with Nature."

RUINS OF OLD PANAMA

CHAPTER I

THE FRONT DOOR TO PANAMA

HE gray sun of a bitter February day was sinking in a swirling sea as the ship doggedly plowed its way southward along the New Jersey coast. One after another the beacons that guard that perilous strip of sand twinkled out, and one after another voyagers unused to ocean's stormiest moods silently disappeared into secretive cabins. "It may be a stern and rockbound coast," said one lady with poetic reminiscence, "but I wish I was on it!" For it must be set down as a melancholy truth that the voyage from New York to Colon is as a rule tempestuous.

Most who seek the Canal Zone as mere sight-seers will choose winter for the trip, at which time wintry gales are the rule as far south as the Bahamas—after which the long smooth rollers of the tropical ocean will sufficiently try the unaccustomed stomach even though the breezes which accompany them be as mild as those of Araby the blest. In brief, to reach in winter our newest possession you must brave the ordinary discomforts of a rough voyage, and three days of biting cold weather as well, unless you sail from New Orleans, or the terminus of Mr. Flagler's new over-sea railroad at Key West.

Despite its isthmian character, the Canal Zone, Uncle Sam's most southerly outpost, may be called an island, for the travelers' purpose. True it is bordered on but two sides by water, and thus far violates the definition of an island. But it is only to be reached by water. The other two sides are walled in by the tangled jungle where vegetation grows so rank and lush that animal life is stunted and beaten in the struggle for existence by the towering palms, clustering ferns and creeping vines. Only things that crawl on their bellies like the serpent accursed in Eden grow to their fullest estate in this network of rustling green. Lions there are, by the talk of the natives at least, but when you encounter them

they turn out to be mere stunted specimens of our northern wild cat. The deer, rarely met, are dwarfed but are the largest animals to be found in the jungle, though one hears reports of giant boas. Indeed the remnants of the age of reptiles are large to our eyes, though puny in comparison with the giants that scientists christened, long centuries after they were extinct and unable to protest, with such names as ichthyosaurus. You will still find lizards or iguana, three to five feet long, if your search of the jungle be thorough. The tapir, or ant eater, too, grows to huge size. But it is not dread of wild animals that keeps man from penetrating the jungle. The swift growing and impenetrable vegetation blocks the paths

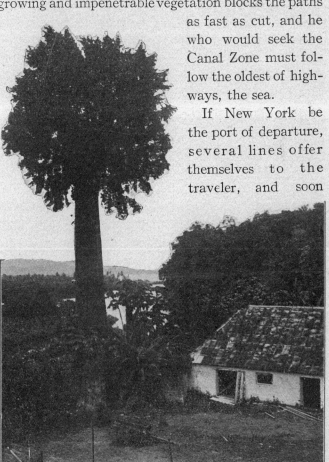

as fast as cut, and he who would seek the Canal Zone must follow the oldest of highways, the sea.

If New York be the port of departure, several lines offer themselves to the traveler, and soon

TREE GROWING OUT OF A CHIMNEY IN JAMAICA

after the canal is opened their number will be increased. At present the Panama Railroad Company, owned by the government, maintains a line of ships mainly for the carriage of supplies and employes of the Canal Commission. There is already discussion of the wisdom of abandoning this line after the construction work is over, on the ground that the United States government has no right to enter into the business of water transportation in competition

CANE RIVER FALLS

with private parties. If sold by the government, however, the line will doubtless be maintained under private ownership. The United Fruit Company, an American corporation with an impressive fleet of ships all flying the British flag, also carries passengers to the Isthmus from New York and New Orleans, as does the Hamburg-American Line, from New York only. My own voyage was by the Royal Mail Steam Packet line, an historic organization chartered in 1839 for the express purpose of bringing England into closer touch with its West Indian colonies. The excellent ships of this line, sailing fortnightly from New York, touch at the little port of Antilla

on the northern shore of Cuba, spend twenty-four hours at Jamaica and reach Colon on the eighth day of the voyage. Thence the ship plows along through our American Mediterranean, touching at Trinidad, St. Kitts, Barbadoes and other British colonial outposts until at last she turns into the open ocean, buffeting her way eastward to Gibraltar and Southampton, her home port.

A real bit of England afloat is the "Oruba" with officers clad on festive occasions in full dress uniforms closely resembling those of the Royal Navy, and stewards who never dropped dishes in a storm but dropped their h's on the slightest provocation. "'E's in the 'old, mum," explained one when a lady inquired for the whereabouts of a missing dog. It is wonderful after all how persistent are the British manners and customs in the places the English frequent. From the breakfast tea, bloaters and marmalade, to the fish knives sensibly served with that course at dinner, but which finicky Americans abjure, all about the table on these ships is typically English. In the colonies you find drivers all turning to the left, things are done "directly" and not "right away," every villa has its tennis court, and Piccadilly, Bond St., and Regent Street are never missing from the smallest colonial towns.

But to return to the voyage. For four days we steamed south along a course as straight as though drawn by a ruler. For three days the wind blew bitter and cutting, the seas buffeted the weather side of the ship with resounding blows, and the big dining saloon displayed a beggarly array of empty seats. Betwixt us and Africa was nothing but a clear course for wind and wave, and both seemed to suffer from speed mania. Strange noises rose from the cabins; stewardesses looked business-like and all-compelling as they glided along the narrow corridors. Hardened men in the smoke room kept their spirits up by pouring spirits down, and agreed that the first leg of a voyage to Colon was always a beastly one.

But by the morning of the fourth day a change comes over the spirit of our dreams. The wind still blows, but it is soft, tempered to the shorn lamb. The ship still rolls, but the mysterious organ called the stomach has become attuned to the motion and ladies begin to reappear on the deck. The deck chairs so blithely rented at New York are no longer untenanted, and we cease to look upon the deck steward who took our money as a confidence man. A glance at the chart at noon shows us off the northern coast of Florida and the deep blue of the water betokens the Gulf Stream. Next morning men begin to don their white suits, and the sailors wander about barefooted. A bright girl suggests

vessel plainly visible—for this is believed to be the first land sighted by Columbus. Of that there is some debate, but there is always debate on shipboard and any event that will furnish a topic is welcome. Everything about the ship now has turned tropical. The shady deck becomes popular, and the 240 pound ship's doctor in immaculate

THE ROAD TO MARKET

A typical highway of Jamaica, followed by natives going to Kingston

that a voyage from New York to the tropics is like a shower bath taken backwards, and we all are glad that the warm water faucet is at last turned on.

The first land we sight after the Jersey coast has faded away is Watling Island, in the Bahamas. Everybody looks at it eagerly—a long, low-lying coast with a slender lighthouse, a fishing village and the wreck of a square rigged

white linen with the cutest little shell jacket after the Royal Navy pattern becomes a subject for wonder and admiration.

Antilla, the first stopping place on the way south, is a cluster of houses on a spacious bay on the northern side of Cuba, connected with Santiago and Havana. Doubtless some day it may become a notable shipping point, and indeed the shores of the bay are dotted with great sugar houses and carpeted with fields of shimmering green cane. But today only a lighter load of timber and a few tropical products are shipped— that is if we except a bunch of tourists who have come this far on the way to Colon by rail and the short sea trip from Florida to Cuba. Most of them were in doubt whether they had improved upon the discomfort of four rough days at sea by

mended by people who don't get sick, now pines for exercise and entertainment. Young men normally sane, bestride an horizontal boom and belabor each other with pillows until one or both fall to the hospitable mattress below. Other youths, greatly encouraged by the plaudits of fair ones, permit themselves to be trussed up like fowls exposed for sale, and, with ungainly hops and lurches, bunt into each other until one

SPORTS ON

electing twenty-four hours of rough riding on the Cuban railway instead.

Past the quarantine station which, with its red-topped hospital, looks like a seashore resort, we steam, and the boat's prow is again turned southward. Jamaica, our next port of call, is thirty-six hours away, and at last we have placid blue water from which the flying fish break in little clouds, and a breeze suggestive of the isles of spice. The ship's company which two days back was largely content with cots, and the innumerable worthless remedies for seasickness, always recom-

THE "ORUBA"

SHIPBOARD

is toppled to the deck. The human cockfight brings loud applause which attains its apogee when some spectator at the critical moment with a shrill cock-a-doodle-doo displays an egg. A ship in the tropics is the truest of playgrounds. We are beginning to feel the content of just living which characterizes the native of the tropics. Indeed when the deck is cleared and waxed, and the weather cloths and colored lights brought forth for the ball, most of the men who left New York full of energy find themselves too languid to participate. I don't know whether the Royal Mail exacts of its officers an aptitude for the dance, but their trim white uniforms were always much in evidence when the two-step was in progress.

Early on the second day out from Cuba a heavy gray mass showed clear on the horizon to the south-west. It is reported by the historians that when Queen Isabella once asked Columbus what Jamaica

to the water. In early morn the crests of the hills are draped with clouds, and from the valleys betwixt them masses of white mist come rolling out as the rays of the sun heat the atmosphere. For forty miles or so you steam along this coast with scarce an acre of level land between the mountains and the deep until in the distance you descry the

BOG WALK, JAMAICA

There are no bogs along this beautiful drive. The name was originally "Bocas del Agua," and has been corrupted to its present form

looked like he crumpled up a sheet of stiff paper in his palm, then partly smoothing it displayed it to the Queen. The illustration was apt. Nowhere does a more crinkly island rise from the sea. Up to a height of 7000 feet and more the mountains rise sheer from the sea with only here and there the narrowest strip of white beach at the base. For the most part the tropical foliage comes unthinned down

hollow in which Kingston lies embedded. A low lying sand bar runs parallel to the shore and perhaps a mile out, forming the barrier for the harbor which is indeed a noble bay well fit to shelter navies. But the barrier, though but a few feet above high water now, is sinking gradually, and the future of Kingston's harbor is somewhat distressing. Once this low sandbar bore the most riotous and wicked town of history, for here stood Port Royal to which flocked the pirates and buccaneers of the Spanish Main, with their booty—doubloons, pieces of eight, beauteous Spanish señoritas and all the other attractive plunder with which the dime novels of our youth made us familiar. A right merry spot was Port Royal in those days and a pistol bullet or a

bloodiest of the savage lot, a baronet and appointed him governor of Jamaica. Now Port Royal has shrunken to a fishing village, bordering upon the abandoned British naval station at the very harbor's mouth.

One sees there the emplacements for guns, but no guns; the barracks for marines, but no men. Even

GOVERNMENT BUILDINGS, KINGSTON
The special type of reënforced concrete buildings with broad arcades is well adapted to the tropics

swift stab in the back, though common enough, only halted the merriment for one man at a time. But fire purged Port Royal, and the pleasant pursuit of piracy began to fall into disrepute. Instead of treating the gallants who sailed under the Jolly Roger as gentlemen adventurers, civilized governments began to hang them—England being the last to do them honor when she made Henry Morgan,

the flagstaff rises dismally destitute of bunting. No sign of military or naval life appears about the harbor. The first time I visited it a small British gunboat about the size of our "Dolphin" dropped anchor and sent four boatloads of jackies ashore for a frolic, but on my second visit the new Governor of the colony arrived on a Royal Mail ship, unescorted by any armed vessel, and was received without military pomp or the thunder of cannon.

The fact of the matter is that the ties uniting Jamaica to the mother country are of the very slenderest, and there are not lacking Jamaicans who would welcome a change in allegiance to the United States. The greatest product of the island is sugar.

Thus far, however, Jamaica has refused this half a loaf, wishing the preferential limited to her products alone.

Meanwhile English writers of authority are openly discussing the likelihood of Jamaica reverting to the United States. In its South American supplement the London *Times* said in 1911, speaking of

KING STREET, KINGSTON, JAMAICA

Our tariff policy denies it entrance to our market, though as I write Congress is debating a lower tariff. The British policy of a "free breakfast table" gives it no advantage in the English markets over the bounty-fed sugar of Germany. Hence the island is today in a state of commercial depression almost mortuary. An appeal to Canada resulted in that country giving in its tariff a 20 per cent advantage to the sugar and fruit of the British West Indies.

the United States: "Its supremacy in the Gulf of Mexico and in the Caribbean Sea is today practically undisputed; there can be little doubt, therefore, that the islands of the West Indies and the outlying units of Spanish America will, upon the completion of the Panama Canal, gravitate in due course to amalgamation with the Great Republic of the North." And Mr. Archibald Colquhoun, an authoritative writer on British West Indian policy, said about the same time: "It is certain that Jamaica, and other West Indian Islands, in view of the local geographical and economic conditions—and especially in view of the change which will be wrought in those conditions by the opening of the Panama Canal—must sooner or later decide between Canada and the United States."

This situation may lead the Imperial Government to throw Jamaica a sop in the shape of heavy expenditures for fortifications, a large resident garrison and a permanent naval station. But it is unlikely. If Kingston is within easy striking distance of the Canal, it is within easier striking distance of our powerful naval base at Guantanamo. The monopoly of striking is not conferred on any one power, and the advantage of striking first would be open to either.

Not impressive as viewed from the water, the town is even less so when considered in the intimacy of its streets. An air of gray melancholy pervades it all. In 1907 an earthquake rent the town into fragments, and the work of rebuilding is but begun. Ruins confront you on every hand, the ruins of edifices that in their prime could have been nothing but commonplace, and in this day of their disaster have none of the dignity which we like to discover in mute memorials of a vanished past. Over all broods a dull, drab mantle of dust. The glorious trees, unexcelled in variety and vigor, have their richly varying hues dulled by the dust, so that you may not know how superb indeed is the coloring of leaf and flower except after one of the short sharp tropical rains that washes away the pall and sets the gutters roaring with a chocolate colored flood.

Making due allowance for the tropical vegetation and the multitudinous negro, there is much that is

JAMAICA, WHERE MOTORING IS GOOD

DUKE STREET, KINGSTON, JAMAICA

Beauty, dignity and pathos abide in the residence streets of the ancient colonial town. Hard times for sugar planters, even more than the earthquake, have cast a gloom over the community.

WOMEN ON THE WAY TO MARKET
"The woman or the donkey furnishes transportation"

characteristically English about Kingston. The houses of the better class of people, however fragile in construction, stand somewhat back from the street, guarded by ponderous brick walls in order that the theory "every Englishman's house is his castle" may be literally maintained. And each house has its name painted conspicuously on its gate posts. The names are emphatically English and their grandeur bears no apparent relation to the size of the edifice. Sometimes they reach into literature. I saw one six-room cottage labeled "Birnamwood," but looked in vain about the neighborhood for Dunsinane.

The town boasts a race course, and the triple pillars of English social life, cricket, lawn tennis and afternoon tea, are much in evidence. The Governor is always an Englishman and his home government,

which never does things by halves, furnishes him with a stately official residence and a salary of £5000 a year. The Episcopal Archbishop of the West Indies resident there is an Englishman. But most of the heads of official departments are Jamaicans, which is quite as it should be, for out of the 850,000 people in the island only about 1660, according to the census of 1911, were born in England, Scotland or Ireland. Furthermore the number of "men from home" is relatively decreasing, although their influence is still potent. Even the native Jamaican of the more cultivated class speaks of England as home, and as a rule he spends his holidays there. Yet the keenest observers declare that the individual Englishman in Jamaica always remains much of a stranger to the native people. He is not as adaptable even as the American, and it is asserted that American influence in the island grows even as British domination is weakened.

One home feature which the English have impressed upon the islands is good roads. The highways leading from Kingston up into the hills and across the island to Port Antonio and other places are models of road making. They are of the highest economic value, too, for in marketing farm products the one railroad is but little used. Nearly everything is brought from farm to market on the heads of the striding women, or in straw panniers slung over the backs of patient donkeys. Amazing are the loads these two patient beasts of burden—biped and quadruped—bear. Once in a while a yoke of oxen, or a one horse cart is seen, but in the main the woman or the donkey furnishes transportation. To the Jamaican there is nothing wrong with the

verbiage of the Tenth Commandment to which our progressive women take violent exception. To him there is nothing anomalous in lumping in his or his neighbor's wife with "his ox or his ass." So the country roads on a market day are an unending panorama of human life, of women plodding to market—often a two days' journey—with a long swinging stride, burden firmly poised on head, or returning with smaller loads gossiping and laughing with much gleaming of white teeth as the stranger passes. The roads are a paradise for automobilists—smooth, of gentle grade, with easy curves and winding through the most beautiful scenery of tropic hillsides and rushing waters. Only the all-pervading dust mars the motorists' pleasure.

If the air is dusty, the prevailing complexion is dusky. For in this island of about 850,000 people

A YARD AND ITS TENANTS
" The huts are inconceivably small, a trifle larger than billiard tables "

only about 15,000 are listed in the census as "white," and the whiteness of a good many of these is admittedly tarnished by a "touch of the tarbrush." As in every country in which any social relation between the races is not remorselessly tabooed —as it is in

COALING TRANSATLANTIC STEAMSHIPS

the pile and emptying it into the ship's bunkers these women received half a cent. There was no merriment about the work, no singing as among our negro roustabouts on the Mississippi. Silently with shoulders squared, hands swinging in rhythm and basket

our southern states—the number of "colored" people increases more rapidly than that of either black or white. There were in 1834, 15,000 whites out of the population of 371,000; there are today 15,605, but the blacks and mongrels have increased to more than 800,000. The gradations in color in any street group run from the very palest yellow to the blackest of Congo black. That is hardly the sort of population which the United States desires to take to its bosom.

The Jamaica negro is a natural loafer. Of course he works when he must, but betwixt the mild climate, the kindly fruits of the earth and the industry of his wife or wives, that dire necessity is seldom forced upon him. My first glimpse of industrial conditions in Jamaica was taken from the deck of a ship warping into dock at Kingston. Another ship, lying at the same dock, was being coaled. Down and up the 1000 feet or so of dock tramped long files of indescribably ragged, black and dirty figures. Those going down bore on their heads baskets piled high with coal, going back they bore the baskets empty. Of the marching figures fully two-thirds were women. With tattered skirts tucked up to the knees and the merest semblance of waists, barefooted, they plodded along. The baskets carried about 65 pounds of coal each, and for taking one from

poised firmly on the head, the women strode along, working thus for perhaps eight or nine hours and then flocking home chatting noisily as they darkened the streets and forced the white-clad tourists to shrink aside from grimy contact. On the country roads you find lines of women carrying fruit and vegetables to market, but seldom a man. Yet thus far that weaker sex has not developed a suffragette, although they support the colony.

There is much head work in Jamaica, even if there be little brain work. The negroes carry everything on their heads. The only hat I saw on a man's kinky poll was an old derby, reversed, filled with yams and thus borne steadily along. A negro given a letter to deliver will usually seek a stone to weight it down, deposit it thus ballasted amidst his wool and do the errand. In Panama an engineer told me of ordering a group of Jamaicans to load a wheel-barrow with stones and take it to a certain spot.

"Would you believe it," he said, "when they had filled that wheel-barrow, two of the niggers lifted it to their companion's head, balanced it and he walked off with it as contented as you please."

The huts in which the negroes live are as a rule inconceivably small. They are just a trifle larger than a billiard table, built of wattled cane, and plastered over with clay. The roof is usually a thatch of palm branches, though sometimes ragged strips of corrugated iron are employed with much less artistic effect. In what corresponds to our tenements, the rooming places of day laborers, the yard rather than the house is the unit. So you will see on a tiny shack about the size of a playhouse for

open air, adds to the gayety of life by grouping so many black families in one corral, reduces the high cost of living as our model tenements never can hope to, but makes one black landlord independent, for the possession of a yard with its rooms all rented leaves nothing needed for enjoyment except a

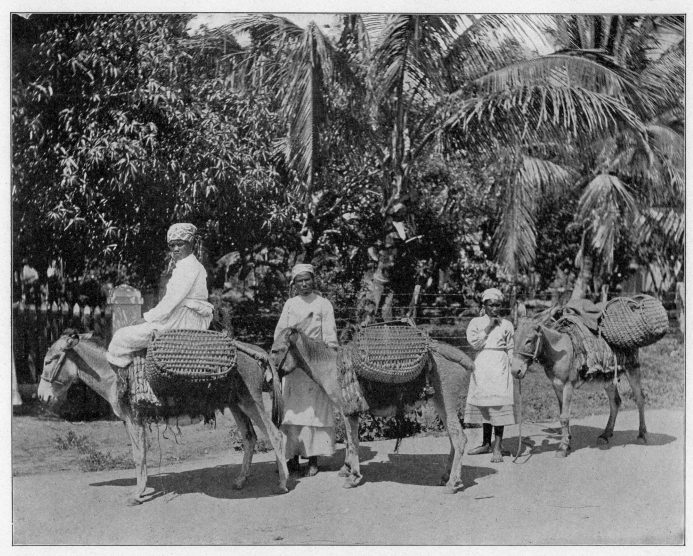

MARKET WOMEN AND THEIR DONKEYS
The true industrial forces of Jamaica.   Men are seldom seen as carriers or sellers of produce

children the sign, "Rooms for Rent," which applies not to the pigmy edifice bearing it, but to the cluster of huts set down helter skelter in the yard. The people sleep in the huts, incidentally barring them so far as the flimsy construction permits against any possible entrance of fresh air. All the other activities of life are conducted in the open—cooking, eating, sewing, gossiping. A yard is the most social place imaginable, and the system not only contributes to health by keeping people in the

phonograph and an ample supply of the rum for which the island is famous.

Racially the Jamaica peasant is a negro, with varying admixtures of white blood. The mongrel breed is steadily increasing and the pure white population relatively decreasing. Economically the peasant is either a day laborer or a servant, and as 40,000 are classed as servants in a population where the employing class is limited, it follows that employers keep many servants and the supply always exceeds the demand. Children come rapidly to the Jamaicans. Marriage is easy and to dispense with it easier still, so that 62 per cent of the births are illegitimate. "My people are very religious," said a missionary proudly, "but, dear me, how immoral they are!"

When girls are about twelve years old the mothers, tired of supporting them, for that task is seldom assumed by the fathers, take them to town on the first market day. The little produce being sold, the pair proceed from house to house seeking some "kine missus" who will take a school girl. In the end the child becomes the property of whoever will clothe, feed and shelter her. Pay is not expected, though when she grows helpful she is sometimes given an occasional gift of silver. The rights of the mistress are patriarchal, and whether or not she spoils the child the rod is seldom spared. When she gets to be seventeen or so the girl suddenly disappears in the night, with a bundle of her clothing. The inevitable man has crossed her path and she has gone to be his companion and slave.

When you think of it there is not much economic change in her situation. She worked for her mistress for nothing— she does the same for her husband, or more commonly for her "friend." He may work spasmodically for her when the need of actual money compels, but as a rule she is the wage earner. Always she tends the little garden and takes its slender produce to market. Sometimes she joins the coal-bearing Amazons down at the steamship docks. Often she goes back to the family which brought her up and offers her services

anew—this time for a wage. Every house has two or three boxes a few feet away serving for servants' quarters, but a girl of this type will decline these, renting instead a shack in a "yard," taking there daily the materials for her dinner usually provided

ONE WAY OF CARRYING BANANAS

At the docks of the United Fruit Co., mechanical carriers, so perfected as not to bruise the fruit, have replaced the leisurely negro

by her mistress. At its door, in a brazier, or a tiny stove, she will cook the meal for the idle "husband" and the children who arrive with mechanical regularity. After supper there is the gossip of the dozen or more women in the yard.

The rebuilding of Kingston, compelled by the earthquake, is proceeding apace. The town will lose much in quaintness, one can see that by the ruins of some of the older structures in which stately colonial outlines can be traced. But it will gain in adaptation to the climate and the ever-present

back from the street, are of a type that suggests the streets of India, and are also of reinforced concrete. It is the belief of the authorities that the comparative lightness of this material coupled with its resistant powers will enable it to survive any earthquake. The whole period of the shock of 1907 barely exceeded ten seconds, but its wreckage will not be repaired in ten years.

The cargo that we have taken on from the spice-scented dock is technically called a "cargo of black ivory," made up of negroes sailing for Colon to work on the "big job." Good-natured, grinning negroes these, though I have heard that, on the smaller ships that carry them by hundreds for the 500 miles for five dollars each, they sometimes riot and make trouble. With us they were inoffensive, though it is perhaps as well that the passenger quarters are to windward of them. The religious sentiment is strong upon them and as the sun goes down in the waste of waters the wail of hymn tunes sung to the accompaniment of a fiddle and divers mouth organs rises over the whistle of the wind and the rumble of the machinery. One can but reflect that ten years ago, before the coming of Col. Gorgas and his sanitation system, three out of five of these

"GWINE TO DE BIG JOB"

earthquake menace. The main business street— King Street, of course, being a British colony— is lined on either side with arcaded concrete buildings of a uniform type. Ceilings are high, windows large and one may walk the three long blocks of the busiest business section without emerging from the shady arcades. The government buildings, occupying two full squares and setting well

happy, cheerful blacks would never return alive from the Canal Zone. Today they invite no more risk than a business man in Chicago going to his office, and when their service is ended the United States government is obligated to return them to Jamaica where for a time their money will make them the idols of the markets, lanes and yards.

CHAPTER II

CRISTOBAL–COLON; AND THE PANAMA RAILROAD

COLON is the most considerable town on the Caribbean Coast north and west of Cartagena. It is in fact two towns, the older one which is still subject to the jurisdiction of the Republic of Panama and which is properly called Colon; and the new or American town which is in the Canal Zone and is called Cristobal. The two are separated only by an imaginary line, though if you want to mail a letter in Colon you must use a Panama stamp, while if you get into trouble—civil or criminal—in that camp of banditti you will have meted out to you the particular form of justice which Panamanian judges keep expressly for unlucky Gringoes who fall into their clutches. The combined towns are called Cristobal-Colon, or in our vernacular Christopher Columbus. The name is half French, half Spanish, and the town is a medley of all nations. For half a century there has been trouble of various sorts about the name of the spot—which is a sort of caldron of trouble any way. The United States wanted to call the port Aspinwall, after the principal promoter of the Panama Railroad which had its terminus there, but Colombia, which at that time controlled the Isthmus, insisted on the name Colon, and finally enforced its contention by refusing to receive at its post office letters addressed to "Aspinwall." This vigorous action was effective and the United States postal authorities were obliged to notify users of the mails that there was no longer any such place on the world's map as Aspinwall.

The dignity of our outraged nation had to be maintained, however, and when, a little later, the commission of our Consul at Colon expired, the State Department refused to replace him because it ignored the existence of such a place as Colon, while Colombia would not admit the existence of an Aspinwall

TORO POINT LIGHT

TORO POINT BREAKWATER
Before its construction northers often made the harbor of Colon untenable for ships

form of Christopher. Hence Cristobal-Colon, the official name which appears on all accurate maps of the present day.

It is one of the traditions of the town that a tramp steamer, commanded by a German, came plowing in from the sea one morning and, passing without attention the docks of Colon, went gaily on up Limon Bay until she ran smack into the land. Being jeered at for his unusual method of navigation the captain produced his charts. "That town is Colon? No? Is it not so? Vell dere are two towns. My port is Colon. Cristobal comes first. I pass it.

within its borders. Thus for some time a good democrat was kept out of a job—it was the period of democratic ascendancy. Perhaps it was pressure for this job that led our government to yield. When the French began digging the canal they chose Limon Bay, the inlet on which Colon stands, as its Atlantic terminus and established a town of their own which they called Cristobal, being the French

THE NEW CRISTOBAL DOCKS

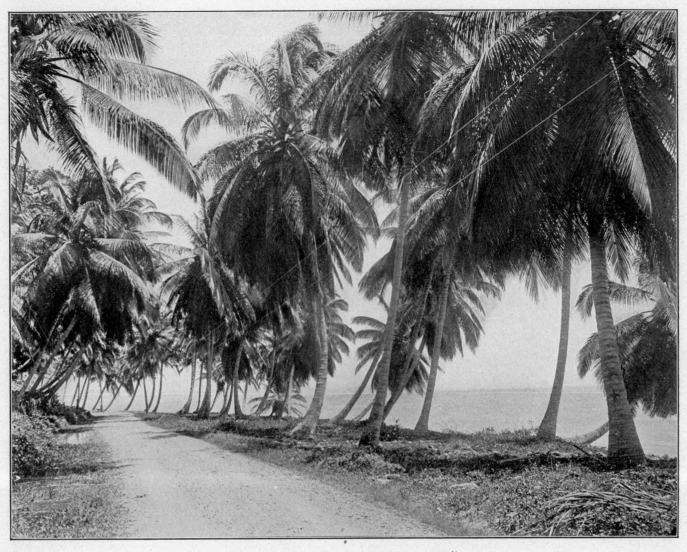

"PALMS WHICH BLEND WITH THE SEA"

I go on to Colon and by thunder dere is no Colon. Nothing but mud." It is recorded that the skipper's explanation was accepted and that he was acquitted of wilfully casting away his vessel.

We reach Colon where lie the docks of the Royal Mail in the early morning. To the right as we steam into Limon Bay is the long breakwater of Toro Point extending three miles into the Caribbean, the very first Atlantic outpost of the canal. For it was necessary to create here a largely artificial harbor, as Limon Bay affords no safe anchorage when the fierce northers sweep down along the coast. In the early days of Colon, when it was the starting point of the gold seekers' trail to Panama, ships in its harbor were compelled to cut and run for the safer, though now abandoned, harbor of Porto Bello some twenty miles down the coast.

That condition the great breakwater corrects. From the ship one sees a line of low hills forming the horizon with no break or indentation to suggest that here man is cutting the narrow gate between the oceans for the commerce of the nations to pass. The town at a distance is not unprepossessing. White houses with red roofs cluster together on a flat island scarcely above the water, and along the sea front lines of cocoanut palms bend before the breeze. No other tree seems so fitly to blend with a white beach and blue sea as this palm. Its natural curves are graceful and characteristic and in a stiff breeze it bows and sways and rustles with a grace and a music all its own.

But the picturesqueness of Colon does not long survive a closer approach. The white houses are seen to be mere frame buildings of the lightest

COLON IN 1884
The author counted twelve ocean liners one day at the docks now standing at this spot

construction which along the seafront stand out over the water on stilts. No building of any distinction meets the eye, unless it be the new Washington Hotel, a good bit of Moorish architecture, owned and conducted by the Panama Railroad which in turn is owned by the United States. The activities of Uncle Sam as a hotel keeper on the Isthmus will be worth further attention.

As we warp into the dock we observe that Colon is a seaport of some importance already. The day I reached there last I counted six British, two German, one French and three American steamships. The preponderance of British flags was not cheering to one's patriotism, and somehow the feeling that except for the Royal Mail ship, all the vessels over which they were waving were owned by American capital did not wholly allay our discontent. It is probable that in the course of the

year every foreign flag appears at Cristobal-Colon, for the ocean tramp ships are ever coming and going. In time, too, the docks, which are now rather rickety, will be worthy of the port, for the government is building modern and massive docks on the Cristobal side of the line.

At present however one lands at Colon, which has the disadvantage of depositing you in a foreign country with all the annoyances of a custom house examination to endure. Though your destination is the Canal Zone, only a stone's throw away, every piece of baggage must be opened and inspected. The search is not very thorough, and I fancy the Panama tariff is not very comprehensive, but the formality is an irritating one. Protective tariffs will never be wholly popular with travelers.

The town which greets the voyager emerging from the cool recesses of the steamship freight house looks something like the landward side of Atlantic City's famous board walk with the upper stories of the hotels sliced off. The buildings are almost without exception wood, two stories high, and with wooden galleries reaching to the curb and there supported by slender posts. It does not look foreign—merely cheap and tawdry. Block after block the lines of business follow each other in almost unvarying sequence. A saloon, a Chinese shop selling dry goods and curios, a kodak shop with curios, a saloon, a lottery agency, another saloon, a money-changer's booth, another saloon and so on for what seems about the hottest and smelliest half mile one ever walked. There is no "other side" to the street, for there run the tracks of the Panama railroad, beyond them the bay, and further along lies the American town of Cristobal where there are no stores, but only the residences and work shops of Canal workers. Between Cristobal and tinder box Colon is a wide space kept clear of houses as a fire guard.

Colon's population is as mixed as the complexions of its people. It must be admitted with regret that pure American names are most in evidence on the signboards of its saloons, and well-equipped students of the social life of the town remark that the American vernacular is the one usually proceeding from the lips of the professional gamblers. Merchandising is in the main in the hands of the Chinese, who compel one's admiration in the tropics by the intelligent way in which they have taken advantage of the laziness of the natives to capture for themselves the best places in the business community.

Most of the people in Colon live over their stores and other places of business, though back from the business section are a few comfortable looking residences, and I noticed others being built on made land, as though the beginnings of a mild "boom" were apparent. The newer houses are of concrete, as is the municipal building and chief public school. The Panama Railroad owns most of the land on

FIRE-FIGHTING FORCE AT CRISTOBAL

THE NEW WASHINGTON HOTEL

ruins stand at the mouth of the Chagres River, looked down upon busy fleets, and fell before the assaults of Sir Henry Morgan and his buccaneers while the coral island that now upholds Colon was tenanted only by pelicans, alligators and serpents. The life of man touched it when in 1850 the American railroad builders determined to make it the Atlantic terminus of the Panama road. Since then it never has lost nor will it lose a true international importance.

Manzanilla Island, on which the greater part of Colon now stands, was originally a coral reef, on which tropical vegetation had taken root, and died down to furnish soil for a new jungle until by the repe-

which the town stands, and to which it is practically limited, and the road is said to be encouraging the use of cement or concrete by builders—an exceedingly wise policy, as the town has suffered from repeated fires, in one of which, in 1911, ten blocks were swept away and 1200 people left homeless. The Isthmian Canal Commission maintains excellent fire-fighting forces both in Cristobal and Ancon, and when the local fire departments proved impotent to cope with the flames both of these forces were called into play, the Ancon engines and men being rushed by special train over the forty-five miles of railroad. Of course the fire was in foreign territory, but the Republic of Panama did not resent the invasion. Since that day many of the new buildings have been of concrete, but the prevailing type of architecture may be described as a modified renaissance of the mining shack.

It is idle to look for points of interest in Colon proper. There are none. But the history of the town though running over but sixty years is full of human interest. It did not share with Panama the life of the Spanish domination and aggression. Columbus, Balboa and the other navigators sailed by its site without heed, making for Porto Bello or Nombre de Dios, the better harbors. San Lorenzo, whose

THE ONLY STONE CHURCH IN COLON
The ritual is of the Church of England; the congregation almost wholly Jamaica negroes

tition of this process through the ages a foot or two of soil raised itself above the surface of the water and supported a swampy jungle. When the engineers first came to locate there the beginnings of the Panama railroad, they were compelled to make their quarters in an old sailing ship in danger at all times

shrubs defying entrance even to the wild beasts common to the country. In the black slimy mud of its surface alligators and other reptiles abounded, while the air was laden with pestilential vapors and swarming with sandflies and mosquitoes. These last proved so annoying to the laborers that unless their

NATURE OF COUNTRY NEAR COLON
Through this water-logged region the Panama railroad was built at heavy cost in money and lives

of being carried out to sea by a norther. In his "History of the Panama Railroad," published in 1862, F. N. Otis describes the site of the present city when first fixed thus:

"This island cut off from the mainland by a narrow frith contained an area of a little more than one square mile. It was a virgin swamp, covered with a dense growth of the tortuous, water-loving mangrove, and interlaced with huge vines and thorny

faces were protected by gauze veils no work could be done even at midday. Residence on the island was impossible. The party had their headquarters in an old brig which brought down materials for building, tools, provisions, etc., and was anchored in the bay."

That was in May, 1850. In March, 1913, the author spent some time in Colon. Excellent meals were enjoyed in a somewhat old-fashioned frame

PANAMA POTTERY SELLERS

far as Gatun, where the great locks now rise, they were carried thither by the railroad. This route proving the more expeditious the news quickly reached New York and the ships began making Colon their port. As a result the town grew as fast and as unsubstantially as a mushroom.

It was a floating population of people from every land and largely lawless. The bard of the Isthmus has a poem too long to quote which depicts a wayfarer at the gate of Heaven confessing to high crimes, misdemeanors and all the sinful lusts of the flesh. At the close of the damning confession he whispered something in the ear of the Saint, whose brow cleared, and beaming welcome took the place of stern rejection. The keeper of the keys according to the poet cried:

> "Climb up, Oh, weary one, climb up!
>   Climb high! Climb higher yet
> Until you reach the plush-lined seats
>   That only martyrs get.
> Then sit you down and rest yourself
>   While years of bliss roll on!
> Then to the angels he remarked,
>   '*He's been living in Colon!*' "

hotel, while directly across the way the finishing touches were being put to a new hotel, of reinforced concrete which for architectural taste and beauty of position compares well with any seashore house in the world. At the docks were ships of every nation; cables kept us in communication with all civilized capitals. Not an insect of any sort was seen, and to discover an alligator a considerable journey was necessary. The completed Panama Railroad would carry us in three hours to the Pacific, where the great water routes spread out again like a fan. In half a century man had wrought this change, and with his great canal will doubtless do more marvelous deeds in the time to come.

Once construction of the road was begun shacks rose on piles amid the swampy vegetation of the island. At certain points land was filled in and a solid foundation made for machine shops. The settlement took a sudden start forward in 1851 when a storm prevented two New York ships from landing their passengers at the mouth of the Chagres River.

The delayed travelers were instead landed at Colon, and the rails having been laid as

HINDOO LABORERS ON THE CANAL
At one time several hundred were employed but they are disappearing

SAN BLAS BOATS AT EARLY DAWN

With the completion of the Pacific railroads in the United States the prosperity of Colon for a time waned. There was still business for the railroad, as there has been to the present day, and as it is believed there will be in the future despite the Canal. But the great rush was ended. The eager men hurrying to be early at the place where gold was to be found, and the men who had "made their pile" hastening home to spend it, took the road across the plains. Colon settled down to a period of lethargy for which its people were constitutionally well fitted. Once in a while they were stirred up by reports of the projected Canal, and the annual revolutions—President Roosevelt in a message to Congress noted 53 in 57 years—prevented life from becoming wholly monotonous. But there was no sign of a renewal of the flush times of the gold rush until late in the '70's the French engineers arrived to begin the surveys for the Canal. By the way, that Isthmus from Darien to Nicaragua is probably the most thoroughly surveyed bit of wild land in the world. Even on our own Canal Zone where the general line of the Canal was early determined each chief engineer had his own survey made, and most of the division

engineers prudently resurveyed the lines of their chiefs.

With the coming of the French, flush times began again on the Isthmus and the golden flood poured most into Colon, as the Canal diggers made their main base of operations there, unlike the Americans who struck at nature's fortifications all along the line, making their headquarters at Culebra about the center of the Isthmus. But though the French failed to dig the Canal they did win popularity on the Isthmus, and there are regretful and uncomplimentary comparisons drawn in the cafés and other meeting-places between the thrift and calculation of the Americans, and the lavish prodigality of the French. Everything they bought was at mining-camp prices and they adopted no such plan as the commissary system now in vogue to save their workers from the rapacity of native shopkeepers of all sorts.

SAN BLAS INDIAN BOYS

At Cristobal you are gravely taken to see the De Lesseps Palace, a huge frame house with two

SAN BLAS LUGGER PUTTING OUT TO SEA

wings, now in the last stages of decrepitude and decay, but which you learn cost fabulous sums, was furnished and decorated like a royal château and was the scene of bacchanalian feasts that vied with those of the Romans in the days of Heliogabalus. At least the native Panamanian will tell you this, and if you happen to enjoy his reminiscences in the environ-

'When the money flowed like likker . . . .
  With the joints all throwed wide open, and no sheriff to
    demur.'

Vice flourished. Gambling of every kind and every other form of wickedness were common day and night. The blush of shame became practically unknown."

THE ATLANTIC FLEET VISITS THE ISTHMUS

ment of a café you will conclude that in starting the Canal the French consumed enough champagne to fill it.

Mr. Tracy Robinson, a charming chronicler of the events of a lifetime on the Isthmus, says of this period: "From the time that operations were well under way until the end, the state of things was like the life at 'Red Hoss Mountain' described by Eugene Field:

The De Lesseps house stands at what has been the most picturesque point in the American town of Cristobal. Before it stands a really admirable work of art, Columbus in the attitude of a protector toward a half-nude Indian maiden who kneels at his side. After the fashion of a world largely indifferent to art the name of the sculptor has been lost, but the statue was cast in Turin, for Empress Eugénie, who gave it to the Republic of Colombia when the

French took up the Canal work. Buffeted from site to site, standing for awhile betwixt the tracks in a railroad freight yard, the spot on which it stood when viewed by the writer is sentimentally ideal, for it overlooks the entrance to the Canal and under the eyes of the Great Navigator, done in bronze, the ships of all the world will pass and repass as

white foam upon the shore, unlike the Pacific which is usually calm. Unlike the Pacific, too, the tide is inconsiderable. At Panama it rises and falls from seventeen to twenty feet, and, retiring, leaves long expanses of unsightly mud flats, but the Caribbean always plays its part in the landscape well. Unhappily this picturesque street—called Roosevelt

ROOSEVELT AVENUE, CRISTOBAL, ABOUT TO LOSE ITS BEAUTY

they enter or leave the artificial strait which gives substance to the Spaniard's dream.

At one time the quarters of the Canal employees —the gold employees as those above the grade of day laborers are called—were in one of the most beautiful streets imaginable. In a long sweeping curve from the border line between the two towns, they extended in an unbroken row facing the restless blue waters of the Caribbean. A broad white drive and a row of swaying cocoanut trees separated the houses from the water. The sea here is always restless, surging in long billows and breaking in

Avenue—is about to lose its beauty, for its water front is to be taken for the great new docks, and already at some points one sees the yellow stacks of ocean liners mingling with the fronded tops of the palms.

Cristobal is at the present time the site of the great cold storage plant of the Canal Zone, the shops of the Panama Railroad and the storage warehouses in which are kept the supplies for the commissary stores at the different villages along the line of the Canal. It possesses a fine fire fighting force, a Y. M. C. A. club, a commissary hotel, and along the water front of Colon proper are the hospital buildings erected by the French but still maintained. Many of the edifices extend out over the water and

THE DE LESSEPS PALACE

the Atlantic side, make a hasty drive about Colon—it really can be seen in an hour—and then go by rail to Panama, anticipating the arrival of their ship there by seven hours and getting some idea of the country en route. Visitors with more time to spare will find one of the short drives that is worth while a trip to the cemetery of Mount Hope where from the very beginning of the town those who fell in the long battle with nature have been laid to rest. The little white headstones multiplied fast in the gay and reckless French days before sanitation was thought of, and when riot and dissipation

the constant breeze ever blowing through their wide netted balconies would seem to be the most efficient of allies in the fight against disease. One finds less distinct separation between the native and the American towns at this end of the railroad than at Panama-Ancon. This is largely due to the fact that a great part of the site of Colon is owned by the Panama Railroad, which in turn is owned by the United States, so that the activities of our government extend into the native town more than at Panama. In the latter city the hotel, the hospital and the commissary are all on American or Canal Zone soil—at Colon they are within the sovereignty of the Republic of Panama.

At present sightseers tarry briefly at Colon, taking the first train for the show places along the Canal line, or for the more picturesque town of Panama. This will probably continue to be the case when the liners begin passing through the Canal to the Pacific. Many travelers will doubtless leave their ships at

were the rule and scarcely discouraged. "Monkey Hill" was the original name of the place, owing to the multitude of monkeys gamboling and chattering

THE NATIONAL GAME—COCK-FIGHTING

in the foliage, but as the graves multiplied and the monkeys vanished the rude unfitness of the name became apparent and it gave place to "Mount Hope." It is pitiful enough in any case; but if you will study the dates on the headstones you will find the years after 1905 show a rapid lessening in the number of tenants.

If you consider the pictures of certain streets of Colon during two phases of their history, you will have little trouble in understanding why the death rate in the town has been steadily decreasing. In a town built upon a natural morass, and on which

reaching a floating board benevolently provided by some merchant who hoped to thus bring custom to his doors. Along the water front between the steamship piers and the railroad there was an effort to pave somewhat as there was heavy freight to be handled, but even there the pavement would sink out of sight overnight, and at no time could it

HOW THE JUNGLE WORKS
Silently but persistently the advance of nature enshrouds man's work in living green

more than eleven feet of water fell annually, there was hardly a foot of paving except the narrow sidewalks. In the wet season, which extends over eight months of the year, the mud in these filthy by-ways was almost waist deep. Into it was thrown indiscriminately all the household slops, garbage and offal. There was no sewage system; no effort at drainage. If one wished to cross a street there was nothing for it but to walk for blocks until

be kept in good condition. The agents of the Panama Railroad and the Royal Mail Steam Packet Company, whose freight houses adjoined, dumped into the seemingly bottomless abyss everything heavy and solid that could be brought by land or water, but for a long time without avail. Under the direction of the United States officers, however, the problem was solved, and today the streets of Colon are as well paved as those of any American city, vitrified brick being the material chiefly used.

In the days when there was no pavement there were no sewers. Today the town is properly drained, and the sewage problem, a very serious one in a town with no natural slope and subject to heavy rains, is efficiently handled. There was no water supply. Drinking water was brought from the

failing died like the flies that swarmed about their food and their garbage indiscriminately. Not until the Americans declared war on filth and appointed Col. W. C. Gorgas commander-in-chief of the forces of cleanliness and health did Colon get cleaned up.

About the base of the Toro light cluster the houses of the engineers employed on the harbor work, and on the fortifications which are to guard

"BOTTLE ALLEY"

A typical Colon street before the Sanitary Department concluded the work of cleaning up

mainland and peddled from carts, or great jars by water carriers. Today there is an aqueduct bringing clear cool water from the distant hills. It affords a striking commentary upon the lethargy and laziness of the natives that for nearly half a century they should have tolerated conditions which for filth and squalor were practically unparalleled. The Indian in his palm-thatched hut was better housed and more healthfully surrounded than they.

Even the French failed to correct the evil and so

the Atlantic entrance of the canal on the west side— other defensive works are building about a mile north of Colon. To these and other forts in course of construction visitors are but grudgingly admitted and the camera is wholly taboo. They are still laughing in Col. Goethal's office at a newly elected Congressman—not even yet sworn in—who wrote that in visiting the Canal Zone he desired particularly to make an exhaustive study of the fortifications, and take many pictures, in order that he might be peculiarly fit for membership on the Military Affairs Committee, to which he aspired.

Toro Point will, after the completion of the Canal work, remain only as the camp for such a detachment of coast artillery as may be needed at the forts. The village will be one of those surrendered to the jungle from which it was wrested. Cristobal will remain a large, and I should judge,

group of children, among whom even the casual observer will detect Spanish, Chinese, Indian and negro types pure, and varying amalgamations of all playing together in the childish good fellowship which obliterates all racial hostilities. The Chinese are the chief business people of the town, and though they intermarry but little with the few families of the old Spanish strain, their unions both legalized

D STREET, COLON, PAVED
Before being sewered and paved this street was as bad as Bottle Alley on preceding page

a growing town. Colon which was created by the railroad will still have the road and the Canal to support it.

Without an architectural adornment worthy of the name, with streets of shanties, and rows of shops in which the cheap and shoddy are the rule, the town of Colon does have a certain fascination to the idle stroller. That arises from the throngs of its picturesque and parti-colored people who are always on the streets. At one point you will encounter a

and free, with the mulattoes or negroes are innumerable. You see on the streets many children whose negro complexion and kinky hair combine but comically with the almond eyes of the celestial. Luckily queues are going out of style with the Chinese, or the hair of their half-breed offspring would form an insurmountable problem.

Public characters throng in Colon. A town with but sixty years of history naturally abounds in early inhabitants. It is almost as bad as Chicago

BACHELOR QUARTERS AT TORO POINT

was a few years ago when citizens who had reached the "anecdotage" would halt you at the Lake Front and pointing to that smoke-bedimmed cradle of the city's dreamed-of future beauty would assure you that they could have bought it all for a pair of boots—but didn't have the boots. One of the figures long pointed out on the streets of Colon was an old colored man—an "ole nigger" in the local phrase—who had been there from the days of the alligators and the monkeys. He worked for the Panama Railroad surveyors, the road when completed, the French and the American Canal builders. A sense of long and veteran public service had invested him with an air of dignity rather out of harmony with his raiment. "John Aspinwall" they called him, because Aspinwall was for a time the name of the most regal significance on the island. The Poet of Panama immortalized him in verse thus:

"Oh, a quaint old moke, is John Aspinwall,
    Who lives by the Dead House gate,
And quaint are his thoughts, if thoughts at all
    Ever lurk in his woolly pate,
For he's old as the hills is this coal-black man,
    Thrice doubled with age is he,
And the days when his wanderings first began
    Are shrouded in mystery."

If you keep a shrewd and watchful eye on the balconies above the cheap john stores you will now and again catch a little glimpse reminiscent of Pekin. For the Chinese like to hang their balconies with artistic screens, bedeck them with palms, illuminate them with the gay lanterns of their home. Sometimes a woman of complexion of rather accentuated brunette will hang over the rail with a Chinese—or at least a Chinesque—baby in the parti-colored clothing of its paternal ancestors. Or as you stroll along the back or side streets more given over to residences, an open door here and there gives a glimpse of an interior crowded with household goods—and household gods which are babies. Not precisely luring are these views. They suggest rather that the daily efforts of Col. Gorgas to make and keep the city clean might well have extended further behind the front doors of the house. They did to a slight degree, of course, for there was fumigation unlimited in the first days of the great cleaning up, and even now there is persistent sanitary inspection. The Canal Zone authorities relinquished to the Panama local officials the paving and sanitation work of the city, but retained it in Colon, which serves to indicate the estimate put upon the comparative fitness for self government of the people of the two towns.

Down by the docks, if one likes the savor of spices and the odor of tar, you find the real society of the Seven Seas. Every variety of ship is there, from the stately ocean liner just in from Southampton or Havre to the schooner-rigged cayuca with its crew of San Blas Indians, down from their forbidden country with a cargo of cocoanuts, yams and bananas. A curious craft is the cayuca. Ranging in size from a slender canoe twelve feet long and barely wide enough to hold a man to a considerable craft of eight-foot beam and perhaps 35 to 40 feet on the water line, its many varieties have one thing in common. Each is hewn out of a single log. Shaped to the form of a boat by the universal

A COLON WATER CARRIER

tool, the machete, and hollowed out partly by burning, partly by chipping, these great logs are transformed into craft that in any hands save those of the Indians bred to their use, would be peremptory invitations to a watery death. But the San Blas men pole them through rapids on the Chagres that would puzzle a guide of our North Woods, or at sea take them out in northers that keep the liner tied to her dock. Some of these boats by the way are hollowed from mahogany logs that on the wharf at New York or Boston would be worth $2,000.

The history of the Panama Railroad may well be briefly sketched here. For its time it was the most audacious essay in railway building the world had known, for be it known it was begun barely twenty years after the first railroad had been built in the United States and before either railroad engineers or railroad labor had a recognized place in industry. The difficulties to be surmounted were of a sort that no men had grappled with before. Engineers had learned how to cut down hills, tunnel mountains and bridge rivers, but to build a road bed firm enough to support heavy trains in a bottomless swamp; to run a line through a jungle that seemed to grow up again before the transit could follow the axe man; to grapple with a river that had been known to rise forty feet in a day; to eat lunch standing thigh deep in water with friendly alligators looking on from adjacent logs, and to do all this amid the unceasing buzz of venomous

AN OPEN SEWER IN A COLON STREET

BY A COCLÉ BROOK

insects whose sting, as we learned half a century later, carried the germs of malaria and yellow fever —this was a new draft upon engineering skill and endurance that might well stagger the best. The demand was met. The road was built, but at a heavy cost of life. It used to be said that a life was the price of every tie laid, but this was a picturesque exaggeration. About 6000 men in all died during the construction period.

Henry Clay justified his far-sightedness by securing in 1835 the creation of a commission to consider the practicability of a trans-isthmian railroad. A commissioner was appointed, secured a concession from what was then New Granada, died before getting home, and the whole matter was forgotten for ten years. In this interim the French, for whom from the earliest days the Isthmus had a fascination, secured a concession but were unable to raise the money necessary for the road's construction. In 1849 three Americans who deserve a place in history, William H. Aspinwall, John L. Stevens and Henry Chauncy, secured a concession at Bogota and straightway went to work. Difficulties beset them on every side. The swamp had no bottom and for a time it seemed that their financial resources had a very apparent one. But the rush for gold, though it greatly increased the cost of their labor, made their enterprise appear more promising to the investing public and their temporary need of funds was soon met.

But the swamp and jungle were unrelenting in their toll of human life. Men working all day deep in slimy ooze composed of decaying tropical vegetation, sleeping exposed to the bites of malaria-bearing insects, speedily sickened and too often died. The company took all possible care of its workmen, but even that was not enough. Working men of

every nationality were experimented with but none were immune. The historian of the railroad reported that the African resisted longest, next the coolie, then the European, and last the Chinese. The experience of the company with the last named class of labor was tragic in the extreme. Eight hundred were landed on the Isthmus after a voyage on which sixteen had died. Thirty-two fell ill almost at the moment of landing and in less than a week eighty more were prostrated. Strangers in a strange land, unable to express their complaints or make clear their symptoms, they were almost as much the victims of homesickness as of any other ill. The interpreters who accompanied them declared that much of their illness was due to their deprivation of their accustomed opium, and for a time the authorities supplied them, with the result that nearly two-

THE MANGOES MARCHING ON STILT-LIKE ROOTS

GOING TO MARKET

Jamaica country roads are gay with women in brightly colored dresses, carrying the products of their little farms to market.   The burden is always borne on the head with the result that peasant women have a graceful and even stately carriage.

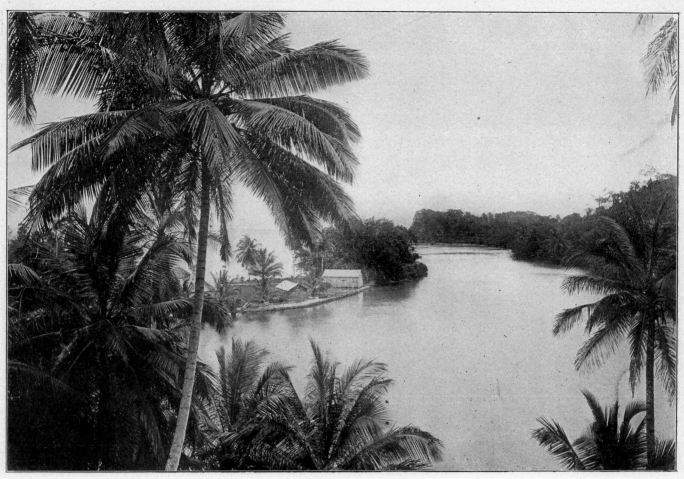

A PICTURESQUE INLET OF THE CARIBBEAN

thirds were again up and able to work. Then the exaggerated American moral sense, which is so apt to ignore the customs of other lands and peoples, caused the opium supply to be shut off. Perhaps the fact that the cost of opium daily per Chinaman was 15 cents had something to do with it. At any rate the whole body of Chinamen were soon sick unto death and quite ready for it. They made no effort to cling to the lives that had become hateful. Suicides were a daily occurrence and in all forms. Some with Chinese stolidity would sit upon a rock on the ocean's bed and wait for the tide to submerge them. Many used their own queues as ropes and hanged themselves. Others persuaded or bribed their fellows to shoot them dead. Some thrust sharpened sticks through their throats, or clutching great stones leaped into the river maintaining their hold until death made the grasp still more rigid. Some starved themselves and others died of mere brooding over their dismal state. In a few weeks but 200 were left alive, and these were sent to

Jamaica where they were slowly absorbed by the native population. On the line of the old Panama Railroad, now abandoned and submerged by the waters of Gatun Lake, was a village called Matachin, which local etymologists declare means "dead Chinaman," and hold that it was the scene of this melancholy sacrifice of oriental life.

The railroad builders soon found that the expense of the construction would vastly exceed their estimates. The price of a principality went into the Black Swamp, the road bed through which was practically floated on a monster pontoon. It is not true, as often asserted, that engines were sunk there to make a foundation for the road, but numbers of flat cars were thus employed to furnish a floating foundation. The swamp which impeded the progress of the road was about five miles south of Gatun and was still giving trouble in 1908, when the heavier American rolling stock was put upon the road. Soundings then made indicate that the solid bottom under the ooze is 185 feet below the surface, and somewhere between are the scores of dump cars and the thousands of tons of rock and earth with which the monster has been fed. The Americans conquered it, apparently, in 1908, by building a trestle and filling it with cinders and other light material. But every engineer was glad when in 1912 the relocation of the road abandoned the Black Swamp to its original diabolical devices.

Even in so great an affair as the building of railroads, chance or good fortune plays a considerable part. So it was the hurricane which first drove two ships bearing the California gold seekers from the mouth of the Chagres down to Colon that gave the railroad company just the stimulus necessary to carry it past the lowest ebb in its fortunes. Before that it had no income and could no longer borrow money. Thereafter it had a certain income and its credit was at the very best. Every additional mile finished added to its earnings, for every mile was used since it lessened the river trip to the Pacific. In January, 1855, the last rail was laid, and on the 28th of that month the first train crossed from ocean to ocean. The road had then cost almost $7,000,000 or more than $150,000 a mile, but owing to the peculiar conditions of the time and place it had while building earned $2,125,000 or almost one-third its cost. Its length was 47 miles, its highest point was 263 feet above sea-level, it crossed streams at 170 points—most of the crossings being of the Chagres River. As newly located by the American engineers a great number of these crossings are avoided.

Traffic for the road grew faster than the road itself and when it was completed it was quite apparent that it was not equipped to handle the business that awaited it. Accordingly the managers determined to charge more than the traffic would bear—to fix such rates as would be prohibitive until they could get the road suitably equipped. Mr. Tracy Robinson

CHILDISH BEAUTY WITHOUT ART

says that a few of the lesser officials at Panama got up a sort of burlesque rate card and sent it on to the general offices in New York. It charged $25 for one fare across the Isthmus one way, or $10 second class. Personal baggage was charged five cents a pound, express $1.80 a cubic foot, second class freight fifty cents a cubic foot, coal $5 a ton,—all for a haul of forty-seven miles. To the amazement of the Panama jokers the rates were adopted and, what was more amazing, they remained unchanged for twenty years. During that time the company paid dividends of 24%, with an occasional stock dividend and liberal additions to the surplus. Its stock at one time went up to 335 and as in its darkest days it could have been bought for a song those who had

A CORNER OF MOUNT HOPE CEMETERY

Names of forgotten French martyrs are carved in the stones

bought it were more lucky than most of the prospectors who crowded its coaches on the journey to the gold fields.

Too much prosperity brought indifference and lax management and the finances of the road were showing a decided deterioration when the French took up the Canal problem. One of the chief values of the franchise granted by New Granada and afterward renewed by Colombia was the stipulation that no canal should be built in the territory without the consent of the railroad corporation. With this club the directors forced the French to buy them out, and when the rights of the French Canal company passed to the United States we acquired the railroad as well.

It is now Uncle Sam's first essay in the government ownership and operation of railroads. Extremists declare that his success as a manager is shown by the fact that he takes a passenger from the Atlantic to the Pacific in three hours for $2.40, while the privately owned Pacific railroads take several days and charge about $75 to accomplish the same result. There is a fallacy in this argument somewhere, but there is none in the assertion that by government officials the Panama Railroad is run successfully

THE SOULFUL EYES OF THE TROPICS

both from the point of service and of profits. Its net earnings for the fiscal year of 1912 were $1,762,000, of which about five-sixths was from commercial business. But it must be remembered that in that year the road was conducted primarily for the purpose of Canal building—everything was subordinated to the Big Job. That brought it abnormal revenue, and laid upon it abnormal burdens. The record shows however that it was directed with a singular attention to detail and phenomenal success. When passenger trains must be run so as never to interfere with dirt trains, and when dirt trains must be so run that a few score steam-shovels dipping up five cubic yards of broken rock at a mouthful shall never lack for a flat car on which to dump the load, it means some fine work for the traffic manager. The superintendent of schools remarked to me that the question whether a passenger train should stop at a certain station to pick up school children depended on the convenience of certain steam-shovels and that the matter had to be decided by Col. Goethals. Which goes to show that the Colonel's responsibilities are varied —but of that more anon, as the story-tellers say.

Within a few years forty miles of the Panama Railroad have been relocated, the prime purpose of the change being to obviate the necessity of crossing the Canal at any point. One of the witticisms of

MARKET DAY AT DAVID

SCENE ON ALMIRANTE BAY

the Zone is that the Panama is the only railroad that runs crosswise as well as lengthwise. This jest is partly based on the fact that nine-tenths of the line has been moved to a new location, but more on the practice of picking up every night or two some thousand feet of track in the Canal bed and moving it bodily, ties and all, some feet to a new line. This is made necessary when the steam-shovels have dug out all the rock and dirt that can be reached from the old line, and it is accomplished by machines called track shifters, each of which accomplishes the work of hundreds of men.

The Panama Railroad is today what business men call a going concern. But it is run with a singular indifference to private methods of railroad management. It has a board of directors, but they do little directing. Its shares do not figure in Wall Street, and we do not hear of it floating loans, scaling down debts or engaging in any of the stock-jobbing operations which in late years have resulted in railroad presidents being lawyers rather than railroad men. The United States government came into possession of a railroad and had to run it. Well? The government proved equal to the emergency and perhaps its experience will lead it to get possession of yet other railroads.

CHAPTER III

NOMBRE DE DIOS, PORTO BELLO AND SAN LORENZO

WITHIN twenty miles, at the very most, east and west of Colon lie the chief existing memorials of the bygone days of Spanish discovery and colonization, and English piratical raids and destruction, on the Isthmus. All that is picturesque and enthralling — that is to say all that is stirring, bloody and lawless—in the history of the Caribbean shore of the Isthmus lies thus adjacent to the Atlantic entrance of the Canal. To the east are Nombre de Dios and Porto Bello—the oldest European settlements on the North American continent, the one being founded about 1510, almost a century and a half before the landing at Plymouth, and the other in 1607, the very year of the planting of Jamestown, Virginia. To the west is the castle of San Lorenzo at the mouth of the Chagres, the gateway to the Pacific trade, built in the latter years of the sixteenth century and repeatedly destroyed. About these Spanish outposts, once thriving market towns and massive fortresses, but now vine-covered ruins where "the lion and the lizard keep their court" clusters a wealth of historical lore.

Let us for the time turn from the Panama of to-day, and from speculation as to its future, and look back upon the Panama of the past. It is a past too full of incident, too replete with stories of battle, murder and sudden death for full justice to be done to it in a chapter. Volumes, libraries almost, have been written about it, for Panama is not one of the happy countries without a history. Of that history the survey here is necessarily the most cursory.

Twenty miles from Colon to the east is the spacious deep water harbor of Porto Bello, visited and named by Colombus in 1502. Earlier still it had harbored the ships of Roderigo de Bastides who landed there in 1500—probably the first European to touch Panama soil. He sought the strait to the Indies, and gold as well. A few miles east and north of Porto Bello is Nombre de Dios, one of the earliest Spanish settlements but now a mere cluster of huts amidst which the Canal workers were only recently dredging sand for use in construction. Few visit Nombre de Dios for purposes of curiosity and indeed it is little worth visiting, for fires, floods and the shifting sands of the rivers have obliterated all trace of the old town. The native village con-

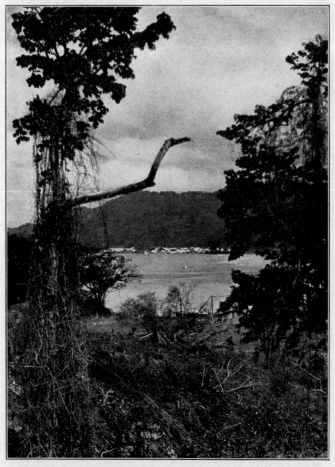

MODERN PORTO BELLO FROM ACROSS THE BAY

sisted of about 200 huts when the American invasion occurred, but a spark from one of the engines set off the dry thatch of one of the huts and a general conflagration ensued. The Americans have since repaired the damages, to the sanitary advantage

TYPICAL NATIVE HUT IN PORTO BELLO DISTRICT

of the place, but at heavy cost to its picturesqueness.

For that quality you must look to its past, for it figured largely in the bloody life of the Isthmus in the 16th century. It was founded by one Don Diego de Nicuesa, who had held the high office of Royal Carver at Madrid. Tired of supervising the carving of meats for his sovereign he sailed for the Isthmus to carve out a fortune for himself. Hurricanes, treachery, jealousy, hostile Indians, mutinous sailors and all the ills that jolly mariners have to face had somewhat abated his jollity and his spirit as well when he rounded Manzanillo Point and finding himself in a placid bay exclaimed: *"Detengamonos aqui, en nombre de Dios"* (Let us stop here in the name of God). His crew, superstitious and pious as Spanish sailors were in those days, though piety seldom interfered with their profanity or piracy, seized on the devout invocation and Nombre de Dios became the name of the port.

The town thus named became for a time the principal Spanish port on the Caribbean coast and one of the two terminals of the royal road to Old Panama. But the harbor was poor, the climate sickly, for the town was shut in on the landward side by mountains which excluded the breeze. It came to be called the Spanish Graveyard. Children died in infancy, and Spanish mothers sent theirs to Cruces to be reared. Difficult of defense by either land or sea it was menaced alternately by the Cimmaroons and the English, and in 1572

ENTRANCE TO PORTO BELLO HARBOR, FROM SPANISH FORT

Nombre de Dios then affords little encouragement for the visits of tourists, but Porto Bello, nearer Colon, is well worth a visit. The visit however is not easily made. The trip by sea is twenty miles steaming in the open Caribbean which is always rough, and which on this passage seems to any save the most hardened navigators tempestuous beyond all other oceans. There are, or rather were, no regular lines of boats running from Colon and one desiring to visit the historic spot must needs plead with the Canal Commission for a pass on the government tug which makes the voyage daily. The visit is well worth the trouble however for the ruins are among the finest on the American continent, while the bay itself is a noble inlet. So at least Columbus thought it when he first visited it in 1502. His son, Fernando, who afterwards wrote of this fourth voyage of the Genoese navigator, tells of this visit thus:

BULLOCK CART ON THE SAVANNA ROAD

Sir Francis Drake took it by assault but gained little plunder by the adventure in which he nearly lost his life. Warned by this, and by other attacks, a distinguished Spanish engineer was sent to examine this, with other Caribbean ports.

He was impressed by Porto Bello and reported "if it might please your Majesty it were well that the city of Nombre de Dios be brought and builded in this harbor." It was so graciously ordered and the "city" having been "brought and builded" at Porto Bello its old site gradually relapsed into wilderness save for the few huts found when the American engineers descended upon it seeking not gold but sand. In the course of this quest they uncovered an old Spanish galleon but did not report any pieces of eight, ingots or doubloons. Indeed looking all over the Canal work we may well say, never was there so much digging for so little treasure, for even in the great Culebra cut no trace of precious metal was found.

MODERN INDIAN, DARIEN REGION
Note characteristic weapons—machete, javelin and shot-gun

or a bow shot one from the other; and it looks like the finest landscape a man can imagine. During seven days we continued there, on account of the rain and ill weather, there came continually canoes from all the country about to trade for provisions, and bottoms of fine spun cotton which they gave for some trifles such as points and pins."

Time changes, and things and places change with it. What are "bottoms of fine spun cotton" and "trifles such as points"? As for the people whose houses then so plentifully besprinkled the landscape round about, they have largely vanished. Slain in battle, murdered in cold blood, or enslaved and worked to death by the barbarous Spaniards, they have given place to a mongrel race mainly negro, and of them even there are not enough to give to Porto Bello today the cheery, well populated air which the younger Columbus noticed more than 400 years ago.

The real foundation date of Porto Bello is fixed at 1607, though probably the moving thither of Nombre de Dios began earlier. Its full name in Spanish was San Felipe de Puertovello, for the pious Spaniards were hard put to it to name a city, a mountain, a cape or a carouse without bringing in a saint. Typically enough San Felipe was soon forgotten and the name became Puerto Bello or beautiful harbor. It grew

"The Admiral without making any stay went on till he put into Puerto Bello, giving it that name because it is large, well peopled and encompassed by a well cultivated country. He entered the place on the 2nd of November (1502), passing between two small islands within which ships may lie close to the shore and turn it out (sic) if they have occasion. The country about the harbor, higher up, is not very rough but tilled and full of houses, a stone's throw

rapidly, for, as already noted, the city of Nombre de Dios was reërected there. By 1618 there were 130 houses in the main town not counting the suburbs, a cathedral, governor's house, kings' houses, a monastery, convent of mercy and hospital, a plaza and a quay. The main city was well-built, partly of stone or brick, but the suburbs, one of which was set aside for free negroes, were chiefly of wattled canes with palm thatch. A few plantations and gardens bordered on the city, but mainly the green jungle came down to the very edge as it does with Chagres, Cruces or other native towns today.

It was the Atlantic port of entry for not Panama alone, but for the entire west coast of South America and for merchandise intended for the Philippines. Its great days were of course the times of the annual fairs which lasted from 40 to 60 days, but even at other times there were 40 vessels and numbers of flat boats occupied in the trade of the port. Yet it was but an outpost in the jungle after all. No man alone dared tread the royal road from the city's gate after nightfall. In the streets snakes, toads and the ugly iguana, which the natives devour eagerly, were frequently to be seen. The native wild cat—called grandiloquently a lion or a tiger—prowled in the suburbs and, besides carrying off fowls and pigs, sometimes attacked human beings. The climate was better than that of Nombre de Dios yet sufficiently unhealthful. Child-birth was so often fatal and the rearing of children attended with so much mortality that all mothers who were able resorted to Panama or Cruces at such a time.

It was for a time a considerable market place and for the privilege of trading there the brokers paid into the public coffer 2,000 ducats a year. Another source of revenue was a tax of two reales on each head of cattle slaughtered in the shambles— a tax still retained in form in the Republic of Panama. He who brought in a negro slave had to pay two pesos for the privilege and from this impost a revenue of some $1,000 a year was obtained, most of which was used in cutting down the jungle and in maintaining roads.

Before Porto Bello had even the beginnings of a town, before even the settlement at Nombre de Dios had been begun, there landed at the former port a Spaniard to whom the Isthmus gave immortality and a violent death—two gifts of fortune which not uncommonly go hand in hand. Vasco Nunez de Balboa was with Bastides in the visit which preceded that of Columbus. Thereby he gained a knowledge of the coast and a taste for seafaring adventure. Having tried to be a planter at Santo Domingo and failed therein, he gave his creditors the slip by being carried in a barrel aboard

NATIVE FAMILY IN CHORRERA

a ship about to explore the Panama coast under the Bachelor Encisco. Though they laughed at him for a time as "*el hombre de casco*", "the man in a cask", his new companions in time came to accept

while: "Here's gold, Spaniards! Here's gold. Take a plenty; drink it down! Here's more gold."

Balboa was a pacifier as well as a fighter and it is recorded of him that even on the warpath he was

SEVENTEENTH CENTURY RUIN AT PORTO BELLO
This edifice, still well preserved, is believed to be the Casa Real, or Custom House

his leadership and ultimately discarded that of Encisco, for besides gallantry Balboa possessed a genius for intrigue. Except for his great achievement of the discovery of the Pacific, and his genius in making friends of the tribes he had subdued, Balboa's career does not differ greatly from that of the leaders of other remorseless Spanish hordes who harried the hapless people of Central America, robbing, enslaving and murdering them with brutal indifference to their rights and totally callous to their sufferings. One can hardly read of the Spaniards in Central America and Peru without sympathizing somewhat with the Indian cacique who, having captured two of the marauders, fastened them to the ground, propped open their jaws and poured molten gold down their throats saying the

not unnecessarily brutal. Indeed one cacique whom he overthrew was so impressed with his forbearance that he entered into alliance with the Spaniard and gave him his favorite daughter. Though he never married the girl Balboa "always lov'd and cherish'd her very much", according to Herrera, which is perhaps more than some wives get with a wedding ceremony.

To anyone who has seen the Isthmian country as it is today, when the stateliest native house is but a hut, and when it would appear that the barest necessities of life are all that are sought by its people, the story told by Herrera, the official historian of the Spanish court, suggests a pitiful deterioration in the standard of native life. Of the home and village of Comagre, the greatest cacique of the Darien region, he writes:

"His palace was more remarkable and better built than any that had yet been seen either on the Islands, or the little that was known of the Continent, being 150 paces in length and eighty in breadth . . . so beautifully wrought that the Spaniards were amaz'd at the sight of it and could not express the Manner and Curiosity of it. There were in it several Chambers and Apartments and one that was like a Buttery was full of such Provisions as the Country afforded, as Bread, Venison, Swine's Flesh, etc. There was another large Room like a Cellar full of earthen Vessels, containing Several sorts of white and red Liquors made of Indian Wheat, Roots, a kind of Palm-Tree and other Ingredients,

drank. The blood they shed, the gold they stole, the houses they burned, the women they violated and the Indians they foully tortured and murdered form a long count in the indictment of civilization against Spain in Central America and the West Indies. That today the Spanish flag waves over not one foot of the territory ravaged by Pizarro, Nicuesa, Cortez, Balboa, and Pedrarias is but the slenderest of justice—the visitation upon the children of the sins of their fathers. It is fair to say that of all the ruffianly spoliators Vasco Nuñez de Balboa was the least criminal. If he fought savagely to overthrow local caciques, he neither tortured, enslaved nor slew them after his victory, but rather strove

STREET IN MODERN PORTO BELLO

the which the Spaniards commended when they drank them!"

How ingenuous the historian's closing line! Doubtless the Spaniards commended as lavishly as they

to make them his friends. He left the provinces somewhat depleted of gold and pearls after his visits, but one of the evidences of the complete lack of the cultivating grace of civilization among the Indians was that they did not care so much for these gew-gaws as they did for their lives, the honor of their women and their liberty. This would of course

about 4000 ounces of gold. As usual the Spaniards were quarreling over the plunder, when a son of the cacique, one Panciano, strode amongst them and, kicking the gold out of his way, addressed them in language thus reported by the historian Quintana:

ANCIENT TRAIL FROM PORTO BELLO
Over this trail Balboa may have led his men on the march that led to the still unknown Pacific

"Christians! why quarrel and make so much turmoil about a little gold, which nevertheless you melt down from beautifully wrought work into rude bars? Is it for such a trifle that you banish yourselves from your country, cross the seas, endure hardships and disturb the peaceful nations of these lands? Cease your unseemly brawl and I will show you a country where you may obtain your fill of gold. Six days' march across yonder country will bring you to an ocean sea like this near which we dwell, where there are ships a little less in size than yours, with sails and oars, and where the people eat out of vessels of gold and have large cities and wealth unbounded."

In the light of our later knowledge we know that he referred to the Pacific and to Peru. At the conclusion of his address he volunteered to lead the Spaniards to the unknown sea, provided they first would aid him and his father in the overthrow of a hostile tribe, and further that they increase their own numbers to 1000 men, for he foresaw hard fighting.

stamp them as sheer barbarians on Fifth Avenue or the Rue de la Paix.

As a matter of fact the Indian scorn of the Spanish greed for gold was the cause of Balboa's first hearing of the Pacific Ocean. He had made an alliance with Careta, a cacique of some power, who gave his daughter to Balboa, together with 70 slaves and

To recuperate his force and add to it Balboa returned to his base at Santa Maria. Here he found trouble of divers kinds. Part of his men were mutinous. Letters from friends at Madrid told that his enemies there were conspiring for his undoing—had even caused a new governor to be sent out to replace him, with orders to send him home for trial. But the most immediate danger was an Indian plot to raid and wholly obliterate the Spanish town—an enterprise which we can hardly blame the oppressed aborigines for cherishing.

An Indian girl, whom a cavalier had first converted to Catholicism, then baptized and then taken for his mistress, revealed the plot to her lover. It had been told her by her brother who, knowing of the wrath to come, in the quaint language of Peter Martyr, "admonyshed her at the days appoynted by sume occasion to convey herselfe oute of the way leste shee shuld bee slayne in the confusion of bataile." Instead of doing this the faithless one, "forgettinge her parentes, her countrie and all her friendes, yea and all the kinges into whose throates Vaschus had thrust his sworde, she opened uppe the matter unto hym, and conceled none of those things which her undiscrete broother had declared unto her."

Balboa was never accused of hesitation. The girl was forced to reveal her brother's hiding place. He was put to the torture and the information thus extorted enabled the Spaniards to strike at once and strike hard. With 150 men he went into the Indian territory of Darien, surprised the natives and put them to total rout. The almost invariable victories of the Spaniards, except when they were taken by surprise, do not indicate superior valor on their part. To begin with they carried fire arms which affrighted the Indians as well as slaughtered them. Further, they wore partial armor—leather gerkins, helmets and cuirasses of steel—so that the unhappy aborigines were not only exposed to missiles, the nature of which they could not comprehend, but saw their own arrows and javelins fall useless from a

Canal Commission Photo

SPANISH FORT AT ENTRANCE TO PORTO BELLO HARBOR

fairly struck target. In one battle the Indians were even reduced to meeting their foes with wooden swords, and, after the inevitable victory, one of the victors to further impress the vanquished with the futility of their defensive weapons ordered the fallen chief to stretch forth his right arm, and with one blow struck it off.

The Indians were superstitious. Anything out of the ordinary filled them with dread. Many refused to stand and fight because Balboa rode into battle on a white horse. Some trained blood hounds that the Spaniards took into battle with them also terrified them. Doing battle with them in the open was almost like slaughtering sheep. Only in ambush were they formidable. It may be noted in passing that not all the barbarities were on the Spanish side. One of Balboa's most trusted lieutenants, Valdivia, was caught in a tempest and his ship wrecked. Those who escaped were captured by the natives, penned up and fattened for a cannibal feast. The day of festivity arriving Valdivia and four of his companions were conducted to the temple and there offered up a sacrifice. Their hearts were cut out with knives of obsidian and offered to the gods while their bodies were roasted and devoured by the savages.

News from Madrid convinced Balboa that he was in disfavor at court. Some great exploit was needed to reëstablish his prestige. He determined to seek without delay that new sea of which he had been told, and to this end gathered an army of 190 Spaniards and about 1,000 Indians. A pack of the trained European war dogs were taken along. The old chroniclers tell singular tales about these dogs. Because of the terror they inspired among the Indians they were held more formidable than an equal number of soldiers. One great red dog with a black muzzle and extraordinary strength was endowed with the rank of a captain and drew the pay of his rank. In battle the brutes pursued the fleeing Indians and tore their naked bodies with their fangs. It is gravely reported that the Captain could distinguish between a hostile and a friendly native.

It is practically impossible to trace now the exact line followed by Balboa across the Isthmus. Visitors to the Canal Zone are shown Balboa Hill, named in honor of his achievement, from which under proper climatic conditions one can see both oceans. But it is wholly improbable that Balboa ever saw this hill. His route was farther to the eastward than the Zone. We do know however that he emerged from the jungle at some point on the Gulf of San Miguel. What or where the hill was from which with "eagle eyes he star'd at the Pacific" we can only guess. It was one of the elevations in the province of Quareque, and before attaining it Balboa fought a battle with the Indians of that tribe who vastly outnumbered his force,

A GROUP OF CHOLO INDIANS

but were not armed to fight Spaniards. "Even as animals are cut up in the shambles," according to the account of Peter Martyr, "so our men, following them, hewed them in pieces; from one an arm, from another a leg, here a buttock, there a shoulder." The chief Porque and 600 of his followers were slain

brush under the glaring tropical sun of a September day. Pious chroniclers set down that he fell on his knees and gave thanks to his Creator—an act of devotion which coming so soon after his slaughter of the Quarequa Indians irresistibly recalls the witticism at the expense of the Pilgrim Fathers, that on

NATIVES GRINDING RICE IN A MORTAR OWNED BY ALL
It never occurred to the Indians to let one man own the mortar and charge all others for its use

and as usual dead and living were robbed of their golden jewelry.

Balboa's force of Spaniards was now reduced to 67 men; the rest were laid up by illness, but notwithstanding the ghastly total of Indian lives taken, no Spaniard had been slain. With these he proceeded a day's journey, coming to a hill whence his native guides told him the sought-for sea might be seen. Ordering his men to stay at the base he ascended the hill alone, forcing his way through the dense under-

landing they first fell upon their knees and then upon the aborigines. Whatever his spirit, Balboa never failed in the letter of piety. His band of cut-throats being summoned to the hilltop joined the official priest in chanting the "Te Deum Laudamus" and "Te Dominum confitur." Crosses were erected buttressed with stones which captive Indians, still dazed by the slaughter of their people, helped to heap. The names of all the Spaniards present were recorded. In fact few historic exploits of so early a day are so well authenticated as the details of Balboa's triumph.

Descending the hill they proceeded with their march for they were then but half way to their goal. Once again they had to fight the jungle and its savage denizens. Later exploring parties, even in

Photo T. J. Marine.

FAMILY TRAVEL ON THE PANAMA TRAIL

our own day, have found the jungle alone invincible. Steel, gunpowder and the bloodhounds opened the way, and the march continued while the burden of gold increased daily. It is curious to read of the complete effrontery with which these land pirates commandeered all the gold there was in sight. From Comagre were received 4000 ounces—"a

gift"; from Panca, ten pounds; Chiapes disgorged 500 pounds to purchase favor; from Cocura 650 pesos worth of the yellow metal and from Tumaco 640 pesos besides two basins full of pearls of which 240 were of extraordinary size. The names of these dead and gone Indian chiefs signify nothing today, but this partial list of contributions shows that as a collector Balboa was as efficient as the Wiskinkie of Tammany Hall. Not counting pearls and girls —of both of which commodities large store was gathered up—the spoil of the expedition exceeded 40,000 pesos in value.

It was September 29, 1513, that at last Balboa and his men reached the Pacific. Being St. Michael's day they named the inlet of the sea they had attained the Gulf of St. Michael. On their first arrival they found they had reached the sea, but not the water, for the tide which at that point rises and falls twenty feet, was out and a mile or more of muddy beach interspersed with boulders intervened between them and the water's edge. So they sat down until the tide had returned when Balboa waded in thigh deep and claimed land and sea, all its islands and its boundaries for the King of Spain. After having thus performed the needful theatrical ceremonies, he returned to the practical by leading his men to the slaughter of some neighboring Indians whose gold went to swell the growing hoard.

The Spaniards made their way along the Pacific coast to a point that must have been near the present site of Panama City, for it is recorded that on a clear day they could see the Pearl Islands in the offing. Balboa wanted mightily to raid these islands, but felt it more prudent to hasten back to the Atlantic coast and send reports of his discovery and tribute of his gold to the King before his enemies should wholly undo him. So he made his way back, fighting and plundering new tribes all the way and leaving the natives seemingly cowed, but actually full of hatred. They had learned the folly of standing against the white man's arms.

rainy season he had marched 190 men through the unknown jungle, fighting pitched battles almost every day, taking food and drink where he could find it or going without, and finally brought all back without losing a man. No expedition since, even the peaceful scientific or surveying ones of our own days, has equaled this record. He had left

DESERTED NATIVE HUT

Note the profusion of pineapples growing wild, without further attention they will thrive and multiply

"Who that had any brains," asked one chieftain touching Balboa's sword, "would contend against this macana which at one blow can cleave a man in two?"

The return was made to Antigua where Balboa was received with loud acclaim. Indeed he had accomplished the incredible. Not only had he discovered a new ocean, not only had he brought home booty worth a dukedom, but in the height of the

the Indians pacified, if resentful, and the letter which he sent off to King Ferdinand was a modest report of a most notable achievement. "In all his long letter," says Peter Martyr, "there is not a single leaf written which does not contain thanks to Almighty God for deliverance from perils and preservation from many imminent dangers."

But Vasco Nunez de Balboa now approached the unhappy and undeserved close of a glorious career.

As his letter went slowly across the seas in a clumsy galleon to Spain, one Pedrarias with a commission to govern Balboa's province and to deal out summary justice to Balboa, who had been represented to the King as a treacherous villain, was on the Atlantic making for the New World. When Ferdinand received Balboa's letter he would have given much to recall his hasty commission to Pedrarias, but there was no wireless in those days, and the new governor, with power of life and death over Balboa, was now well out at sea.

The blow did not fall at once. On arrival at Santa Maria de la Antigua in June, 1514, Pedrarias sent a courier to Balboa to announce his coming and his authority. The devoted followers of Vasco Nunez were for resisting the latter, assuring him that the King could not have received the report of his notable discovery, else he would not thus have been supplanted. Balboa however submitted gracefully, promising the newcomer implicit obedience. Pedrarias, though charged to try Balboa for treason, concealed his orders until he had gathered all the useful information that the old chieftain could impart and won many of his followers to his own personal support. Then he arrested Balboa and put him on trial, only to have him triumphantly acquitted. Pedrarias was disgusted. He hated Balboa and feared his influence in the colony. For his own part he was tearing down the little kingdom his predecessor had erected.

WHAT THEY STILL CALL A ROAD IN PANAMA

Balboa had fought the Indian tribes to their knees, then placated them, freed them without torture and made them his allies. Pedrarias applied the methods of the slave trader to the native population. Never was such misery heaped upon an almost helpless foe, save when later his apt pupil Pizarro invaded Peru. The natives were murdered, enslaved, robbed, starved. As Bancroft says, "in addition to gold there were always women for baptism, lust and slavery." The whole Isthmus blazed with war, and where Balboa had conquered without losing a man Pedrarias lost 70 in one campaign. One of these raids was into the territory now known as the Canal Zone. On one raid Balboa complained to the King there "was perpetrated the greatest cruelty ever heard of in Arabian or Christian country in any generation. And it is this. The captain and the surviving Christians, while on this journey, took nearly 100 Indians of both sexes, mostly women and children, fastened them with chains and afterwards ordered them to be decapitated and scalped."

Ill feeling rapidly increased between Pedrarias and Balboa. The former with the jealousy and timidity of an old man continually suspected Balboa of plotting against him. His suspicion was not allayed when royal orders arrived from Spain creating Balboa adelantado and governor of the newly discovered Pacific coast. The title sounded well but he would have to fight to establish his government over the

Indians and even then Pedrarias would be his superior. But he determined to make the effort, though with the whole Isthmus in war-paint because of the cruelties of Pedrarias he would have to fight every inch of his way. Moreover he tried to carry across the isthmus the hulls of four brigantines, constructed on the Atlantic coast and designed to be put together on the Pacific. Just why he attempted this exploit is perplexing, for there were as good timber and better harbors for shipyards on the Pacific side. Nearly 2000 Indian lives were sacrificed in the heart-rending task of carrying these heavy burdens through the jungle, and when the task was ended it was found that the timbers of two of the ships were useless, having been honeycombed by worms. Two however were seaworthy and with them he put forth into the Pacific, but a great school of whales encountered near the Pearl Islands, where even today they are frequently seen, affrighted his men who made him turn back.

In his party was a man who had fallen in love with Balboa's beautiful mistress, the daughter of the Indian cacique Careta. She had been annoyed by his advances and complained to Vasco Nunez, who warned the man to desist, accompanying the warning with remarks natural to the situation. This man overheard a conversation, really concerning some pitch and iron for the ships but which might be distorted to convey the impression that Balboa was plotting the overthrow of Pedrarias. By an unlucky chance the eavesdropper was chosen as one of a party to carry dispatches to Pedrarias, and had no sooner reached the presence of that bloodthirsty old conquistadore than he denounced Balboa as a traitor. Moreover he roused the old man's vanity by telling him that Balboa was so infatuated with his mistress that he would never marry the governor's daughter—a marriage

OUTDOOR LIFE OF THE NATIVES
The tree is a mango so loaded with fruit that the boughs droop. The fruit is seldom liked by others than natives

which had been arranged and announced as an affair of state.

In a rage Pedrarias determined to put an end to Balboa. Accordingly he wrote a pleasant letter, beseeching him to come to Santa Maria for a conference. That Balboa came willingly is evidence enough that he had no guilty knowledge of any plot. Before he reached his destination however he was met by Pizarro with an armed guard who arrested him. No word of his could change the prearranged

name more than any other's deserves to be linked with that of Columbus in the history of the Isthmus of Panama. It was in 1517 and Balboa was but forty-two years old.

Had the bungling and cruel Pedrarias never been sent to the Isthmus that part of the country known as the Darien might by now be as civilized as the Chiriqui province. As it was, the thriving settlements of Acla and Antigua languished and disappeared, and the legacy of hatred left by the Indians

NATIVE HUT AND OPEN-AIR KITCHEN

program. He was tried but even the servile court which convicted him recommended mercy, which the malignant Pedrarias refused. Straightaway upon the verdict the great explorer, with four of his men condemned with him, were marched to the scaffold in the Plaza, where stood the block. In a neighboring hut, pulling apart the wattled canes of which it was built that he might peer out while himself unseen Pedrarias gloated at the sight of the blood of the man whom he hated with the insane hatred of a base and malignant soul. There the heads of the four were stricken off, and with the stroke died Vasco Nunez de Balboa, the man whose

of that day is so persistent that the white man has never been able to establish himself on the eastern end of the Isthmus.

Fate has dealt harshly with the memory of Balboa. Keats, in his best known and most quoted sonnet, gives credit for his discovery to Cortez. Local tradition has bestowed his name on a hill he never saw, and Panamanian financial legislation has given his name to a coin which is never coined—existing as a fictitious unit like our mill. He did not himself realize the vastness of his discovery, and gave the misleading name of the South Sea to what was the Pacific Ocean. But time is making its amends.

COCOANUT GROVE ON THE CARIBBEAN COAST

something of a glamour about the person of the victim, so that unconsciously we tend to emphasize his merits while we touch lightly upon his faults. But after all, this effect is no more than that which his personality wrought upon the minds of contemporary witnesses, who were unanimous in their expressions of esteem for Balboa, and of condemnation for the manner of his taking off."

And finally the United States government has acted wisely and justly when in decreeing a great port, lined with massive docks, the stopping place for all the argosies of trade entering or leaving the Canal at its Pacific end, they conferred upon it the name Balboa. It will stand a fitting monument to the great soldier and explorer whose murder affected for the worse all Central America and Peru.

History will accord with the verdict of John Fiske who said of him:

"Thus perished in the forty-second year of his age the man who, but for that trifle of iron and pitch, would probably have been the conqueror of Peru. It was a pity that such work should not have fallen into his hands, for when at length it was done, it was by men far inferior to him in character and caliber. One cannot but wish that he might have gone on his way like Cortez, and worked out the rest of his contemplated career in accordance with the genius that was in him. That bright attractive figure and its sad fate can never fail to arrest the attention and detain the steps of the historian as he passes by. Quite possibly the romantic character of the story may have thrown

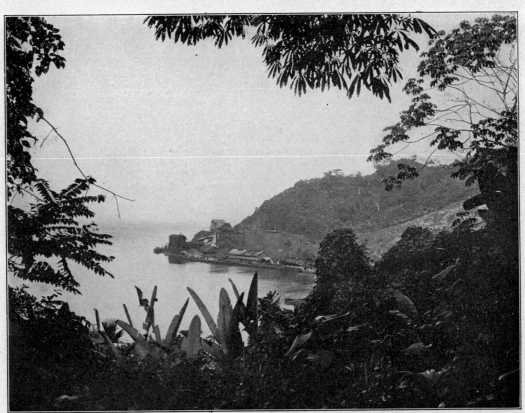
Ramsay, Photo
CANAL COMMISSION STONE CRUSHER, PORTO BELLO

NATIVE HUTS NEAR PORTO BELLO

The Indians of this region are fishermen and famous navigators.   They ship on vessels leaving Colon for far distant ports

But to return to Porto Bello. Balboa's own association with that settlement was of the very briefest, but the influence of his discovery was to it all important. For the discovery of the Pacific led to the conquest of Peru under Pizarro, the founding of Old Panama and the development at Porto Bello of the port through which all the wealth wrung from that hapless land of the Incas found its Atlantic outlet.

The story of Old Panama may be reserved for a later chapter, even though the rise and fall of both Nombre de Dios and Porto Bello were chiefly dependent upon the chief Spanish city of the Pacific coast. For great as was the store of gold, silver and jewels

torn from the Isthmian Indians and sent from these Spanish ports back to Spain, it was a mere rivulet compared to the flood of gold that poured through the narrow trails across the Isthmus after Pizarro began his ravishment of Peru. With the conquest of the Land of the Incas, and the plunder thereof that made of the Isthmus a mighty treasure house attracting all the vampires and vultures of a predatory day, we have little to do here. Enough to point out that all that was extorted from the Peruvians was sent by ship to Panama and thence by mule carriage either across the trail to Nombre de Dios or Porto Bello, or else by land carriage to some point on the Chagres River, usually Venta Cruces, and

AN INDIAN FAMILY OF THE DARIEN

thence by the river to San Lorenzo and down the coast to Porto Bello. Nor did the mules return with empty packs. The Peruvians bought from the bandits who robbed them, and goods were brought from Spain to be shipped from Panama to South America and even to the Philippines.

perts" of whom we are hearing so much these days, it might be worth while to add some experts in enterprise.

As this Spanish trade increased the French and English corsairs or buccaneers sprung into being— plain pirates who preyed however on Spanish com-

Photo by Underwood and Underwood

RUINED SPANISH FORT AT PORTO BELLO

Now used as an American cemetery. The site is one of infinite beauty, but the cemetery is neglected

It seems odd to us today with "the Philippine problem" engaging political attention, and with American merchants hoping that the canal may stimulate a profitable Philippine trade, that three hundred years ago Spanish merchants found profit in sending goods by galleons to Porto Bello, by mule-pack across the Isthmus and by sailing vessel again to Manila. Perhaps to the "efficiency ex-

merce alone, the English finding excuse in the fact that the Spaniards were Catholics, and the French in the assertion that Spain had no right to monopolize all American trade. The excuses were mere subterfuges. The men offering them were not animated by religious convictions, nor would they have engaged in the American trade if permitted. For them the more exciting and profitable pursuit of

Photo by Underwood and Underwood
SAN BLAS LUGGERS AT ANCHOR

was in progress, and the newly laden galleons were creeping along the coast to Nombre de Dios and Porto Bello, word had been sent to Lima for the plate fleet to come to Panama bearing the tribute to the King—gold stripped from the walls of temples, pearls pried from the eyes of sacred images, ornaments wrested from the arms and necks of native women by a rude and ribald soldiery. With the plate fleet came also numerous vessels taking advantage of the convoy, though indeed there was little danger from pirates on the Pacific. The Atlantic, being nearer European civilization, swarmed with these gentry.

At Panama all was transferred to mules and started for the Atlantic coast. So great was the volume of treasure and of goods to be transported that the narrow trail along which the mules proceeded in single file, usually 100 in a caravan or train, was occupied almost from one end to the other, and the tinkling of the mule-bells, and

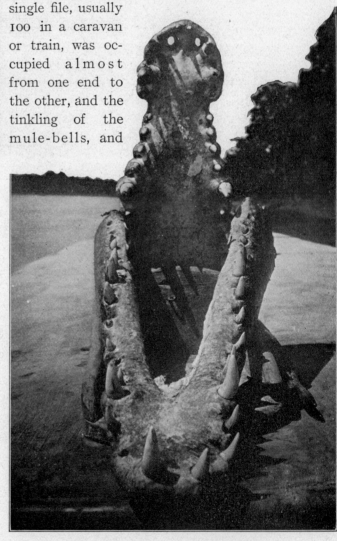

THE TEETH OF THE TROPICS
Skeletonized jaws of a Bayano river crocodile

piracy, and this they pushed with such vigor that by 1526 the merchant vessels in the trade would sail together in one fleet guarded by men-of-war. At times these fleets numbered as many as forty sail, all carrying guns. The system of trade—all regulated by royal decree—was for the ships to sail for Cartagena on the coast of Colombia, a voyage occupying usually about two months. Arrived there, a courier was sent to Porto Bello and on to Panama with tidings of the approach of the fleet. Other couriers spread the tidings throughout the northern provinces of South America.

The fleet would commonly stay at Cartagena a month, though local merchants often bribed the general in command to delay it longer. For with the arrival of the ships the town awoke to a brief and delirious period of trading. Merchants flocked to Cartagena with indigo, tobacco and cocoa from Venezuela, gold and emeralds from New Granada, pearls from Margarita and products of divers sorts from the neighboring lands. While this business

NATIVE BRIDGE IN THE DARIEN

the cries of the muleteers were seldom stilled. Indians sometimes raided the trail and cut out a loaded mule or two, and the buccaneers at one time, finding robbery by sea monotonous, landed and won rich booty by raiding a treasure caravan. The bulkier articles of commerce were packed in carts at Panama and sent to Venta Cruz where they were transferred to flat boats, and taken down the river to San Lorenzo and thence to Porto Bello by sea. When the galleons had cast anchor at that port, and the merchants and caravans were all arrived the little town took on an air of bustle and excitement astonishing to the visitor who had seen it in the hours of its normal life.

"The spectator," says Alcedo, "who had just before been considering Porto Bello in a poor, unpeopled state, without a ship in the port and breathing nothing but misery and wretchedness, would remain thunderstruck at beholding the strange alteration which takes place at the time of this fair. Now he would see the houses crowded with people, the square and the streets crammed with chests of gold and silver, and the port covered with vessels; some of these having brought by the river Chagres from Panama the effects of Peru, such as cacao, bark (quina), vicuna wool, bezoar stone, and other productions of these provinces. He would see others bringing provisions from Cartagena; and he would reflect that, however detestable might be its climate, this city was the emporium of the riches of the two worlds, and the most considerable commercial depot that was ever known."

The visitor to Porto Bello today may see still standing the long stone façade of the aduana, or custom house, facing the ancient plaza. In that square the merchants erected cane booths and tents made of sails, while all available space was filled with bales of goods drawn thither on sledges. With the fleet came 5000 or 6000 soldiers, who besides the sailors needful to man the vessels, the merchants and their clerks, the porters, the buyers of all nationalities and the native sightseers crowded the little town of a few hundred houses so that it appeared to be in possession of a mob.

An itinerant preacher, Thomas Gage, who has left some entertaining reminiscences of his experiences on the Isthmus, tells quaintly of seeking lodgings during the fair:

"When I came into the Haven I was sorry to see that as yet the Galeons were not come from Spaine, knowing that the longer I stayed in that place, the greater would be my charges. Yet I comforted myselfe that the time of year was come, and that they could not long delay their coming. My first thoughts were of taking up a lodging, which at that time were plentifull and cheape, nay some were offered me for nothing with this caveat, that when the Galeons did come, I must either leave them, or pay a dear rate for them. A kind Gentleman, who was the Kings Treasurer, falling in discourse with me, promised to help me, that I might be cheaply lodged even when the ships came, and lodgings were at the highest rate. He, interposing his authority, went with me to seeke one, which at the time of the fleets being there, might continue to be mine. It was no bigger than would containe

Copyright, 1912, National Geographic Magazine, Washington, D. C.
Photo by Henry Pittier

CHOCO INDIAN GIRLS

Note the toes. With them they pick up the smallest objects

a bed, a table, a stoole or two, with roome enough beside to open and shut the doore, and they demanded of me for it during the aforesaid time of the fleet, sixscore Crownes, which commonly is a fortnight. For the Towne being little, and the Soldiers, that come with the Galeons for their defence at least four or five thousand; besides merchants from Peru, from Spain and many other places to buy and sell, is causes that every roome though never so small, be dear; and sometimes all the lodgings in the Towne are few enough for so many people, which at that time doe meet at Portobel. I knew a Merchant who gave a thousand Crownes for a shop of reasonable bignesse, to sell his wares and commodities that yeer I was there, for fifteen daies only, which the Fleet continued to be in that Haven. I thought it much for me to give the sixscore Crownes which were demanded of me for a room, which was but as a mouse hole, and began to be troubled, and told the Kings Treasurer that I had been lately robbed at sea, and was not able to give so much, and bee besides at charges for my diet, which I feared would prove as much more. But not a farthing would be abated of what was asked; where upon the good Treasurer, pitying me, offered to the man of the house to pay him threescore Crownes of it, if so be that I was able to pay the rest, which I must doe, or else lie without in the street. Yet till the Fleet did come I would not enter into this deare hole, but accepted of another faire lodging which was offered me for nothing. Whilst I thus expected the Fleets coming, some money and offerings I got for Masses, and for two Sermons which I preached at fifteen Crownes a peece. I visited the Castles, which indeed seemed unto me to be very strong; but what most I wondered at was to see the requa's of Mules which came thiether from Panama, laden with wedges of silver; in one day I told two hundred mules laden with nothing else, which were unladen in the publicke Market-place, so that there the heapes of silver wedges lay like heapes of stones in the street, without any feare or suspition of being lost. Within ten daies the fleet came, consisting of eight Galeons and ten Merchant ships, which forced me to run to my hole. It was a wonder then to see the multitude of people in those streets which the weeke before had been empty.

"Then began the price of all things to rise, a fowl to be worth twelve Rialls, which in the mainland within I had often bought for one; a pound of beefe then was worth two Rialls, whereas I had in other places thirteen pounds for half a Riall, and so of all other food and provisions, which was so excessively dear, that I knew not how to live but by fish and Tortoises,

which were very many, and though somewhat deare, yet were the cheapest meat I could eate."

On this annual fair, and on trade with the back country, both Nombre de Dios and Porto Bello waxed prosperous and luxurious. Prosperity was a dangerous quality for a town or a man to exhibit in those days when monarchs set the example of theft and extortion, and private plunderers were quick to follow it. So Nombre de Dios was early made the point of a piratical raid by Sir Francis Drake. Though this gentleman was a pirate he is given a measure of immortality by a statue in Baden the inscription on which celebrates him as the introducer of potatoes into Europe. Plunder, not potatoes, however, engaged his chief attention, though as a side issue he engaged in the slave trade. July 29, 1572, he made a descent upon Nombre de Dios with 73 men armed, according to a writer of the time, with "6 Targets; 6 Fire Pikes; 12 Pikes; 24 Muskets and Callivers; 16 Bowes and 6 Partizans; 2 Drums and 2 Trumpets." His men landed from pinnaces and after encountering "a jolly hot volley of shot" in the plaza put the Spaniards to flight. At the point of a sword a captive was forced to lead the raiders to the Governor's house where to his joy Drake discovered a stack of silver ingots worth a million pounds sterling. But 'twas an embarrassment of riches, for the bars

INDIAN HUTS NEAR PORTO BELLO

COUNTRY BACK OF PORTO BELLO

a more profitable raid. This was to be nothing less than a land expedition to cut off one of the treasure caravans just outside of old Panama on its way down the Nombre de Dios trail. Had the Indian population been as hostile to the English then as they became in later days this would have been a more perilous task. But at this time the men who lurked in the jungles, or hunted on the broad savannas

were of 40 pounds weight each and therefore hard to move, so Drake sought the King's Treasure House where he hoped to find more movable wealth. As the door was being broken down he fainted from loss of blood, and as he lay speechless on the sill the Spaniards rallied and attacked the invaders. Though Drake reviving sought to hold his men up to the fight, they had lost their dash, and despite his protestations carried him bodily to the boats. The men were wiser than their leader because it was the chance arrival of some soldiers from Panama that had rallied the populace of the town, and the English, deprived of Drake's leadership, would certainly have been overwhelmed. That leader however grieved sincerely when a Spanish spy told him later that there was 360 tons of silver in the town and many chests of gold in the Treasure House.

With his appetite whetted for plunder Drake retired to plan

had one beast of prey they feared and hated more than the lion or the boa—the Spaniard. Whether Indian or Cimmaroon—as the escaped slaves were called —every man out in that tropic wilderness had some good ground for hating the Spaniards, and so when Drake and his men came, professing themselves enemies of the Spaniards likewise, the country folk made no war upon them but aided them to creep down almost within sight of Panama. Halting here, at a point which must have been well within the

NATIVE WOMEN OF THE SAVANNAS BEARING BURDENS

Canal Zone and which it seems probable was near the spot where the Pedro Miguel locks now rise, they sent a spy into the town who soon brought back information as to the time when the first mule-train would come out.

All seemed easy then. Most of the travel across the isthmus was by night to avoid the heat of the day. Drake disposed his men by the side of the trail—two Indians or Cimmaroons to each armored Englishman. The latter had put their shirts on outside of their breastplates so that they might be told in the dark by the white cloth—for the ancient chroniclers would have us believe them punctilious about their laundry work. All were to lie silent in the jungle until the train had passed, then closing in behind cut off all retreat to Panama—when ho! for the fat panniers crammed with gold and precious stones!

The plan was simplicity itself and was defeated by an equally simple mischance. The drinks of the Isthmus which, as we have seen, the Spaniards commended mightily when they drank, were treacherous in their workings upon the human mind—a quality which has not passed away with the buccaneers and cimmaroons, but still persists. One of Drake's jolly cutthroats, being over fortified with native rum for his nocturnal vigil, heard the tinkle of mule bells and rose to his feet. The leading muleteer turned his animal and fled, crying to the saints to protect him from the sheeted specter in the path. The captain in charge of the caravan was dubious about ghosts, but, there being a number of mules loaded with grain at hand, concluded to send them on to see if there were anything about the ghosts which a proper prayer to the saint of the day would exorcise. So the Englishmen again heard the tinkling mule bells, waited this time in low breathing silence to let the rich prize pass, then with shouts of triumph dashed from the jungle, cut down or shot the luckless muleteers, and swarmed about the caravan eager to cut the bags and get at the booty—and were rewarded with sundry bushels of grain intended to feed the crowds at Nombre de Dios.

The disaster was irreparable. The true treasure train at the first uproar had fled back to the walls of Panama. Nothing was left to Drake and his men but to plod back empty handed to Cruces,

CAMINA REALE, OR ROYAL ROAD NEAR PORTO BELLO

A LADY OF THE SAVANNA

where they had left their boats. Of course they raided the town before leaving but the season was off and the warehouses barren. Back they went to the coast and relieved their feelings by plundering a few coastwise towns and hurling taunts at the governor of Cartagena. Shortly thereafter they renewed their enterprise and did this time capture the treasure train, getting perhaps $100,000 worth of plunder, with but little loss. Some French pirates under Captain Tetu, who had joined in the adventure, suffered more severely and their captain, wounded and abandoned in the forest, was put to death by the Spaniards with certain of their favorite methods of torture.

After a time in England Drake returned to the Caribbean with a considerable naval force, harried the coast, burned and sacked some towns, including Nombre de Dios, and extorted heavy ransom from others. He put into the harbor of Porto Bello with the intent of taking it also, but while hesitating before the formidable fortresses of the place was struck down by death. His body, encased in lead, was sunk in the bay near perhaps to the ancient ships which our dredges have brought to light. The English long revered him as a great sailor and commander—which indeed he was, but a pirate withal. His most permanent influence on the history of the Isthmus was his demonstration that Nombre de Dios was incapable of defense, and its consequent disappearance from the map.

Such greatness as had pertained to Nombre de Dios was soon assumed by Porto Bello, which soon grew far beyond the size attained by its predecessor. It became indeed a substantially built town, and its fortresses on the towering heights on either side of the beautiful bay seemed fit to repel any invader—

notwithstanding which the town was repeatedly taken by the English. Even today the ruins of town and forts are impressive, more so than any ruins readily accessible on the continent, though to see them at their best you must be there when the jungle has been newly cut away, else all is lost in a canopy of green. Across the bay from the town, about a mile and a half, stand still the remnants of the "Iron Castle" on a towering bluff, Castle Gloria and Fort Geronimo. These defensive works were built of stone, cut from reefs under the water found all along the coast. Almost as light as pumice stone and soft and easily worked when first cut, this stone hardens on exposure so that it will stop a ball without splitting or chipping. When Admiral Vernon, of the British navy, had captured the town in 1739, he tried to demolish the fort and found trouble enough. "The walls of the lower battery," he recorded, "consisting of 22 guns, were nine foot thick and of a hard stone cemented with such fine

NATIVE CHILDREN, PANAMA PROVINCE

mortar that it was a long work to make any impression in it, to come to mine at all, so that the blowing up took sixteen or eighteen days." Even today the relics of the Iron Fort present an air of bygone power and the rusty cannon still lying by the embrasures bring back vividly the days of the buccaneers.

Inheriting the greatness and prosperity of Nombre de Dios, Porto Bello inherited also its unpleasant prominence as a target for the sea rover. French filibusters and British buccaneers raided it at their fancy while the black Cimmaroons of the mainland lay in wait for caravans entering or leaving its gates. To describe, or even to enumerate all the raids upon the town would be wearisome to the reader. Most savage, however, of the pests that attacked the place was Sir Henry Morgan, the English buccaneer, whose ex-

come or go from Spain; by reason of the unhealthiness of the air, occasioned by certain vapors that exhale from the mountains. Notwithstanding their chief warehouses are at Porto Bello, howbeit their habitations be all the year long at Panama; whence they bring the plate upon mules at such times as the fair begins, and when the ships, belonging to the Company of Negroes, arrive here to sell slaves."

Morgan's expedition consisted of nine ships and about 460 men, nearly all English—too small a force to venture against such a stronghold. But the intrepid commander would listen to no opposition. His ships he anchored near Manzanillo Island where now stands Colon. Thence by small boats he con-

BULL-RIDER AND NATIVE CAR AT BOUQUETTE, CHIRIQUI

ploits are so fully and admiringly related by Esquemeling that we may follow his narrative, both of the sack of Porto Bello, and the later destruction of the Castle of San Lorenzo.

It was in 1668 that Morgan made his first attack upon Porto Bello. "Here," wrote Esquemeling, "are the castles, almost inexpugnable, that defend the city, being situated at the entry of the port; so that no ship or boat can pass without permission. The garrison consists of three hundred soldiers, and the town is constantly inhabited by four hundred families, more or less. The merchants dwell not here, but only reside for awhile, when the galleons

veyed all save a few of his men to a point near the landward side of the town, for he feared to attack by sea because of the great strength of the forts. Having taken the Castle of Triana he resolved to shock and horrify the inhabitants of the town by a deed of cold-blooded and wholesale murder, and accordingly drove all the defenders into a single part of the castle and with a great charge of gunpowder demolished it and them together. If horrified, the Spaniards were not terrified, but continued bravely the defense of the works they still held. For a time the issue of the battle looked dark for Morgan, when to his callous and brutal mind

THE INDIANS CALL HER A WITCH

there occurred an idea worthy of him alone. Let us follow Esquemeling's narrative again:

"To this effect, therefore, he ordered ten or twelve ladders to be made, in all possible haste, so broad that three or four men at once might ascend them. These being finished, he commanded all the religious men and women whom he had taken prisoners to fix them against the walls of the castle. Thus much he had before hand threatened the governor to perform, in case he delivered not the castle. But his answer was: 'He would never surrender himself alive'. Captain Morgan was much persuaded that the governor would not employ his utmost forces, seeing religious women and ecclesiastical persons exposed in the front of the soldiers to the greatest dangers. Thus the ladders, as I have said, were put into the hands of religious persons of both sexes; and these were forced at the head of the companies, to raise and apply them to the walls. But Captain Morgan was deceived in his judgment of this design. For the governor, who acted like a brave and courageous soldier, refused not, in performance of his duty, to use his utmost endeavors to destroy whosoever came near the walls. The religious men and women ceased not to cry unto him and beg of him by all the Saints of Heaven he would deliver the castle, and hereby spare both his and their own lives. But nothing could prevail with the obstinacy and fierceness that had possessed the governor's mind. Thus many of the religious men and nuns were killed before they could fix the ladders. Which at last being done, though with great loss of the said religious people, the pirates mounted them in great numbers, and with no less valour; having fireballs in their hands and earthen pots full of powder. All which things, being now at the top of the walls, they kindled and cast in among the Spaniards.

"This effort of the pirates was very great, insomuch as the Spaniards could no longer resist nor defend the castle, which was now entered. Hereupon they all threw down their arms, and craved quarter for their lives. Only the governor of the city would admit or crave no mercy; but rather killed many of the pirates with his own hands, and not a few of his own soldiers because they did not stand to their arms. And although the pirates asked him if he

A CUNA-CUNA FAMILY NEAR PORTO BELLO

A NATIVE VILLAGE

These villages are now scattered throughout the Canal Zone but will disappear as the order expelling natives from the Zone is more thoroughly enforced.

would have quarter, yet he constantly answered: 'By no means; I had rather die as a valiant soldier, than be hanged as a coward'. They endeavored as much as they could to take him prisoner. But he defended himself so obstinately that they were forced to kill him; notwithstanding all the cries and tears of his own wife and daughter, who begged him upon their knees he would demand quarter and save his life. When the pirates had possessed themselves of the castle, which was about night, they enclosed therein all the prisoners they had taken, placing the women and men by themselves, with some guards upon them. All the wounded were put into a certain apartment by itself, to the intent their own complaints might be the cure of their disease; for no other was afforded them."

For fifteen days the buccaneers held high carnival in Porto Bello. Drunk most of the time, weakened with debauchery and riot, with discipline thrown to the winds, and captains and fighting men scattered all over the town in pursuit of women and wine, the outlaws were at the mercy of any determined assailant. Esquemeling said, "If there could

A TRAIL NEAR PORTO BELLO

have been found 50 determined men they could have retaken the city and killed all the pirates. Less than fifty miles away was Panama with a heavy garrison and a thousand or more citizens capable of bearing arms. Its governor must have known that the success of the raid on Porto Bello would but arouse the English lust for a sack of his richer town. But instead of seizing the opportunity to crush them when they were sodden and stupefied by debauchery he sent puerile messages asking to be informed with what manner of weapons they could have overcome such strong defenses. Morgan naturally replied with an insult and a threat to do likewise to Panama within a twelvemonth.

For fifteen days the revel was maintained, every citizen who looked as if he had money being put to the torture to compel him to confess where he had hidden it. When all had been extorted that seemed possible the buccaneers made ready to depart. But first Morgan demanded 100,-000 pieces of eight, in default of which he would burn the city and blow up the castles. The wretched citizens sought aid of the President of Panama who was as un-

A CHOLO MOTHER AND DAUGHTER

A GROUP OF CUEPA TREES

willing to help them with gold as with powder and lead. In some miraculous way they raised it, and Morgan and his men departed, making their way to that town of revelry, Port Royal, of which I have already spoken, at the entrance to Kingston harbor. Perhaps it is fair to contrast with Esquemeling's story of the exploit Morgan's official report—for this worthy had a royal commission for his deeds. The Captain reported that he had left Porto Bello in as good condition as he found it, that its people had been well treated, so much so that "several ladies of great quality and other prisoners who were offered their liberty to go to the President's camp refused, saying they were now prisoners to a person of quality who was more tender of their honors than they doubted to find in the President's camp; and so voluntarily continued with him."

Captain Morgan's own testimony to his kindness to prisoners and his regard for female honor impresses one as quite as novel and audacious as his brilliant idea of forcing priests and nuns to carry the scaling ladders with which to assault a fortress defended by devout Catholics. Yet except for little incidents of this sort the whole crew—Spanish conquistadores, French filibusters and English buccaneers were very tenacious of the forms of religion and ostentatious piety. The Spaniards were always singing Te Deums, and naming their engines of war after the saints; Captain Daniels, a French filibuster, shot dead a sailor for irreverent behavior during mass; the English ships had divine service every Sunday and profanity and gambling were sometimes prohibited in the enlistment articles. All of which goes to show that people may be very religious and still a pest to humanity—nor is it necessary to turn to the buccaneers for instances of this fact.

CHAPTER IV

SAN LORENZO AND PANAMA

TWO years of the joys of Port Royal emptied the pockets of the buccaneers. The money that passed from hand to hand over the gambling tables went thence into the pockets of the hordes of women from Spain, France and even England who flocked to that den of thieves, and from them into the coffers of merchants who took it back to Europe. As the money slowly disappeared the men clamored to be led on another raid. So great a reputation had Captain Morgan won that desperadoes from all corners of the world flocked to Jamaica seeking enrollment in his service. He had but to give out the tidings that he was ready to lead an expedition against Panama to have his rolls crowded, and as fine an assortment of picturesque cutthroats begging for enlistment as ever appeared outside the pages of a dime novel.

He designated the south side of the island of Tortuga—ever a favorite lurking place for pirates—as a rendezvous, writing at the time to certain gentry whom Esquemeling in a matter of fact way calls "the ancient and expert Pirates there abiding", asking their coöperation. By the 24th of October, 1670, he had gathered together 37 ships fully armed

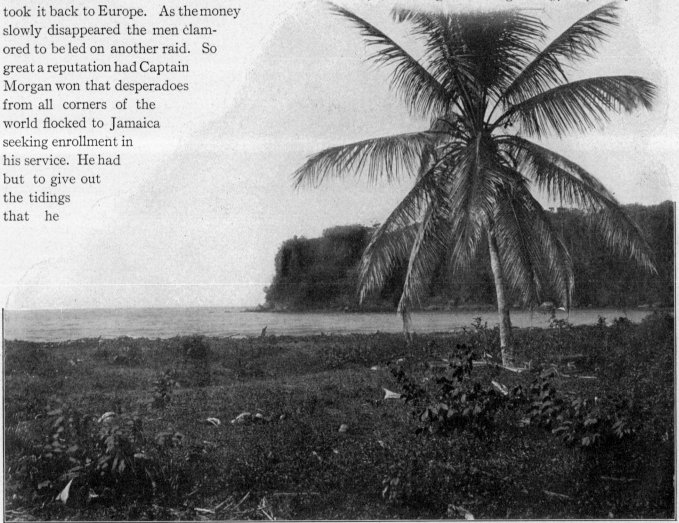

MOUTH OF THE CHAGRES RIVER

San Lorenzo stands on the brow of the cliff. The watch tower may be seen faintly uplifted.

75

and victualled, with 2000 fighting men besides mariners and boys. The chief ship mounted 22 great guns and six small brass cannon.

With this force Morgan first attacked the island of San Caterina, expecting to capture there some Indian or Spaniard who would guide him to Panama, by the Chagres River route, probably in order to take with him heavy artillery which could scarcely be dragged through the jungle. The first step toward the navigation of the river was the capture of Fort Lorenzo which stood on a high bluff at its mouth. Against this famous fort-

MOUTH OF THE CHAGRES FROM THE FORT
The upper picture shows the sea beach on the Pacific Coast littered with drift-wood

for the sack of that city had been determined upon in preference to either Vera Cruz or Cartagena, because it was richer. The people of the island were in no condition to resist the overwhelming force of the English, but the governor begged Morgan to make a sham attack in order that his credit and that of his officers might be maintained at home, and accordingly much powder was ineffectively burned. It sounds like a cheap device but it was employed again at Manila in 1898, the parties to the agreement being the Spanish governor and certain high officers of the United States army and navy.

Having secured his guides, by the easy process of putting on the rack all the Indians captured until one was found willing to lead the raiders through his native land, Morgan determined to move on Panama

ress, therefore, he sent Col. Bradley (or Brodley as he is sometimes called) with four ships and about 400 men, while he himself remained at St. Catherine to conceal from the Spaniards his ultimate design against Panama.

The visitor to Colon should not fail, before crossing to the Pacific side of the Isthmus, to visit the ruins of the Castle of San Lorenzo. The trip is not an easy one, and must usually be arranged for in advance, but the end well repays the exertion. The easiest way, when the weather permits, is to charter a tug or motor boat and make the journey by sea—a trip of two or three hours at most. But the Caribbean is a tempestuous and a treacherous sea. One may wait days for weather permitting the trip to be made in comfort, and even then may find a stormy afternoon succeed to a calm morning. For this reason it is essential that a seaworthy boat be procured and, if not essential, very desirable that the company be not subject to the qualms of seasickness.

To my mind the more interesting way to visit the ruins is to take the railroad out to Gatun, and there at the very base of the roaring spillway, board a power boat and chug down the sluggish Chagres to the river's mouth where stands the ancient fort. The boats obtainable are not of the most modern model and would stand a slender chance in speed contests. But in one, however slow, you are lost to all appearance of civilization five minutes after you cast off from the clay bank. At Gatun, the canal which has been carried through the artificial lake made by damming the Chagres River, turns sharply away from that water course on the way to the new port of Balboa. The six or eight miles of the tropical river which we are to traverse have been untouched by the activities of the canal builders. The sluggish stream flows between walls of dense green jungle, as silent as though behind their barrier

only a mile or two away there were not men by the thousands making great flights of aquatic steps to lift the world's ocean carriers over the hills. Once in awhile through the silent air comes the distant boom of a blast in Culebra, only an infrequent reminder of the presence of civilized man and his explosive activities. Infrequent though it is, however, it has been sufficient to frighten away the more timid inhabitants of the waterside—the alligators, the boas and the monkeys. Only at rare intervals are any of these seen now, though in the earlier days of the American invasion the alligators and monkeys were plentiful. Today the chief signs of animal life are the birds—herons, white and blue, flying from pool to pool or posing artistically on logs or in shallows; great comorant ducks that fly up and down midstream, apparently unacquainted with the terrors of the shotgun; kingfishers in bright blue and paroquets in gaudy colors. The river is said to be full of fish, including sharks, for the water is saline clear up to the Gatun locks.

I know of no spot, easy of access, on the Isthmus where an idea of the beauty and the terror of the jungle can be better gained than on the lower Chagres. The stout green barrier comes flush to the

Photo by T. J. Marine

THE SALLY-PORT AT SAN LORENZO

An unusual picture because of the clearing away of the jungle. Ordinarily the walls are hidden water's edge, the mangroves at places wading out on their stilt-like roots into the stream like a line of deployed skirmishers. That green wall looks light, beautiful, ethereal even, but lay your boat alongside it and essay to land. You will find it yielding indeed, but as impenetrable as a wall of adamant. It will receive you as gently as the liquid amber welcomes the fly, and hold you as inexorably in its beautiful embrace when you are once entrapped. The tender fern, the shrinking sensitive plant, the flowering shrub, the bending sapling, the sturdy and towering tree are all tied together by lithe, serpentine, gnarled and unbreakable vines which seem to spring from the ground and hang from the highest branches as well. There are not enough inches of ground to support the vegetation so it grows from the trees living literally on the air. Every green thing that can bear a thorn seems to have spines and prickers to tear the flesh, and to catch the clothing and hold the prisoner fast. Try it and you will see why no large mammals roam in the jungle; only the snakes and the lizards creeping down below the green tangle can attain large size and move.

And how beautiful it all is! The green alone would be enough, but it is varied by the glowing orange poll of a lignum vitæ tree, the bright scarlet of the hibiscus, the purple of some lordly tree whose name the botanist will know but not the wayfarer. Color is in splotches on every side, from the wild flowers

CHURCH AT CHAGRES
Up the steep path in the foreground the buccaneers charged upon Fort Lorenzo

close to the river's brink to great yellow blossoms on the tops of trees so tall that they tower over the forests like light-houses visible for miles around. Orchids in more delicate shades, orchids that would set Fifth Avenue agog, are here to be had for a few blows of a machete. It is a riot and a revel of color—as gay as the decorations of some ancient arena before the gladiatorial combats began. For life here is a steady battle too, a struggle between man and the jungle and woe to the man who invades the enemy's country alone or strays far from the trail, shadowy and indistinct as that may be.

"A man ought to be able to live quite a while lost in the jungle," said a distinguished magazine writer who was with me on the upper Chagres once. We had been listening to our guide's description of the game, and edible fruits in the forest.

"Live about two days if he couldn't find the trail or the river's bank," was the response of the Man Who Knew. "If he lived longer he'd live crazy. Torn by thorns, often poisoned, bitten by venomous insects, blistered by thirst, with the chances against his finding any fruit that was safe eating, he would probably die of the pain and of jungle madness before starvation brought a more merciful death. The jungle is a cat that tortures its captives; a python that embraces them in its graceful folds and hugs them to death; a siren whose beauty lured them to perdition. Look out for it."

The native Indian knows it and avoids it by doing

most of his traveling by canoe. On our trip to the river's mouth we passed many in their slender cayucas, some tied by a vine to the bank patiently fishing, others on their way to or from market with craft well loaded with bananas on the way up, but light coming back, holding gay converse with each other across the dark and sullen stream. Here and there through breaks in the foliage we see a native

OLD SPANISH MAGAZINE

house, or a cluster of huts, not many however, for the jungle is too thick and the land too low here for the Indians who prefer the bluffs and occasional broad savannas of the upper waters. As we approach its outlet the river, about fifty or sixty yards wide thus far, broadens into a considerable estuary, and rounding a point we see before us the blue Pacific breaking in white foam on a bar which effectually closes the river to all save the smallest boats, and which you may be sure the United States will never dredge away, to open a ready water-way to the base of the Gatun locks. To the left covering a low point, level as if artificially graded, is a beautiful cocoanut grove, to the right, across a bay perhaps a quarter of a mile wide is a native village of about fifty huts with an iron roofed church in the center— beyond the village rises a steep hill densely covered with verdure, so that it is only by the keenest searching that you can pick out here a stone sentry tower, there the angle of a massive wall—the ruins of the Castle of San Lorenzo.

"Cloud crested San
    Lorenzo guards
  The Chagres en-
    trance still,
Though o'er each
    stone the moss
    hath grown
  And earth his
    moat doth fill.
His bastions feeble
    with decay
  Steadfastly view
    the sea,
And sternly wait
    the certain fate
  The ages shall de-
    cree."

We land in the co-

SPANISH RUINS, PORTO BELLO

coanut grove across

OUR GUIDE AT SAN LORENZO

office setting forth the mysterious occult powers of a wizard and soothsayer who, among other services to mankind, recounted a number of rich marriages which had been made by the aid of his philters and spells.

We made our way from the village attended by volunteer guides in the scantiest of clothing, across a little runway at the bottom of a ravine, and so into the path that leads up the height crowned by the castle. It was two hundred and fifty years ago, almost, that the little hollow ran with a crimson fluid, and the bodies of dead Spaniards lay in the rivulet where now the little native boys are cooling their feet. The path is steep, rugged and narrow. Branches arch overhead and as the trail has served as a runway for the downpour of innumerable tropical rains the soil is largely washed away from between the stones, and the climbing is hard.

"Not much fun carrying a steel helmet, a heavy leather jacket and a twenty-pound blunderbuss up this road on a hot day, with bullets and arrows whistling past," remarks a heavy man in the van, and the picture he conjures up of the Spanish assailants on that hot afternoon in 1780 seems very vivid. Although the fort, the remains of which are now standing, is not the one which Morgan destroyed, the site, the natural defenses and the plan of the works are identical. There was more wood in the original fort than in that of which the remains are now discernible—to which fact its capture was due.

the river from the ruins we have come to see and the uninitiated among us wonder why. It appears however that the descendants of the natives who so readily surrendered dominion of the land to the Spaniards are made of sterner stuff than their ancestors. Or perhaps it was because we had neither swords or breastplates that they reversed the 16th century practice and extorted tribute of silver from us for ferrying us across the stream in cayucas when our own boats and boat-men would have given us a greater sense of security. Landed in the village we were convoyed with great ceremony to the alcalde's hut where it was demanded that we register our names and places of residence. Perhaps that gave us a vote in the Republic of Panama, but we saw no political evidences about unless a small saloon, in a hut thatched with palmetto leaves and with a mud floor and basket work sides might be taken for a "headquarters". Indeed the saloon and a frame church were about the only signs of civilization about the town if we except a bill posted in the alcalde's

THE AUTHOR AT SAN LORENZO

LOOKING UP THE CHAGRES FROM SAN LORENZO

The villagers every now and then cut away the dense underbrush which grows in the ancient fosse and traverses and conceals effectually the general plan of the fortress from the visitor. This cleaning up process unveils to the eye the massive masonry, and the towering battlements as shown by some of the illustrations here printed. But, except to the scientific student of archæology and of fortification, the ruins are more picturesque as they were when I saw them, overgrown with creeping vines and shrubs jutting out from every cornice and crevice, with the walls so masked by the green curtain that when some sharp salient angle boldly juts out before you, you start as you would if rounding the corner of the Flatiron Building you should come upon a cocoanut palm bending in the breeze. Here you come to great vaulted chambers, dungeons lighted by but one barred casemate where on the muddy ground you see rusty iron fetters weighing forty pounds or more to clamp about a prisoner's ankle or, for that matter, his neck.

The vaulted brick ceiling above is as perfect as the day Spanish builders shaped it and the mortar betwixt the great stones forming the walls is too hard to be picked away with a stout knife. Pushing through the thicket which covers every open space you stumble over a dismounted cannon, or a neat conical pile of rusty cannon balls, carefully prepared for the shock of battle perhaps two hundred years ago and lying in peaceful slumber ever since—a real Rip Van Winkle of a fortress it is, with no likelihood of any rude awakening. In one spot seems to have been a sort of central square. In the very heart of the citadel is a great masonry tank to hold drinking water for the besieged. It was built before the 19th century had made its entrance upon the procession of the centuries, but the day I saw it the still water that it held reflected the fleecy clouds in the blue sky, and no drop trickled through the joints of the honest and ancient masonry. Back and forth through narrow gates, in and out of vaulted chambers, down dark passages behind twenty-foot walls you wander, with but little idea of the topography of the place until you come to a little watch tower jutting out at one corner of the wall. Here the land falls away sharply a hundred feet or more to the sea and you understand why the buccaneers

they found the garrison reënforced until it nearly equaled the English. So slight was the disparity in numbers that it seems amazing that the English could have sustained the rigors of the assault. It was, of course, impossible to attack the castle on its sea front, and the invaders accordingly left their boats about a league from the castle, making their way painfully through the jungle toward the place of action. Esquemeling describes the fortification which they were to overthrow thus:

"This castle is built upon a high

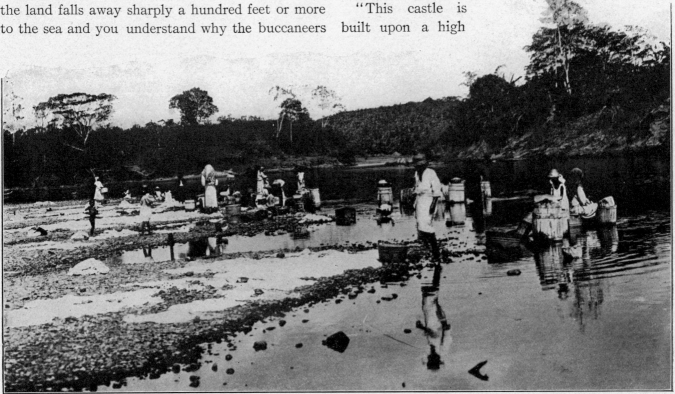

THE TRUE NATIVE SOCIAL CENTER

were forced to attack from the landward side, though as you were scaling that toilsome slope you wondered that any race of humans ever dared attack it at all.

In their story of the assault on Fort Lorenzo, as indeed in the narrative of all the doings of the buccaneers, the historians have followed the narrative of Esquemeling, a young Dutch apothecary who joined the sea rovers as a sort of assistant surgeon, and wrote a book which has kept his memory alive, whatever may have been the effect of his surgery on his patients. News of the advance of the English had reached the Governor of Panama so that when the assailants reached the battlefield

mountain, at the entry of the river, and surrounded on all sides with strong palisades, or wooden walls; being very well terrepleined, and filled with earth; which renders them as secure as the best walls made of stone or brick. The top of this mountain is in a manner divided into two parts, between which lies a ditch of the depth of thirty feet. The castle itself has but one entry, and that by a drawbridge which passes over the ditch aforementioned. On the land side it has four bastions, that of the sea containing only two more. That part thereof which looks towards the South is totally inaccessible and impossible to be climbed, through the infinite asperity of the mountain.

"The North side is surrounded by the river, which hereabouts runs very broad. At the foot of the said castle, or rather mountain, is seated a strong fort, with eight great guns, which commands and impedes the entry of the river. Not much lower are to be seen two other batteries, whereof each hath six pieces of cannon to defend likewise the mouth of the said river. At one side of the castle are built two great store-houses, in which are deposited all sorts of war-like ammunition and merchandise, which are brought hither from the inner parts of the country. Near these houses is a high pair of stairs, hewed out of the rock, which serves to mount to the top of the castle. On the West side of the said fortress lies a small port, which is not above seven or eight fathoms deep, being very fit for small vessels and of very good anchorage. Besides this, there lies before the castle, at the entry of the river, a great rock, scarce to be perceived above water, unless at low tide."

If the English had hoped to take the garrison by surprise they were speedily undeceived. Hardly had they emerged from the thicket into the open space on which stands now the village of Chagres than they were welcomed with so hot a volley of musketry and artillery from the castle walls that many fell dead at the first fire. To assault they had to cross a ravine, charge up a bare hillside, and pass through a ditch thirty feet deep at the further

bank of which stood the outer walls of the fort made of timber and clay. It was two in the afternoon when the fighting began. The buccaneers charged with their usual daredevil valor, carrying fire balls

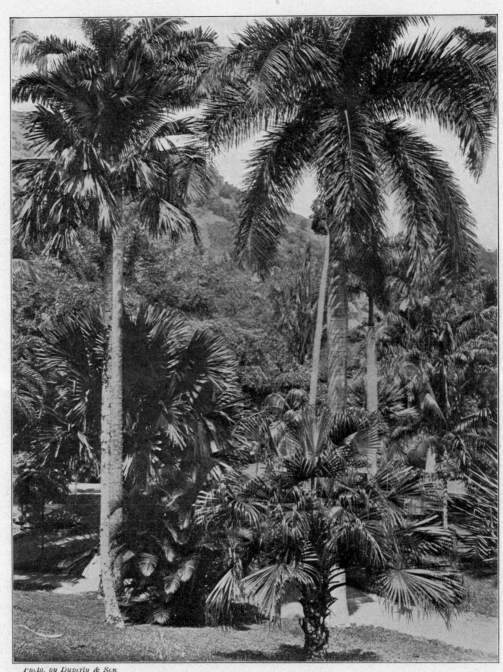

Photo. by Duperly & Son

TROPICAL FOLIAGE ON THE CARIBBEAN

along with their swords and muskets. The Spaniards met them with no less determination, crying out:

"Come on ye English dogs, enemies to God and our King; let your other companions that are behind come too; ye shall not go to Panama this bout."

All the afternoon and into the night the battle raged and the assailants might well have despaired of success except for an event which Esquemeling thus describes:

"One of the Pirates was wounded with an arrow in his back which pierced his body to the other side. This instantly he pulled out with great valor at the side of his breast; then taking a little cotton that he had about him, he wound it about the said arrow, and putting it into his musket, he shot it back into the castle. But the cotton being kindled by the powder occasioned two or three houses that were within the castle, being thatched with palm leaves, to take fire, which the Spaniards perceived not so soon as was necessary. For this fire meeting with a parcel of powder blew it up, and hereby caused great ruin, and no less consternation to the Spaniards, who were not able to account for this accident, not having seen the beginning thereof."

The fire within the fort not only disconcerted its defenders but greatly aided the assailants, for by its flames the Spaniards could be seen working their guns and were picked off by the English sharp-shooters. The artillery of the invaders made breaches in the walls and the debris thus occasioned dropped into the ditch making its crossing practicable for a storming party. Though the gallant governor of the castle threw himself into the breach and fought with the greatest desperation, he was forced back and into his citadel. There a musket shot pierced his brain and the defense which was becoming a defeat became in fact a rout. Spaniards flung themselves from the lofty cliffs upon the rocks below or into the sea rather than trust to the mercy of their conquerors. All but thirty of the garrison of 314 were slain, not one officer escaping, and only a few escaped to steal up the river and through the jungle carrying to Panama the dismal tale of the fall of its chief outpost.

NATIVE PANAMA WOMAN

Nor did the English win their triumph easily. Their force was in the neighborhood of 400, of whom more than 100 were killed and 70 wounded. A round shot took off both legs of Colonel Bradley and from the wound he died a few days later. The church of the castle was turned into a hospital, the Spaniards were made to bury their own dead, which was done by dropping them over the cliff into the sea, and word was sent to Morgan that the way was clear for his march upon Panama.

We may for a time turn aside from Buccaneer Morgan and his ravenous raid to consider the later history of the two strongholds — Porto Bello and San Lorenzo — which lie to the east and west of Colon. It was not the rude shock of war which reduced them to the state of desolation and ruin in which visitors now find them — though of such shocks they certainly experienced enough. Morgan on his return from Panama blew up San Lorenzo and left it a wreck, but the Spaniards rebuilt it stronger than ever and

ON THE UPPER CHAGRES

A CHARACTER OF COLON

it long continued to mount guard over the entrance to the Chagres. So too with the forts at Porto Bello. But about 1738 one Edward Vernon, after whom it is said Mount Vernon, the home of Washington, was named, rose in the English parliament and declared that he could take Porto Bello with only six ships. Parliament took him at his word, commissioned him admiral, gave him seven ships and dispatched him on the enterprise. Being a gentleman of spirit and a true sport, Admiral Vernon, on approaching the Isthmus, sent one of his ships into other waters, "disdaining to appear before Porto Bello with one ship more than he had engaged to take it with." Success came to him with ease. Only four of his ships were engaged and the only considerable loss was among a landing party which stormed the lower battery of the Iron Fort. The Spaniards showed but little stomach for the fight, and it is worth noting that in the recurrent affrays in the West Indies and Central America the English whipped them with the same monotonous certainty with which the latter had beaten the Indians. Any one desiring to draw broad generalizations as to the comparative courage of nations is welcome to this fact.

After refitting at Jamaica, Admiral Vernon, with a somewhat larger fleet, proceeded against San Lorenzo. Again his triumph was easy, for after a leisurely bombardment to which the Spaniards replied but languidly, the white flag was displayed and the English entered into possession. The warehouses in Chagres were plundered and the fort blown up. The spluttering war between England and Spain in which these actions occurred became known as "the war of Jenkins' ear." A too zealous guarda costa lopped off the ear of a certain Captain Jenkins who, though unknown to fame prior to that outrage, so made the welkin ring in England, even exhibiting the mummified member from which he had been thus rudely divorced, that Parliament was forced to declare a war in retaliation for his ear or have its own talked off.

The buccaneers and pirates really caused the final abandonment of Porto Bello and San Lorenzo, though not by direct attack. They made trade by the Caribbean and along the Spanish Main so perilous that the people of the Pacific coast found it more profitable in the long run to make the voyage around the Horn or through the Straits of Magellan. The economics of trade are unvarying. It seeks the cheapest before the shortest routes, and one of the studies of our canal authorities will be to so fix their tolls that they will

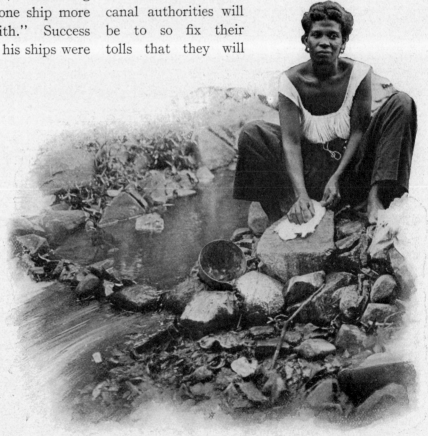

WOMAN OF THE CHAGRES REGION

not, like Morgan, L'Olonais and others, frighten trade away from the Isthmus.

Though the forts were rebuilt to their original strength in 1751, they never regained importance. Porto Bello disappeared when the Royal Road to Panama lost its traffic, and the Chagres only resumed a brief importance in 1844 when the Royal Mail Steampacket Co. made San Lorenzo a port of call. When Colon, however, appeared as a port and the terminus of the Panama railroad, the fate of all other ports on the Atlantic side of the Isthmus was sealed. Left to brood over the days of their greatness—though indeed they never repelled any serious attack—the Iron Fort and San Lorenzo were abandoned by their Columbian garrisons and given over to the insidious and irresistible conquest of the jungle. Picturesque and dignified, they well repay the visit of the tourist.

> " Still standeth San Lorenzo there,
>   Aye, faithful at his post,
> Though scoffing trees in every breeze
>   Their prime and vigor boast;
> His garrison is but the shades
>   Of soldiers of the past,
> But it pleaseth him, alone and grim,
>   To watch unto the last."

CHAPTER V

THE SACK OF OLD PANAMA

THE week after the fall of San Lorenzo, Morgan with his full force appeared at the mouth of the Chagres River. Before leaving St. Catherine he had dismantled the forts and burned all the houses for no particular reason except the seemingly instinctive desire of a buccaneer to destroy all that he could not steal. At once he began his preparations for the ascent of the Chagres to its head of navigation, where, disembarking, he would take the trail for Old Panama. Cruces, which was the point of debarkation, had grown to a considerable town at this time, being the point of transshipment of goods destined for Nombre de Dios, or Porto Bello, from the mules that had brought them thus far, to the boats that would float them down to tide water. The town, an inconsiderable hamlet of thatched huts, remained in 1913, but the rise of Gatun Lake was expected to practically blot it out of existence.

Old Panama, for which Morgan was preparing the grim experience of a battle and a sack, had been founded in 1519 by that Pedrarias of whom we have told as the executioner of Balboa. It had grown rapidly, built up by the trade resulting from the invasion of Peru. At the time of Morgan's raid Esquemeling writes of the city:

"There belonged to this city (which is also the head of a bishopric) eight monasteries, whereof seven were for men and one for women; two stately churches and one hospital. The churches and monasteries were all richly adorned with altar-pieces and paintings, huge quantity of gold and silver, with other precious things. . . . Besides which ornaments, here were to be seen two thousand houses of magnificent and prodigious building, being all of the greatest part inhabited by merchants of that country, who are vastly rich. For the rest of the inhabitants of lesser quality and tradesmen, this city contained five thousand houses more. Here were also great numbers of stables, which served for the horses and mules, that carry all the plate, belonging as well unto the King of Spain as to private men, towards the coast of the North Sea. The neighboring fields belonging to this city are all cultivated and fertile plantations, and pleasant gardens, which afford delicious prospects unto the inhabitants the whole year long."

NEAR A CONVENT AT OLD PANAMA

Correal fixes the number of private houses as between seven and eight thousand. The pious Thomas Gage whom we have seen haggling for rooms at Porto Bello visited Panama about 1538 and even then credits it with five thousand inhabit-

CASA REALE OR KING'S HOUSE
Its heavy walls show that it was planned for defense but the Spaniards abandoned it

ants, and at least eight cloisters of nuns and friars. Unfortunately the good evangelist found that "the Spaniards are in this city much given to sinne, looseness and venery," for which reason, or perhaps because he "feared much the heats," he made haste to leave the town and left us none of those graphic descriptions of which his pen was capable.

The country round about Panama was then, and still is, arable and well-fitted for grazing. The rural population was but small, more meager indeed than one would think would have been necessary for raising vegetables for so considerable a town. In the back country were great numbers of Cimmaroons, or escaped slaves who are described as living in communities, ruled over by a black king. They went naked and were armed with bows and arrows, spears, darts and machetes. They lived on plunder and as when captured were they killed, or, at the best, enslaved anew, they fought with great desperation. Merchandise trains were their chief victims, though they often raided cattle ranches, or cut off individuals in the outskirts of the city. The English supplied them with weapons and could always be sure of their aid against the Spaniards, who had been their masters and whom they hated.

The harbor was wretched, useful only for small vessels which at high tide could come straight to the sea-wall, being left there by the receding tide, high and dry, so that by quick action they could be unloaded before the waters returned. A very considerable part of the food of the town was fish brought thither by Indians from Taboga and nearby islands.

Such was the town which Morgan raided. Because of the colossal disaster which befell it, a disaster without parallel since the days when the Goths and Vandals swept down over the pleasant plains of Italy, there has been a tendency to magnify the size, wealth and refinement of Panama at the time of its fall. But studied calmly, with no desire to exaggerate the qualities which made it so rich a prize, Panama may fairly be described as a city of about 30,000 people, with massive churches, corvents and official buildings of masonry, with many stately houses of the type esteemed luxurious in the tropics, and peopled largely by pure-blooded Span-

iards of the better type. It was too early a date for
the amalgamation of races now so much in evidence
on the Isthmus to have proceeded far, and the ancient records show that the Spaniards of substance
in the town had mainly come thither from Seville.

Morgan started up the river from San Lorenzo,
where he left 500 men to serve as a garrison, on the
18th of January, 1761. His force comprised 1200
men in five boats with artillery and thirty-two
canoes. The raiders planned to live on the country
and hence took small store of provisions—an error
which nearly wrecked the expedition. The first day
they covered about eighteen miles. This was by
nature made the easiest part of their journey, for
this stretch of the Chagres is deep, with but a slow
current and much of the way they may have been
aided by the incoming tide. If the chronicler who
fixed their distance covered at eighteen miles was
correct, they must have pitched their camp the
first night not very far from where Gatun Dam now
rears its mighty bulk across the valley and makes of
the Chagres a broad lake. Their troubles however
came with their first nightfall. Leaving their boats
and scattering about the surrounding country they
found that the Spaniards had raked it clean of
provisions of every sort. The Indian villages were
either smoking ruins or clusters of empty huts, the
cattle ranches were bare of cattle, and even the
banana and yam patches were stripped. By noon
on the second day, according to Esquemeling,
"they were compelled to leave their boats and canoes
by reason the river was very dry for want of rain,
and the many trees that were fallen into it." Hence-
forth at that point the Chagres River transformed
into a lake will be in the neighborhood of forty feet
deep the year round. Apparently, however, the
abandonment of the boats was only partial, the
main body of troops marching through the woods
while others waded, pushing the boats over the
shallows as is done today. The advance was
continued in this fashion, partly by water and partly
through the jungle, all with the greatest difficulty,
at a snail's pace and on stomachs daily growing
emptier. Twice they came upon signs that the
Spaniards had prepared an ambuscade for them,
but becoming faint-hearted had fled. Thereat the
buccaneers grumbled mightily. They were better at
fighting than at chopping paths through the jungle,

Photo by Burtis & Elliott

THE RUINED TOWER OF SAN AUGUSTINE

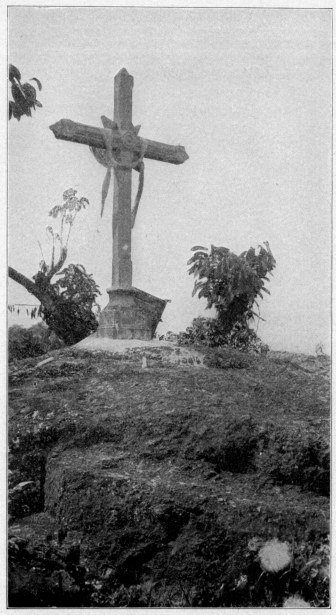

WAYSIDE SHRINE ON THE SAVANNA ROAD

never were out of their mothers' kitchens, may ask how these pirates could eat, swallow and digest those pieces of leather, so hard and dry. To whom I only answer: That could they once experiment what hunger, or rather famine, is, they would certainly find the manner, by their own necessity, as the pirates did. For these first took the leather and sliced it in pieces. Then did they beat it between two stones, and rub it, often dipping it in the water of the river to render it by these means supple and tender. Lastly they scraped off the hair, and roasted or broiled it upon the fire. And, being thus cooked, they cut it into small morsels, and eat it, helping it down with frequent gulps of water, which by good fortune they had near at hand."

Once only did they meet with any resistance; that was near Cruces where several hundred Indians ambushed them in the jungle, and while avoiding any direct combat, killed several with arrows. As the Indians fled they cried out in Spanish, "Ho, ye dogs! Go to the savanna; to the savanna," from which, as from like warnings uttered by stragglers, the invaders concluded that battle was to be given them on the broad plain before the city.

It had taken six days for the expedition to reach Cruces—a trip which could readily be made today by train to Camboa and thence by cayuca in five or six hours. Arrived there they prepared for the last stage of the journey, for there they finally left their boats and took up the Royal Road. Cruces is eight miles from Panama, and at the moment of Morgan's descent upon it, was at the period of its greatest prosperity. Of its rise to greatness and its final disappearance under the rising waters of Gatun Lake I shall have more to say in the chapter concerning the Chagres River. The English found the frame houses already ablaze, and the larders swept clean, the Spaniards having followed their invariable custom of leaving no food for the invaders. Some wretched dogs and cats which hung about the deserted dwellings were killed and eaten, and in the storehouses a number of jars of wine were found, upon drinking which the buccaneers became deathly sick. They claimed it was poisoned, but more probably their stomachs, which had been struggling to digest leather scraps, were in no condition for the strong wines of the tropics.

From this point onward the invaders saw many of

and were so hungry that if they had slain a few Spaniards they would quite probably have cooked and eaten them. For six days they struggled with the jungle without finding any food whatsoever, then they discovered a granary stored with maize which they ate exultingly. Leather scraps became a much prized article of food, just as in a very different climate Greely's men in the Arctic circle kept alive on shreds cut from their sealskin boots. Of leather as an article of diet Esquemeling writes:

"Here again he was happy, that had reserved since noon any small piece of leather whereof to make his supper, drinking after it a good draught of water for his greatest comfort. Some persons, who their enemies, but the Indians only offered active resistance, firing upon the advancing column from ambuscades, and at one or two made a determined stand. As the invaders were strung out in single file along a narrow road (Esquemeling complains that only ten or twelve men could walk in a file) it would have been easy to so impede their progress, and harass them with attacks from the bush, as to defeat their purpose wholly. For it is to be remembered that the English were almost starved, footsore and weary, dragging cannon along the rocky roads and bearing heavy equipment under the scorching sun. But the Spaniards contented themselves with shouting defiance and daring the invaders to meet them "a la savanna." At the first danger of a fight they ran away.

Gaining on the ninth day of their march the top of a hill, still known as "El Cerro de los Buccaneeros" (The Hill of the Buccaneers), the pirates had the joy of seeing for the first time the Pacific, and thus knowing that Panama must be at hand. Upon the plain below they came upon a great body of cattle. Some historians say that the Spaniards had gathered a great herd of savage bulls to be driven upon the English lines in expectation of putting them to rout. The tradition seems doubtful, and to any one who has seen the mild and docile bulls of the Panama savannas it is merely ridiculous. However the cattle came there it was an ill chance for the Spaniards, for they furnished the hearty food necessary to put fight again into the famished bodies of the buccaneers. Esquemeling's description of the banquet on the plains is hardly appetizing:

"Here while some were employed in killing and flaying cows, horses, bulls and chiefly asses, of which there was greatest number, others busied themselves in kindling of fires and getting wood wherewith to roast them. Thus cutting the flesh of these animals into pieces, or gobbets, they threw them into the fire, and half carbonadoed or roasted, they devoured them with incredible haste and appetite. For such was their hunger that they more resembled cannibals than Europeans at this banquet, the blood many

ARCHED BRIDGE AT OLD PANAMA, ALMOST 400 YEARS OLD
There was no Horatius to hold this strait path against the invaders

times running down from their beards to the middle of their bodies."

Gorged to their gullets, the cutthroats lay down to rest. Morgan had a sharp watch kept, and sounded at least one false alarm that the men might not sleep too securely. But the Spaniards on the eve of their crushing disaster left their foes to rest in peace except for a noisy cannonade which did no damage, and shouts of "Corros! Nos Veremos"—"Dogs! We will see you again," which they certainly did, finding the meeting most unpleasant.

On the morrow, the tenth day after leaving San Lorenzo, and either the 18th or 27th of January, 1671, for contemporary writers differ about the date, the attack on the city began. The buccaneers disappointed the Spanish at the very outset by not taking the road which lay plain and open to them and which was well commanded by the Spanish batteries and ambuscades, but came upon them through the woods. This violation of the rules of the game embarrassed the Spaniards from the very first.

But even so, they had every advantage on their side—except courage. They largely outnumbered

Photo by Prof. Otto Lutz

FOLIAGE ON THE CANAL ZONE

the assailants, though the estimate of the hostile generals differ greatly, as they always have in history. We must reasonably suppose that in a battle on the issue of which directly depended their lives, the lives and honor of their womenfolk, their homes, their fortunes, their liberty and the continued existence of their city the people of Panama would have turned out to a man. Yet the President of Panama reported to the Spanish court that he had but 1200 men, mostly negroes, mulattoes and Indians, armed with fowling pieces and his only artillery three wooden cannon bound with rawhide. Dr. C. L. G. Anderson, to whose painstaking study of the old Spanish chroniclers all present-day students of Panama history must be largely indebted, says, and reasonably, "The Spanish army was made up not merely of merchants, planters and servants, but contained besides many regular troops; veterans of the wars in Flanders, Sicily and other countries of Europe." Whatever the precise figures may have been there is no question that the assailants were largely outnumbered by the defenders who, fighting for wives and children, homes and firesides, might have been

THE CHAGRES ABOVE SAN LORENZO

expected to show desperate valor. Instead of which the buccaneers put the Spaniards to rout in two hours' fighting on the plain to which the pirates had been so scornfully invited.

The Spanish plan of battle savored largely of the theatrical. As the circus opens its performance with a grand entry of mounted performers, so the Spaniards ushered in the fight with a grand charge of cavalry. Admirable cavalrymen, they are said to have been, well mounted on trained cattle ponies and in all about 400 strong. Unhappily there appeared to have been no preliminary study of the English position, and a morass impenetrable by horsemen guarded its flanks. Only in front could the English line be reached and there the trained marksmen of the buccaneers, or cattle hunters, dropping on one knee, picked off the Spanish horsemen before they could close. The cavalry hardly reached the buccaneers' first line though they charged twice with the utmost gallantry. An infantry charge that followed was beaten back with like slaughter. Seeing this the Spaniards are said to have resorted to a device as ridiculous in its outcome as it was in its conception. This was the driving against the buccaneers' lines of a herd of a thousand bulls driven by fifty vaqueros. With great shouting and cracking of whips the herd was urged against the invaders. But the Central American bull as a ferocious beast is a disappointment—

which perhaps explains the placidity with which Panama agreed to the request of the United States that it abolish bull fighting. If not vicious, however, they can be obstinate, and about as many bulls charged into the already shattered Spanish lines as upon the buccaneers. Morgan showed quick wit by ordering his men to let the bulls pass, but kill the vaqueros, and so, with the exception of a few bovines who lingered to rend the British flags, being enraged by their scarlet hue, the greater part of the herd trotted off to a quieter part of the savanna where they might placidly graze while the foolish men who had sought to drag them into the quarrel went on killing each other. This virtually ended the Spanish defense. After another charge the defenders of the city gave up any effort at organized opposition to the invaders and fled into the city, or to the shelter of the neighboring jungle. The English, exhausted with their long march and the shock of the battle, did not immediately follow up their advantage but rested for some hours. There is much conflict of authority on the question of loss in the battle. Morgan claimed to have lost only five men killed and ten wounded, and fixed the Spanish loss at about 400. Esquemeling says there were 600

IN THE CRYPT OF OLD SAN AUGUSTINE

cavalry on the savanna, and three hours sufficed for the English to make themselves masters of the whole city. During the fighting flames broke out in several quarters of the town, some think set purposely by the assailants, which was denied by Morgan. However caused, the fires raged for days, were still smoldering when the buccaneers left three weeks later, and consumed nearly all except the masonry edifices in the city. Imagination balks at the effort to conceive the wretched plight of the 30,000 people of this city, subjected for three weeks to the cruelty, cupidity and lust of the "experienced and ancient pyrates" and the cutthroats of all nationalities that made up the command of Morgan. Little more than a thousand of the raiders could have remained alive, but all the fighting men of the city were slain, wounded or cowed into unmanly subjection. After the first riotous orgy of drunkenness and rapine—though indeed Morgan shrewdly strove to keep his men sober by spreading the report that all the wine had been poisoned — the business of looting was taken

Spaniards dead upon the field beside the wounded and prisoners. Whatever the comparative losses the Spanish defeat was decisive, nor did the survivors regain sufficient morale to offer any effective opposition to the buccaneers as they moved upon the city.

One would think that the final defense would have been dogged and desperate in the extreme. The Spaniards knew what to expect in the way of murder, rapine, plunder and enslavement. They had the story of Porto Bello fresh in their memories, and, for that matter, they had enjoyed such fruits of victory themselves too often to hug the delusion that the English would now forego them. Nor even after the decisive thrashing they had sustained on the plain need they have despaired. On three sides Panama was defended by the sea and its inlets, and on the fourth could only be approached along a single road and over an arched bridge, the sturdy masonry of which still stands, and forms a favorite background for photographic groups of tourists. Though not walled, as was its successor, Old Panama had a great plenty of heavy masonry buildings, the ruins of which show them to have been constructed with a view to defense. The churches, the eight convents, the official buildings and many of the private residences were built of stone with heavy barred windows and, if stoutly defended in conjunction with barricades in the streets, might well have balked the invaders of their prey. But the Spanish spirit seemed crushed by the defeat of their choice

A WOMAN OF OLD PANAMA

up seriously. First the churches and government houses had to be ransacked for precious ornaments and treasure, and herein the robbers met with their first serious disappointment, for on the news of their coming much of the plate had been put on ships and sent out to sea. A brig aground in the harbor was seized by Morgan and sent in pursuit, but the delights of the Island of Taboga, From ceremonial plate to the seamstress's thimble; from the glittering necklace to the wedding ring, everything was raked together into the great common store of plunder. What was easily found was not enough. Wells were searched, floors torn up, walls ripped open and, after all other devices had been employed, prisoners were put to the torture to make them reveal the hiding places of their own and

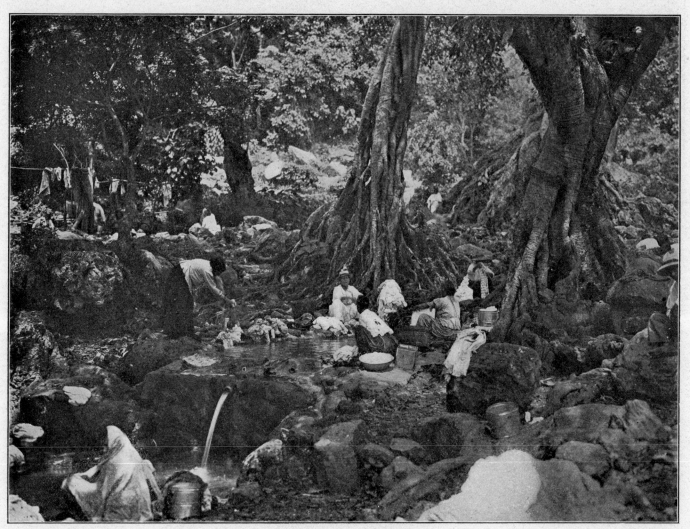

WASH DAY AT TABOGA

then as now a pleasure resort, proved superior even to the avariciousness of the Spaniards, and they lingered there over wine cups until the treasure ships had vanished. Rumors still linger that much of the treasure had been buried at Taboga, and that one richly freighted ship had been sunk some place nearby. But frequent treasure-hunting expeditions have come home empty handed.

After raking the government buildings from garret to vaults the pirates turned to the private houses.

others' valuables. Capt. Morgan led in this activity, as indeed he appears to have been the most villainous of all his crew in the mistreatment of women. After all that could be gathered by these devices had been taken the several thousand prisoners were informed that if they wanted to retain their lives and regain their liberty they must pay ransom, fixed in amount according to the standing in the community and the wealth of the captive. Of course the community was gone and the buccaneers had taken all of the wealth, but the luckless prisoner was expected to pay nevertheless and a surprising number of them did so. With all these expedients for the extraction of wealth from a subjugated town, the buccaneers were fain to be satisfied, and, weak from wounds and revelry, according to Esquemeling:

A STREET IN CRUCES

"On the 24th of February, of the year 1761, Captain Morgan departed from the city of Panama, or rather from the place where the city of Panama did stand. Of the spoils whereof he carried with him one hundred and seventy-five beasts of carriage, laden with silver, gold and other precious things, besides 600 prisoners more or less, between women, children and slaves."

So they plodded back to San Lorenzo whence they had started on their piratical expedition. It affords a striking illustration of the strictly business methods of these pirates that before reaching the castle Morgan ordered a halt, and had every man searched for valuables, submitting himself to the inquisition. So thorough was the search that even the guns were shaken, upside down, lest precious stones might be concealed in their barrels. However the buccaneers came to jeer at Morgan's apparent fairness in being searched with the rest, and putting his personal pilferings into the common lot as a piece of duplicity. For the loot of the Panama expedition has been reckoned at several millions of dollars, and indeed a town of that size, famous for wealth and at a period when the amassing of gold and jewels was a passion, should certainly have produced that much. But when it came to the vital operation of dividing the spoils the ordinary fighting men found that for their four months' campaign, they received about $100 apiece. "Which small sum," says the literary apothecary Esquemeling, who was "buncoed" with the rest, "they thought too little reward for so much labor and such huge and manifest dangers they had so often exposed their lives unto. But Captain Morgan was deaf to all these and many other complaints of this kind, having designed in his mind to cheat them of as much as he could."

BREAKING WAVES AT OLD PANAMA

Henry Morgan was indeed a practical pirate, who, had he but lived four hundred years later, could have made vastly more money out of a town of 30,000 people by the mild devices of franchises and bonds, than he did out of Panama with murder, the rack, robbery and rapine for his methods. After setting the example of loyally putting his all into the common store, he assumed the duty of dividing that store. This accomplished to his liking, and knowing that idleness breeds discontent, and that discontent is always hurtful to capital, he set his men to work pulling the Castle of San Lorenzo to pieces. While they were thus engaged, one dark night with favoring winds he hove anchor and with four ships, filled with his English favorites, and laden with the lion's share of the booty, he sailed away from Chagres and from buccaneering forever. He left behind all the French, Dutch and mongrel pirates—those ancient and experienced ones. He left them some of the poorer ships — much as an efficient gang of street railway looters leave some rusty rails and decrepit cars to a town they have looted—but saw to it that none was left that could possibly catch up with his fleet.

OLD BELL AT REMEDIOS, 1682

So the deserted buccaneers first fought awhile among themselves, then dispersed. Some in an amateurish way sacked the town of Keys in Cuba. Others went to Campeche and Honduras. Esquemeling with a small band went up to Bocadel Toro, now the Panama headquarters of the United Fruit Company, whence he made his way back to Europe. There he wrote his "History of the Buccaneers," which became one of the world's "best sellers," and in which he gave his Captain Morgan "the worst of it"—a species of satisfaction which is often the only recourse of the literary man who gets tangled up with Big Business.

As for Captain Morgan, he was made much of at Jamaica, where the crown's share of the proceeds of his piracy was cheerfully accepted by the governor. But in England there was some embarrassment, for there was no war with Spain and the complete destruction of a Spanish city by a force bearing British flags was at least embarrassing. So by way of showing its repentance and good intent the government announced its purpose to suppress buccaneering and all piracy, and to that end created Henry Morgan a baronet and put the commission in his hands—much as we have

THE BEETLING CLIFFS OF THE UPPER CHAGRES

THE ROOTS REACH DOWN SEEKING FOR SOIL

excellent road laid and maintained by the Republic of Panama. If you go by horseback the old trail which the pirates used is still traceable and at low tide one can ride along the beach. For the majority the drive along the road, which should be taken in the early morning, is the simpler way, though there was promise in 1913 that within a few months a trolley line would still further simplify the trip.

been accustomed to put politicians on our civil service commissions, and protected manufacturers on our tariff boards. So as *Sir* Henry Morgan this most wholesale robber and murderer Central America ever knew ended his days in high respectability.

While the ruins of Old Panama compare but unfavorably with those of Porto Bello or San Lorenzo, their proximity to the city of Panama make them a favorite point of interest for tourists. Half a day is ample to give to the drive out and back and to the inspection of the ruins themselves. The extended area over which they are scattered testifies to the size of the obliterated city, while the wide spaces, destitute of any sign of occupation, which intervene between the remaining relics, shows clearly that the greater part of the town must have been built of perishable materials easily swept away at the time of the fire, or slowly disintegrating during the flood of years that have since rolled by. The tower of the Cathedral of St. Augustine alone among the relics still remaining affords any suggestion of grandeur or even of architectural dignity.

To reach the ruins you take a horse, a carriage or an automobile for a ride of about five miles over an

From Balboa, the Pacific opening of the Panama Canal, and the newest of the world's great ports, to the ruins of Old Panama, founded in 1609 and obliterated by pirates in 1671, by trolley in two hours! Was ever the past more audaciously linked to the present? Were ever exhibits of the peaceful commerce of today and the bloody raids of ancient times placed in such dramatic juxtaposition?

The road to Old Panama runs through a peaceful grazing country, with a very few plantations. One or two country residences of prosperous Panamanians appear standing well back from the road, but signs of life and of industry are few. The country lies high, is open and free from jungle and in almost any North American state, lying thus close to a town of 40,000 people and adjacent to a district in which the United States is spending some millions of dollars a month, would be platted in additions for miles around, and dotted with the signs of real estate dealers. But the Panamanian mind is not speculative, or at any rate soars little above the weekly lottery ticket. So all Uncle Samuel's disbursements in the Zone have thus far produced nothing remotely resembling a real estate boom.

However as we turn off from the main road toward the sea and the square broken tower of the old cathedral, or Church of St. Augustine, with the ferns springing from the jagged top, and vines twisting out through the dumbly staring windows, real estate and "booms" seem singularly ignoble topics in the presence of this mute spectator of the agonies of a martyred people.   For even the dulling mists of the interposing centuries, even our feeling that the Spaniards suffered only the anguish and the torments which they had themselves meted out to the real owners of the lands they had seized upon, cannot wholly blunt the sense of pity for the women and children, for the husbands and fathers in the city which fell under Morgan's blight. It would be no easy task to gather in the worst purlieus of any American city today a band so wholly lost to shame, to pity and to God as the ruffians who followed Morgan. What they did to the people on whom their hands reeking with blood were laid must be left to

the imagination.   The only contemporary record of the sack was written by one of their own number to whom apparently such scenes had become commonplace, for while his gorge rises at the contemplation of his own hard fortune in being robbed and deserted by his chief, he recounts the torture of men and the violation of women in a matter-of-fact way as though all in the day's work.

Driving on we come to the arched bridge which formed the main entrance to the town in the day of its downfall. Sturdy it is still, though the public road no longer passes over it, defying the assaults of time and the more disintegrating inroads of the tropical plants which insinuate themselves into every crevice, prying the stone apart with tender fingers ever hardening. At once the bridge, none too wide for three to cross abreast, awakens wonder that no Horatius was in all the Spanish armies to keep the bridge as did he of ancient Rome. But after all the rivulet which today makes its sluggish way under the arch is no Tiber to hold the invading army at bay. Perhaps it was bigger in Morgan's time; today it would be easily

BLUFF NEAR TORO POINT
Photographing this scene is now prohibited as a United States fort is to be erected here

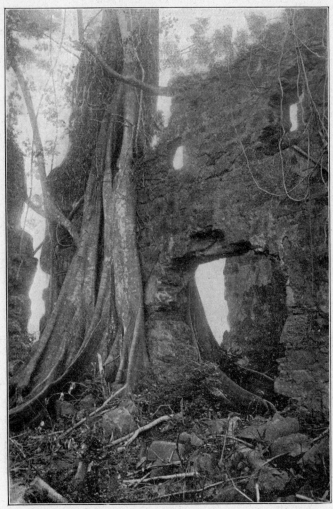

"WHETHER THE TREE OR THE WALL IS STOUTER IS A PROBLEM"

Continuing toward the sea the visitor next comes upon the ruins of the Cathedral, which are in so shattered a state as to justify the belief that either the invaders or the Spaniards themselves employed gunpowder to wreck so massive an edifice. The flames and the work of the vegetation could hardly have accomplished such complete destruction. The tower alone retains definite form, rising about fifty feet from a dense jungle, and lined within with vines and clinging trees that use the ancient walls as a support and hasten their disintegration in so doing. It is difficult even to trace the lines of the great church, so thoroughly have its walls been demolished. Some of the massive arches still stand all pendulous with vines.

At the water's edge one still finds steps leading down into the sea, and the remains of the old paved road to which at high tide the boats could come with their cargoes of fish and country produce. If one happens to visit the spot at low tide the view looking seaward is as ugly as could well be imagined. The hard sand beach extends only to high water mark. Beyond that for more than a mile seaward extends a dismal range of black mud of about the consistency of putty. Near the shore it is seen to be full of round holes from which crawl unsightly worms and small crabs. E. C. Stedman puts its unsightly appearance in two lines:

"The tide still ebbs a league from quay,
    The buzzards scour the empty bay."

Along the strand still stand fragments of the old seawall, and at a considerable distance from the Cathedral ruins you come upon another large building of which little more than the lower walls and the subterranean vaults still have form and coherence. The dungeon into which visitors usually make their way is peculiarly dark, damp and dismal, and the general air of ghoulishness is mightily enhanced by the myriads of bats that hang from the ceiling and whirl and whiz away when intruders light matches to study the moldering masonry. A most interesting feature of this crypt is the great roots of the trees and shrubs that sprung from seeds that had fallen into some crevice and found there soil enough to germinate, but not sufficient to support life as the plant grew larger. The roots twist and creep along the walls, reaching out for earth below as unerringly as a giant boa creeps sinuously through the jungle.

forded, almost leapt. At any rate no "Dauntless Three" like those Macaulay sung were there to stay the onrolling tide of foemen.

Hardly have we passed the bridge than a massive vine-embedded ruin on the left of the road stands mute evidence that the Spaniards had forts, if they had but possessed the courage to defend them. This is the Casa Reale, or government house. Its walls of rubble masonry are full two feet thick and have the appearance of having been pierced for musketry. If the buccaneers had any artillery at all, which is doubtful, it was hardly heavy enough to have had any effect against such a wall. Secure within the Casa Reale such a handful of men as held the Alamo against the Mexicans could have resisted Morgan's men indefinitely. But the spirit was lacking. The stout walls of the Casa Reale stand now as evidences of the character of the defenses the people of Panama had if they but had the pluck to use them.

CHAPTER VI

REVOLUTIONS AND THE FRENCH REGIME

T HE history of the Isthmus from the fall of Old Panama to the time when the government of the United States, without any particular pomp or ceremony, took up the picks and shovels the French had laid down and went to work on the Canal, may be passed over here in the lightest and sketchiest way. It is of Panama of the Present, rather than Panama of the Past, that I have to tell even though that past be full of picturesque and racy incident. Curious enough is the way in which through all those centuries of lawless no-government, Spanish mis-government, and local self-government, tempered by annual revolutions, there appears always the idea that some day there will be a waterway across the neck of the continent. It was almost as hard for the early Spaniards to abandon the idea that such a natural waterway

existed as it has been in later years to make the trans-continental railroads understand that the American people intended to create such a strait.

The search for the natural waterway had hardly been abandoned when discussion arose as to the practicability of creating an artificial one. In its earlier days this project encountered not only the physical obstacles which we had to overcome, but others springing from the rather exaggerated piety of the time. Yet it was a chaplain to Cortez who first suggested a canal to Philip II of Spain in words that have a good twentieth-century ring to them, though their form be archaic: "It is true." he wrote, "that mountains obstruct these passes, but if there be mountains there are also hands." That is the spirit in which Uncle Sam ap-

SAN PABLO LOCK IN FRENCH DAYS

PART OF THE SEA WALL AT PANAMA

proached the Big Job. But when the sturdy chaplain's appeal came to King Philip he referred it to the priests of his council, who ruled it out upon the scriptural injunction, "What God hath joined together let no man put asunder," and they were backed up by a learned prelate on the Isthmus, Fray Josef de Acosta, who averred, "No human power will suffice to demolish the most strong and impenetrable mountains, and solid rocks which God has placed between the two seas, and which sustain the fury of the two oceans. And when it would be to men possible it would in my opinion be very proper to fear the chastisement of heaven for wishing to correct the works which the Creator with greatest deliberation and foresight ordained in the creation of this universe."

Doubtless the Fray de Acosta was the more orthodox, but we like better the spirit of the cleric who held the somewhat difficult post of spiritual adviser to Cortez. His belief that "if there are mountains there are also hands" is good doctrine, and we can believe that the good father would have liked to have seen some of Col. Goethal's steam shovels biting into those mountains at five cubic yards a bite.

It seems strange that the four canal routes over the respective merits of which the Senate of the United States was engaged in seemingly interminable wrangle only a few years ago—Nicaragua, Darien, Panama and Tehuantepec—should have been suggested by Cortez in the sixteenth century. Nearly 250 years before the birth of the republic destined to dig the canal this stout explorer from old Spain laid an unerring finger upon the only routes which it could follow. Doubtless it was as well that no effort was made at the time, yet it would be unwise for us with smug twentieth-century self-sufficiency to assert that no other age than ours could have put the project through. Perhaps the labor and skill that raised the mighty city of Palmyra, or built the massive aqueducts that in ruins still span the Roman Campagna, or carved the Colossi of the Egyptian desert, might have been equal to the Panama problem.

In 1814 the Spanish cortes ordered surveys made for a canal, but nothing came of it, and the great project lay quiescent as long as Spain's power in the Isthmus remained unshaken. More by the indifference of other nations than by any right of their own, the Spanish had assumed sovereignty over all of South and Central America. That they held the country by virtue of a papal bull—such as that may be—and by right of conquest is undeniable. But men begun to say that the Pope had given Spain something he never owned, while so far as conquest was concerned Morgan had taken from the Spanish all they ever won by force of arms on the Isthmus. He did not hold what he had taken because he was a pirate not a pioneer.

The only serious effort to colonize in the Panama region by any people, save Spaniards, was the founding of a colony of Scotch Presbyterians, headed by one William Patterson, who had occupied a Scotch pulpit. Beside theology he must have known something of finance, for he organized, and was one of the first directors of, the Bank of England. His colonization project in Panama was broadly conceived, but badly executed. Taking the rich

East India Company for a model he secured a franchise from Scotland, granting him a monopoly of Scottish trade in the Indies in return for an annual tribute of one hogshead of tobacco. Capitalizing his company for $600,000, he backed the shares with his reputation as a founder of the bank and saw the capital over-subscribed in London. But the success woke up his rivals. They worked on the King, persuaded him to denounce the action taken in Scotland and pushed a law through the English Parliament outlawing the Scotch company in England. In every country the people interested in the established companies fought the interloper who was trying to break into their profitable demesne. But the Scotch stuck to their guns. They rallied at first about Patterson as in later years the French flocked to the support of De Lesseps. Ships were built in Amsterdam, pistols were bought by wholesale, brandy and bibles were both gathered in large quantities, and in 1768 volunteers were called for to join the expedition. Every settler was promised fifty acres of agricultural land and one fifty-foot town lot.

Politics had bothered Patterson at the outset by arraying the English against the Scotch. Now religion added to the dissension. The church and the kirk factions—or the Episcopalians and the Presbyterians—fell afoul of each other. The kirk carried the executive council and Patterson, the

THE PELICANS IN THE BAY OF PANAMA

only man who knew anything about the expedition, was permitted to accompany it only as an ordinary settler. Graft stepped in and though the colonists paid for six months' provisions they discovered when far out at sea that they had but enough for two. Moreover nobody on the ships knew where they were going to settle, for they sailed under sealed orders. When these were opened and the tidings

Spaniards from the land. But illness held the 900 colonists gripped, and malaria, the ruling pest of those tropical shores, is not wont to stimulate a militant spirit. They had settled on the Atlantic coast in the Darien region, as far from the rich traffic of the East Indies as though they were in their old Caledonian homes. Curiously enough they made no effort to get across to the Pacific,

ROAD FROM PANAMA TO LA BOCA

spread that Panama and not the East Indies was the destination, there was renewed distrust and disaffection.

The story of this luckless enterprise is short and dismal. On the voyage out forty-four of the adventurers died, and after landing the deaths continued with melancholy regularity. They were spared trouble with the Indians who, on learning that they were no friends to the Spaniards, welcomed them warmly, and urged them to join in driving the

whence only could trade be conducted, but perhaps that was as well, for the Spaniards though much broken by the recent invasion of the buccaneers would have resisted such an advance to their utmost.

So the unhappy colonists of New Caledonia found themselves on a miasmatic bit of land, remote from anything like civilization, with no sign of trade to engage their activities, an avowed enemy at their back and surrounded by Indians, the price of whose friendship was a declaration of war upon the Span-

OLD FRENCH CANAL AT MOUNT HOPE

Our engineers abandoned the French canal except as a docking place for vessels and a waterway for carrying material to the foot of Gatun locks.

THE CITY PARK OF COLON

iards. To make matters worse, the King issued a proclamation prohibiting all governors of English colonies in the West Indies from giving them aid or comfort, denouncing them as outlaws.

Disheartened, the first colony broke up and sailed away, just when the Company was dispatching two more ships from Scotland. The fugitives sailed for New York, and on one of their ships carrying 250 men, 150 are said to have died before reaching that port. As for the new colonists, they reached the deserted fort of St. Andrew, and saw the mute evidences of death and despair. From the Indians they learned the details of the story, and a great majority voted to sail away without further delay. Twelve however elected to stop, and being landed with a generous supply of provisions, kept foothold in the colony until the third expedition arrived. This consisted of four ships, which had left the Clyde with about 1300 colonists. About 160 however died on the way out, and the survivors were mightily distressed when instead of finding a thriving colony of a thousand or more awaiting them, they discovered only twelve Scotchmen living miserably in huts with the Indians.

The imaginative prospectus writer seems to have been no less active and engaging at that time than in these days of mining promotions, and many of the new colonists had come in the expectation of finding a land watered by springs, the waters of which were 'as soft as milk and very nourishing," a land wherein people lived 150 years, and to die at 125 was to be cut off in the flower of one's youth. What they found was twelve haggard Scotchmen in a primeval forest, ill-fed, unclothed, dependent largely on the charity of the Indians, and who, so far from looking confidently forward to an hundred more years of life cried dolorously to the newcomers, "Take us hence or we perish."

The new colonists, however, had pluck. Stifling their disappointment, they disembarked and settled down to make the colony a success. According to the records they had brought five forces for disintegration and failure along with them—namely four ministers and a most prodigious lot of brandy. The ancient chroniclers do not say upon which of these rests the most blame for the disasters that followed. The ministers straightaway set up to be rulers of the colony. When stockades should be a-building all were engaged in erecting houses for them. As but two could preach in the space of one Sunday, they designated two holy days weekly whereon they preached such resounding sermons that "the regular service frequently lasted twelve hours without any interruption." Nor would they do other work than sermonizing. As for the brandy, all the records of the colony agree that much too much of it and of the curious native drinks was used by all, and that the ministers themselves were wont to reinvigorate themselves after their pulpit exertions by mighty potations.

Yet the colony was not wholly without a certain

CHILDREN IN A NATIVE HUT

sturdy self reliance.   Seeing it persist despite all obstacles, the Spaniards dispatched a force of soldiers from Panama to destroy it.   Campbell

the East India Company, whose monopoly was threatened, the plenteousness of the brandy and the zeal of the four ministers.

THE WATER FRONT OF PANAMA

After the expulsion of the Scotch, the domination of the Isthmus by the Spaniards was never again seriously menaced by any foreign power.   All the vast South and Central American domain was lost to Spain, not by the attacks of her European neighbors, but by the revolt of their people against a government which was at one time inefficient

waylaid them in the jungle and overthrew them. Then the King of Spain became alarmed and sent eight Spanish men-of-war to make an end of these interlopers—the King of England and Scotland coldly leaving them to their fate.   But they fought so bravely that in the end the Spanish, though their fleet had been reënforced by three ships, were obliged to grant them capitulation with the honors of war, and they "marched out with their colors flying and drums beating, together with arms and ammunition, and with all their goods."

So ended the effort to make of Darien an outpost of Scotland. In the effort 2000 lives and over £200,000 had been lost.   Macaulay explains it by saying, "It was folly to suppose that men born and bred within ten degrees of the Arctic circle would enjoy excellent health within ten degrees of the equator."   But Lord Macaulay forgot to reckon on the hostility of

and tyrannical.   The French Revolution and the Napoleonic upheaval in Europe found their echo in South America, where one after another the various states threw off the Spanish yoke.   But Panama,

THE WATER GATE OF PANAMA

then known as Terra Firma, was slow to join in the revolutionary activities of her neighbors.   It is true that in 1812 the revolutionists became so active in Bogota, the capital of the province, that the seat of government was temporarily removed to Panama City.   But the country as a whole was sluggish.

Four classes of citizens, European Spaniards, their sons, born on the Isthmus, and called creoles, the Indians and the negroes, made up the population and were too diverse by birth and nature to unite for any patriotic purpose. Accordingly through the period of breaking shackles, which made Bolivar famous the world over and created the great group of republics in South America, the state of which the Isthmus was a part remained quiescent. In 1814 revolutionists vainly tried to take Porto Bello, but that famous fortress which never resisted a foreign foe successfully, beat off the patriots. Panama was at this time in high favor at Madrid because of its loyalty and the Cortes passed resolutions for the building of a canal, but went no further. But all the time the revolutionary leaven was working beneath the surface. In 1821 a field marshal from Spain, charged with the task of crushing out the revolution in Colombia and Ecuador, stripped Porto Bello, San Lorenzo and Panama of the greater part of their garrisons and took them to Guayaquil. By bribes and promises the local patriots persuaded the few soldiers remaining to desert and, with no possibility of resistance, the independence of Panama from Spain was declared. Early in 1822 Panama became the Department of the Isthmus in the Republic of Colombia.

It would be idle to describe, even to enumerate, all the revolutions which have disquieted the Isthmus since it first joined Colombia in repudiating the Spanish rule. They have been as thick as insects in the jungle. No physical, social or commercial ties bound Panama to Colombia at any time during their long association. A mountain range divided the two countries and between the cities of Panama and Bogota there was no communication by land. In foreign commerce the province of Panama exceeded the parent state, while the possession of the shortest route across the Isthmus was an asset of which both Bogotans and Panamanians keenly realized the value.

Revolutions were annual occurrences, sometimes hard fought, for the people of Panama have plenty of courage in the field; sometimes ended with the first battle. The name of the parent state has been sometimes Colombia, sometimes New Granada; Panama has at times been independent, at others a state of the Federation of New Granada; at one time briefly allied with Ecuador and Venezuela. In 1846 the volume of North American travel across the

Photo by Underwood & Underwood

ENTRANCE TO MT. HOPE CEMETERY

Isthmus became so great that the United States entered into a treaty with New Granada in which we guaranteed to keep the Isthmus open for transit. That and the building, by American capital of the Panama Railroad, made us a directly interested party in all subsequent revolutions. Of these there were plenty. President Theodore Roosevelt defending in 1903 the diplomatic methods by which he "took" Panama, enumerated no fewer than fifty-three revolutions in the fifty-seven years that had elapsed since the signing of the treaty. He summed up the situation thus:

"The above is only a partial list of the revolutions, rebellions, insurrections, riots, and other outbreaks that have occurred during the period in question; yet they number fifty-three for the last fifty-seven years. It will be noted that one of them lasted nearly three years before it was quelled; another for nearly a year. In short, the experience of nearly half a century has shown Colombia to be utterly incapable of keeping order on the Isthmus. Only the active interference of the United States has enabled her to preserve so much as a semblance of sovereignty. Had it not been for the exercise by the United States of the police power in her interest, her connection with the Isthmus would have been severed long ago."

We are apt to think of these revolutions as mere riots, uprisings somewhat after the sort of Falstaff's seven men in buckram, and savoring much of the opera bouffe. Such, to a great extent they were, and curiously enough none of them, except for its outcome, was less serious or dignified than the final one which won for Panama its freedom from Colombia, and for the United States the ten miles' strip across the ocean called the Canal Zone. That was perhaps the only revolution in history by which was created a new and sovereign state, and the issue of which was finally determined by the inability of a

CATHEDRAL PLAZA, PANAMA
The building in the center was by turns the French and the American Administration Building

AVENIDA CENTRALE
The building with the rounded corner balcony is the American Consulate

commanding general to pay the fares for his troops over forty-eight miles of railroad. Of that, however, more hereafter.

Of course, during all the revolutions and counter revolutions the idea of the canal had steadily grown. England at one time took a mild interest in it and sent one Horatio Nelson to look over the land. The young naval officer's health failed him and he returned to become in later years the hero of Trafalgar and the Nile. Later, the great German scientist, Baron von Humboldt, in the course of a famous voyage to South America, spent some time on the Isthmus, and wrote much of its natural features, enumerating nine routes for a canal including of course the one finally adopted. Louis Napoleon, though never on the Isthmus, dreamed out the possibilities of a canal when he was a prisoner in the fortress

of Ham. Had he succeeded in maintaining Maximilian on the throne of Mexico he might have made the Isthmian history very different. Among our own people, De Witt Clinton, builder of the Erie Canal, and Henry Clay, were the first to plan for an American canal across the Isthmus, but without taking practical steps to accomplish it.

Canal schemes, however, were almost as numerous as revolutions in the years preceding 1903. Darien, Panama, Tehuantepec, Nicaragua have all been considered at various times, and the last named for some time was a very close second to Panama in favor. There is reason to believe that the government of the United States deliberately "nursed" the Nicaragua project in order to exact better terms from Colombia, which held the Panama route at an exorbitant figure.

ANCON HILL AT SUNSET

The honor of actually inaugurating the canal work must ever belong to the French, as the honor of completing it will accrue to us. It is not the first time either that the French and the Americans worked together to accomplish something on this continent. Yorktown and Panama ought to be regarded as chapters of the story of a long partnership. In 1876 Ferdinand de Lesseps, with the glory of having dug the Suez Canal still untarnished, became interested in the Panama situation as the result of representations made by a French engineer, Napoleon B. Wyse. Lieut. Wyse had made a survey of the Isthmus and, in connection with Gen. Stephen Turr, a Hungarian, had secured a concession from Colombia to run ninety-nine years after the completion of the canal, with a payment to Colombia of $250,-000 annually after the

seventy-fifth year had expired. This franchise was transferable by sale to any other private company but could not be sold to a government—a proviso which later complicated greatly the negotiations with the United States.

De Lesseps was instantly interested. The honors which had been heaped upon him as the result of his successful operation at Suez were very grateful to him. The French temperament is particularly avid of praise and public honor. Moreover, he sincerely believed in the practicability of the plan and, neither at the outset or later, did any one fully enlighten him as to the prodigious obstacles to be encountered. Lieut. Wyse had interested a group of financiers who scented in the scheme a chance for great profits, and to their project the name of De Lesseps was all important. For advertising purposes it had the value of that of Roosevelt today. To

Photo by Underwood & Underwood

ABANDONED FRENCH MACHINERY ON THE CANAL

launch the project successfully money was needed, and this they found. Some sort of professional approval, in addition to the De Lesseps name was desirable and this they provided by calling together an International Scientific Congress at Paris to discuss the great undertaking. One hundred and sixty-four delegates were present, of whom forty-two were engineers and only eleven Americans. It was charged at the time that the congress was more political than scientific and furthermore that it was "packed" so as to register only the will of De Lesseps, who in turn recommended in the main such measures as the syndicate putting up the money desired. However, the Congress gave

OVERWHELMED BY THE JUNGLE

a decision which the French themselves were forced to reverse and which the United States definitely abandoned early in its work.   In the French Congress there were less than 100 of the 164 delegates present when the vote was taken. Seventy-eight voted for sea-level and a majority of the engineers voted against it.

a quasi-public and scientific appearance to a project which was really conceived only as a money-making proposition by a group of financiers.   There was and has since been bitter criticism of the vote by which the Congress declared for a sea-level canal—

In my description of the canal work the funda-

A LOTTERY TICKET SELLER

mental differences between the respective advantages of the sea-level and the lock type of canal will continually reappear. At this moment it is enough to say that the obstacles to the sea-level plan are to be found in Culebra Hill and the Chagres River. In the lock type of canal the cut at Culebra is 495 feet below the crest of Gold Hill and 364 feet below the crest of Contractor's Hill opposite. The top width of this cut is over half a mile. To carry the canal to sea-level would mean a further cut of eighty-five feet with vastly enhanced liability of slides. As for the Chagres River, that tricky stream crosses the line of the old French canal twenty-three times. As the river is sometimes three or four feet deep one day and nearly fifty feet deep at the same point the next—a turbid, turbulent, roaring torrent, carrying trees, huts and boulders along with it—the canal could obviously not exist with the

Chagres in its path. The French device was to dam the stream some miles above the point at which the canal first crossed it and lead it away through an artificial channel into the Pacific instead of into the Atlantic, where it now empties. This task the American engineers have avoided by damming the Chagres at Gatun, and making a great lake eighty-five feet above the level of the sea through which the canal extends and which covers and obliterates the twenty-three river crossings which embarrassed the engineers of the sea-level canal.

It is fair to say, however, that today (1913), with the lock canal approaching completion, there is a very large and intelligent body of Americans who still hold that the abandonment of the sea-level plan was an error. And it is a curious fact that while De Lesseps was accused of "packing" his congress so as to vote down the report for a lock canal which a majority of the engineers voting favored, Roosevelt, after a majority of his "International Board of Consulting Engineers" had voted for a sea-level canal, set aside their recommendation and ordered the lock type instead.

Immediately after the adjournment of the International Congress at Paris the stock of the canal company, $60,000,000 as a first issue, was offered to the investing public. It was largely over-subscribed. The French are at once a thrifty and an emotional people. Their thrift gives them instant

MACHINERY SEEMINGLY AS HOPELESS AS THIS WAS RECOVERED AND SET TO WORK

THE POWER OF THE JUNGLE

Note how the tree has grown around and into this steel dump car at San Pablo command of such sums of ready cash as astound financiers of other nations. Their emotionalism leads them to support any great national enterprise that promises glory for *La Patrie*, has in it a touch of romance and withal seems economically safe. The canal enterprise at the outset met all these conditions, and

LA FOLIE DINGLER

This house, built by the French for $150,000, was sold for $25.00 by the Americans

work done by the Frenchmen actually on the Isthmus while riveting attention on the blackmailers and parasites in Paris who were destroying the structure at its very foundations. It is significant that none of the real workers on the canal do this. Talk with the engineers and you will find them enthusiastic over

the commanding figure of De Lesseps at its head, the man who had made Africa an island and who dogmatically declared, "the Panama Canal will be more easily begun, finished and maintained than the Suez Canal," lured the francs from their hiding places in woolen stockings or under loose hearth stones.

It has been the practice of many writers upon the canal to ridicule the unsuccessful effort of the French to complete it; to expatiate upon the theatrical display which attended their earlier operations, and the reckless extravagance which attended the period when the dire possibility of failure first appeared to their vision; to overlook the earnest and effective

the engineering work done by the French. Those sturdy, alert Americans who are now putting the Big Job through will take pains to give their predecessors the fullest credit for work done, for dirt moved, for surveys made and for machinery designed—a great lot of it is in use on the line today, including machines left exposed in the jungle twenty years. Hundreds of their buildings are still in use. If, after listening to the honest and generous praise expressed by our engineers, the visitor will go out to the cemetery of Mount Hope, near Cristobal, and read the lines on the headstones of French boys who came out full of hope and ambition to be cut down at twenty-two, twenty-five—all

NEAR THE PACIFIC ENTRANCE TO THE CANAL

The suction dredge is an inheritance from the French and still working boyish ages—he will reflect that it is ill to laugh because the forlorn hope does not carry the breast-works, but only opens the way for the main army. And there are many little French graveyards scattered about the Isthmus which make one who comes upon them unawares feel that the really vital thing about the French connection with the canal was not that the first blast which it had been prepared to celebrate with some pomp failed to explode, or that the young engineers did not understand that cham-

largely by our force in carrying material for the Gatun dam. At the Pacific entrance they had dug a narrow channel three miles long which we are still using. We paid the French company $40,000,000 for all its rights on the Isthmus. There are various rumors as to who got the money. Some, it is believed, never went far from New York, for with all their thrift the French are no match for our high financiers. But whoever got the money we got a good bargain. The estimate of our own commission

WHERE THE FRENCH DID THEIR BEST WORK

The greatest amount of excavations by the French was in Culebra Cut

pagne mixed but badly with a humid and malarial climate, but that the flower of a great and generous nation gave their lives in a struggle with hostile nature before science had equipped man with the knowledge to make the struggle equal.

Today along a great part of our canal line the marks of the French attainments are apparent. From Limon Bay, at the Atlantic end of the canal, our engineers for some reason determined upon an entirely new line for our canal, instead of following the French waterway, which was dug for seven miles to a depth of fifteen feet, and for eight miles further, seven feet deep. This canal has been used very

in 1911 values the physical property thus transferred at $42,799,826.

Bad luck, both comic and tragic, seemed to attend the French endeavors. Count De Lesseps, with a national fondness for the dramatic, arranged two ceremonies to properly dignify the actual beginning of work upon the canal. The first was to be the breaking of ground for the Pacific entrance, which was to be at the mouth of the Rio Grande River in the Bay of Panama. A distinguished company gathered on the boat chartered for the occasion at Panama, and there was much feasting, speaking and toasting. Every one was so imbued with enthusiasm

AN OLD SPANISH CHURCH

This edifice, still standing at Nata, is said to be the oldest church in Panama

historic sod was to be turned. Accordingly, excavation was begun *pro forma* in a champagne box filled with earth on the deck of the ship. The little daughter of De Lesseps dealt the first blow of the pick, followed by representatives of Colombia. To complete the ceremony the Bishop of Panama gravely blessed the work thus auspiciously begun, and the canal builders steamed back to Panama.

Later, the same party assembled to witness the first blast at Culebra —for the French made the first attack on that redoubtable fortress, which after the lapse of thirty-five years is stubbornly resisting our American sappers and miners. But after due preparations, including wine, the fair hand of Mlle. Ferdinande De Lesseps pressed the button—and nothing happened. Some fault in the connections made the electric spark impotent, and the chroniclers of the time do not record exactly when the blast was actually fired. But in the official canal paper the ceremony was described as "perfectly successful," and the reporter added that picturesque detail which Koko said "imparts an artistic verisimilitude to an other-

that no one thought of so material a thing as the tide. On the Pacific coast the tide rises and falls twenty feet or more, and while the guests were emptying their glasses the receding tide was emptying the bay whither they were bound. When they arrived they found that nearly two miles of coral rock and mud flats separated them from the shore where the

Photo by Underwood & Underwood

JUNCTURE OF FRENCH AND AMERICAN CANALS

The American Canal is the wider, and affords the more direct route to the sea

PART OF THE TOLL OF LIFE
This cemetery on the westerly slope of Ancon Hill is one of the Zone's pathetic spots

wise bald and uninteresting statement of fact," by saying that the rocks were "much less resistant than we had expected."

These needless ceremonies and the false reports which attended them were merely what in our cynical age and nation are called press-agent "stunts," and were necessitated by the need for interesting the French people in the work, lest they let the market for the shares slump. They were early symptoms of the evil that culminated in the revelations of blackmail and forced tribute paid the French press when the final collapse was impending and inevitable.

De Lesseps indeed was a master in the art of "working the press," and had he confined his activities to that, without interfering with his engineers, history might have told a different story of his canal management. But lest doubt should seize upon would-be investors, he continually cut down

the estimates of his engineers, and issued flamboyant proclamations announcing triumphs that had not been won and prophesying a rate of progress that never could be attained. When his very capable Technical Commission, headed by Col. George M. Totten, the builder of the Panama Railroad, estimated the total cost of the canal at $168,600,000, he took the report to his cabin on shipboard and there arbitrarily, with no possible new data, lopped off about $37,000,000. Even at that, he calmly capitalized his company at 600,000,000 francs or $120,-000,000, though his own estimate of the cost of the canal exceeded that amount by more than $12,000,-000. One-half of his capital stock or $60,000,000 the Count had reserved for the United States, but sold not a dollar's worth. The $60,000,000 first offered in France was, however, eagerly subscribed. Of course it was wholly insufficient.

We know, what the unfortunate French investors

THE ANCON HOSPITAL GROUNDS
The beauty of the grounds is due to early French planning

riers of disease germs was not dreamed of. Beyond building excellent hospitals for the sick, some of which we still use, and dosing both sick and well liberally with quinine, they had no plan of campaign against "Yellow Jack." As a result, death stalked grimly among them, and the stories written of his ravages are ghastly. On the south side of Ancon Hill, where the quarry has gashed the hillside, stood, until recently, a large frame house, built for Jules Dingler, first director-general of canal work. It

could not, and their directors probably did not know, that the canal could never be built by a private company seeking profit. Neither could it be built by private contract, as we discovered after some discouraging experiences of our own. The French builders were at the mercy of the stock market. A hurtful rumor, true or false, might at any time shut off their money supplies. Experience has pretty thoroughly demonstrated that the confidence of the investing public cannot long be maintained by false reports or futile promises, but both of these devices the French worked until the inevitable catastrophe.

Disease on the Isthmus coöperated with distrust in Paris to bring about failure. The French in 1880 knew nothing of the modern scientific systems for checking yellow-fever contagion and the spread of malaria. The part mosquitoes play as car-

A SUNKEN RAILROAD
Nine feet below the boat is the roadbed of the old Panama railroad

A ZONE WORKING VILLAGE

The low houses were built by the French: all screening added by Americans

cost $150,000, though perhaps worth a third of that sum, and was called "La Folie Dingler." But it was a rather tragic folly for poor Dingler, for before he had fairly moved into it his wife, son and daughter died of yellow fever and he returned to Paris to die too of a broken heart. His house, in which he anticipated such happiness, became a smallpox hospital, and was finally sold for $25 with the stipulation that the purchaser remove it.

A dinner was given M. Henri Boinne, secretary-general of the company. Some one remarked that there were thirteen at the table, whereupon the guest of honor remarked gaily that as he was the last to come he would have to pay for all. In two weeks he was dead—yellow fever. Others at the dinner followed him. Of the members of one surveying party on the upper waters of the Chagres—a region I myself visited without a suggestion of ill effects—every one, twenty-two in all, were prostrated by disease and ten died. Bunau-Varilla, whose name is closely linked with the canal, says: "Out of every one hundred individuals arriving on the Isthmus, I can say without exaggeration that only twenty have been able to remain at their posts at the working stations, and even in that number

many who were able to present an appearance of health had lost much of their courage."

Col. Gorgas tells of a party of eighteen young Frenchmen who came to the Isthmus, all but one of whom died within a month. The Mother Superior of the nursing sisters in the French hospital at Ancon lost by fever twenty-one out of twenty-four sisters who had accompanied her to the Isthmus.

How great was the total loss of French lives can only be guessed. The hospital records show that at Ancon, 1041 patients died of yellow fever. Col. Gorgas figures that as many died outside the hospital. All the French records are more or less incomplete and their authenticity doubtful because apprehension for the tender hopes and fears of the shareholders led to the suppression of unpleasant facts. The customary guess is that two out of every three Frenchmen who went to the Isthmus died there. Col. Gorgas, who at one time figures the total loss during the French régime at 16,500, recently raised his estimate to 22,000, these figures of course including negro workmen. Little or no effort was made to induce sanitary living, as under the Americans, and so ignorant were the French—as indeed all physicians were at that time—of the causes of the spread of yellow fever, that they set the legs of the hospital beds in shallow pans of water to keep the ants from creeping to the beds. The ants were stopped, but the water bred hosts of wrigglers from which came the deadly *stegomyia* mosquito, which carries the yellow-fever poison from the patient to the well person. Had the hospital been designed to spread instead of to cure disease its managers could not have planned better.

It is a curious fact that, in a situation in which the toll of death is heaviest, man is apt to be most reckless and riotous in his pleasures. The old drinking song of the English guardsmen beleaguered during the Indian mutiny voices the almost universal desire of strong men to flaunt a gay defiance in the face of death:

> "Stand! Stand to your glasses steady,
>   'Tis all we have left to prize,
> One cup to the dead already,
>   Hurrah, for the next that dies".

Wine, wassail and, I fear, women were much in evidence during the hectic period of the French activities. The people of the two Isthmian towns still speak of it as the *temps de luxe*. Dismal thrift was banished and extravagance was the rule. Salaries were prodigious. Some high officials were paid from $50,000 to $100,000 a year with houses, carriages, traveling expenses and uncounted incidentals. Expenditures for residences were lavish, and the nature of the structures still standing shows

NEGRO QUARTERS, FRENCH TOWN OF EMPIRE
Paving and sanitary arrangements due to American régime

that graft was the chief factor in the cost. The director-general had a $40,000 bath-house, and a private railway car costing $42,000—which is curiously enough almost exactly $1000 for each mile of the railroad it traversed. The hospital buildings at Colon cost $1,400,000 and one has but to look at them today to wonder how even the $400,000 was spent.

The big graft that finally was one of the prime factors in wrecking the company was in Paris, but enough went on in Colon and Panama to make those two towns as full of easy money as a mining camp after a big strike. The pleasures of such a society are not refined. Gambling and drinking were the less serious vices. A French commentator of the time remarks, "Most of the commercial business of Panama is transacted standing and imbibing cocktails—always the eternal cocktail! Afterward, if the consumer had the time and money to lose, he had only to cross the hall to find himself in a little room, crowded with people where roulette was going on. Oh this roulette, how much it has cost all grades of canal employees! Its proprietor must make vast profits. Admission is absolutely free; whoever wishes may join in the play. A democratic mob pushes and crowds around the table. One is elbowed at the same time by a negro, almost in rags, anxiously thrusting forward his ten sous, and by a portly merchant with his pockets stuffed with piasters and bank notes".

These towns, which bought and consumed French champagnes and other wines by the shipload, could not afford to build a water system. Water was peddled in the streets by men carrying great jars, or conducting carts with tanks. There were millions for roulette, poker and the lottery, but nothing for sewers or pavements and during the wet season the people, natives and French both, waded ankle deep in filth which would have driven a blooded Berkshire hog from his sty. When from these man-created conditions of drink and dirt, disease was bred and men died like the vermin among which they lived, they blamed the climate, or the Chagres River.

Amidst it all the work went on. So much stress has been laid upon the riot in the towns that one forgets the patient digging out on the hills and in the jungle. In 1912 the Secretary of the United States Canal Commission estimated the amount of excavation done by the French, useful to our canal, at 29,709,000 cubic yards worth $25,389,000. That by no means represented all their work, for our

shift in the line of the canal made much of their excavation valueless. Between Gold Hill and Contractor's Hill in the Culebra Cut, where our struggle with the obstinate resistance of nature has been fiercest, the French cut down 161 feet, all of it serviceable to us. Their surveys and plats are invaluable, and their machinery, which tourists seeing some pieces abandoned to the jungle condemn in the lump, has been of substantial value to us both for use and for sale.

But under the conditions as they found them, the French could never have completed the canal. Only a government could be equal to that task. President Roosevelt found to his own satisfaction at least that neither private contract nor civilian management was adequate. Most emphatically, if the desire for profit was to be the sole animating force the canal could never be built at all. When the

FILTH THAT WOULD DRIVE A BERKSHIRE FROM HIS STY
A typical scene in the negro quarters of Colon during the period of French activity in Panama

CANAL VALLEY NEAR PEDRO MIGUEL

Through the line of hills in the background extends the deepest part of the Culebra Cut

discovery that the canal enterprise would never be a "big bonanza" dawned on the French stockholders distrust was rapidly succeeded by panic. Vainly did De Lesseps repeat his favorite formula, "The canal will be built." Vainly did the officers of the company pay tribute to the blackmailers that sprung up on every side—journalists, politicians, discharged employees, every man who knew a weak point in the company's armor. Reorganizations, new stock issues, changes of plan, appeals for government aid, bond issues, followed one after another. The sea-level canal was abandoned and a lock canal substituted. After repeated petitions the French Chamber of Deputies, salved with some of the spoil, authorized an issue of lottery bonds and bankruptcy was temporarily averted. A new company was formed but the work languished, just enough in fact being done to keep the concession alive. After efforts to enlist the coöperation of the United States, the company in despair offered to sell out altogether to that government, and after that proffer the center of interest was transferred from Paris to Washington.

The French had spent in all about $260,000,000 and sacrificed about 2000 French lives before they drew the fires from their dredges, left their steam shovels in the jungle and turned the task over to the great American Republic.

CHAPTER VII

THE UNITED STATES BEGINS WORK

 HE probable failure of the French became apparent some years before the actual collapse occurred and public opinion in the United States was quite ready for the assumption of the work and its expense by our government. Of course that opinion was not wholly spontaneous—public opinion rarely is, notwithstanding the idealists. There were many parties in interest who found it profitable to enlist various agencies for awakening public opinion in this country to the point of buying the French property and saving something out of the wreck for the French stockholders. But, as a matter of fact, little artificial agitation was needful. The people of the United States readily agreed that a trans-isthmian canal should be built and owned by the United States government. There was honest difference of opinion as to the most practicable route and even today in the face of the victory over nature at Panama there are many who hold that the Nicaragua route would have been better.

Naturally the start made by the French had something to do with turning the decision in favor of the Isthmus, but it was not decisive. The French had no rights that they could sell except the right of veto conferred by their ownership of the Panama Railroad. Their franchise from Colombia expressly prohibited its transfer to any other government, so it was unsalable. But the charter of the Panama Railroad, which the French had acquired, provided that no interoceanic canal should be built in Co-

Photo by Underwood & Underwood

PANAMA SOLDIERS GOING TO CHURCH

lombia without the consent of the railroad corporation. This to some extent gave the French the whiphand. What they had to sell was the controlling stock of the railroad company, the land they had acquired in Colombia, the machinery on the spot and the work they had completed. But all of this was of little value without a franchise from Colombia and the one the French held could not be transferred to a government, and was of little worth anyway as it would expire in 1910, unless the canal were completed by that year —a physical impossibility.

In 1898 the race of the battleship "Oregon" around Cape Horn to join the United States fleet off Cuba in the Spanish - American war offered just the graphic and specific argument necessary to fix the determination of the American people to dig that canal and to own it. That voyage of 10,000 miles which might have been avoided by a ditch fifty miles long revolted the common sense of the nation, and the demand for instant action on the canal question was universal.

THE OFFICIAL UMPIRE, COCLE

Accordingly in 1899 President McKinley appointed what was known as the Walker Commission, because headed by Admiral John G. Walker, to investigate all Central American routes. They had the data collected during almost a century at their disposal and very speedily settled down to the alternative between the Panama and the Nicaragua routes. Over this choice controversy raged long and noisily. While it was in progress the bullet of an assassin ended the life of President McKinley and Theodore Roosevelt succeeded him.

The Isthmian Canal was precisely the great, epoch-marking spectacular enterprise to enlist the utmost enthusiasm and energy of this peculiarly dynamic President. A man of strong convictions he favored the Panama route—and got it. He believed in a lock canal—and enforced his beliefs over the report of the engineers whose expert professional opinions he invited. Of a militant temperament he thought the canal should be dug by the army—and that is the way it was built. Not over tolerant of other people's rights he thought the United States should have a free hand over the canal and adjacent territory—and when Colombia, which happened to own that territory, was slow in accepting this view he set up out of nothing over night the new Republic of Panama, recognized it as a sovereign state two days afterwards, concluded a treaty with it, giving the United States all he thought it should have, and years later, in a moment of frankness declared "I took Panama, and left Congress to debate it later."

About the political morality and the personal ethics of the Roosevelt solution of the diplomatic problem there will ever be varying opinions. Colombia is still mourning for her ravished province of Panama and refuses to be comforted even at a price of $10,000,000 which has been tentatively offered as salve for the wound. But that the canal in 1913 is just about ten years nearer completion than it would be had not Roosevelt been President in 1903 is a proposition generally accepted. History—which is not always moral—is apt to applaud results regardless of methods, and

THE MAN AND THE MACHINE

President Roosevelt and the monster steam shovel figure largely in the story of Panama the Republic and Canal of Panama are likely to be Roosevelt's most enduring monuments—though the canal may outlast the Republic.

Prior to this time there had been several sporadic negotiations opened with different nations of Central America for canal rights. The most important one was a treaty signed at Bogotá in 1870 by an envoy especially authorized by President Grant. But this treaty was never ratified by our Senate, and was amended out of acceptable form by the Colombian Senate. For the purposes of this narrative we may well consider the diplomatic history of the canal to begin with the passage of the Spooner act in 1902. This act, written by Senator John C. Spooner of Wisconsin, authorized the Panama route if the French property could be bought for $40,000,000 and the necessary right of way secured from Colombia. Failing this the Commission of seven members created by the act was authorized to open negotiations with Nicaragua. Events made it quite apparent that the Nicaragua clause was inserted merely as a club to be used in the negotiations with Co-

THE TRAIL NEAR CULEBRA

lombia and the French company. With the latter it proved highly effective, for although the American attorney for the company, Mr. William Nelson Cromwell, fixed a price at first upon the property of $101,141,500 an apparently active opening of negotiations with Nicaragua caused an immediate drop to the prescribed $40,000,000. With that offer in hand the Commission unanimously reported to the President in favor of the Panama route.

The Republic of Colombia was less tractable, and naturally so as it held a stronger hand. When negotiations began the French concession had but seven years more of life. If their progress could be prolonged for that period practically all that the United States would have paid the French would be paid to Colombia. Meanwhile the French property was wholly unsalable without a Colombian franchise. The one weak point in the Colombian armor was the possibility that the United States might finally turn to Nicaragua, but this contingency was made unlikely by the report of the Commission, and by the general desire of the American people which was undoubtedly for the Panama route.

In 1903 the Colombian Minister at Washington negotiated with Senator Hay a treaty which by a lucky chance failed of ratification in the Panama Senate. It never reached our Senate, but it is quite incredible that it could have succeeded there, for it had several features that would have led to endless disagreement between the two countries— might indeed have resulted in the United States annexing Colombia altogether. For example the Canal Zone was to be governed by a joint commission of the two countries—Colombia remaining

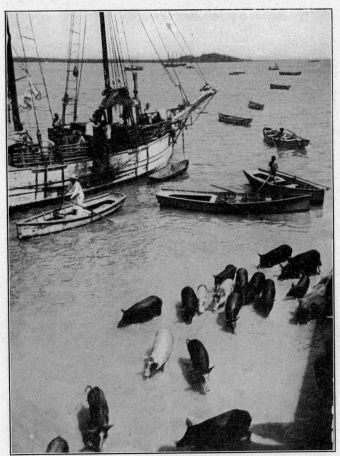

LANDING PIGS FOR MARKET

sovereign over the territory. The United States was to explicitly guarantee the sovereignty of Colombia against all the world. Colombia was to police the Zone. Each of these sections was big with possibilities of trouble. That Colombia did not speedily ratify this treaty would be inexplicable, for it was all to the Colombian good, except for the fact that by delaying any action for seven years the French property along the line of the canal, valued at $40,000,000, would drop into the Colombian treasury.

Delay, however, while good enough for the Colombians, did not suit the Panamanians, nor did it please Theodore Roosevelt, whom Providence, while richly endowing him otherwise, had not invested with patience in the face of opposition. The Panamanians, by whom for the purposes of this narrative I mean chiefly the residents of Colon and the city

of Panama, wanted to see some American money spent in their various marts of trade. The French were rapidly disappearing. The business of all their commercial institutions from dry goods stores down to saloons was falling off. Even the lottery did not thrive as of yore and the proprietors of the lesser games of chance, that in those days were run quite openly, were reduced to the precarious business of robbing each other. All these and other vested interests called for immediate negotiation of any sort of a treaty which would open the spigots of Uncle Sam's kegs of cash over the two thirsty Isthmian towns. It was irksome too to think that the parent state of Colombia would make the treaty and handle the cash accruing under it. The Yankees were ready to pay $10,000,000 down, and it was believed a further rental of $250,000 for the right to build a canal every foot of which would be on

IN THE BANANA COUNTRY, ON THE COAST NEAR BOCAS DEL TORO

the territory of the Province of Panama. If Panama was a sovereign state instead of merely a province, all this money would be used for the benefit of but 400,000 people, including Indians and negroes, who of course could not be expected to have much to say about its use. If employed in public works, it would only have to spread over about 32,000 square miles, or a territory a little smaller than Indiana. But of course it would chiefly go to the two cities. On the other hand if Colombia made this treaty the capital city Bogotá would get the lion's share of the spoil, and for that matter all the provinces would share in the division with Panama, which had the goods for sale.

What more natural than that the Panamanians should turn their thoughts toward secession from Colombia. It was no novel channel for their meditations, for, as has been pointed out already, there had been 53 revolutions in Colombia in 57 years. Red revolution had become a commonplace except for the poor fellows who got themselves killed in them, or the widows and children thrown on the charity of a rather uncharitable people. Always hitherto the result of the revolutions had been the same—Panama had either been whipped into subjection, or had voluntarily returned to the domination of Colombia. But that was before there was a $10,000,000 prize at stake.

In several of these revolutions the United States had interfered, always in behalf of Colombia and always with fatal effect upon the hopes of the revolutionists. For the key to the military situation in Panama was the railroad. In every well ordered revolution—for the business of revolting had become a science—the conspirators began by corrupting the federal soldiers at Panama city where alone any garrison was maintained. This done they proclaimed Panama a free and independent state. As there was no land communication between Bogotá and the Isthmus the federal government was compelled to send its troops to Colon and thence across the Isthmus to Panama by railroad. If the revolutionists could destroy or obstruct the railroad their chances for success would be greatly enhanced.

But under a treaty with Colombia in 1846 the United States guaranteed the neutrality of the railroad and this guarantee was sensibly constructed to include the task of keeping the line open for traffic. In several revolutions, therefore, United States marines were detailed to guard the line, and Colombia being thus enabled to pour its superior forces into Panama crushed out rebellion with comparative ease. If the experience of the 53 revolutions counted for anything, it indicated that Panama could not throw off the Colombian yoke as long as the United States kept the railroad open for Colombian troops.

Let us consider the situation toward the midsummer of 1903. In Washington was the Roosevelt administration keenly eager to have the canal work begun as a great deed to display to the nation

Photo by Underwood & Underwood
THE BEST RESIDENCE SECTION, COLON

ANCON HILL FROM HARBOR OF PANAMA

The town nestles under the northeast side of the hill which is precipitous and cuts off the sun's rays early in the afternoon. From the crest the most beautiful view in Panama may be enjoyed.

in the coming presidential campaign. In New York was Mr. William Nelson Cromwell, representing the French company and quite as keen for action which would enable him to sell the United States $40,-000,000 worth of French machinery and uncompleted canal. At Bogotá was the Colombian legislature talking the Hay-Herrara treaty to death and giving every indication of a purpose of killing it. Spanning the Isthmus was the all important railroad which was part of the property the French so greatly desired to sell. And at Panama and Colon were groups of influential men, high financiers in a small way—a leader among them was the owner of the Panama lottery—exceedingly anxious to have the handling of that $10,000,-000 which the United States would pay for a franchise, and quite desirous to have the country tributary to those two towns suddenly populated by 40,000 to 50,000 canal workmen, all drawing money from the United States and spending it there.

What happened was inevitable. Under the conditions existing only two things could have prevented the successful revolution which did occur—the quick ratification of a satisfactory treaty between the United States and Colombia, or an observance by the United States of the spirit as well as the letter of neutrality in the inevitable revolution.

Neither of these things happened. The Congress at Bogotá failed to ratify the treaty. In Panama

THE OLD FIRE CISTERN, PANAMA

and Colon the revolutionary Junta conspired, and sent emissaries to Washington to sound the government there on its attitude in case of a revolution. To their aid came Mr. Cromwell and M. Bunau-Varilla, a highly distinguished French engineer also interested in the plight of his countrymen. Dr. Amador was chosen to sound the then Secretary of State John Hay. He was told, according to trustworthy reports, that while the United States guaranteed Colombia against foreign aggression it did not bind itself to protect the sovereignty of that state against domestic revolution. In the event of such an uprising all it was bound to do was to see that traffic over the railroad was unimpeded. This sounded and still sounds fair enough, but there were minds among the revolutionists to see that this policy opened the way for a successful revolution at last.

For this is the way in which the policy worked when put to the test—and indeed some of the incidents indicate that the Roosevelt administration went somewhat beyond the letter of the rule Secretary Hay had laid down. Our government knew before the revolutionary blow was struck that it was imminent. It is said indeed that when the revolutionists suggested September 22nd as the date for the spontaneous uprising of the people the Secretary sagaciously suggested that the Congress of Colombia would not then have adjourned and that it might seem irregular to base a revolution on the omission of the legislature to act when it was still in session and could correct that omission. For this, or some other reason, the revolution was postponed until November 5th. The Colombian minister at Washington kept his government advised of the suspicious activity there of the agents of the Junta and warmly advised the heavy reënforcement of the garrison at Panama. But his home government was slow to follow his advice. When it did move it was checked by the French managers of the railroad.

Colombia's only considerable seaport on the Pacific is Buenaventura and at this point troops were collected to reënforce Panama. Two Colombian gunboats in harbor at Panama were ordered to go after the troops. Coal was needed for the voyage. The only source of coal supplies on the Isthmus was the Panama Railroad which had long made a practice of selling the fuel to all comers. But to the request of the Colombian navy for coal at this time the railroad agent, evidently primed for the occasion, put in a reluctant negative. All his coal was at Colon, and the pressure of commercial business was so great that he could not move it across

Photo by Underwood & Underwood
THE TWO PRESIDENTS; ROOSEVELT AND AMADOR

the Isthmus in season to be of use to the gunboats. So those troops stayed at Buenaventura and the Junta at Panama went on with its plotting.

Now Colombia tried another plan to reënforce its Panama garrison—or to replace it, for by this time the troops that had been there were won over to the smoldering conspiracy. About four hundred soldiers were sent down by the Gulf and landed at Colon. That they were landed at all seems like a slight error in carrying out the Roosevelt policy, for in the harbor of Colon lay the United States cruiser "Nashville" and gunboat "Dixie" whose commanders had this desptach from the Secretary of the Navy:

"Maintain free and uninterrupted transit. If interruption is threatened by armed force occupy line of railroad. Prevent landing of any armed force with hostile intent either government or insurgent, either at Colon, Porto Bello or other points."

Now there are some curious features about this despatch. On November 2nd, its date, there was no insurrection, therefore no insurgents. If the administration intended to take official cognizance of the activities of the Junta it must have known that the conspirators had no ships and could not therefore plan landing any forces. The order then was plainly designed to prevent Colombia from landing troops in its own territory—a most extraordinary policy to adopt toward a friendly nation. It was furthermore an order equivalent to assuring the success of the foreshadowed revolution, for as there was no way except by sea for Colombia to send

CHOLO CHIEF AND HIS THIRD WIFE
The Chief is said to have poisoned her two predecessors

troops to put down the insurgents, it was evident that for the United States by its superior force to close the sea against her was to give Panama over to the revolutionists.

However 400 troops were landed on the 3rd of November. The commander of the "Nashville" probably thought his orders only operative in case of an outbreak of insurrection and thus far there had been none. It became time for the railroad company to declare its second check—which in this case was checkmate. When the two generals in command of the Colombian forces ordered special trains to transport their men to Panama the agent blandly asked for prepayment of the fares—something above $2000. The generals were embarrassed. They had no funds. It was of course the business of the road, under its charter from Colombia, to transport the troops on demand, and it was the part of the generals to use their troops to compel it to do so. Taking the matter under advisement they went alone across to Panama to investigate the situation. There they were met by Gen. Huertas, in command of the garrison who first gave them a good dinner and then put them under arrest informing them that Panama had revolted, was now an independent republic, and that he was part of the new régime. There was no more to it in Panama. The two generals submitted gracefully. The Junta arrested all the Colombian officials in Panama, who thereupon readily took oath of fealty to the new government. A street mob, mainly boys, paraded cheering for Panama Libre. The Panama flag sprung into being, and the revolution was complete.

Out in the harbor lay three Colombian gunboats. Two swiftly displayed Panama flags which by singular good fortune were in their lockers. The third with a fine show of loyalty fired two shells over the insurgent city, one of which, bursting, slew an innocent Chinaman smoking opium in his bunk. The city responded with an ineffective shot or two from the seawall and the sole defender of the sovereignty of Colombia pulled down its flag.

Photo by Prof. Lutz

NATIVE HOUSE AND GROUP AT PUERTA PINAS

At the other end of the line the situation was more serious and might well have caused bloodshed. Col. Torres, in charge of the troops there, on hearing the news from Panama demanded a train at once, threatening that unless it was furnished he would attack the Americans in the town. He had more than 400 armed men, while on the "Nashville" were but 192 marines. In such a contest the Colombians could have relied upon much assistance from the natives. With a guard of 42 marines employees of the railroad prepared its stone freight house for defense while American women and children were sent to vessels in the harbor. The Colombian colonel had fixed two o'clock as the hour for beginning hostilities but when that time arrived he invited a conference, and it was finally agreed that both parties should retire from Colon, while he went to Panama to consult with the jailed generals. During his absence the "Dixie" arrived with 400 marines, and a little later the "Atlanta" with 1000. With this overwhelming force against him Col. Torres recognized that the United States was back of the railroad's refusal of transportation and so yielded. With his troops he sailed again for Cartagena.

Two days after the revolution—bloodless save for the sleeping Chinaman—the United States recognized the Republic of Panama. Twelve days later, with M. Bunau-Varilla who had by cable been appointed minister to Washington, a treaty was concluded by which

HINDOO MERCHANTS ON THE ZONE

the United States was granted all it desired for the furtherance of the canal project. Much of the subsequent time of President Roosevelt was taken up in arguing that he had not gone beyond the proper bounds of diplomacy in getting this advantage, but the world though accepting the result has ever been incredulous of his protestations of good faith. And the end is not yet. Colombia has not condoned the part taken by the United States, and the State Department has long been endeavoring to discover some way, not too mortifying to our national self-esteem, by which we may allay Colombia's discontent. And as for that nation it has persistently refused to recognize Panama as independent, one of the results of which has been that the perpetrators of crime on the Isthmus may skip blithely over the line to Bo-

WHAT THEY CALL A STREET IN TOBAGA

gotá or Cartagena and enjoy life free from dread of extradition.

Briefly summarized the terms of the treaty thus expeditiously secured are:

1. The guaranty of the independence of the Republic of Panama.

2. The grant to the United States of a strip of land from ocean to ocean, extending for five miles on each side of the canal, to be called the Canal Zone and over which the United States has absolute jurisdiction. From this Zone the cities of Panama and Colon are explicitly excluded.

3. All railway and canal rights in the Zone are ceded to the United States and its property therein is exempted from taxation.

4. The United States has the right to police, garrison and fortify the Zone.

5. The United States is granted sanitary jurisdiction over the cities of Panama and Colon, and is vested with the right to preserve order in the Republic, should the Panamanian government in the judgment of the United States fail to do so.

6. As a condition of the treaty the United States paid to Panama $10,000,000 in cash, and in 1913 began the annual payment of $250,000 in perpetuity.

Thus equipped with all necessary international authority for the work of building the canal President Roosevelt plunged with equal vehemence and audacity into the actual constructive work. If he strained to the breaking point the rights of a friendly nation to get his treaty, he afterwards tested even further the elasticity of the power of a President to act without Congressional authority.

We may hastily pass over the steps forward. Mr. Cromwell was paid the $40,000,000 for the French stockholders, and at once there arose a prodigious

CHAME BEACH, PACIFIC COAST
Where sand is obtained for locks on the Pacific division

outcry that the Frenchmen got but little out of it; that their stock had been bought for a few cents on the dollar by speculative Americans; that these Americans had financed the "revolution" and that some of the stock was held by persons very close to the administration. None of these charges was proved, but all left a rather bad impression on the public mind. However the United States received full value for the money. April 28, 1904, Congress appropriated the $10,000,000 due Panama, and with

Photo by Underwood & Underwood

FRENCH DRY DOCK, CRISTOBAL

WHAT THE WORK EXPENDED ON THE CANAL MIGHT HAVE DONE

Build a Chinese wall from San Francisco to New York, or dig a ditch 10 feet deep and 55 feet wide across the United States at its widest part

the title thus clear Lieutenant Mark Brooke, U. S. A., at 7:30 A. M. May 4th, formally took over the territory in the name of the United States. An excellent opportunity for pomp and ceremony, for fuss and feathers was thus wasted. There were neither speeches, nor thundering salutes and the hour was obviously unpropitious for champagne. "They order these things better in France," as "Uncle Toby" was wont to say.

When little more than a decade shall have rolled away after that wasted ceremonial moment the visitor to the Isthmus will gaze upon the greatest completed public work of this or any other past age. To conceive of some task that man may accomplish in future that will exceed in magnitude this one is in itself a tax upon the most vivid imagination. To what great work of the past can we compare this one of the present?

The great Chinese wall has been celebrated in all history as one of man's most gigantic efforts. It is 1500 miles long and would reach from San Francisco to St. Louis. But the rock and dirt taken from the Panama Canal would build a wall as high and thick as the Chinese wonder, 2500 miles long and reach from San Francisco to New York in a bee-line.

We cross thousands of miles of ocean to see the great Pyramid of Cheops, one of the Seven Wonders of the ancient world. But the "spoil" taken from the canal prism would build sixty-three such pyramids which put in a row would fill Broadway from the Battery to Harlem, or a distance of nine miles.

The Panama Canal is but fifty miles long, but if we could imagine the United States as perfectly level, the amount of excavation done at Panama would dig a canal ten feet deep and fifty-five feet wide across the United States at its broadest part.

Courtesy Scientific American

A GRAPHIC COMPARISON

The "spoil" taken from the canal would build 63 pyramids the size of Cheops in Broadway from the Battery to Harlem

New York City boasts of its great Pennsylvania terminal, and its sky-piercing Woolworth Building; Washington is proud of its towering Washington Mon- ument, the White House and the

WHAT THE PANAMA CONCRETE WOULD DO

buildings adjacent thereto. But the concrete used in the locks and dams of the canal would make a pyramid 400 feet high, covering the great railway station; the material taken from Culebra cut alone would make a pyramid topping the Woolworth tower by 100 feet, and covering the city from Chambers to Fulton Street, and from the City Hall to West Broadway; while the total soil excavated in the Canal Zone would form a pyramid 4200 feet or four fifths of a mile high, and of equal base line obliterating not only the Washington Monument but the White House, Treasury, the State, War and Navy Buildings and the finest part of official Washington as well.

Jules Verne once, in imagination, drove a tunnel through the center of the earth, but the little cylindrical tubes drilled for the dyna-mite cartridges on "the line" (as people at Panama refer to the Canal Zone) would, if placed end to end, pierce this great globe of ours from side to side; while the dirt cars that have carried off the material would, if made up in one train, reach four times around the world.

But enough of the merely big. Let us consider the spectacle which would confront that visitor whom, in an earlier chapter, we took from Colon to view Porto Bello and San Lorenzo. After finishing those historical pilgrimages if he desired to see the canal in its completed state—say after 1914—he would take a ship at the great concrete docks at Cristobal which will have supplanted as the resting places

for the world's shipping the earlier timber wharves at Colon. Steaming out into the magnificent Limon Bay, the vessel passes into the channel dredged out some three miles into the turbulent Caribbean, and protected from the harsh northers by the massive Toro Point breakwater. The vessel's prow is turned toward the land, not westward as one would think of a ship bound from the Atlantic to the Pacific, but almost due south. The channel through which she steams is 500 feet wide at the bottom, and 41 feet deep at low tide. It extends seven miles to the first interruption at Gatun, a tide water stream all the way. The shores are low, covered with tropical foliage, and littered along the water line with the débris of recent construc-tion work. After steaming about six miles someone familiar with the line will be able to point out over the port side of the ship the juncture of the old French canal with the com-pleted one, and if the jun-gle has not grown up too thick the narrow channel of the former can be traced reaching back to Colon by the side of the Panama Rail-road. This canal was used by the Americans throughout the con-struction work.

At this point the shores rise higher and one on the bridge, or at the bow, will be able to clearly discern far ahead a long hill sloping gently upward on each side of the canal, and cut at the center with great masses of white ma-sonry, which as the ship comes nearer are seen to be gigantic locks, rising in pairs by three steps to a total height of 85 feet.

Courtesy Scientific American

PROPORTIONS OF SOME
OF THE CANAL WORK

UNITED STATES

ATLANTIC OCEAN

EUROPE

AFRICA

SOUTH AMERICA

PACIFIC OCEAN

TOTAL LENGTH OF BORE HOLES WOULD PASS THROUGH CENTER OF THE EARTH

A TRAIN OF FLAT CARS TO CARRY EXCAVATED MATERIAL WOULD ENCIRCLE THE EARTH FOUR TIMES

Courtesy Scientific American

THE "SPOIL" FROM CULEBRA CUT WOULD DO THIS

IN A TYPICAL LOCK

The bridge across is temporary, for construction purposes only.   Gates are still skeletonized awaiting the steel sheathing

For 1000 feet straight out into the center of the canal extends a massive concrete pier, the continuation of the center wall, or partition, between the pairs of locks, while to right and left side walls flare out, to the full width of the canal, like a gigantic U, or a funnel guiding the ships toward the straight pathway upward and onward.   A graceful lighthouse guides the ships at night, while all along the central pier and guide wall electric lights in pairs give this outpost of civilization in the jungle something of the air at night of a brightly lighted boulevard.

Up to this time the ship had been proceeding under her own steam and at about full speed.   Now slowing down she gradually comes to a full stop alongside the central guide wall.   Here will be waiting four electric locomotives, two on the central, two on the side wall.   Made fast, bow and stern, the satellites start off with the ship in tow.   It will take an hour and a half to pass the three locks at Gatun and arrangements will probably be made for passengers to leave the ship and walk by its side if desired, as it climbs the three steps to the waters of Gatun Lake 85 feet above.

Probably the first thing the observant passenger will notice is that as the ship steams into the open lock the great gates which are to close behind her and hold the water which flows in from below, slowly lifting her to the lock above, are folded flush with the wall, a recess having been built to receive them.   The chamber which the vessel has entered is 1000 feet long, if the full water capacity be employed, 110 feet wide and will raise the ship $28\frac{1}{3}$ feet.   If the ship is a comparatively small one the full length of the lock will not be used, as intermediate gates are provided which will permit the use of 400 or 600 feet of the lock as required—thus saving water, which means saving power, for the water that raises and lowers the ships also generates electric power which will be employed in several ways.

Back of each pair of gates is a second pair of emergency gates folded back flush with the wall and only to be used in case of injury to the first pair.   On the floor of the canal at the entrance to the lock lies a great chain, attached to machinery which, at the first sign of a ship's becoming unmanageable, will raise it and bar the passage.   Nearly all serious accidents which have occurred to locks have been due to vessels of which control has been lost, by some error in telegraphing from the bridge to the engine room. For this reason at Panama vessels once in the locks will be controlled wholly by the four locomotives on the lock walls which can check its momentum at the slightest sign of danger. Their own engines will be shut down. Finally at the upper entrance to the locks is an emergency dam built on the guide wall.   It is evident that if an accident should happen to the gates of the upper lock the water on the upper level would rush with destructive force against the lower ones, perhaps sweeping away one after the other and wrecking the canal disastrously. To avert this the emergency dams are swung on a pivot, something like a drawbridge, athwart the lock and great plates let down one after the other, stayed by the perpendicular steel framework until the rush of the waters is checked. A caisson is then sunk against these plates, making the dam complete.

The method of construction and operation of these locks will be more fully described in a later chapter. What has been outlined here can be fully observed by the voyager in transit.   The machinery by which all is operated is concealed in the masonry crypts below, but the traveler may find cheer and certainty of safety in the assurance of the engineer who took me through the cavernous passages—"It's all made fool proof".

Leaving the Gatun locks and going toward the Pacific the ship enters Gatun Lake, a great artificial body of water 85 feet above tide water. This is the ultimate height to which the vessel must climb, and it has reached it in the three steps of the Gatun locks.   To descend from Gatun Lake to the Pacific level she drops down one lock at Pedro Miguel, $30\frac{1}{3}$ feet; and two locks at Miraflores with a total descent of $54\frac{2}{3}$ feet. Returning from the Pacific to the Atlantic the locks of course are taken in reverse order, the ascent beginning at Miraflores and the complete descent being made at Gatun.

LOCK AT PEDRO MIGUEL UNDER CONSTRUCTION

The picture shows strikingly the construction of the locks in pairs, the inner pair being for precautionary purposes

Gatun Lake constitutes really the major part of the canal, and the channel through it extends in a somewhat tortuous course for about twenty-four miles. So broad is the channel dredged—ranging from 500 to 1000 feet in width and 45 to 85 in depth—that vessels will proceed at full speed, a very material advantage, as in ordinary canals half speed or even less is pre-

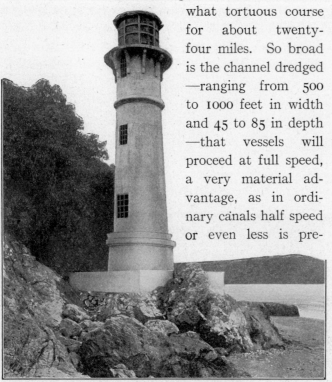

RANGE TOWER AT PACIFIC ENTRANCE

scribed in order to avoid the erosion of the banks.

The lake which the voyager by Panama will traverse will in time become a scenic feature of the trip that cannot fail to delight those who gaze upon it. But for some years to come it will be ghastly, a living realization of some of the pictures emanating from the abnormal brain of Gustave Doré. On either side of the ship gaunt gray trunks of dead trees rise from the placid water, draped in some instances with the Spanish moss familiar to residents of our southern states, though not abundant

on the Isthmus. More of the trees are hung with the trailing ropes of vines once bright with green foliage and brilliant flowers, now gray and dead like the parent trunk. Only the orchids and the air plants will continue to give some slight hint of life to the dull gray monotony of death. For a time, too, it must be expected that the atmosphere will be as offensive as the scene is depressing, for it has been found that the tropical foliage in rotting gives out a most penetrating and disagreeable odor. The scientists have determined to their own satisfaction that it is not prejudicial to health, but the men who have been working in the camps near the shores of the rising lake declare it emphatically destructive of comfort.

The unfortunate trees are drowned. Plunging their roots beneath the waters causes their death as infallibly, but not so quickly, as to fill a man's lungs with the same fluid brings on his end. The Canal Commission has not been oblivious to the disadvantages, both aesthetic and practical, of this great body of dead timber standing in the lake, but it has found the cost of removing it prohibitive. Careful estimates fix the total expense for doing quickly what nature will do gratis in time at $2,000,000. The many small inlets and backwaters of the lake more-

BIRD'S EYE VIEW OF PEDRO MIGUEL LOCKS

over will afford breeding places for the mosquitos and other pestilent insects which the larvacide man with his can and pump can never reach, and no earthly ingenuity can wholly purify.

One vegetable phenomenon of the lake, now exceedingly common, will persist for some time after the ocean-going steamers begin to ply those waters, namely the floating islands. These range from a few feet to several acres in extent, and are formed by portions of the spongy bed of the lake being broken away by the action of the water, and carried off

Florida and Louisiana. Conditions in Gatun Lake are ideal for it and the officials are studying methods of checking its spread from the very beginning.

The waters of the lake cover 164 square miles and are at points eighty-five feet deep. In the main this vast expanse of water, one of the largest of artificial reservoirs, containing about 183 billion cubic feet of water, is supplied by the Chagres River, though several smaller streams add to its volume. Before the dam was built two or three score yards measured the Chagres at its widest point. Now the

Photo by Critchlow.

THE VEGETABLE MARTYRS

The trees in the district flooded by Gatun Lake are being slowly drowned and will finally disappear

by the current, or the winds acting upon the aquatic plants on the surface. They gradually assume a size and consistency that will make them, if not combated, a serious menace to navigation. At present the sole method of dealing with them is to tow them down to the dam and send them over the spillway, but some more speedy and efficacious method is yet to be devised. However as the trees now standing fall and disintegrate, and the actual shores of the lake recede further from the canal the islands will become fewer, and the space in which they can gather without impediment to navigation greater. Another menace to a clear channel which has put in an appearance is the water hyacinth which has practically destroyed the navigability of streams in

waters are backed up into the interior far beyond the borders of the Canal Zone, along the course of every little waterway that flowed into the Chagres, and busy launches may ply above the sites of buried Indian towns. The towns themselves will not be submerged, for the cane and palm-thatched huts will float away on the rising tide. Indeed from the ships little sign of native life will appear, unless it be Indians in cayucas making their way to market. For the announced policy of the government is to depopulate the Zone. All the Indian rights to the soil have been purchased and the inhabitants remorselessly ordered to move out beyond the five-mile strip on either side of the canal. This is unfortunate as it will rob the trip of what might have been a scenic feature, for the Indians love to build their villages near the water, which is in fact their principal highway, and but for this prohibition would probably rebuild as near the sites of their obliterated towns as the waters would permit.

In passing through the lake the canal describes eight angles, and the attentive traveler will find interest in watching the range lights by which the ship is guided when navigating the channel by day or by night — for there need be no cessation of passage because of darkness. These range lights are lighthouses of reënforced concrete so placed in pairs that one towers above the other at a distance back of the lower one of several hundred feet. The pilot keeping these two in line will know he is keeping to the center of his channel until the appearance of two others on either port or starboard bow warns him that the time has come to turn. The towers are of graceful design, and to come upon one springing sixty feet or more into the air from a dense jungle clustering about its very base is to have a new experience in the picturesque. They will need no resident light keepers, for most are on a general electric light circuit. Some of the more inaccessible

however are stocked with compressed acetylene which will burn over six months without recharging. The whole canal indeed from its beginning miles out in the Atlantic to its end under the blue Pacific will be lighted with buoys, beacons, lighthouses and light posts along the locks until its course is almost as easily followed as a "great white way."

Sportsmen believe that this great artificial lake will in time become a notable breeding place for fish and game. Many of our migratory northern birds, including several varieties of ducks, now hibernate at the Isthmus, and this broad expanse of placid water, with its innumerable inlets penetrating a land densely covered with vegetation, should become for them a favorite shelter. The population will be sparse, and mainly as much as five miles away from the line of the canal through which the great steamers will ceaselessly pass.

During the period of its construction that portion of the canal which will lie below the surface of Gatun Lake was plentifully sprinkled with native villages, and held two or three considerable construction towns. Of the latter Gorgona was the largest, which toward the end of canal construction attained a population of about 4000. In the earlier history of the Isthmus Gorgona was a noted stopping place for those crossing the neck, but it seems to have been famed chiefly for the badness of its ac-

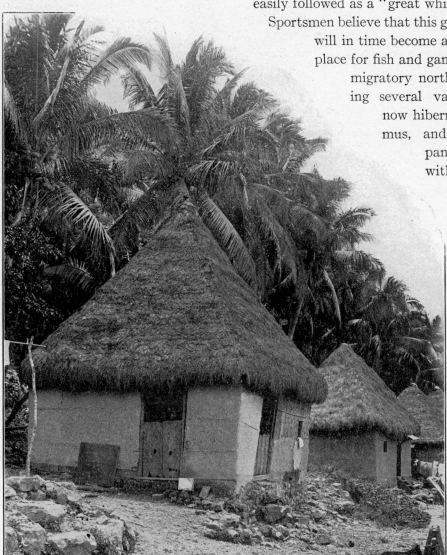

NATIVE STREET AT TABOGA

comodations. Otis says of it, "The town of Gorgona was noted in the earlier days of the river travel as the place where the wet and jaded traveler was accustomed to worry out the night on a rawhide, exposed to the insects and the rain, and in the morning, if he was fortunate regale himself on jerked beef and plantains."

The French established railroad shops here which the Americans greatly enlarged. As a result this town and the neighboring village of Matachin became considerable centers of industry and Gorgona was one of the pleasantest places of residence on "the line." Its Y. M. C. A. clubhouse was one of the largest and best equipped on the whole Zone, and the town was well supplied with churches and schools. By the end of 1913 all this will be changed. The shop will have been moved to the great new port of Balboa; such of the houses and official buildings as could economically be torn down and reërected will have been thus disposed of. Much of the two towns will be covered by the lake, but on the higher portions of the site will stand for some years deserted ruins which the all-conquering jungle will finally take

THE Y. M. C. A. CLUB HOUSE AT GATUN

for its own. The railroad which once served its active people will have been moved away to the other side of the canal and Gorgona will have returned to the primitive wilderness whence Pizarro and the gold hunters awakened it. Near its site is the hill miscalled Balboa's and from the steamships' decks the wooden cross that stands on its summit may be clearly seen.

Soon after passing Gorgona and Matachin the high bridge by which the railroad crosses the Chagres at Gamboa, with its seven stone piers will be visible over the starboard side. This point is of some interest as being the spot at which the water was kept out of the long trench at Culebra. A dyke, partly artificial, here obstructed the canal cut and carried the railroad across to Las Cascadas, Empire, Culebra and other considerable towns all abandoned, together with that branch of the road, upon the completion of the canal.

Now the ship passes into the most spectacular part of the voyage—the Culebra Cut. During the process of construction this stretch of the work vied with the great dam at Gatun for the distinction of being the most interesting and picturesque part of

GAMBOA BRIDGE WITH CHAGRES AT FLOOD
For contrasting picture showing the river in dry season, see page 192

the work. Something of the spectacular effect then presented will be lost when the ships begin to pass. The sense of the magnitude of the work will not so greatly impress the traveler standing on the deck of a ship, floating on the surface of the canal which is here 45 feet deep, as it would were he standing at the bottom of the cut. He will lose about 75 feet of the actual height, as commanded by the earlier traveler who looked up at the towering height of Contractors Hill from the very floor of the colossal excavation. He will lose, too, much of the almost barbaric coloring of the newly opened cut where bright red vied with chrome yellow in startling the eye, and almost every shade of the chromatic scale had its representative in the freshly uncovered strata of earth.

The tropical foliage grows swiftly, and long before the new waterway will have become an accustomed path to the ships of all nations the sloping banks will be thickly covered with vegetation. It is indeed the purpose of the Commission to encourage the growth of such vegetation by planting, in the belief that the roots will tie the soil together and lessen the danger of slides and washouts. The hills that here tower aloft on either side of the canal form part of the great continental divide that, all the way from Alaska to the Straits of Magellan divides the Pacific from the Atlantic watershed. This is its lowest point. Gold Hill, its greatest eminence, rises 495 feet above the bottom of the canal, which in turn is 40 feet above sea level. The story of the gigantic task of cutting through this ridge, of the new problems which arose in almost every week's work, and of the ways in which they were met and overcome will necessitate a chapter to itself. Those who float swiftly along in well-appointed steamships through the almost straight channel 300 feet wide at the bottom, between towering hills, will find the sensation the more memorable if they will study somewhat the figures showing the proportions of the work, the full fruition of which they are enjoying.

At Pedro Miguel a single lock lets the ship down to another little lake hardly two miles across to Miraflores where two more locks drop it down to tide water. From Miraflores the traveler can see the great bulk of Ancon Hill looming up seven miles

Photo by Underwood & Underwood

WORKING IN CULEBRA CUT

The picture is taken at a comparatively quiet time, only two dirt trains being visible

Photo by Underwood & Underwood

MIRAFLORES LOCK IN MARCH, 1913

This lock is in two stories with a total lift of 56⅔ feet; the Pacific tides rise in the canal to the lower lock

away, denoting the proximity of the city of Panama which lies huddled under its Pacific front. Practically one great rock is Ancon Hill, and its landward face is badly scarred by the enormous quarry which the Commission has worked to furnish stone for construction work. At its base is the new port of Balboa which is destined to be in time a great distributing point for the Pacific coast of both North and South America. For the vessels coming through the canal from the Atlantic must, from Balboa, turn north or south or proceed direct across the Pacific to those Asiatic markets of which the old-time mariners so fondly dreamed. Fleets

of smaller coastwise vessels will gather here to take cargoes for the ports of Central America, or for Ecuador, Colombia, Peru and other Pacific states of South America. The Canal Commission is building great docks for the accommodation of both through

NAOS, PERICO AND FLAMENCO ISLANDS TO BE FORTIFIED

and local shipping; storage docks and pockets for coal and tanks for oil. The coaling plant will have a capacity of about 100,000 tons, of which about one-half will be submerged. One dry dock will take a ship 1000 feet long and 105 feet wide—the width of the dock itself being 110 feet. There will be also a smaller dock. One pier, of the most modern design, equipped with unloading cranes and 2200 feet long is already complete, and the plans for additional piers are prepared. The estimated cost of the terminals at Balboa is $15,000,000.

The Suez Canal created no town such as Balboa is likely to be, for conditions with it were wholly different. Port Said at the Mediterranean end and Aden at the Red Sea terminus are coaling stations, nothing more. Geographical considerations however are likely to give to both Balboa and Cristobal—particularly the former—prime importance as points of transshipment.

The machine shops long in Gorgona and Matachin have been removed to Balboa, and though since the completion of the canal the number of their employes has been greatly decreased, the work of repairing and outfitting vessels may be expected to maintain a large population of mechanics. The administration offices now at Culebra will also be moved to Balboa, which in fact is likely to become the chief town of the Canal Zone. Here is to be an employes' club house, built of concrete blocks at a cost of $52,000. Like the other club houses established during the construction period it will be under the direct administration of the Y. M. C. A. The town of Balboa, and the club house will be in no small degree the fruit of the earnest endeavor of Col. Goethals

to build there a town that shall be a credit to the nation, and a place of comfort for those who inhabit it. His estimate presented to Congress of the cost and character of the houses to be furnished to officers of various grades and certain public buildings may be interesting here. The material is all to be concrete blocks:

Governor's house	$25,000
Commissioners' and high officials' houses, each	15,000

Houses of this type to have large center room, a sitting room, dining room, bath, kitchen and four bed rooms.

Families drawing $200 a month	6,000
Families drawing less, in 4-family buildings	4,000
Bachelor quarters, for 50	50,000

Besides these buildings for personal occupance Balboa will contain—unless the original plans are materially modified:

Hotel	$22,500
Commissary	63,000
School	32,000
Police station and court	37,000

When Col. Goethals was presenting his estimates to Congress in 1913 the members of the Committee on Appropriations looked somewhat askance on the club-house feature of his requests, and this colloquy occurred:

"The Chairman: 'A $52,000 club house?'

"Col. Goethals: 'Yes, sir. We need a good club house, because we should give them some amusement, and keep them out of Panama. I believe in the club-house principle.'

"The Chairman: 'That is all right, but you must contemplate a very elaborate house?'

"Col. Goethals: 'Yes, sir. I want to make a town there that will be a credit to the United States government.'"

Looking out to sea from the prow of a ship entering the Pacific Ocean you will notice three conical

BEGINNING OF NEW BALBOA DOCKS

islands rising abruptly from the waves, to a height of three or four hundred feet. To be more precise the one nearest the shore ceased to be an island when the busy dirt trains of the Canal Commission dumped into the sea some millions of cubic yards of material taken from the Culebra Cut, forming at once a great area of artificial land which may in ensuing centuries have its value, and a breakwater which intercepts a local current that for a time gave the canal builders much trouble by filling the channel with silt. The three islands, Naos, Flamenco, and Perico are utilized by the United States as sites for powerful forts. The policy of the War Department necessarily prevents any description here of the forts planned or their armament. Every government jealously guards from the merely curious a view of its defensive works, and the intruder with a camera, however harmless and inoffensive he may be, is severely dealt with as though he had profaned the Holy of Holies. Despite these drastic precautions against the harmless tourist it is a recognized fact that every government has in its files plans and descriptions of the forts of any power with which it is at all likely to become involved in war.

It may be said, however, without entering into prohibited details, that by the fortifications on the islands, and on the hills adjacent to the canal entrance, as well as by a permanent system of submarine mines the Pacific entrance to the canal is made as nearly impregnable as the art of war permits. The locks at Miraflores are seven miles inland and the effective range of naval guns is fourteen miles, so that but for the fortifications and a fleet of our own to hold the hostile fleet well out to sea the very keystone of the canal structure would be menaced. Our government in building its new terminal city at Balboa had before it a very striking illustration of the way in which nations covet just such towns. Russia on completing her trans-Siberian railroad built at Port Arthur a terminal even grander and more costly than our new outpost on the Pacific. But the Japanese flag now waves over Port Arthur— and incidentally the fortifications of that famous terminal were also considered impregnable. Perhaps the impregnable fort like the unsinkable ship is yet to be found.

THE PACIFIC GATEWAY

The gun points to canal entrance; high hills in the background are beyond the canal

At Balboa the trip through the completed canal will be ended. It has covered a fraction over fifty miles, and has consumed, according to the speed of the ship and the "smartness" of her handling in locks, from seven to ten hours. He who was fortunate enough to make that voyage may well reflect on the weeks of time and the thousands of tons of coal necessary to carry his vessel from Colon to Balboa had the canal not existed.

From Balboa to the ancient and yet gay city of Panama runs a trolley line by which the passenger, whose ship remains in port for a few days, or even a few hours, may with but little cost of time or money visit one of the quaintest towns on the North American continent. If the climate, or the seemingly ineradicable sluggishness of the Panamanian do not intervene the two towns should grow into one, though their governments must remain distinct, as the Republic of Panama naturally clings to its capital city. But seemingly the prospect of a great new port at his doors, open to the commerce of all the world, where ships from Hamburg and Hong Kong, from London and Lima, from Copenhagen and from Melbourne may all meet in passing their world-wide ways, excites the Panamanian not a whit. He exists content with his town as it is, reaching out but little for the new trade which this busy mart next door to him should bring. No new hotels are rising within the line of the old walls; no new air of haste or enterprise enlivens the placid streets and plazas. Perhaps in time Balboa may be the big town, and Panama as much outworn as that other Panama which Morgan left a mere group of ruins. It were a pity should it be so, for no new town, built of neat cement blocks, with a Y. M. C. A. club house as its crowning point of gaiety, can ever have the charm which even the casual visitor finds in ragged, bright-colored, crowded, gay and perhaps naughty Panama.

Photo by Underwood & Underwood

COMPLETED CANAL AT COROZAL

CHAPTER VIII

THE FORMATIVE PERIOD

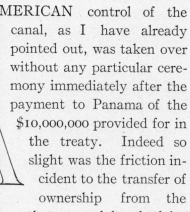MERICAN control of the canal, as I have already pointed out, was taken over without any particular ceremony immediately after the payment to Panama of the $10,000,000 provided for in the treaty. Indeed so slight was the friction incident to the transfer of ownership from the French to the Americans that several hundred laborers employed on the Culebra Cut went on with their work serenely unconscious of any change in management. But though work was uninterrupted the organization of the directing force took time and thought. It took more than that. It demanded the testing out of men in high place and the rejection of the unfit; patient experimenting with methods and the abandonment of those that failed to produce results. There was a long period of this experimental work which sorely tried the patience of the American people before the canal-digging organization fell into its stride and moved on with a certain and resistless progress toward the goal.

In accordance with the Spooner act President Roosevelt on March 8, 1904, appointed the first Isthmian Canal Commission with the following personnel:

Admiral John G. Walker, U. S. N., *Chairman*,
Major General George W. Davis, U. S. A.,
William Barclay Parsons,
William H. Burr,
Benjamin M. Harrod,
Carl Ewald Gunsky,
Frank J. Hecker.

In 1913 when the canal approached completion not one of these gentlemen was associated with it. Death had carried away Admiral Walker, but official mortality had ended the canal-digging careers of the

Photo by Underwood & Underwood

TUNNEL FOR THE OBISPO DIVERSION CANAL

147

others. Indeed under the rule of President Roosevelt the tenure of office of Isthmian Commissioners was exceedingly slender and the whole commission as originally designed was finally abolished being replaced by one made up, with one exception, of officers of the army and navy. The first commission visited the Isthmus, stayed precisely 24 days, ordered some new surveys and returned to the United States. The most important fact about its visit was that it was accompanied to the scene of work by an army surgeon, one Dr. W. C. Gorgas, who had been engaged in cleaning up Havana. Major Gorgas, to give him his army title, was not at this time a member of the Commission but had been appointed Chief Sanitary Officer. I shall have much to say of his work in a later chapter; as for that matter Fame will have much to say of him in later ages. Col. Goethals, who will share that pinnacle was not at this time associated with the canal work. Coincidently with the Commission's visit the President appointed as chief engineer, John F. Wallace, at the moment general manager of the Illinois Central Railroad. His salary was fixed at $25,000 a year.

In telling the story of the digging of the Panama Canal we shall find throughout that the engineer outshines the Commission; the executive rather than the legislative is the ruling force. The story therefore groups itself into three chapters of very unequal length—namely the administrations as chief engineers of John F. Wallace, from June 1, 1904, to June 28, 1905; John F. Stevens, June 30, 1905, to April 1, 1907, and Col. George W. Goethals from April 1, 1907, to the time of publication of this book and doubtless for a very considerable period thereafter.

Each of these officials encountered new problems, serious obstacles, heartbreaking delays and disappointments. Two broke down under the strain; doubtless the one who took up the work last profited by both the errors and the successes of his predecessors. It is but human nature to give the highest applause to him who is in at the death, to immortalize the soldier who plants the flag on the citadel, forgetting him who fell making a breach in the outer breastworks and thereby made possible the ultimate triumph.

Wallace at the very outset had to overcome one grim and unrelenting enemy which was largely subdued before his successors took up the work. Yellow fever and malaria ravaged the Isthmus, as they had done from time immemorial, and although Sanitary Officer Gorgas was there with knowledge of how to put that foe to rout the campaign was yet to be begun. They say that Wallace had a lurking dread that before he could finish the canal the canal would finish him, and indeed he had sound reasons for that fear. He found the headquarters of the chief engineer in the building on Avenida Centrale now occupied by the United States legation, but prior to his time tenanted by the French Director-General. The streets of the town were unpaved, ankle deep in foul mire in the rainy season, and covered with germ-laden dust when dry. There

Photo by Underwood & Underwood

THE TWO COLONELS

W. C. Gorgas and George W. Goethals, whose combined work gave the canal to the world

A WALK AT ANCON

of serviceable machinery it had been abandoned in the open and required careful overhauling before being fit for use; the railroad was inadequate in track mileage and in equipment. Above all the labor problem was yet to be successfully solved. In his one year's service Wallace repaired 357 French houses and built 48 new ones, but the task of housing the employees was still far from completed. Men swarmed over the old French machinery, cutting away the jungle, dousing the metal with kerosene and cleaning off the rust. Floating dredges were set to work in the channel at the Atlantic end—which incidentally has been abandoned in the completed plans for the canal though it was used in preliminary construction. The railroad was reëquipped and extended and the foundation laid for the thoroughly up-to-date road it now is. Meanwhile the surveying parties were busy in the field collecting the data from which after a prolonged period of discussion, the vexed question of the type of canal should be determined.

being no sewers the townsfolk with airy indifference to public health emptied their slops from the second-story windows feeling they had made sufficient concession to the general welfare if they warned passersby before tilting the bucket. Yellow fever was always present in isolated cases, and by the time Wallace had been on the job a few months it became epidemic, and among the victims was the wife of his secretary.

However, the new chief engineer tackled the job with energy. There was quite enough to enlist his best energies. It must be remembered that at this date the fundamental problem of a sea level *vs.* a lock canal had not been determined—was not definitely settled indeed until 1906. Accordingly Engineer Wallace's first work was getting ready to work. He found 746 men tickling the surface of Culebra Cut with hand tools; the old French houses, all there were for the new force had been seized upon by natives or overrun by the jungle; while the French had left great quantities

IN THE HOSPITAL GROUNDS

Two factors in the situation made Wallace's job the hardest. The Commission made its headquarters in Washington, 2000 miles or a week's journey away from the job, and the American people, eager for action, were making the air resound with cries of "make the dirt fly!" In a sense Wallace's position was not unlike that of Gen. McClellan in the opening months of the Civil War when the slogan of the northern press was "On to Richmond," and no thought was given to the obstacles in the path, or the wisdom of preparing fully for the campaign before it was begun. There are many who hold today that if Wallace had been deaf to those who wanted to see the dirt fly, had taken the men off the work of excavation until the type of canal had been determined and all necessary housing and sanitation work had been completed, the results attained would have been better, and the strain which broke down this really capable engineer would have been averted.

Red tape immeasurable wound about the Chief Engineer and all his assistants. Requisitions had to go to the Commission for approval and the Commission clung to Washington tenaciously, as all federal commissions do wherever the work they are commissioned to perform may be situated. During the Civil War days a story was current of a Major being examined for promotion to a colonelcy.

"Now, Major," asked an examiner, "we will consider, if you please, the case of a regiment just ordered into battle. What is the usual position of the colonel in such a case?"

"On Pennsylvania Avenue, about Willard's Hotel," responded the Major bravely and truthfully.

The officers who directed Wallace's fighting force clung to Pennsylvania Avenue and its asphalt rather than abide with Avenida Centrale and its mud. So too did succeeding commissions until Theodore Roosevelt, who had a personal penchant for being on the firing line, ordered that all members of the Commission should reside on the Isthmus. At that he had trouble enforcing the order except with the Army and Navy officers who made up five-sevenths of the Commission.

How great was the delay caused by red tape and absentee authorities cannot be estimated. When requisitions for supplies reached Washington the regulations required that bids be advertised for. I rather discredit the current story that when a young Panamanian arrived at Ancon Hospital and the mother proved unable to furnish him with food, the doctor in charge was officially notified that if he bought a nursing bottle without advertising thirty days for bids he must do so at his own expense. That story seems too strikingly illustrative of red-tape to be true. But it is true that after Col.

FRENCH COTTAGES ON THE WATER FRONT, CRISTOBAL

Gorgas had worked out his plans for furnishing running water to Panama, and doing away with the cisterns and great jars in which the residents stored water and bred mosquitoes, it took nine months to get the iron pipes, ordinary ones at that, to Panama. Meanwhile street paving and sewerage were held up and when Wallace wired the Commission to hurry he was told to be less extravagant in his use of the cable.

PAY DAY FOR THE BLACK LABOR

ever anything was to be done on the canal line the first word from Washington was always criticism — the policy instantly applied was delay.

Allowing for the disadvantages under which he labored Mr. Wallace achieved great results in his year of service on the Isthmus. But his connection with the canal was ended in a way about which must ever hang some element of mystery. He complained bitterly, persistently and

No man suffered more from this sort of official delay and stupidity than did Col. Gorgas. If any man was fighting for life it was he—not for his own life but that of the thousands who were working, or yet to work on the canal. Yet when he called for wire netting to screen out the malarial mosquitos he was rebuked by the Commission as if he were asking it merely to contribute to the luxury of the employees. The amount of ingenuity expended by the Commission in suggesting ways in which wire netting might be saved would be admirable as indicative of a desire to guard the public purse, except for the fact that in saving netting they were wasting human lives. The same policy was pursued when appeals came in for additional equipment for the hospitals, for new machinery, for wider authority. When-

justly about the conditions in which he was compelled to work and found in President Roosevelt a sympathetic and a reasonable auditor. Indeed, moved by the Chief Engineer's appeals, the President endeavored to secure from Congress authority to substitute a Commission of three for the unwieldy body of seven with which Wallace found it so hard to make headway. Failing in this the President characteristically enough did by indirection what Congress would not permit him to do directly. He demanded and received the resignations of all the original commissioners, and appointed a new board with the following members:

Theodore P. Shonts, *Chairman*,
Charles E. Magoon, *Governor of the Canal Zone*,
John F. Wallace, *Chief Engineer*,

Mordecai T. Endicott,
Peter C. Hains,
Oswald H. Ernst,
Benjamin M. Harrod.

As in the case of the earlier commissioners none of these remained to see the work to a conclusion.

This commission, though similar in form, was vastly different in fact from its predecessor. The President in appointing it had directed that its first three members should constitute an executive committee, and that two of these, Gov. Magoon and Engineer Wallace, should reside continuously on the Zone. To further concentrate power in Mr. Wallace's hands he was made Vice-President of the Panama Railroad. The President thus secured practically all he had asked of Congress, for the executive committee of three was as powerful as the smaller commission which Congress had refused him. In all this organization Mr. Wallace had been consulted at every step. He stayed for two months in Washington while the changes were in progress and expressed his entire approval of them. It was therefore with the utmost amazement that the President received from him, shortly after his return to the Isthmus, a cable requesting a new conference and hinting at his resignation.

At the moment that cable message was sent Panama was shuddering in the grasp of the last yellow fever epidemic that has devastated that territory. Perhaps had Col. Gorgas secured his wire netting earlier, or Wallace's appeals for water pipes

Photo by Underwood & Underwood
IN WALLACE'S TIME
Sanitation work in Panama City

met with prompter attention it might have been averted. But in that May and June of 1905 the fever ravaged the town and the work camps almost as it had in the days of the French. There had been, as already noted, some scattered cases of yellow fever in the Zone when the Americans took hold, but they were too few and too widely separated to cause any general panic. The sanitary authorities however noted with apprehension that they did not decrease, and that a very considerable proportion were fatal. It was about this time that the Commission was snubbing Col. Gorgas because of his insatiable demands for wire screening. In April there were seven cases among the employees in the Commission's headquarters in Panama. Three died and among the 300 other men employed there panic spread rapidly. Nobody cared about jobs any longer. From all parts of the Zone white-faced men flocked to the steamship offices to secure passage home. Stories about the ravages of the disease among the French became current, and the men at work shuddered as they passed the little French cemeteries so plentifully scattered along the Zone.

The sanitary forces wheeled out into the open and went into the fight. Every house in Panama and Colon was fumigated, against the bitter protests of many of the householders who would rather face yellow fever then the cleansing process, and who did not believe much in these scientific ideas of the "gringoes" anyway. An army of inspectors made house to house canvasses of the towns and removed, sometimes by force, all suspected victims to the iso-

THE WASHING PLACE AT TABOGA

Taboga, site of the Commission sanitarium, is the most picturesque point readily accessible from Panama City.
The laundry place is the gathering point for the women of the village.

lation hospitals. The malignant mosquitoes, couriers of the infection, were pursued patiently by regiments of men who slew all that were detected and deluged the breeding places with larvacide. The war of science upon sickness soon began to tell. June showed the high-water mark of pestilence with sixty-two cases, and six deaths. From that point it declined until in December the last case was

reaching New York he met the then Secretary of War, afterwards President, William Howard Taft, to whom he expressed dissatisfaction with the situation and asked to be relieved at the earliest possible moment. Secretary Taft declined to consider his further association with the canal, for a moment, demanded that his resignation take effect at once and reproached him for abandoning the work in words

THE FUMIGATION BRIGADE
When the members of this command finished with a district in Panama the mosquito was done for

registered. Since then there has been no case of yellow fever originating on the Isthmus, and the few that have been brought there have been so segregated that no infection has resulted.

It was, however, when the epidemic was at its height that Mr. Wallace returned from Washington to the Isthmus. Almost immediately he cabled asking to be recalled and the President, with a premonition of impending trouble, so directed. On

that stung, and which when reiterated in a letter and published the next day put the retiring engineer in a most unenviable position. From this position he never extricated himself. Perhaps the fear of the fever, of which he thought he himself had a slight attack, shook his nerve. Perhaps, as the uncharitable thought and the Secretary flatly charged, a better position had offered itself just as he had become morally bound to finish the canal work. Or

TYPICAL SCREENED HOUSES

perhaps he concluded in the time he had for cool reflection on the voyage to Panama that the remedies offered for the red tape, divided authority and delay that had so handicapped him were inadequate. His communication to the press at the time was unconvincing. The fairest course to pursue in the matter is to accept Mr. Wallace's own statement made to a congressional investigating committee nearly a year later, in answer to a question as to the cause of his resignation:

"My reason was, that I was made jointly responsible with Mr. Shonts and Mr. Magoon for work on the canal, while Mr. Shonts had a verbal agreement with the President that he should have a free rein in the management of all matters. I felt Mr. Shonts was not as well qualified as I was either as a business man or an administrator, and he was not an engineer. . . . I thought it better to sacrifice my ambitions regarding this work, which was to be the crowning event of my life, than remain to be humiliated, forced to disobey orders, or create friction."

The Wallace resignation was at the moment most unfortunate. There had for months been an almost concerted effort on the part of a large and influential section of the press, and of men having the public ear to decry the methods adopted at Panama, to criticize the men engaged in the work and to magnify the obstacles to be overcome. Perhaps this chorus of detraction was stimulated in part by advocates of the Nicaragua route hoping to reopen that controversy. Probably the transcontinental railroads, wanting no canal at all, had a great deal to do with it. At any rate it was loud and insistent and the men on the Isthmus were seriously affected by it. They knew by Mr. Wallace's long absence that some trouble was brewing in Washington. His sudden departure again after his return from the capital and the rumor that he had determined to take a more profitable place added to the unrest. Probably the rather savage letter of dismissal with which Secretary Taft met the Chief Engineer's letter of resignation, and the instantaneous appointment in his place of John F. Stevens, long associated with James J. Hill in railroad building, at a salary $5000 a year greater, was the best tonic for the tired feeling of those on the Isthmus. It indicated that the President thought those who had accepted positions of command on the Canal Zone had enlisted for the war, and that they could not desert in the face of the enemy without a proper rebuke. It showed furthermore that the loss of one man would not be permitted to demoralize the service, but that the cry familiar on the line of battle "Close up! Close up,

A STREET AFTER PAVING

Before paving it was of the sort shown on page 39

men! Forward"! was to be the rallying cry in the attack on the hills of Panama.

Despite the unfortunate circumstances attending Mr. Wallace's retirement, his work had been good, so far as it went. In office a little more than a year he had spent more than three months of the time in Washington or at sea. But he had made more than a beginning in systematizing the work, in repairing the railroad, in renovating the old machinery and actually making "the dirt fly". Of that objectionable substance—on the line of the canal, if anywhere, they applaud the definition "dirt is matter out of place" —he had excavated 744,644 yards. Not much of a showing judged by the records of 1913, but excellent for the machinery available in 1905. The first steam shovel was installed during his régime and before he left nine were working. The surveys, under his direction,

HOSPITAL BUILDINGS, UNITED FRUIT CO.

were of great advantage to his successor who **never** failed to acknowledge their merit.

Mr. Stevens, who reached the canal, adopted at the outset the wise determination to reduce construction work to the minimum and concentrate effort on completing arrangements for housing and feeding the army of workers which might be expected as soon as the interminable question of the sea level or lock canal could be finally determined. From his administration dates much of the good work done in the organization of the

STOCKADE FOR PETTY CANAL ZONE OFFENDERS

BEGINNING THE NEW DOCKS, CRISTOBAL

Commissary and Subsistence Department, and the development of the railroad. The inducement of free quarters added to high wages to attract workers also originated with him. At the same time Gov. Magoon was working over the details of civil administration, the schools, courts, police system and road building. The really fundamental work of canal building, the preparation of the ground for the edifice yet to be erected, made great forward strides at this period. But the actual record of excavation was but small.

One reason for this was the hesitation over the type of canal to be adopted. It is obvious that several hundred thousand cubic yards of dirt dug out of a ditch have to be dumped somewhere. If deposited at one place the dump would be in the way of a sea-level canal while advantageous for the lock type. At another spot this condition would be reversed. Already the Americans had been compelled to move a second time a lot of spoil which the French had excavated, and which, under the American plans, was in danger of falling back into Culebra Cut. "As a gift of prophecy is withheld from us in these latter days," wrote Stevens plaintively in reference to the vacillation concerning the plans, "all we can do now is to make such arrangements as may look proper as far ahead as we can see."

President Roosevelt meanwhile was doing all he could to hasten determination of the problem.

Just before the appointment of Mr. Stevens he appointed an International Board of Advisory Engineers, five being foreign and nine American, to examine into the subject and make recommendations. They had before them a multiplicity of estimates upon which to base their recommendations and it may be noted eight years after the event that not one of the estimates came within one hundred million dollars of the actual cost. From which it appears that when a nation undertakes a great public work it encounters the same financial disillusionments that come to the young homebuilder when he sets out to build him a house from architect's plans guaranteed to keep the cost within a fixed amount.

Poor De Lesseps estimated the cost of a sea-level canal at $131,000,000, though it is fair to say for the French engineers whose work is so generally applauded by our own that their estimate was several million dollars higher. The famous International Congress had estimated the cost of a sea-level canal at $240,000,000. In fact the French spent $260,000,000 and excavated about 80,000,000 cubic yards of earth! Then came on our estimators. The Spooner act airily authorized $135,000,000 for a canal of any type, and is still in force though we have already spent twice that amount. The Walker Commission fixed the cost of a sea-level canal with a dam at Alhajuela and a tide lock at Miraflores at $240,000,000. The majority of President Roose-

Photo by Underwood & Underwood

A BACK STREET IN COLON
This street is as clean and well paved as any in the United States

velt's Board of Advisory Engineers reported in favor of a sea-level canal and estimated its cost at $250,-000,000; the minority declared for a lock canal fixing its cost "in round numbers" at $140,000,000. Engineer Wallace put the cost of a sea-level canal at $300,000,000 exclusive of the $50,000,000 paid for the Canal Zone. Col. Goethals came in in 1908, with the advantage of some years of actual construction, and fixed the cost of the sea-level canal at $563,000,000 and the lock type at $375,000,000. He guesses best who guesses last, but it may be suggested in the vernacular of the streets that even Col. Goethals "had another guess coming".

On all these estimates the most illuminating comment is furnished by the Official Handbook of the Panama Canal for 1913 showing total expenditures to November 1, 1912, of $270,625,624 exclusive of fortification expenditures. The Congressional ap-

propriations to the same date, all of which were probably utilized by midsummer of 1913, were $322,551,448.76.

The action of his Advisory Board put President Roosevelt for the moment in an embarrassing position. A swinging majority declared for a sea-level canal, and even when the influence of Engineer Stevens, who was not a member of the Board, was exerted for the lock type it left the advocates of that form of canal still in the minority. To ask a body of eminent scientists to advise one and then have them advise against one's own convictions creates a perplexing situation. But Roosevelt was not one to allow considerations of this sort to weigh much with him when he had determined a matter in his own mind. Accordingly he threw his influence for the lock type, sent a resounding message to Congress and had the satisfaction of seeing his views approved

STEAM SHOVEL AT WORK

the Panama railroad as the original bed would
be covered by the new lake. The development
of the commissary system which supplied every
thing needful for the daily life of the employee,
the establishment of quarters, the creation of
a public school system, were all well under way.
Then arose a new issue which split the second Commission and again threatened to turn things topsy-
turvy.

Chairman Shonts, himself a builder of long experience and well accustomed to dealing with contractors, was firmly of the opinion that the canal
could best be built by letting contracts to private
bidders for the work. In this he was opposed by
most of his associates, and particularly by Mr.
Stevens who had been working hard and efficiently
to build up an organization that would be capable
of building the canal without the interposition of
private contractors looking for personal profit. The
employees on the Zone, naturally enough, were with
Stevens to a man, and time has shown that he and

by that body June 29, 1906. It had been two years
and two months since the Americans came to
Panama, and though at last the form of canal was
determined upon there are not lacking today men
of high scientific and political standing who hold
that an error
was made, and
that ultimate-
ly the great
locks will be
abandoned
and the canal
bed brought
down to tide
water.

The Ameri-
cans on the
Isthmus now
got fairly into
their stride.
Determina-
tion of the
type of canal
at once deter-
mined the
need for the
Gatun Dam,
spillway and
locks. It ne-
cessitated the
shifting of the
roadbed of

THE BALBOA ROAD
The trolley line shown will extend from Balboa, through Panama and Ancon to the ruins of Old Panama

A DRILL BARGE AT WORK

The sea and tidal waters are underlaid with coral rock necessitating much submarine blasting

they were right. There is something about working for the nation that stirs a man's loyalty as mere private employment never can. But in this instance Mr. Shonts was in Washington, convenient to the ear of the President while Mr. Stevens was on the Zone. Accordingly the President approved of the Chairman's plan, and directed the Secretary of War, Mr. Taft, to advertise for bids. Mr. Stevens was discontented and showed it. That his judgment would be justified in the end he could not know. That it had been set aside for the moment he was keenly aware, and that he was being harassed by Congress and by innumerable rules such as no veteran railroad builder had ever been subjected to did not add to his comfort.

His complaints to the Secretary of War were many, and not of a sort to contribute to that official's peace of mind. When the bids came in from the would-be contractors they were all rejected on the ground that they did not conform to the specifications, but the real reason was that the President at heart did not believe in that method of doing the work, and was sure that the country agreed with him. This should have allayed Mr. Stevens' rising discontent. It certainly offended Chairman Shonts, who stood for the contract system, and when the bids were rejected and that system set aside promptly resigned. The President thereupon consolidated the offices of Chairman of the Commission and Chief Engineer in one, Mr. Stevens being appointed that one. Given thus practically unlimited power Mr. Stevens might have been expected to be profoundly contented with the situation. Instead he too resigned on the first of April, 1907.

About his resignation as about that of Mr. Wallace there has always been a certain amount of mystery. He himself made no explanation of his act, though his friends conjectured that he was not wholly in harmony with the President's plan to abolish the civilian commission altogether, and fill its posts by appointments from the Army and Navy. On the Isthmus there is a story that he did not intend to resign at all. Albert Edwards, who heard the story early, tells it thus:

"One of the canal employees, who was on very friendly terms with Stevens, came into his office and found him in the best of spirits. When the business in hand was completed he said jovially:

Photo by S. H. Elliott

PACIFIC ENTRANCE TO THE CANAL

"'Read this. I've just been easing my mind to T. R. It's a hot one—isn't it?' And he handed over the carbon copy of his letter. His visitor read it with great seriousness.

"'Mr. Stevens', he said, 'that is the same as a resignation'.

"And Stevens laughed.

"'Why, I've said that kind of thing to the Colonel a dozen times. He knows I don't mean to quit this job'.

"But about three hours after the letter reached Washington Mr. Stevens received a cablegram: 'Your resignation accepted'".

At any rate the Stevens resignation called forth no such explosive retort as had been directed against the unhappy Wallace, and he showed no later signs of irritation, but came to the defense of his successor in a letter strongly approving the construction of certain locks and dams which were for the moment the targets of general public criticism.

Two weeks before Stevens resigned the other members of the Commission, excepting Col. Gorgas, in response to a hint from the President had sent in their resignations. Mr. Roosevelt had determined that henceforward the work should be done by army and navy officers, trained to go where the work was to be done and to stay there until recalled; men who had entered the service of the nation for life and were not looking about constantly to "better their conditions". He had determined further that the government should be the sole contractor, the only employer, the exclusive paymaster, landlord and purveyor of all that was needful on the Zone. In short he had planned for the Canal Zone a form of administration which came to be called socialistic and gave cold chills to those who stand in dread of that doctrine. To carry out these purposes he appointed on April 1, 1907, the following commission:

Lieut.-Col. George W. Goethals, *Chairman and Chief Engineer*,

Major D. D. Gaillard, U. S. A.,

Major William L. Sibert, U. S. A.,

Mr. H. H. Rousseau, U. S. N.,

Col. W. C. Gorgas, U. S. A., Medical Corps,

Mr. J. C. S. Blackburn,

Mr. Jackson Smith,

Mr. Joseph Bucklin Bishop, *Secretary*.

A majority of this commission was in office at the time of publication of this book, and gave evidences of sticking to the job until its completion. Senator Blackburn resigned in 1910 and was succeeded by Hon. Maurice H. Thatcher, also of Kentucky; and Mr. Smith retired in favor of Lieut. Col. Hodges in 1908.* With the creation of this commission began the forceful and conclusive administration of Col. Goethals, the man who finished the canal.

*In June, 1913, President Wilson announced the pending appointment of Richard L. Metcalfe of Nebraska to succeed Commissioner Thatcher, but at the time of the publication of this book the appointment had not been consummated.

CHAPTER IX

COL. GOETHALS AT THE THROTTLE

Photo by Underwood & Underwood

COL. GOETHALS AT HIS DESK

THE visitor to the Canal Zone about 1913 could hardly spend a day in that bustling community without becoming aware of some mighty potentate not at all mysterious, but omnipresent and seemingly omniscient, to whom all matters at issue were referred, to whom nothing was secret, whose word was law and without whose countenance the mere presence of a visitor on the Zone was impossible. The phrases most in use were "see the Colonel," "ask the Colonel" and "the Colonel says". If there had been a well-conducted newspaper on the Zone these phrases would have been cast in slugs in its composing room for repeated and ready use. No President of the United States, not even Lincoln in war times, exerted the authority he daily employed in the zenith of his power. The aggrieved wife appealed to his offices for the correction of her marital woes, and the corporation with a $600,000 steam crane to sell talked over its characteristics with the Colonel.

He could turn from a vexed question of adjusting the work of the steam shovels to a new slide in the Culebra Cut, to compose the differences of rival dancing clubs over dates at the Tivoli Hotel ballroom. On all controverted questions there was but one court of last resort. As an Isthmian poetaster put it:

"See Colonel Goethals, tell Colonel Goethals,
 It's the only right and proper thing to do.
Just write a letter, or even better
 Arrange a little Sunday interview".

Engineer Stevens in a speech made at the moment of his retirement before a local club of workers said:

"You don't need me any longer. All you have to do now is to dig a ditch. What you want is a statesman".

A statesman was found and his finding exemplifies strikingly the fact that when a great need arises the man to meet it is always at hand, though frequently in obscurity. Major George W. Goethals of the General Staff, stationed at Washington was far from being in the public eye. Anyone who knows his Washington well knows that the General Staff is a sort of general punching bag for officers of the Army who cannot get appointments to it, and for newspaper correspondents who are fond of describing its members as fusty bureaucrats given to lolling in the Army and Navy Club while the Army sinks to the level of a mere ill-ordered militia. But even in this position Major Goethals had not attained sufficient eminence to have been made a target for the slings and arrows of journalistic criticism. As a member of the Board of Fortifications,

PRESIDENT TAFT ARRIVES

however, he had attracted the attention of Secretary Taft, and through him had been brought into personal relations with President Roosevelt.

Of course when a man has "made good" everybody is quick to discern in him the qualities which compel success. But Roosevelt must have been able to discover them in the still untested Goethals, for when the Stevens resignation reached Washington the President at once turned to him with the remark, "I've tried two civilians in the Canal and they've both quit. We can't build the canal with a new chief engineer every year. Now I'm going to give it to the Army and to somebody who can't quit."

John F. Stevens resigned April 1, 1907, and on the

Photo by Underwood & Underwood
RAILWAY STATION AT GATUN
The Panama Railroad is being equipped with stations and rolling stock of the first-class

same day Col. Goethals became Chief Engineer of the Panama Canal, and the supreme arbiter of the destinies of all men and things on the Canal Zone. Everybody with a literary turn of mind who goes down there describes him as the Benevolent Despot, and that crabbed old philosopher Thomas Carlyle would be vastly interested could he but see how the benevolent despotism which he described as ideal but impossible is working successfully down in the semi-civilized tropics.

Before describing in detail Col. Goethals' great work, the digging of the canal, let me relate some incidents which show what manner of man it was that took the reins when the Americans on the ditch swung into their winning stride.

This is the way they tell one story on the Isthmus:

A somewhat fussy and painfully perturbed man bustled into the office of Col. Goethals one morning and plunged into his tale of woe.

"Now I got that letter of yours, Colonel", he began but stopped there checked by a cold gaze from those quiet blue eyes.

"I beg your pardon", said the Colonel suavely, "but you must be mistaken. I have written you no letter".

"Oh, yes, Colonel, it was about that work down at Miraflores".

"Oh, I see. You spoke a little inaccurately. You

meant you received my orders, not a letter. You have the orders, so that matter is settled. Was there anything else you wished to talk with me about"?

But the visitor's topic of conversation had been summarily exhausted and, somewhat abashed, he faded away.

And again: A high official of the Isthmian Commission had been somewhat abruptly translated from the Washington office to Ancon. There was no

He spoke of his fears to the Colonel at lunch one day.

"Let's walk over to the site and see", remarked that gentleman calmly. It may be noted in passing that walking over and seeing is one of the Colonel's favorite stunts. There are mighty few, if any, points on the Canal Zone which he has not walked over and seen, with the result that his knowledge of the progress of the work is not only precise but personal. But to return to the house a-building.

COL. GOETHALS REVIEWING THE MARINES AT CAMP ELLIOTT

house suitable for his occupancy and the Colonel ordered one built to be ready, let us say, October first. Meanwhile the prospective tenant and his family abode at the Tivoli Hotel which, even to one enjoying the reduced rates granted to employees, is no inexpensive spot. Along about the middle of August he began to get apprehensive. A few foundation pillars were all that was to be seen of the twelve-room house, of the type allotted to members of the Commission, which was to be his.

On arrival there three or four workmen were found plugging away in a leisurely manner under the eye of a foreman to whom the Colonel straightway addressed himself, "You understand the orders relative to this job"? he said to the foreman, tentatively.

"Oh, yes, Colonel", responded that functionary cheerfully, "it is ordered for October first, and we are going to do our very best".

"Pardon me", blandly but with a suspicion of

satire, "I was afraid you did not understand the order and I see I was right. Your order is to have this house ready for occupancy October first. There isn't anything said about doing your best. The house is to be finished at the time fixed".

Turning, the Colonel walked away, giving no heed to the effort of the foreman to reopen the conversation. Next day that individual called on the prospective tenant.

"Say", he began ingratiatingly, "you don't really need to be in that house October first, do you? Would a few days more or less make any difference to you"?

"Not a bit".

"Well, then", cheering up, "won't you just tell the Colonel a little delay won't bother you"?

"Not I! I want to stay on this Isthmus. If you want to try to get the Colonel's orders changed you do it. But none of that for me".

And the day before the time fixed the house was turned over complete.

It is fair to say however that peremptory as is Col. Goethals in his orders, and implacable in his insistence on literal obedience, he

PRESIDENT TAFT AND "THE COLONEL"

yields to the orders of those who rank him precisely what he exacts from those whom he commands. The following dialogue from a hearing before the House Committee on Appropriations will illustrate my point. The subject matter was the new Washington Hotel at Colon.

"*The Chairman:* Did you ever inquire into the right of the Panama Railroad Company, under the laws of the State of New York, to go into the hotel business?

"*Col. Goethals:* No sir; I got an order from the President of the United States to build that hotel and I built it".

This military habit of absolute command and implicit obedience is not attended in Col. Goethals' case with any of what civilians are accustomed to call "fuss and feathers". On the Zone he was never seen in uniform, and it is said, indeed, that he brought none to Panama. His mind in fact is that of the master, not of the martinet. If he compels obedience, he commands respect and seems to inspire real affection. In a stay of some weeks at Panama during which time I associated in-

Photo by Underwood & Underwood

The upper part shows a 16-inch rifle being tested at Sandy Hook. The gun, which is of the type adopted for the Canal defenses, throws a 2,400 pound shell to an extreme range of 22 miles. It could drop a shell into Wall Street from Sandy Hook. One shell striking a battleship fairly would put her out of business. The lower part of picture shows comparative size of the gun

COL. GOETHALS ENCOURAGES THE NATIONAL GAME

timately with men in every grade of the Commission's service I heard not one word of criticism of his judgment, his methods or even his personality. This is the more remarkable when it is considered how intimately his authority is concerned with the personal life of the Isthmian employees. If one wishes to write a magazine article pertaining to the Canal Zone the manuscript must be submitted to the Colonel. If complaint is to be made of a faulty house, or bad commissary service, or a negligent doctor, or a careless official in any position it is made to the Colonel. He is the Haroun al Raschid of all the Zone from Cristobal to Ancon. To his personal courts of complaint, held Sunday mornings when all the remainder of the canal colony is at rest, come all sorts and conditions of employees with every imaginable grievance.

The court is wholly inofficial but terribly effective. There is no uniformed bailiff with his cry of "Hear ye! Hear ye"! No sheriff with jingling handcuffs. But the orders of that court, though not registered in any calf-bound law books for the use of generations of lawyers, are obeyed, or, if not obeyed, enforced. Before this judge any of the nearly 50,000 people living under his jurisdiction, speaking 45 different languages, and citizens in many cases of nations thousands of miles away, may come with any grievance however small. The court is held of a Sunday so as not to interfere with the work of the complainants, for you will find that on the Zone the prime consideration of every act is to avoid interference with work. The Colonel hears the complaints patiently, awards judgment promptly and sees that it is enforced. There is no system of constitutional checks and balances in his domain. He is the legislative, judicial and executive branches in one—or to put it less technically but more understandably, what the Colonel says goes. It is, I think, little less than marvelous that a man in the continual exercise of such a power should awaken so little criticism as he. It is true that those who displease him he may summarily deport, thus effectually stilling any local clamor against his policy, but I am unable to discover that he has misused, or even often used, this power.

A young man comes in with an important problem affecting the social life of the Zone. His particular dancing club desires to use the ball room at the Tivoli Hotel on a certain night, but the room was engaged for that date and the other nights suggested did not fit the convenience of the club, so there was nothing to do but to put it up to the Colonel, who put aside the responsibilities of the head of a $400,000,000 canal job and President of the Panama Railway to fix a date whereon the young folk of that aspiring social club might Turkey trot and Tango to their hearts' content. So far as I know the Colonel has not yet been appealed to by the moralists of the Zone to censor the dances.

Troubles between workmen and their bosses of course make up a considerable share of the business before the court. Once a man came in with an

evident air of having been ill-used. He had been discharged and the Colonel promptly inquired why.

"Because I can't play baseball", was the surprising response of the discharged one, who had been a steamshoveler.

Photo by Underwood & Underwood

THE COLONEL'S DAILY STROLL

It appeared on inquiry that the drill men had challenged the steamshovelers to a match at the national game, and dire apprehensions of defeat filled the minds of the latter because they had no pitcher. At this juncture there providentially appeared a man seeking a job who was a scientific twirler whether he knew much about steamshoveling or not. The American sporting spirit was aroused. The man with the job who couldn't pitch lost it to the man who could but had no job. So he came to the Colonel with his tale of woe.

Now that sagacious Chief Engineer knows that the American sporting spirit is one of the great forces to be relied upon for the completion of the canal. The same sentiment which led the shovelers to use every device to down the drillers at baseball would animate them when they were called to fight with the next slide for possession of Culebra Cut. Some employ-

OLD FRENCH LADDER DREDGES STILL USED

ers would have sent the man back to his boss with a curt order of reinstatement—and the shovelers would have lost the game and something of their spirit. So after a moment of reflection the Colonel said quietly to the man:

"They want shovelers on the Pacific end. Go over there in the morning and go to work".

The feudal authority, the patriarchal power which Col. Goethals possesses over the means of livelihood of every man on the Zone, nay more, over their very right to stay on the Zone at all, gives to his decisions more immediate effect than attends those of a court. The man who incurs his displeasure may lose his job, be ousted from his lodgings and deported from the Isthmus if the Colonel so decrees. A Jamaican negress came in to complain that her husband took her earnings away from her; would not work himself but lived and loafed on the fruits of her industry. The Colonel ordered the man to allow her to keep her earnings. The man demurred saying sullenly that the English law gave a husband command over his wife's wages.

"All right," said the Colonel, "you're from Jamaica. I'll deport you both and you can get all the English law you want".

The husband paid back the money he had confiscated and the pair stayed.

Family affairs are aired in the Colonel's court to a degree which must somewhat abash that simple and direct warrior. What the dramatists call "the eternal triangle" is not unknown on the Zone, nor is the unscriptural practice of coveting your neighbor's wife wholly without illustration. For such situations the Colonel's remedy is specific and swift—

A SIDE DRILL CREW AT WORK

deportation of the one that makes the trouble. Sometimes the deportation of two has been found essential, but while gossip of these untoward incidents is plentiful in the social circles of Culebra and Ancon the judge in the case takes no part in it.

It is not in me to write a character sketch of Col. Goethals. That is rather a task for one who has known him intimately and has been able to observe the earlier manifestations of those qualities that led President Roosevelt to select him as the supreme chief of the canal work. All his life he has been an army engineer, having a short respite from active work in the field when he was professor of engineering at West Point. Fortifications and locks were his specialties and fortifications and locks have engaged his chief attention since he undertook the Panama job. Perhaps it is due to his intensely military attitude that the public has insensibly come to look upon the canal in its quality as an aid to national defense rather than a stimulus to national commerce. For the Colonel any discussion of the need for fortifying the canal was the merest twaddle, and he had his way. He begged long for a standing army of 25,000 men on the Zone, but it is doubtful whether he will win this fight. Moreover he would so subordinate all considerations to the military one that he urges the expulsion from the Zone of all save canal employees that the danger of betrayal may be less. How far that policy shall be approved by Congress is yet to be determined. Thus far however the Colonel has handled Congress with notable success and even there his dominant spirit may yet triumph.

Power on the Zone, however, autocratic and absolute, Col. Goethals possesses. It was conferred

THE COLONEL'S FIRE WORKS
A big blast in Culebra Cut.   In one year 27,252 tons of dynamite were used

covering therefore nine months of the Stevens administration, and was dated at the end of the fiscal year, June 30, 1907. He reported that 80 per cent. of the plant necessary for completing the work was on the ground or had been ordered. When he arrived the high water-mark for excavating in Culebra Cut was 900,000 cubic yards a month, and since his rule began it has never fallen below the million mark, except in May, 1908. It may be noted in passing, that during the first two years of his administration the average for excavation

on him formally by the order of Jan. 6, 1908, giving the Chairman authority to reorganize the service at his own discretion, subject of course to review by the President or Secretary of War. The first effect of this was the abolition of a large list of departments with high sounding names, and concentration of their functions in the quartermaster's department with Major C. A. Devol at its head. The Colonel developed in fact a rage for abolishing and concentrating departments. He did not go quite as far as Nero who wished that Rome had but one neck that he might strike off its head at a blow, but he certainly reduced the number of responsible chiefs to such a point that it was easy to place the fault if work lagged or blunders multiplied.

Col. Goethals' first annual report was issued after he had been in command only three months,

along the whole line exceeded three million cubic yards a month. During the whole administration of Messrs. Wallace and Stevens only six million yards had been removed. The contrasting figures are given not as reflecting on the earlier engineers, but as indicating the rapidity with which the equip-

Photo by Underwood & Underwood

A HEAVY BLAST UNDER WATER

ment and efficiency of the canal organization were increased when the battle of the levels was ended and the civilian commission done away with.

In this report Col. Goethals argued vigorously against turning over the canal work to private contractors — a matter which the President had asked him to report upon in detail. He pointed out that the canal required special equipment for which no contractor could find use after the expiration of his contract and which therefore the government might just as well buy and own itself. The force of this argument became particularly apparent as the work approached completion. Projects for the utilization of the plant were sent into Congress from every section of the country. It was strongly urged that the plant be sent *en bloc* to Alaska to build railroads and open that rich, but long shut-in territory to settlement and development. Other friends of the reclamation service urged that it be employed in draining semi-submerged lands in the Mississippi Valley and digging irrigating ditches in the Southwest. The floods of the spring of 1913 caused an active demand for its employment on Ohio rivers. It is fair to note that Mr. Stevens made the first energetic fight for the establishment of the system under which the government owns this colossal and almost invaluable plant, while Col. Goethals' recommendation put upon it the final

Photo by Underwood & Underwood

THE COLONEL'S DAILY MEAL

stamp of official approval.

This act has importance which will long outlive the construction period of the canal. By the time that work is completed it will have demonstrated beyond doubt that the United States government is perfectly capable of doing its own construction work without the intervention of private contractors; that it not only can build the biggest dam in the world, erect the mightiest locks that ever raised a ship, and dig a channel through the backbone of a continent, but is quite able to perform the lesser functions incident thereto. It can, and did, successfully conduct hotels and a railroad and steamship line, maintain eating-houses and furnish household supplies. After the Panama exhibit it will take either a brave or a singularly stupid man to preach

"THE GOETHALS' OWN" IN ACTION
Attacking a stronghold of the Culebra Slide with a regiment of men and a battery of machines

the ancient dread of a paternalistic government.

Early in Col. Goethals' régime the great department of engineering and construction was split into three subdivisions, namely,

The Atlantic Division, comprising the canal from

deep water in the Caribbean to, and including, the Gatun locks and dam. In all this covered about seven miles of the canal only, but one of its most difficult and interesting features.

The Central Division, including Gatun Lake and the Culebra Cut to the Pedro Miguel lock, or about 32 miles of canal.

The Pacific Division, including the Pedro Miguel and Miraflores locks, and the canal from the foot of the latter to deep water in the Pacific.

Under this classification will be described the construction work on the canal, work which at the time of the author's visit was clear to view, impressive in its magnitude, appalling in the multiplicity of its details, and picturesque in method and accomplishment. With the turning of the water into the channel all this will be hidden as the works of a watch disappear when the case is snapped shut. The canal, they say, and rightly, will be Goethals' monument—though there are those who think it a monument to Col. Gorgas, while quite a few hold

that the fame of Theodore Roosevelt might be further exalted by this work. But whomsoever it may commemorate as a monument it was even more impressive in the building than in the completed form.

One Sunday late in my stay on the Isthmus I was going over the line from Ancon to Culebra. As we approached the little tunnel near Miraflores I noticed an unusual stir for the day, for on the Canal Zone the day of rest is almost religiously observed. Men were swarming along the line, moving tracks, driving spikes, ramming ballast. I asked one in authority what it all meant. "Oh", said he, "we're going to begin running dirt trains through the tunnel, and that necessitates double tracking some of the line. The Colonel said it must be done by tomorrow and we've got more than 1000 men on the job this quiet Sunday. The Colonel's orders you know".

Yes, I knew, and everybody on the Canal Zone knows.

Photo by S. H. Elliott

BAS OBISPO END OF CULEBRA CUT

CHAPTER X

GATUN DAM AND LOCKS

ENTERING the Panama Canal from the Atlantic, one finds the beginning of that section called by the engineers the Atlantic Division, four miles out at sea in Limon Bay, a shallow arm of the Caribbean on the shore of which are Colon and the American town of Cristobal. From its beginning, marked only by the outermost of a double line of buoys, the canal extends almost due south seven miles to the lowest of the Gatun Locks. Of this distance four miles is a channel dredged out of the bottom of Limon Bay and the bottom width of the canal from its beginning to the locks is 500 feet. Its depth on this division will be 41 feet at mean tide. For the protection of vessels entering the canal at the Atlantic end, or lying in Colon harbor, a great breakwater 10,500 feet, or a few feet less than two miles long, made of huge masses of rock blasted along the line of the Canal, or especially quarried at Porto Bello, extends from Toro Point to Colon light. In all it will contain 2,840,000 cubic yards of rock and its estimated cost is $5,500,000.

In the original plans for the harbor of Cristobal

ENTRANCE TO GATUN LOCKS
The rafts in the foreground carry pipes through which suction dredges discharge material removed

I. COLON: THESE PICTURES IN ORDER FORM A PANORAMA OF THE COLON WATER FRONT

a second breakwater was proposed to extend at an angle to the guard one, but the success of the former in breaking the force of the seas that are raised by the fierce northers that blow between October and January has been so great that this may never be needed. Its need is further obviated by the construction of the great mole of stone and concrete which juts out from the Cristobal shore for 3500 feet at right angles to the Canal. From this mole five massive piers will extend into the harbor, jutting out like fingers on a hand, each 1000 feet long and with the space between them 300 feet wide so that two 1000 foot ships may dock at one time in each slip. The new port of Cristobal starts out with pier facilities which New York had not prepared for the reception of great ships like the "Vaterland"

III. COLON: PANAMA RAILROAD AND ROYAL MAIL DOCKS

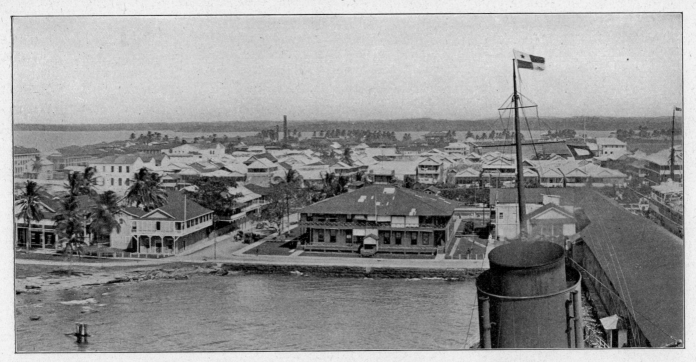

II. COLON: PART OF THE RESIDENTIAL DISTRICT ON THE WATER FRONT

and the "Aquitania" at the time of their launching.

From the shore of the bay to the first Gatun lock is a little less than four miles. The French dug a canal penetrating this section, a canal which forms today part of our harbor and which has been used to some extent for the transportation of material for the Gatun dam. Our engineers however abandoned it as part of our permanent line, and it is rapidly filling up or being over-grown by vegetation. At its best it was about fifteen miles long, 15 feet deep as far as Gatun, and 7 feet deep thence to the now vanished village of Bohio.

The Canal from the seaboard to the Gatun locks was straightaway excavation, through land little higher than the water, with tidewater following so

IV. COLON   THE DE LESSEPS HOUSE IN THE DISTANCE SHOWS LOCATION OF NEW DOCKS

that the work could be done by floating dredges.
No novel problems were presented to the engineer,
nor are interesting achievements displayed to the
tourist until the great dam itself is reached.

The simplest way of reaching the Gatun dam is
of course by train from Colon, a ride of perhaps
twenty minutes. But a more spectacular one is by
launch, either up the Canal, or around by the
Chagres River from its mouth. The latter is a
difficult trip however and seldom essayed. One
advantage of taking the Canal is that it gives a
much clearer idea of the construction of the dam
than can be derived by approaching it by railroad.
The first significant fact forced upon your attention
in thus coming upon the dam is that it does not
look like a dam at all, but rather like a long and
gently sloping hill pierced at one point by a sort
of masonry gate which upon closer approach reveals
itself as a system of mighty locks.

Not very long ago there was a wide-spread apprehension in the United States, bred of a rather shallow
newspaper criticism very widely republished, that
the Gatun dam would prove inadequate to the pressure of the waters impounded behind it and might

Photo by Underwood & Underwood
SOUTH APPROACH WALL, GATUN LOCKS

collapse, or "topple over". If all who have been
impressed by that gruesome prophecy could see the
dam itself their apprehensions would be speedily
quieted. One might as well talk of toppling over
the pyramids, or Murray Hill, New York (not the
structures on it, but the hill itself) or the Treasury
Building at Washington. Elevations, natural or
artificial, the base of which is eight to ten times
their height, cannot topple over while the force of
gravity continues to operate. Now the height of

GATUN LOCKS OPENING INTO THE LAKE
The skeleton structure on the left is the frame-work of the emergency dam which swings directly athwart the lock

Gatun dam is 105 feet, and from its crest the filling of clay and rock slopes gently away on the landward side for nearly half a mile. There are more abrupt eminences on many of our rolling prairies. The face on the lake side descends somewhat more abruptly, but is still several hundred feet long before its slope ends with the bed of the lake. This face is covered with broken stone down to the "toe"— as they call the walls of rough rock between which the dirt dam was built.

The method of building the dam was simple enough even though it sounds complicated in the telling. When Congress acquiesced in the minority report of the Board of International Engineers, approved by the President and recommending a lock type canal, it meant that instead of simply digging a ditch across the Isthmus we would create a great artificial lake 85 feet above sea level, confined by dams at either ends, with locks and two short canals to give communication with the oceans. To create this lake it was determined to impound the waters of the Chagres, and a site near the village of Gatun, through which the old French canal passed, was selected for this purpose. Conditions of topography of course determined this site. The Chagres valley here is 7,920 feet wide, but the determining fact was that about the center of the valley was a hill of

BIRD'S EYE VIEW OF GATUN DAM
In the foreground the locks, only two of the three steps being fully shown. In the middle distance the spillway, through which surplus water flows into the Chagres and old French Canal

rock which afforded solid foundation for a concrete dam for the spillway. Geologists assert that at one time the floor of the valley was 300 feet higher than now, and that in the ages the Chagres River cut away the shallow gorges on either side of the rocky hill. These, it was determined, could readily be obstructed by a broad earth dam of the type determined upon, but for the spillway with its powerhouse and flood gates a rock foundation was essential and this was furnished by the island.

The first step in the construction of the dam was to dam the Chagres then flowing through its old channel near the site chosen for the

Photo by Thompson

GATUN LAKE SEEN FROM THE DAM

CONSTRUCTION WORK ON GATUN DAM

The space between two rock walls has been filled with mud, which having hardened, supports dirt trains bringing spoil from Culebra Cut to build up the dam to required dimensions

was piled upon it, compressing it and squeezing out the remaining moisture. As this surface became durable the railroad tracks were shifted to it, and when I visited the dam in 1913 the made land of the dam was undistinguishable from the natural ground surrounding it. Over it scores of locomotives were speeding, dragging ponderous trains heavy laden with "spoil" from the Culebra Cut. From the crest on the one hand the dam sloped away in a gentle declivity nearly half a mile long to the original spillway, and through the old French canal. This was accomplished by building parallel walls, or "toes" of broken stone and filling the space between with jungle on the one side, and a lesser distance on the other, to the waters of the Gatun Lake then less than half filled. When the main body of the dam had

fluid mud pumped from the old channel of the stream. A new channel of course was provided called the "west diversion". The toes are about a quarter of a mile apart and rise about 30 feet high. They were built by the customary devices of building trestles on which dump trains bearing the material were run. After the core of fluid silt pumped in between the walls had begun to harden, dry earth

PUMPING MUD INTO THE CORE OF GATUN DAM

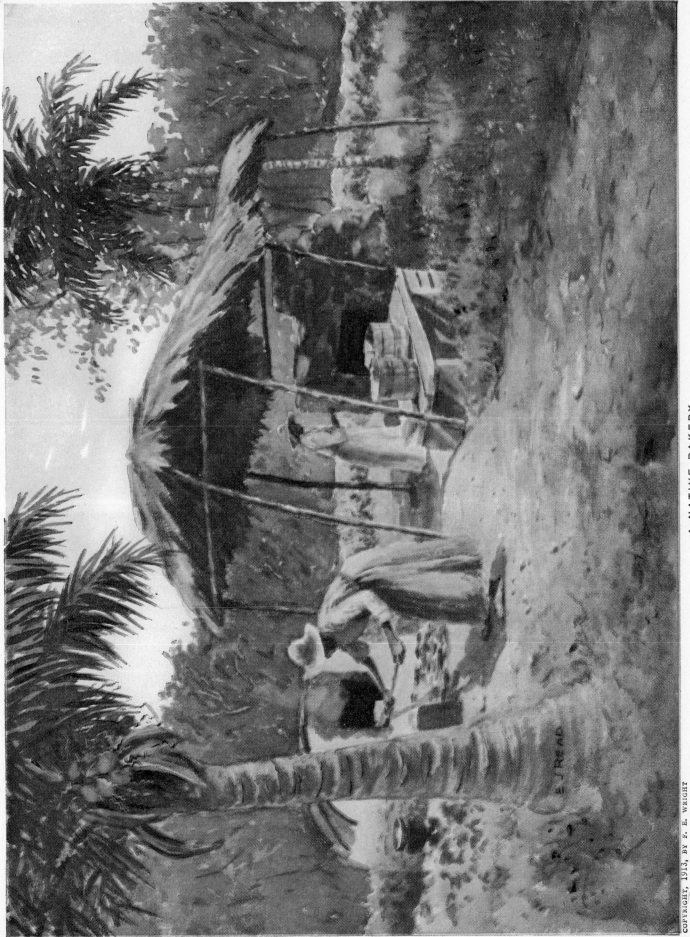

A NATIVE BAKERY

The Panamanian never does anything indoors that he can do in the open. The village bakery, the village mortar or mill and the village laundry are social meeting places used by all.

GATUN UPPER LOCK

same time, hoping to distribute on such dams the head formed during construction. An unlimited amount of waste rock was available for this work. The banks of the channels were first made secure by dumping rock at the end of the trestles. After the channel was contracted to some extent, a considerable current developed; rock dumped from the trestles was carried some distance down stream, forming a rock apron in the bed of the stream below the dam. Quite deep holes, however, were dug by the water below this rock apron. When the work on the two dams had progressed so that a channel about 80 feet wide and 6 feet deep was left in the center, it was found impracticable to make any headway. Stone dumped from the trestles would be rolled down stream. The rainy season was then about to commence.

been completed and the spillway was ready to carry off the waters of the Chagres then flowing through the "west diversion" the task of damming the latter was begun. This was the first effort to stem the current of the Chagres, the river dreaded for so many reasons, and the description by Lieutenant Colonel William L. Sibert, the engineer in charge of this division, will be of interest:

"The elevation of the spillway channel is 10 feet above sea level, consequently in any attempt to stop the flow of the Chagres and force it through this channel, a rise of about 14 feet of water had to be encountered. The banks and bottom of the west diversion were soft clay. The plan adopted was to drive trestles across this channel on the 30-foot contour on each face of the dam, and to build, by dumping rock directly into the stream, two dams at the

Photo by Underwood and Underwood

CENTER: GATUN CENTER LIGHT; LOWER CORNER: EMERGENCY GATES

Photo by Underwood & Underwood

SPILLWAY UNDER CONSTRUCTION

Concrete is dumped directly from the railway into the moulds. Pipes to the power house are shown

The lower part of the bents of the trestles being well supported with rock, it was then decided to dump a carload or two of crooked rails above the trestles in such a way that they would form an entanglement and stop the rock, thus insuring either the construction of the dam or the taking out of the trestle. By this means the two dams were finally completed and the Chagres River successfully diverted.

To the unprofessional observer the Gatun dam is a disappointment as a spectacle. It does not look like a dam at all, but merely like a continuation of one of the hills it connects. But as a matter of fact it is the greatest dam in the world—a mile and a half long, 105 feet high, half a mile thick at its base, 398 feet at the surface of the lake and 100

feet wide at the top. It is longer and higher than the Assouan dam which the British built across the Nile though the latter, being all of masonry, is vastly the more picturesque. Into the entire work will go about 21,000,000 cubic yards of material.

One day while the Gatun dam was in the earlier stages of its construction in 1908, a newspaper correspondent was temporarily detained at Gatun while crossing the Isthmus. Idly, to pass the time away, he strolled out on the dam to where he saw a group of men gathered. He found them discussing a small break at the edge of the dam upstream; a break not caused by any pressure of the water, for the water had not reached that point, but by the weight of the heavy superstructure pressing upon the semi-fluid core of the dam which then had not had sufficient time for drainage and drying.   The dispatch which the correspondent sent north as the result of his casual observation of the slide, was seized upon by the advocates of the sea-level canal as a text from which to argue the entire impracticability of the lake-level project.   The agitation became so general and so menacing that President Roosevelt was impelled to appoint a commission of seven engineers of high professional standing and technical knowledge of dam building to visit the spot and report upon the menace. Their verdict was that the Canal engineers had gone far beyond the necessary point in making the dam ponderous and safe.   Secretary of War Taft, who happened to be on the Isthmus when the break occurred, declared that it was "insignificant when one takes into consideration the whole size of the dam".

When the tricky Chagres gets on one of its rainy season rages the spillway by which the dam is pierced at about its center will be one of the spectacular points on the Canal line.   That river drains a basin covering 1,320 square miles, and upon which

the rains in their season fall with a persistence and continuity known in hardly any other corner of the earth.   The Chagres has been known to rise as much as 40 feet in 24 hours, and though even this great flood will be measurably lowered by being distributed over the 164 square miles in Gatun Lake, yet some system of controlling it by outlets and flood gates was of course essential to the working and the safety of the Canal.   The spillway is the center of this system, the point at which is the machinery by which the surface of Gatun Lake can be at all times kept within two feet of its normal level, which is 85 feet above the level of the sea.

Fundamentally the spillway is a channel 1,200 feet long and 285 feet wide cut through the solid rock of the island which at this point bisects the now obliterated Chagres Valley.   Though cut through rock it is smoothly lined and floored with cement; closed at its upper end by a dam, shaped like the arc of a circle so that, while it bars an opening of only 285 feet, its length is 808 feet.   For the benefit of the unprofessional observer it may be noted that by thus curving a dam in the direction

PARTLY COMPLETED SPILLWAY, 1913
The river was low when this picture was taken.   At high water it will flow over the completed structure shown at the right

of the force employed against it, its resisting power is increased. It resists force exerted horizontally precisely as an arch resists force, or weight, exerted from above. The dam at the spillway extends solidly across the opening to a height of 69 feet. But this is 16 feet below the normal level of the Lake. From the top of the solid dam rise thirteen concrete piers to a height as planned, of 115 feet above sea level, that is the piers will rise 46 feet above the top of the dam. Between each two of these piers will be mounted regulating gates of steel sheathing, made water tight and movable up or

Photo by Underwood & Underwood

THE GIANT PENSTOCKS OF THE SPILLWAY

down as the state of the Chagres level requires a free or a restricted passage for the water. Nor will those operating the gates await the visual appearance of the flood before throwing wide the passage for its onrush. At divers points along the Chagres, and throughout its water shed are little stations whence observers telephone at regular intervals throughout the day to the office at the spillway the result of their observations of the river's height. With these figures at hand the controller of the gates can foresee the coming of a flood hours before it begins to beat against the gates.

THE SPILLWAY AT HIGH WATER

A comparison with the picture on page 179 will show the varying stages of the river

Photo by Underwood & Underwood

LOCK GATES APPROACHING COMPLETION

The spillway further serves a useful and an essential purpose in that it harnesses the water power of the useful Chagres, and turns it into electric power to open and shut the colossal gates of the various locks; to propel the electric locomotives that tow the great ships through the concrete channels; to light the canal towns and villages, and the lighthouses on the line; to run the great cranes at Balboa and Cristobal; to run the machinery in the shops at Balboa; to furnish motive power, if so determined for the Panama Railroad, and to swing the great guns at Toro Point and Naos Island until their muzzles bear with calm yet frightful menace upon any enemy approaching from either the Caribbean or the Pacific. There will be power for all these functions, and power too to light Panama and Colon, to run the Panama tramway and perform other useful functions if the present

grip of private Panama monopoly upon these public services shall be relinquished. The water drops 75 feet through huge penstocks to great turbines in the spillway hydro-electric station with a capacity of 6,000 kilowatts, but the amount of water power is sufficient for double that current, and turbines to supply the addition can be installed whenever the need for the power develops.

The Gatun locks are built at the very eastern end of Gatun dam, at the point where it joins the mainland bordering the Chagres valley. Of their superficial dimensions I have already spoken, and have described their appearance as seen from the deck of a ship in passage. It will be hard however for one who has not stood on the concrete floor of one of these massive chambers and looked upward to their crest, or walking out on one of the massive gates peered down into their depths, to appreciate

THE WATER KNOCKING AT GATUN GATES

they plied, and whole trains of loaded dump cars swallowed up in a single lock chamber, one got some idea of the magnitude of the work. A track for a travelling crane extended down the center of the chamber and the monster rumbled back and forth carrying loads of material to their appointed destinations. Across the whole width of the Canal below the locks stretched cable carriers upheld by skeleton devices of steel mounted on rails so that the pair of them, though separated by 500 feet of space, spanned by the sagging cables, could be moved in unison. Out on the swinging cables ran the loaded cars or buckets, filled with concrete and dumped with a crash and a roar at the chosen place. Giant mixers ground up rock from Porto Bello, sand from Nombre de Dios, and cement from divers states of our union into a sort of Brobdignagian porridge with which the hungry maws of the moulds were ceaselessly fed. Men wig-wagged signals with flags across gaping chasms.

their full size. It is all very well to say that the Imperator, the greatest of ships now afloat, could find room in one of these locks with five feet at each side, and fifty feet at each end to spare, but then few of us have seen the Imperator and nobody has seen her in the lock. It is all very well to figure that a six story house would not rise above the coping of one of these locks, but imagination does not visualize the house there, and moreover there are stories and stories in height. Yet as one stood on the floor of one of these great monolithic tanks as they were being rushed to completion in 1913, and saw locomotives dwarfed by the ponderous walls betwixt which

WALL OF GATUN LOCK SHOWING ARCHED CONSTRUCTION

TRAVELLING CRANES AT WORK

Mounted on rails these cranes carry the heaviest burdens. Those shown are placed for delivering concrete to the forms. One crane will cost $60,000

its weight, which rests on piles of 60 feet long capped and surrounded with concrete. This wall was built by slow stages and allowed to stand in order that its settlement might be uniform. An examination of the picture below will make clear the method of constructing the lock walls, for in it are shown the completed monoliths and a steel form half completed with men preparing it for the concrete therein. Col. Sibert describes the details of the work thus:

"The locks proper are founded on rock and the heavy masonry is completed. This rock foundation was not of sufficient extent, however, at available elevations, for supporting the guide walls. Under that guide wall extending into the lake the underlying rock at the south end is about 150 feet below sea level, and the overlying material is soft. This wall is cellular in construction. It is composed of four longitudinal walls about 2 feet thick with cross walls about 17 feet apart, all built of reinforced concrete.

"The natural ground underlying the wall was about

Steam whistles blew shrill warnings and cryptic orders. Wheels rumbled. Pulleys creaked. It seemed that everything a man could do was being done by machine, yet there was an army of men directing, correcting and supplementing the mechanical labor.

Into the locks at Gatun will go 2,000,000 cubic yards of concrete if the original estimate is adhered to. A statistician estimates that it would build a wall 8 feet wide and 12 feet high and 133 miles long—which would just about wall off the state of Delaware from the rest of the Union.

The side walls of each of the locks are practically monoliths, constructed of concrete poured into great steel frames or moulds where it hardens into a solid mass. They are based in the main on bed rock, though it was found on making tests that the bed rock was not of sufficient extent to support the guide walls as well, so one of these is therefore made cellular to lighten

BUILDING A MONOLITH

A CULVERT IN THE LOCK WALL

8 feet above sea level. On this ground a wide fill with a very flat slope was constructed to elevation plus 35, and through this piles about 60 feet long, 4-foot centers, were driven and a heavy reinforced concrete slab built around the heads of the piles, on which was erected the cellular structure. There was a continual slow settlement of this wall as its construction progressed. It was brought to a height of 61 feet above sea level through its entire length in order that the settlement might extend over the whole base before any part was brought to full height.

"The north guide and flare walls are yet to be built. It will be necessary to go to a depth of about 70 feet below sea level through very soft material in order to uncover the rock on which to build the flare walls. Under the guide wall itself the rock is at a still lower elevation, and a pile foundation will probably be constructed, the piling going to rock. The material in this space was too soft to hold up steam shovels, and it was decided to do the general excavation by suction dredges. These dredges cut their way into the space where the walls in question are to be built, making a channel just wide and deep enough for their passage. They then widened out the cut and deepened it to 41 feet below sea level. An earthen dam was then built across the narrow entrance cut,

shutting off the connection with the sea, and as the dredges worked they were lowered. They are now floating at an elevation of 32 feet below sea level and can remove the material to the depth required. After the excavation is completed it is proposed to have the dredges excavate a sump 65 feet below sea level and lower the water to 50 feet below sea level in order to test the stability of the sides of the cut. If there is no sliding the pit will be filled with water; the dredges floated out; the dam across the entrance channel replaced and the excavation unwatered for the construction of the walls first referred to.

"The masonry of the Gatun locks was largely placed by cableways, having a span of 800 feet, covering the entire space to be occupied by the

DIAGRAM OF LOCK-GATE MACHINERY

locks. The stone and sand for the concrete were obtained, respectively, 20 and 40 miles down the Caribbean coast, and were brought in barges up the old French Canal as closely as possible to the lock

TOWING LOCOMOTIVE CLIMBING TO UPPER LOCK

site, and were unloaded by cableways into large stock piles near the bank. The material, however, was still 3,500 feet away and 60 feet below the center of lock construction. This situation caused the adoption of a central mixing plant near the central portion of the locks, consisting of eight 2-yard mixers. An automatic, electric, loop-line railroad, each car carrying the material for a batch of concrete, was installed, passing under the cement shed, under the sand and stone piles; and over the mixers. The mixed concrete was delivered to the cableways requiring it by an electric line, the flat cars of which were handled by electric locomotives. Steel forms were used in constructing the walls of the locks".

A vital feature of the locks is, of course, getting the water into and out of them, and the method of operating the gigantic gates. The former is simple enough of explanation, though the *modus operandi* will be entirely concealed when the locks are in operation. Through each of the side walls, and through the center walls which divide the pairs of locks, runs a tunnel 18 feet in diameter. To put it more graphically a tunnel large enough to take a mogul locomotive of the highest type. From this main tunnel smaller ones branch off to the floors of the locks that are to be served, and these smaller chutes are big enough for the passage of a farmer's wagon with a span of horses. These smaller chutes extend under the floor of the lock and connect with it by valved openings, the valves being operated by electricity. There is no pumping of the water. Each lock is filled by the natural descent of the water from the lock above or from the lake. By the use

of the great culvert in the central wall the water can be transferred from a lock on the west side of the flight to one on the east, or vice versa. Though it hardly seems necessary, every possible device for the conservation of the water supply has been provided.

We will suppose a vessel from the Atlantic reaches Gatun and begins to climb to the lake above. The electric locomotives tow her into the first lock, which is filled just to the level of the Canal. The great gates close behind her.

How do they close? What unseen power forces those huge gates of steel, shut against the dogged resistance of the water? They are 7 feet thick, 65 feet long and from 47 to 82 feet high. They weigh from 390 to 730 tons each. Add to this weight the resistance of the water and it becomes evident that large power is needed to operate them. At Gatun in the passing of a large ship through the locks, it will be necessary to lower four fender chains, operate six pairs of miter gates and force them to miter, open and close eight pairs of rising stem gate valves for the main supply culverts, and thirty cylindrical valves. In all, no less than 98 motors will be set

THE HEAVY WHEEL SHOWN IS THE "BULL WHEEL"
By its revolution it thrusts or withdraws the arm at the right which moves the gate

THE TANGLED MAZE OF STEEL SKELETONS THAT ARE A LOCK IN THE MAKING

in motion twice during each lockage of a single ship, and this number may be increased to 143, dependent upon the previous position of the gates, valves and other devices. Down under the surface of the lock wall, packed into a little crypt which seems barely to afford room for its revolving, is a great cogwheel 5 feet in diameter, revolving slowly and operating a ponderous steel arm which thrusts out or pulls back the gate as desired. The bull wheel, they call it, is driven by a 27 horse power motor, while a smaller motor of 7½ horse power locks the gates tight after they are once in position. Two of these bull wheels, and two each of the motors are needed for each pair of gates.

The ship then is in the lowest lock, one pair of gates closed tightly behind her. Another pair confronts her holding back the water in the lock above, which if filled, will be just 28⅓ feet above the surface of that on which she floats. But the water about her is now slowly rising. Another set of electric motors concealed in the concrete wall have set in motion the valves in the floor of the lock,

and the water is flowing in from the tunnels, raising the ship and at the same time lowering the water in the lock above. When the vessel's keel is higher than the sill of the lock above the upper gates swing slowly back and fold in flat with the wall. The ship is now in a chamber 2000 feet long filled to a level. The locomotives pull her forward a thousand feet or so. Again great gates close behind her. Again the water rises slowly about her lifting her with it. The first process is repeated and she enters the third lock. By the time she has been drawn out into the lake and the locomotives have cast her off, more than 100 electric motors with a horse power ranging from 7½ to 50 each will have contributed to her progress. Altogether over 1000 individual motors will be required for the different locks. Indeed the whole interior of those massive lock walls is penetrated by lighted galleries strung with insulated wires bearing a death-dealing current. Men will be stationed at the various machinery rooms, but the whole line of machinery can be operated from a central operating tower on the lock above.

CHAPTER XI

GATUN LAKE AND THE CHAGRES RIVER

THAT section of the Canal, which for the convenience of engineering records and directions is known as the Central Division, comprises within its boundaries two of the great spectacular features of the Isthmus—Gatun Lake and the Culebra Cut. I have already described the scenic characteristics of this lake, but some discussion of the part it plays in the economy of the Canal will not be out of place.

In the first place the creation of the lake depended on the type of canal to be selected. A sea-level canal could not exist with the lake; a lock canal could not have been built without it. The meanderings of the Chagres, crossing and recrossing the only practicable line for the Canal, and its passionate outbursts in the rainy season made it an impossible obstacle to a sea-level canal, and all the plans for a canal of that type contemplated damming the stream at some point above Gatun—at Bohio, Gamboa or Alhajuela—and diverting its outflow into the Pacific. On the other hand the lock canal could not be built without some great reservoir of water to repeatedly fill its locks, and to supply the waterpower whereby to operate them. Hence Gatun Lake was essential to the type of canal we adopted.

The lay reader will probably be surprised when he hears how carefully the area of the Chagres watershed and the average rainfall were studied, and the height of the dam and the spillway adjusted to make certain a sufficient supply of water for the

THE CHAGRES, SHOWING OBSERVER'S CAR

From the swinging car the observer measures the crest of the flood and rapidity of the current

187

FLUVIOGRAPH AT BOHIO, NOW SUBMERGED

Panamanian as the Rhine is German and there have been watches on the Chagres, too, when buccaneers and revolutionists urged their cayucas along its tortuous highway. It was the highway by which the despoilers of Peru carried their loot to the Atlantic on the way to Spain, and along its tide drifted the later argonauts who sought the golden fleece in California in the days of '49. The poet too has sung it, but not in words of praise. Listen to its most famous lyric from the pen of James Henry Gilbert. Panama's most famous bard and most cruel critic.

locks. The only locks with which these could be compared are those at the "Soo", or outlet of Lake Superior. That canal, the busiest one in the world for eight months in the year, averaged 39 lockages a day during that period on the American side and a smaller number through the Canadian locks. The water in Gatun Lake will be sufficient for 41 passages, if the full length of the locks is used or 58 if only the partial length is used, which will be the case with steamships of less than 15,000 tons—and in ships of this class the bulk of the world's trade is conducted. If the limit of 41 lockages seems low, it must be remembered that time is quite as much a factor in the case as is the water supply. It will take an hour and a half to put a ship through the locks. That time therefore technically constitutes a "passage". In the 24 hours there would be 36 passages possible, and under the circumstances that would draw most heavily on the lake there will be water enough for 41.

For the creation of this lake our engineers found the Chagres River available. It had dug the valley in which would be stored the vast volume of water needed, and the unfailing flow from its broad watershed could be relied upon at all seasons—though indeed in the rainy season its contribution is sometimes embarrassingly lavish.

Every land comes to be judged largely by its rivers. Speak of Egypt and you think of the Nile; India suggests the Ganges; England the Thames; and France the Seine. The Chagres is as truly

AUTOMATIC FLUVIOGRAPH ON GATUN LAKE

Photo by Underwood & Underwood

THE VILLAGE OF BOHIO, NOW SUBMERGED

"Beyond the Chagres River
    Are the paths that lead to death—
To the fever's deadly breezes,
    To malaria's poisonous breath!
Beyond the tropic foliage,
    Where the alligator waits,
Are the mansions of the Devil—
    His original estates.

"Beyond the Chagres River
    Are the paths fore'er unknown,
With a spider 'neath each pebble
    A scorpion 'neath each stone.
'Tis here the boa-constrictor
    His fatal banquet holds,
And to his slimy bosom
    His hapless guest enfolds!

"Beyond the Chagres River
    'Tis said—the story's old—
Are paths that lead to mountains
    Of purest virgin gold;
But 'tis my firm conviction,
    Whatever tales they tell,
That beyond the Chagres River
    All paths lead straight to Hell"!

A much maligned stream is the River Chagres. Pioneers, pirates, prospectors and poets have vied with each other in applying the vocabulary of contumely and abuse to it, and the practitioners of medicine have attached its name to a peculiarly depressing and virulent type of tropical fever. But the humble native loves it dearly and his homes, either villages of from ten to forty family huts, or mere isolated cabins cling to its shores all the way from Fort Lorenzo to the head waters far beyond the boundary of the Canal Zone. The native too has something of an eye for the picturesque. Always his huts are erected on a bluff of from 15 to 40 feet rise from the river, with the ground cleared before them to give an unblocked view of the stream. Whether by accident or because of a real art instinct he is very apt to choose a point at a bend in the river with a view both up and down the stream. Possibly however art had less to do with his choice than an instinct of self-defense, for in the days of Isthmian turbulence, or for that matter today, the rivers were the chief highways and it was well to

STEPS LEADING TO FLUVIOGRAPH STATION AT ALHAJUELA
This is one of the more distant stations, being ten or more miles outside the Canal Zone

its origin there will presently be water enough to wash out all the stains of blood. In 1913 the place was one of the principal zone villages, with large machine shops and a labor colony exceeding 1500 in number. All vanishes before the rising lake, which will be here a mile wide.

The native craft by which alone the Chagres could be navigated prior to the creation of the lake are long, slender canoes be on guard for hostile forces coming from either direction.

I saw the upper Chagres in the last days of its existence as a swirling stream full of rapids, rushing along a narrow channel between banks sometimes rising in limestone cliffs 60 feet high and capped by dense tropical foliage ascending perhaps as much higher into the blue tropical sky. The river was at its best and most picturesque as at the opening of the dry season we poled our way up from Matachin towards its source. Then Matachin was a hamlet of canal workers, and a weekly market for the natives who brought thither boat loads of oranges, bananas, yams and plantains. Sometimes they carried stranger cargoes. I heard a commission given one native to fetch down a young tiger for somebody who wanted to emulate Sarah Bernhardt in the choice of pets. Iguanas, the great edible lizard of Panama, young deer, and cages of parrots or paroquets occasionally appear. But as a market Matachin is doomed, for it is to be submerged. With it will go an interesting discussion of the etymology of its name, one party holding that it signifies "dead Chinamen" as being the spot where imported Chinese coolies died in throngs of home-sickness during the construction of the Panama Railroad. But the word also means "butcher" in Spanish and some think it commemorates some massacre of the early days. However sanguinary fashioned usually from the trunks of the espevé tree, hollowed out by fire and shaped within and without with the indispensable machete. It is said that occasionally one is hewn from a mahogany log, for the native has little idea of the comparative value of the different kinds of timber. Mahogany and rosewood logs worth thousands of dollars in New York are doing humble service in native huts in Panama. But the native has a very clear understanding of the comparative labor involved in hewing out a hardwood log, and the cayucas are therefore mainly of the softer espevé, a compact wood with but little grain which does not crack or splinter when dragged roughly over the rocks of the innumerable rapids. The river cayuca is about 25 feet along with an extreme beam of

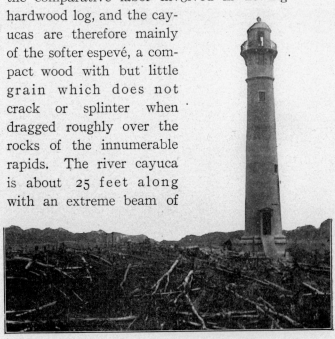

A LIGHT HOUSE IN THE JUNGLE

about 2½ feet and a draft of 6 to 10 inches. Naturally it is crank and can tip a white man into the
stream with sin-
gular celerity,
usually righting
itself and speed-
ing swiftly away
with the rushing
current. But the
natives tread it
as confidently as
though it were a
scow. For up-
stream propulsion
long poles are
used, there being
usually two men
to a boat, though
one man standing
in the stern of a
30-foot loaded ca-
yuca and thrust-
ing it merrily up
stream, through
rocky rapids and
swirling whirl-
pools is no un-
common sight.

Our craft was
longer—35 feet in
all, and in the of-
ficial service of
the Canal com-
mission had risen
to the dignity of a
coat of green paint
besides having a
captain and a
crew of two men.
Our captain,
though but in his
nineteenth year,
was a person of
some dignity, con-
veying his orders

linen in the streams, upon their slightly concealed
charms. The corrupt Spanish they spoke made it

THE RIVERSIDE MARKET AT MATACHIN

to the crew in tones of command, though not averse
to joining in the lively badinage with which they
greeted passing boatmen, or rallied maidens, washing

difficult to do more than catch the general import of
these playful interchanges. Curiously enough the
native peasant has no desire to learn English, and

frequently conceals that accomplishment, if he has attained it, as though it were a thing of which to be ashamed. This attitude is the more perplexing in view of the fact that the commission pays more to English speaking natives.

"This boy Manuel", said my host to me in low tones, "understands English and can speak it after a fashion, but rarely does so. I entrapped him once in a brief conversation and said to him, 'Manuel, why don't you speak English and get on the roll of English speaking employees? You are getting $62.50 gold a month now; then you'd get $75 at least'.

"Manuel dropped his English at once. 'No quiero aprender a hablar ingles', said he, 'Para mi basta el espanol'". (I don't care. Spanish good enough for me.)

Manuel indeed was the son of the alcalde of his village, and the alcalde is a person of much power and of grandeur proportionate to the number of thatched huts in his domain. The son bore himself as one of high lineage and his face indeed, Caucasian in all save color, showed that Spanish blood predominated over the universal admixture of negro. He saved his money, spending less than $10 a month and investing the rest in horses.

A QUIET BEACH ON THE CHAGRES

From Matachin up to Cruces the river is comparatively commonplace, spanned at one point by the Gamboa bridge up at which the voyager looks reflectively from below as he hears that when the spillway is closed and the lake filled up there will be but 15 feet headway above the river's crest, where at the moment there is more than 60. Higher up are the towers, housing the machinery for recording the river's rise, one of them a relic of the French régime, while a slender wire spanning the stream carries the pendulous car in which observers will go out at flood time to measure the height of the tide's crest and the speed of the current. A stream of many moods is the Chagres, sometimes rising 40 feet in 24 hours. Accordingly along its banks and those of its principal tributaries are fluviographic stations whence watchers may telephone to the keepers of the flood gates of the dam warnings of the coming of any sudden freshet.

In the matter of conserving the waters of the Chagres, estimating the total capacity of the watershed and in providing for swift forwarding of in-

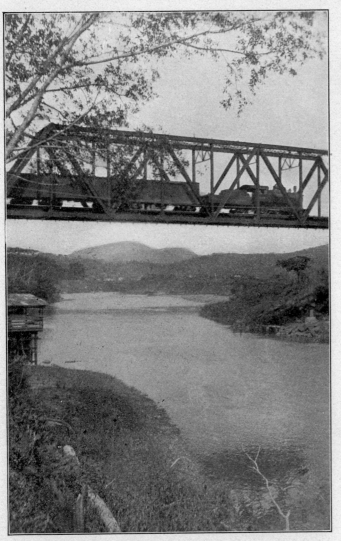

RAILROAD BRIDGE OVER THE CHAGRES AT GAMBOA
River is at low water. For picture showing it at flood, see page 141

THE RIVER AND VILLAGE OF CHAGRES

The little hamlet of rude thatched huts with a frame Catholic church in the middle has seen history in its time. The Spanish fortress of San Lorenzo on the hill was taken by Sir Henry Morgan's buccaneers and later by the British under Admiral Vernon after hard fighting.

formation concerning sudden rises we shall always be under great obligations to the French. Their hydrographic observations and records are invaluable, and their stations established before we assumed control are still used, with much of their machinery. Stations are maintained far up the valleys of the Chagres and tributary rivulets, and all are connected with the central control at Gatun dam by telephone. Some of the stations are equipped with automatic machinery which, in the event of a rise during the night summons the keeper by ringing an alarm bell. The life of the keeper of a fluviograph station, miles perhaps of jungle isolating him from the nearest human habitation, is lonesome enough. Yet its monotony is sometimes relieved by lively incident. The irascible Chagres, for example, once caught the keeper at Alhajuela with a sudden rise, and compelled him to camp out a night and day in a tree top and see his house, pigs and poultry swept away on the rushing tide. There was a fair chance that the tree would follow.

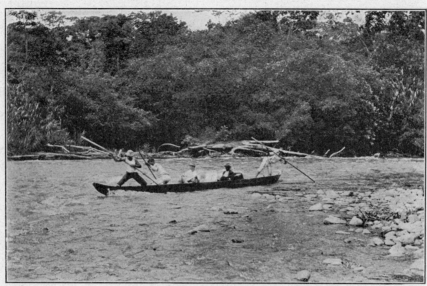

POLING UP THE RAPIDS

On our way up the river to visit some of the fluviographs we landed at Cruces, went a brief space into the jungle and cleared away with machetes the tangled vegetation until the old trail, or Royal Road to Panama, was laid bare. Three to four feet wide or thereabouts it was, and at points rudely paved with cobble stones. The nature and dimensions of the trail show that it was not intended for wheeled carriages, and indeed a native vehicle is a rarity on the Isthmus today, except in the towns. Time came when with the growing power and cruelty of the Spaniards this Camina Reale, or King's Highway, was watered with the blood of Indian slaves, bearing often their own possessions stolen from them by the Spaniard who plied on their bent backs his bloody lash. It may have been over this trail that Balboa carried, with incredible labor, the frames of three ships or caravels, which he after-

Photo by S. H. Elliott

CONSTRUCTION WORK ON THE SPILLWAY

WATER GATES IN LOCK WALL
Through these gates the water is admitted to the great conduit in the center wall of the lock

announced—quietly interfered. The anchors were removed to some safe spot and in due time will form part of the historic decorations of the new city of Balboa.

Doubtless by the standards of these days the wealth that was carried back and forth along the Royal Road by men crushed low like termite ants beneath their heavy burdens, was not great. Yet one gets some idea of the volume of the trade from Bancroft's statement that in the year 1624, just four years after the landing of the Mayflower, goods to the amount of 1,446,346 pesos d'oro (practically an equal number of dollars), were registered at the Casa, or custom house, while

wards erected and launched in the Pacific. Several years ago there were found in the jungle near Cruces two heavy anchors, with 14-foot shafts and weighing about 600 pounds which had been carried thus far on the way to the Pacific and there dropped and left to the kindly burial of the tropical jungle. When they were discovered a too loyal graduate of our military academy at West Point in charge of some engineering work on the Isthmus, thought it would be a fine thing to send them up there and have them preserved on the parade ground of the academy. Without announcing his intention he had them removed from the spot where they were found and had taken them as far as the steamship wharf at Colon when Col. Goethals—who has a habit of hearing of things that are not

probably 7½ millions of dollars' worth of goods were smuggled through. There were great warehouses then and a stone church with a neighboring monastery to which it was customary to send the children of the richer people at Nombre de Dios to be kept until they had attained their seventh year. For that piously named town was almost a plague spot

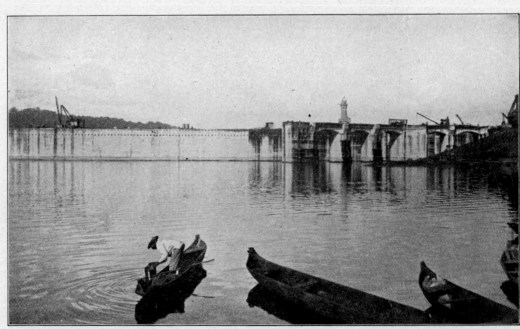

THE LAKE ABOVE GATUN

and its miasmatic atmosphere was fatal to tender infants.

The paved trail echoes no more with the muleteer's cry, or the clatter of hoofs, nor are there wine shops to tempt the traveller for there are none to be tempted. But even in its palmiest days Cruces could have been but a dismal spot. Gage a soldier of fortune and an itinerant preacher visited the village in 1638 and left us this record:

"Before ten of the clock we got to Venta de Cruces where lived none but mulattoes and blackmores who belong unto the flat boates that merchandize to Portobel. There I had much good entertainment by the people who desired me to preach unto them the next Sabbath day and gave me twenty crownes for my sermon and procession. After five days of my abode there, the boats set out, which were much stopped in their passage down the river, for in some places we found the water very low, so that the boats ran upon the gravel; from whence with poles and the strength of the blackmores they were to be lifted off again".

After the lapse of almost four centuries we found the shallows still there and the blackmores—or their descendants—ready to carry our boat past their fall. But the people who paid the early traveler twenty crowns for a sermon had vanished as irrevocably as the city's public edifices, and no descend-

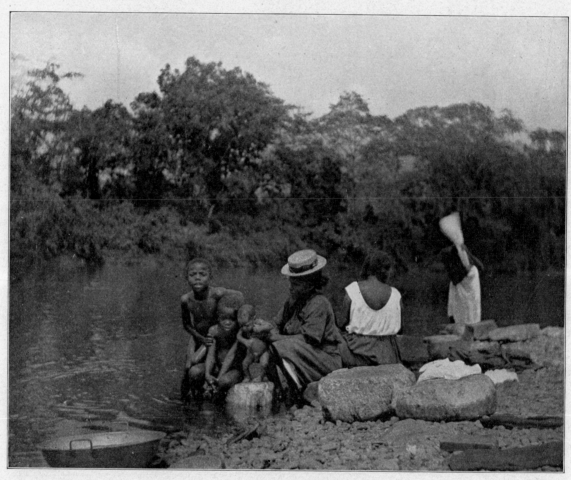

HOW THEY GATHER AT THE RIVER

ants of like piety remain. Morgan's fierce raiders swept through the village in 1670, and its downfall may have begun then, for the stout Protestantism of the buccaneers manifested itself in burning Catholic churches and monasteries in intervals of the less pious, but more pleasing, occupation of robbing the Spaniards or torturing them to extort confessions of the hiding places of their wealth.

Sir Henry Morgan, however, was not the only famous man of battles to pass through Cruces. In 1852 a very quiet young captain in the army of the United States, one Ulysses S. Grant, was there in command of a company of the Fourth Regiment of Infantry, U. S. A., proceeding from New York to San Francisco. Cholera broke out among the men and the loss while on the Isthmus was heavy. At Cruces the men were detained for days, the roster of the sick growing daily, while rascally contractors who had agreed to furnish mules to the army sold them at higher prices to private parties eager to

WASHERWOMEN'S SHELTERS BY THE RIVER
For protection against the burning sun they erect small shanties of palms

spring of 1913, with a population of at least 3,000, is to be abandoned to the rising tide of Gatun Lake, and such portions of it as escape submergence by the water will be overwhelmed by the equally irresistible jungle.

Charles T. Bidwell, an English traveler who crossed the Isthmus in 1853 by way of the Gorgona route, says of the pleasures of a sojourn in that town, "The place contained a few stores and more drinking saloons, most of which were kept by the 'enterprising Yankee'. The Gorgona road to Panama was just then open, it being passable only in the dry season, and it was estimated that 2,000 persons had passed through this place on their way to or from California. * * * We decided to take the Gorgona road and arranged to have saddle mules ready in the morning to convey us to Panama for $20 each and to pay 16½ cents a pound additional for the conveyance of our luggage". (The distance now by rail, which closely follows the old trail is 16 miles, the fare 80 cents.) "We then went to inspect 'a free ball' which had been got up with all available splendor in honor of some feast, and

get away from the pest hole. According to the surgeon's report the situation was saved by Grant, who made a new contract and enforced it—the latter being a practice that grew on him in later days.

For a brief space in the days of the gold rush to California in 1848–'54, Cruces bade fair to regain its early importance. Once the half-way place on the trail of Spaniards marching to steal gold from the Peruvians, and Englishmen following to rob and murder the robbers in turn, it became the meeting place of prospectors going out to California full of hope, and of miners returning, some laden with gold but more bowed with disappointment. Again Cruces became the point at which people and freights were transferred from the river to the trail, or vice versa. But another trail reached the river's bank at Gorgona and this village became a considerable rival to the older and larger place higher up stream. Here were several rambling wooden houses dignified by the name of hotels of which no trace remains today. The whole village, a considerable one in the

A FERRY ON THE UPPER CHAGRES

here we had a rare opportunity of seeing assembled many shades of color in the human face divine; a gorgeous display of native jewelry and not the most happy mixture of bright colors in the toilettes of those who claimed to be the 'fair sex'. Dancing however, and drinking too, seemed to be kept up with no lack of spirit and energy to the inharmonious combination of a fiddle and a drum; and those of the assembly whose tastes led them to quieter pursuits had the opportunity of losing at adjoining gaming tables the dollars they had so easily and quickly extracted from the travelers who had had occasion to avail themselves of their services. These tables too were kept by the enterprising Yankee. Having seen all this, and smoked out our cigars, we sought our beds, when we found for each a shelf or bunk in a room which our host boasted had at a push contained twenty-five or thirty people. * * * On awakening at daylight I found a basin and a pail of water set out in the open air on an old pianoforte, which some traveler had probably been tempted to bring thus far on the road".

The writer goes on to say that it took a little over two days to traverse the distance to Panama, the guides having stolen the mules they had rented and made off during the night.

Above Cruces the banks of the Chagres begin to rise in perpendicular limestone cliffs, perhaps 60 or 70 feet high while from their crests the giant tropic trees, the wild fig, the Panama, the Ceiba and the sentinel rise yet another one hundred feet into the bright blue sky. Amongst them flash back and forth bright colored parrots and paroquets, kingfishers like those of our northern states, only

gaudier, and swallows innumerable. Up and down the river fly heavy cormorants disturbed by the clank of the poles among the stones of the river bottom, but not too shy to come within 50 feet or so of our boat where, much to my satisfaction, there is no gun. White and blue herons stand statuesque in the shallows with now and then an aigret. Of life other than feathered one sees but little here. A few fish leaped, but though the river was crystalline and my guide assured me it was full of fish I saw none lurking in either deeps or shallows. Yet he must have been right for the natives make much

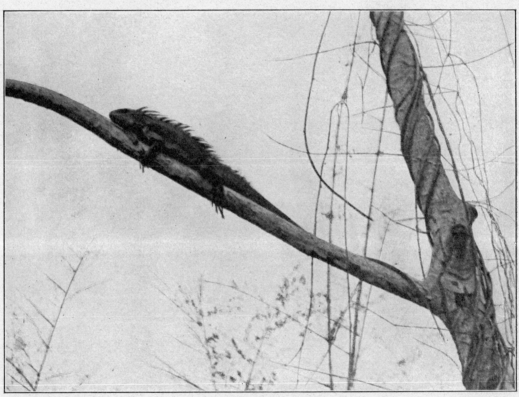

Photo by W. T. Beyer

THE MUCH PRIZED IGUANA

This lizard, which attains a length of five feet, is esteemed a delicacy in Panama

of fish as an article of diet, catching them chiefly by night lines or the unsportsmanlike practice of dynamiting the stream, which has been prohibited by the Panama authorities, although the prohibition is but little enforced.

Now and then an alligator slips lazily from the shore into the stream but they are not as plentiful here as in the tidal waters of the lower river. Occasionally, too, a shrill cry from one of our boatmen, taken up by the other two at once, turns attention to the underbrush on the bank, where the ungainly form of an iguana is seen scuttling for

CRUCES—A LITTLE TOWN WITH A LONG HISTORY

point is a spot which should become a shrine for Progressive Republican pilgrims. A low cliff of white limestone, swept clear of vegetation and polished by the river at high water describes an arc of a circle hollowed out by the swift river which rushes underneath. Springs on the bluff above have sent out little rivulets which trickling down the face of the stone have scarred it with parallel vertical grooves a foot or two apart. Seen from the further side of the stream it bears a startling likeness to a huge human upper jaw with glistening teeth. With a fine sense of the fitness of things the river men have named it "Boca del Roosevelt"—Roosevelt's mouth.

safety. Ugliest of beasts is the iguana, a greenish, bulbous, pop-eyed crocodile, he serves as the best possible model for a dragon to be slain by some St. George. The Gila monster of Arizona is a veritable Venus of reptiles in comparison to him, and the devil fish could give him no lessons in repulsiveness. Yet the Panamanian loves him dearly as a dish. Let one scurry across the road, or, dropping from a bough, walk on the surface of a river—as they literally do—and every dark-skinned native in sight will set up such a shout as we may fancy rose from oldtime revellers when the boar's head was brought in for the Yuletide feast. Not more does the Mississippi darkey love his possum an' sweet 'taters, the Chinaman his bird's nest soup and watermelon seeds, the Frenchman his absinthe or the German his beer than does the Panamanian his iguana.

In a mild way the Chagres may lay claim to being a scenic stream, and perhaps in future days when the excellence of its climate in the winter becomes known in our United States, and the back waters of the lake have made its upper reaches navigable, excursion launches may ply above Cruces and almost to Alhajuela. Near the latter

Some of the fluviograph stations are located far beyond the limits of the Canal Zone, but by the terms of the treaty with the Republic of Panama the Canal Commission has over such headwaters and reaches of the Chagres such jurisdiction as may be necessary for the protection and regulation of Gatun Lake. We went to one of these stations some 20 miles of poling up the Chagres beyond

A NATIVE CHARCOAL BURNER

Alhajuela. The keeper was a native of the Canary Islands who had mastered English sufficiently to make his reports over the 'phone. His wife, who greeted us in starched cotton with a pink hair ribbon, pink shoes and a wealth of silver ornaments, was a native, dark of complexion as a Jamaica negress, but her sister who was there on a visit was as white as a Caucasian. Doctors on the Zone say that these curious variations in type in the same family are so common that they can never foretell within several shades, the complexion of a baby about to be born.

The keeper of this station was paid $65.50 monthly and the Commission supplied his house, which was of the native type and cost about $85. Though many children, pickaninnies, little Canaries or whatever clustered about his door, his living expenses were practically nothing. Expense for clothing began only when the youngsters had reached 11 or 12 years of age and thereafter was almost negligible—as indeed were the clothes. The river furnished fish, the jungle iguanas, wild pigs and birds; the little garden patch yams, bananas, mangoes and other fruits. He was far removed from the temptations of Matachin, or other riotous market places and he saved practically all of his pay. His ambition was to get enough to return to his native isles, buy a wine-shop and settle down to a leisurely old age—though no occupation could much outdo for laziness the task of watching for the rising of the Chagres in the dry season.

Returning from the upper waters of the Chagres one reaches Gatun Lake at Gamboa where the railway bridge crosses on seven stone piers. A little above is a fluviograph station fitted with a wire cable extending across the stream and carrying a car from which an observer may take measurements of the crest of any flood. Indeed the river is watched and measured to its very sources. It long ago proved itself unfit for trust, and one who has seen it in flood time, 40 feet higher than normal, bearing on its angry, tawny bosom houses, great trees, cayucas stolen from their owners, and dead animals, sweeping away bluffs at bends and rolling great boulders along its banks, will readily understand why the builders of the Canal stationed scouts and

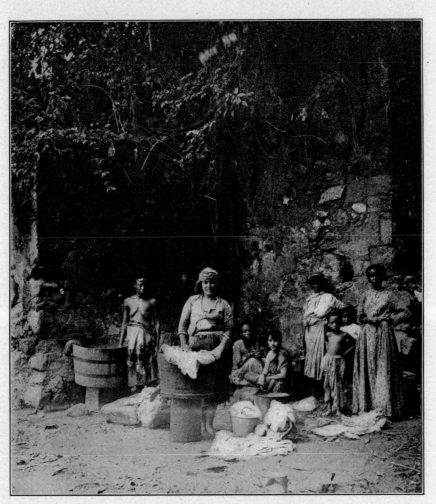

THE NATIVES' AFTERNOON TEA

spies throughout the Chagres territory to send ample and early warning of its coming wrath.

Leaving the Chagres, turning into Gatun Lake and directing our course away from the dam and toward the Pacific end of the Canal, we traversed a broad and placid body of water interspersed with densely wooded islands, which very soon narrows to the normal width of the Canal. In midsummer, 1913, when the author conducted his inspection, a broad dyke at Bas Obispo cut off Gatun Lake and its waters from the Canal trench, then dry, which

PIERS OF THE ABANDONED PANAMA RAILWAY

here extends in an almost straight line, 300 feet wide, through steadily rising banks to the continental divide at Culebra. The railroad then crossed upon this dyke to the western side of the Canal and passed through several construction towns and villages, abandoned later when the Canal was filled and the railroad moved to the other side. Tourists with an eye for the spectacular used to stand on this dyke and speculate upon the thrilling sight when a huge blast of dynamite should rend the barrier, and in a mighty wave the waters of Gatun Lake should rush down the broad channel betwixt the eternal hills to make at last the long desired waterway from Orient to Occident. But unhappily Col. Goethals and his associates unsentimentally put the picturesque aside for the practical. No dynamite blast, no surging charge of waters through the cut, entered into their program. Instead with mighty siphons the water was to be lifted over the barrier and poured into the Canal for days until the two bodies of water were nearly at a level. Then by the prosaic use of floating dredges the dyke would be removed and the Canal opened from Gatun Locks to the locks at Pedro Miguel.

CHAPTER XII

THE CULEBRA CUT.

TECHNICALLY what is known as the Culebra Cut extends from Bas Obispo to the locks at Pedro Miguel, a distance of nine miles. To the general public understanding, however, the term applies only to the point of greatest excavation between Gold Hill and Contractor's Hill. But at Bas Obispo the walls of the Canal for the first time rise above the water level of Gatun Lake. At that point the cutting begins, the walls rising higher and higher, the Canal pressing stubbornly onward at a dead level, until the supreme height of the continental divide is attained at Gold Hill. Thenceforward on the line toward Panama City the hills grow lower until at the entrance to the locks at Pedro Miguel the banks sink practically to the water level. Out of this nine mile stretch there had been taken up to January 1, 1913, just 88,531,237 cubic yards of material and it was then estimated that there then remained to be excavated 5,351,419 cubic yards more. But the later estimate was destined to be largely increased for, after the date at which it was made, the number and extent of "slides" in the deepest part of the cut increased to staggering proportions. Col. D. D. Gaillard, Member of the Commission and Division Engineer in charge of the Culebra Cut, estimated in 1912 that in all 115,000,000 cubic yards would have to be removed.

To the general public the slides seemed to menace the very existence and practicability of the Canal, though the engineers knew that they began even with the superficial excavating done by the French, and had therefore made allowance for them in their estimates. Not sufficient allowance however was made, and as month after month brought tidings of new slides, with terrifying details of such incidents as whole forests moving, vast cracks opening in the earth, large buildings in imminent danger of being swept into the Cut, the bottom of the Canal mysteriously rising ten to fifteen feet in the air, while smoke oozed from the pores of the adjacent earth—when such direful reports filled the newspapers the public became nervous, almost abandoning hope of the success of the great enterprise.

This attitude of apprehension on the part of the public is scarcely surprising. If the Capitol Park at Washington, with the National Capitol cresting it, should suddenly begin to move down into Pennsylvania Avenue at the rate of about three feet a day the authorities of the city would naturally feel some degree of annoyance. And if the smooth and level asphalt of that historic thoroughfare should, over night, rise up into the air 18 feet in spots those responsible for traffic might not unreasonably be somewhat worried.

Such a phenomenon would not be so startling in mere magnitude as the slides which added so greatly to the work of the engineers on the Canal, and made tourists, wise with the ripe fruits of five days' observation, wag their heads knowingly when Col.

WORKING ON THREE LEVELS

THE ORIGINAL CULEBRA SLIDE

A Y. M. C. A. club had to be moved to escape this slide which in 1913 was still moving

Goethals calmly repeated his assertion that the water would be turned in by August. The Colonel, however, had not withdrawn or even modified this prophecy so late as June 10, 1913. Despite the almost daily news of increased activity of the slides he clung with tenacity to his purpose of putting a ship through in October.

If these slides were an entirely new and unexpected development for which no allowance of either time or money had been made in the estimates of the Canal builders they would of course justify the apprehension they have awakened in the non-professional mind. But the slides were in fact anticipated. The first slide recorded during our work on the Isthmus was in 1905; the others have only been bigger, and have been bigger only because the Canal being dug deeper has weakened the bases of even bigger hills along the banks. All the same, the proportions of the slides are terrifying and the chief geologist declared that they would not cease until the angle of the Canal bank became so gentle that gravity would not pull the crest down.

The slides are of two sorts. The simpler is a mere swift rush of all the loose surface dirt, sand, gravel and stone down the surface of the bank. These gravity slides, mere dirt avalanches, though trouble-

some, present no new problems. To stop them it is necessary only to carry the crest of the bank further back so that the angle will be less steep. But the great, troublesome slides are those caused by the pressure of the hill-top on its undermined and weakened base. These originate at the top of the hill, making their presence known by gaping fissures opening in the earth and extending in lines roughly parallel to the Canal. Once started the whole mass, acres in extent, moves slowly toward the cavity of the Canal, three feet a day being its swiftest recorded progress. At Culebra the slides compelled the moving of a large part of the town away from the edge of the Cut, lest it be swept into the gorge. The Culebra Y. M. C. A. clubhouse, the largest on the Zone had to be torn down to escape this peril.

As the slide moves slowly downward, its colossal weight applied at points where nature had made no provision for it, forces the earth upward at the point where it can offer the least resistance, namely the bed of the Canal. Sometimes this upheaval, so mysterious to the non-technical mind, attains a height of eighteen feet. Again, the friction of this huge mass of stone and gravel creates heat, which turns into steam the rills of water that everywhere percolates through the soil. The upheaval of the Canal bed, and the occasional outpourings of steam have led at times to exaggerated and wholly unfounded reports in the newspapers of volcanic action being one of the new problems with which the Canal builders had to grapple.

The story told about the extent of the slides is sufficiently alarming, but the calmness with which Col. Goethals and his lieutenants meet the situation is reassuring. According to the official report there were twenty-six slides and breaks in Culebra Cut to January 1, 1913 with a total area of 225 acres. Since that date many others have occured. It is estimated that because of slides between 21,000,000 and 22,000,000 cubic yards of material in excess of the original estimate will have been taken out of the Cut before completion. This is just about one-fifth of the total amount of excavation, dry and wet, estimated originally for the whole Canal. But the attitude of the engineers toward this addition to their labors was merely one of calm acceptance of the inevitable and a dogged determination to get the stuff out of the way. The slides were an obstacle; so was the whole isthmus for that matter.

But all that was necessary was to keep the shovels working and the slides would be removed and the isthmus pierced.

To my mind one of the finest evidences of the spirit animating the Canal force was the fashion in which this problem of the slides has been approached. It was at first disappointing, almost demoralizing, to find over night the work of weeks undone and the day when "finis" could be written to the volume put far over into the future. But the only effect was a tighter grip on the pick and the shovel, a new determination to force through the Canal. Culebra was approached as Grant approached Vicksburg. To reduce it and to open the Canal to traffic, as Grant opened the Mississippi to the steamboats of the nation, took more time than was at first expected, but it had to be done. The dirt could not always slide in faster than it could be carted out, for in time there would be no dirt left to slide. And so, undismayed and intent upon success, the whole force from Col. Goethals to the youngest engineer moved on Culebra and the doom of that stubborn block to progress was sealed.

To the unscientific mind the slides are terrifying

SLIDE ON WEST BANK OF THE CANAL NEAR CULEBRA

Picture shows about 1,000,000 cubic yards of material moving toward the cut at about three yards a day

ATTACKING THE CUCARACHA SLIDE

This slide has filled the Cut from side to side. A partial Cut has been dug through its center and the shovels are seen working on either side. The tracks are moved nightly as the material is removed.

in their magnitude and in the evidence they give of irresistible force. Man can no more check their advance than he can that of a glacier which in a way they resemble. When I was on the Isthmus the great Cucaracha slide was in progress, and had been for that matter since 1907. It had a total area of 47 acres and extended up the east bank of the Canal for about 1900 feet from the axis of the Canal. When it began its progress was disconcertingly rapid. Its base, foot, or "toe"—these anatomical terms in engineering are sometimes perplexing—moved across the canal bed at the rate of 14 feet a day. All that stood in its path was buried, torn to pieces or carried along with the resistless glacier of mud. Not content with filling the Canal from one side to the other, the dirt rose on the further side to a height of about 30 feet. Not only was the work of months obliterated, but work was laid out for years to come. Indeed in 1913 they were still digging at the Cucaracha slide and the end was not in sight. This slide was wholly a gravity slide, caused by a mass of earth slipping on the inclined surface of some smooth and

slippery material like clay on which it rests. The nature of the phenomenon is clearly shown by the diagram printed on the next page in which the slide marked C is of the type just described.

On the west bank of the Canal occurred a slide of the second type caused by the crushing and squeezing out of underlying layers of soft material by the prodigious pressure of the high banks left untouched by the steam shovels. This slide is usually accompanied by the uprising of the bed of the Canal sometimes to a height of thirty feet. Col. Gaillard tells of standing on the bed of the Canal, observing the working of a steam shovel, when it gradually dawned upon him that he was no longer on the level of the shovel. At first he thought that the shovel must have been placed upon a bit of boggy land and was slowly sinking, but on investigation he discovered that the point on which he was standing had been slowly rising until within five minutes he had been lifted six feet without jar and with no sensation of motion. A perfectly simple illustration of the way in which this elevation of the bed of the Canal is caused may be obtained by pressing the hand upon a pan of dough. The dough will of course rise at the side of the hand. On the "big job" the towering hills furnished the pressure, the bed of the Canal rose like the dough. In the diagram already referred to, the slide to the right marked "B" is of the type here described. To cope with it, the work of the shovels and dirt trains in the Canal carrying the débris away is supplemented by others above removing the crest of the slide and thus lightening the pressure. In the diagram shovels are shown thus working on two levels, but I have seen four terraces of the same slide bearing steam shovels and rumbling dirt trains hurrying the débris away to where it will no longer be a menace.

The Culebra slide possessed a certain remorselessness which was not manifested by any of the others in quite so picturesque a way. For this slide, with apparently human malice, attacked not only the work done on the Canal proper, but like a well directed army moved on the headquarters of its foe. Its first manifestation appeared in the form of a wide crack in the earth at the crest of the hill on which sits the town of Culebra, and directly in front of the building used by Col. Gaillard as division headquarters for the engineers. Retreat was the only course possible in the face of such an enemy and the building was sacrificed. The Culebra Y. M. C. A. clubhouse too was a point of attack for the remorseless foe. It stood on the very crest of the hill, a beautiful building on a most beautiful site. The serpent of Culebra Cut—the word "culebra" means snake—saw this pleasant place of rest and marked it for his own. Nothing remained but to rally a force of men and tear the

DIAGRAM OF CULEBRA CUT SLIDES

C. is a slide moving over a slippery surface; the mass B breaks on a line of cleavage and crushes the underlying material, forcing it up at A. The steam shovels are working to reduce pressure on B

Courtesy of Scientific American

A ROCK SLIDE NEAR EMPIRE

About 400,000 cubic yards of rock broke away, half filling the cut and opening it to the water of the Obispo Diversion Canal

THE AUTHOR AT CULEBRA CUT

in August, 1912. Here about 400,000 cubic yards of rock slipped into the Cut, wrecking cars, destroying tracks and machinery and flooding the Canal with water from the Obispo diversion. It is not generally known that parallel to the Canal at various points are dug smaller canals, or big ditches, for the purpose of catching and carrying off the heavy annual rainfall on the canal watershed. These diversion ditches cost much in time and labor. One was constructed by the French. Another, 5¼ miles long, known as the Obispo diversion, cost $1,250,000 and was absolutely essential to the construction of the Canal. The rock slide, above referred to, broke down the barrier between the Canal cut and the diversion ditch and filled the former with an untimely flood which it took time to stay and pump out.

From all parts of the United States citizens interested in the progress of the Canal—and only those at the work can tell how widespread and patriotic that interest is—have sent suggestions for checking these slides. Practically all have been impracticable—a few only indeed have been thought worthy of being put to the test. One that for a time seemed worth trying was the suggestion that the wall of the cut be plastered with concrete, binding its surface together in a solid mass. But upon that being done it was demonstrated that the slides were not superficial but basic, and concrete face and all went down to one general destruction when the movement began. One curious

building down for reërection at some other point. It was probably the largest and most attractive clubhouse on the Zone, but where it once stood there was a nearly sheer drop of about sixty feet, when first I visited the scene of the slide. Before the spot, too, on which the engineering headquarters had stood, there was a patch of lawn that had slid some eighty feet down into the Cut. With it traveled along a young eucalyptus tree waving its leaves defiantly in the face of the enemy that was bearing it to irrevocable disaster. Whether the Culebra slide had attained its fullest proportions in 1913 could not be told with certainty though the belief was current that it had. While the crest of the hill had not been fully reached, the top of the slide began at the edge of a sort of jog or terrace that extended away from the Cut some distance on a level before the ground began to slope upward again. Should it extend further a very considerable and beautiful part of the town would be destroyed, but as it is to be abandoned in any event on the completion of the Canal, this phase of the matter does not give the Commission much concern.

A third slide, of lesser proportions which seriously complicated the work of the engineers, occurred near Empire

CUTTING AT BASE OF CONTRACTORS HILL

This shows the point at which the Cut is deepest. The actual level of canal bed was not reached at the time this photograph was taken fact about the slides is that they do not invariably slide *down* throughout their entire course. Occasionally they take a turn upward. One tree at Cucaracha was pointed out to me which after moving majestically down for a space was carried upward over a slope for 100 feet, and then having passed the crest of the hill started down again.

upon time and labor however has been heavy enough. Within the $8^{1}/_{3}$ miles of the Culebra Cut fully 200 miles of track have been covered up, destroyed or necessarily rebuilt because of slides, and at one point tracks had to be maintained for nearly two years on ground moving from three or four inches to several feet a day. Of course this necessitated the constant work of repair gangs and track layers. When the Canal is completed nearly 22% of the excavation will have been of material put in the way by slides—a fact which seems to give some belated support to the prophecy of the early Spanish theologians that God would not permit the Isthmus to be pierced, but would array new and unexpected forces against so blasphemous an effort to interfere with His perfect work.

A ROCK SLIDE AT LAS CASCADES
A steam shovel was wholly demolished but its operators escaped.   The slides have seldom cost lives

The slides are by no means wholly in the wet season despite the popular impression to that effect, though it was in the height of that season that the one at Cucaracha began. Yet I have seen a slide moving slowly in January when the shovels digging fiercely at its base were enshrouded in clouds of dust. Curiously enough though tracks have been torn up, machinery engulfed and wrung into indistinguishable tangles of steel, no man was caught in any of these avalanches prior to May, 1913, when three were thus lost. The tax they have put

One feature of the slides which would surely have awed the pious prophets of the Spanish day, and which did indeed considerably perplex our more prosaic engineers, was the little wisps of smoke that arose from the slowly moving soil. That this was volcanic few believed, except some newspaper correspondents in eager search for sensations. The true explanation that heat generated by friction working upon the water in the earth caused the steam was all very well and complete as an explanation of that particular phenomenon. But it left a certain worried feeling in the minds of the men who spent their days in putting hundreds of plugs of dynamite into holes drilled in the rock which the scientists declared superheated. Dropping a dynamite cartridge into a red-hot rock is apt to create a menace to the continued life and health of the dropper which even the excellent sanitary brigade of Col. Gorgas could scarcely control successfully. For a time there was a halt in the blasting operations and indeed two blasts were fired prematurely by this natural heat, but fortunately without loss of life. Finally the scheme was devised of thrusting an iron pipe into the drill hole and leaving it there a few minutes. If it was cool to the touch on withdrawal all was well; if hot a stream of water was kept playing in the hole while the charge was inserted and tamped down.

Dynamite has been man's most useful slave in this great work, but like all slaves it now and then rises in fierce and murderous revolt. "Though during the past three and one-quarter years, in work under the writer's charge", writes Col. Gaillard, "over 20,000,000 pounds of

Photo by Underwood & Underwood
HOW TOURISTS SEE THE CUT
The picture shows Vincent Astor's party in the observation car

dynamite were used in blasting, but eight men have been killed, three of whom failed to go to a safe distance and were killed by flying stones, and two by miscounting the number of shots which had gone off in a 'dobe' group, and approaching the group before the last shot had exploded".

Something like 12,000,000 pounds of dynamite a year was imported from "the states" to keep the job going, over 6,000,000 pounds a year being used in Culebra Cut alone, and many an unsuspecting passenger danced over the tossing Atlantic waves with a cargo beneath him explosive enough to blow him to the moon. On the Zone the stuff is handled with all the care that long familiarity has shown to be necessary, but to the uninitiated it looks careless enough. It is however a fact that the accidents are continually lessening in number and in fatalities caused. The greatest accident of all occurred December 12, 1908, when we had been only four years on the job. It was at Bas Obispo, and in order to throw over the face of a hill of rock that rose from the west bank of the Canal at that point nearly 44,000 pounds of dynamite had been neatly tamped away in the holes drilled for that purpose. Actually the last hole of this prodigious battery was being tamped when it exploded and set off all the others. A colossal concussion shook all the face of the earth. The side of the hill vanished in a cloud of smoke and dust from which flying rocks and trees rose into the air. When the roar of the explosion died away cries of anguish rose on the trembling air. About the scene of the explosion an army of men had been working, and of these 26 had been killed outright and a host more wounded. No such disaster has ever occurred again though there have been several small ones, and many narrow escapes from large ones.

Photo by Underwood & Underwood
SLICING OFF THE CHIEF ENGINEER'S OFFICE

Once a steam shovel taking its accustomed bite of four or five cubic yards of dirt, engulfed at the same time about a bushel of dynamite left from the French days. Again the teeth of a shovel bit upon the fulminate cap of a forgotten charge. In both these cases the miraculous happened and no explosion occurred. When one reads in the Official Handbook issued by the Commission that a pound of dynamite has been used to about every two cubic yards of material blasted, and compares it with the total excavation of about 200,000,000 cubic yards one thinks that even the undoubted sins of the Isthmus during its riotous days are expiated by such a vigorous blowing up.

One day at Matachin an engineer with whom I was talking called a Span-

HANDLING ROCK IN ANCON QUARRY

iard and sent him off on an errand. I noticed the man walked queerly and commented on it. "It's a wonder that fellow walks at all", said my friend with a laugh. "He was sitting on a ledge once when a blast below went off prematurely and Miguel, with three or four other men, and a few tons of rock, dirt and other débris went up into the air. He was literally blown at least 80 feet high. The other men were killed, but we found signs of life in him and shipped him to the hospital where he stayed nearly eight months. I'd hesitate to tell you how many bones were broken, but I think the spine was the only one not fractured and that was dislocated. His job is safe for the rest of his life. He loves to tell about it. Wait 'till he gets back and I'll ask him".

Presently Miguel returned, sideways like a crab, but with agility all the same. "Tell the gentleman how it feels to be blown up", said the engineer.

"Caramba! I seet on ze aidge of ze cut, smoke my pipe, watch ze work when—Boom! I fly up in air, up, up! I stop. It seem I stop long time. I see ozzair sings fly up past me. I start down— I breathe smoke, sand. Bang! I hit ground. When I wake I in bed at hospital. Can't move. Same as dead"!

"Miguel never fails to lay stress on the time he stopped before beginning his descent", comments my friend, "and on the calmness with which he viewed the prospect, particularly the other things

JAMAICANS OPERATING A COMPRESSED AIR DRILL

going up. His chief sorrow is that no moving pic-ture man took the incident".

Incidents of heroic self-sacrifice are not unknown among the dynamite handlers. Here is the story of Angel Alvarez, an humble worker on the Big Job. He was getting ready a surface blast of dyna-mite and all around him men were working in calm assurance that he would notify them before the ex-plosion. Happening to glance up he saw a great boulder just starting to slip down the cut into the pit where he stood with two open boxes of dynamite. He knew that disaster impended. He could have jumped from the pit and run, saving himself but sacri-ficing his comrades. Instead he shouted a frantic warning, and seizing the two boxes of dynamite thrust them aside out of the way of the falling boulder. There was no hope for him. The rock would have crushed him in any event. But one stick of dyna-mite fell from one of the boxes and was exploded—though the colossal explosion that might have oc-curred was averted. They thought that Alvarez was broken to bits when they gathered him up, but the surgeons patched him up, and made a kind of a man out of him. Not very shapely or vigorous is Angel Alvarez now but in a sense he carries the lives of twenty men he saved in that moment of swift decision.

The visitor to the Cut during the period of con-struction found two types of drills, the tripod and the well, busily preparing the chambers for

the reception of the dynamite. Of the former there were 221 in use, of the latter 156. With this battery over 90 miles of holes have been excavated in a month, each hole being about 27 feet deep. The drills are operated by compressed air supplied from a main running the length of the Cut and are in batteries of three to eight manned by Jamaica negroes who look as if the business of standing by and watching the drill automatically eat its way into the rock heartily agreed with their conception of the right sort of work.

He who did not see the Culebra Cut during the mighty work of excavation missed one of the great spectacles of the ages—a sight that at no other time, or place was, or will be, given to man to see. How it was best seen many visits left me unable to determine. From its crest on a working day you looked down upon a mighty rift in the earth's crust, at the base of which pigmy engines and ant-like forms were rushing to and fro without seeming plan or reason. Through the murky atmosphere strange sounds rose up and smote the ear of the onlooker with resounding clamor. He heard the strident clink, clink of the drills eating their way into the rock; the shrill whistles of the locomotives giving warning of some small blast, for the great charges

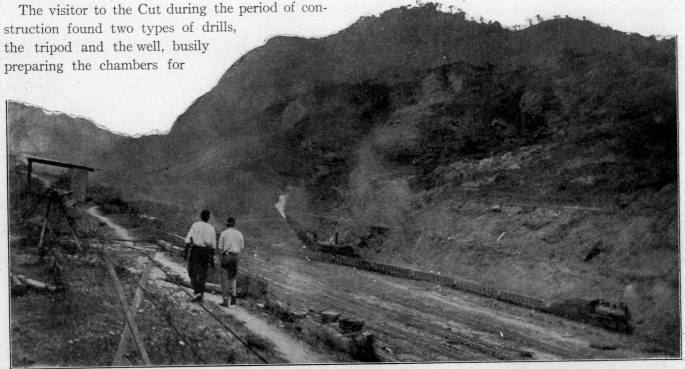

IN THE CUCARACHA SLIDE

were set off out of working hours when the Cut
was empty; the constant and uninterrupted rumble
that told of the dirt trains ever plying over the
crowded tracks; the heavy crash that accompanied
the dumping of a six-ton boulder onto a flat car;
the clanking of chains and the creaking of machinery
as the arms of the steam shovels swung around looking for another load; the cries of men, and the boom-
ing of blasts. Collectively the sounds were harsh,
deafening, brutal such as we might fancy would arise
from hell were the lid of that place of fire and tor-
ment to be lifted.

But individually each sound betokened useful
work and service in the cause of man and progress
as truly as could the musical tinkle of cow bells, the
murmur of water over a village millwheel, or the
rude melody of the sailors' songs as they trim the
yards for the voyage to the distant isles of spice.
The hum of industry that the poets have loved to
tell about loses nothing of its significance when from
a hum it rises to a roar. Only not all the poets can
catch the meaning of its new note.

So much for the sounds of the Culebra Cut on a
work day. The sights are yet more wonderful.
One who has looked upon the Grand Canyon of the
Colorado will find in this man-made gash in the
hills something of the riot of color that characterizes
that greatest of natural wonders, but he who has
had no such preparation will stand amazed before
the barbaric wealth of hues which blaze forth from
these precipitous walls. Reds predominate—red
as deep a crimson as though Mother Earth's bosom
thus cruelly slashed and scarred was giving up its
very life's blood; red shading into orange, tropical,
hot, riotous, pulsing like the life of the old Isthmus
that is being carved away to make place for the
new; red, pale, pinkish, shading down almost to
rose color as delicate as the hue on a maiden's
cheek, typifying perhaps the first blush of the bride
in the wedding of the Atlantic to the Pacific. Yellow too from the brightest orange to the palest
ochre, and blue from the shade of indigo which Columbus hoped to bring across this very Isthmus
from the bazaars of Cathay; purple as royal as
Ferdinand and Isabella ever wore, or the paler
shades of the tropic sky are there. As you look
upon the dazzling array strung out before you for
miles you may reflect that imbedded in those parti-

BROW OF GOLD HILL, CULEBRA CUT

colored rocks and clays are semi-precious stones of varied shades and sorts—beryls, moss agates, blood-stones, moonstones which the workmen pick up and sell to rude lapidaries who cut and sell them to tourists. But in all this colossal tearing up of the earth's surface there has been found none of the gold for which the first white men lusted, nor any precious stone or useful mineral whatsoever.

Again I looked on the Cut from above one morning before the breeze that blows across the Isthmus from nine o'clock in the morning until sundown, had driven out of it the mists of early dawn. From unseen depths filled with billowy vapor rose the clatter of strenuous toil by men and machines, softened somewhat by the fleecy material through which they penetrated. Of the workers no sign appeared until the growing heat of the sun and the freshening breeze began to sweep the Cut clear in its higher reaches, and there on the topmost terrace of Gold Hill, half a mile across the abyss from where I stood, was revealed a monster steam shovel digging away at the crest of the hill to lighten the weight that was crowding acres upon acres of broken soil into the canal below. It seemed like a mechanical device on some gigantic stage, as with noiseless

"EVERY BITE RECORDED AT HEADQUARTERS"

ferocity it burrowed into the hillside, then shaking and trembling with the effort swung back its long arm and disgorged its huge mouthful on the waiting flat cars. The curtain of mist was slowly disappearing. From my lofty eyrie on an outjutting point of Contractor's Hill it seemed as if the stage was being displayed, not by the lifting of a curtain, but rather by the withdrawal of a shield downward so that the higher scenery became first visible. One by one the terraces cut into the lofty hillsides were exposed to view, each with its line of tugging steam shovels and its rows of motionless empty cars, or rolling filled ones rumbling away to the distant dump. Now and again a sudden eruption of stones and dirt above the shield of fog followed in a few seconds by a dull boom told of some blast. So dense was the mist that one marvelled how in that narrow lane below, filled with railroad tracks, and with busy trains rushing back and forth men could work save at imminent danger of disaster. Death lurked there at all times and the gray covering of fog was more than once in the truest sense a pall for some poor mutilated human frame.

Perhaps the most impressive view of the Cut in the days of its activity was that from above. It was the one which gave the broadest general sense of the prodigious proportions of the work. But a more terrifying one, as well as a more

Photo by Underwood & Underwood

A DIRT-SPREADER AT WORK

precise comprehension of the infinity of detail coupled with the magnitude of scope of the work was to be obtained by plodding on foot through the five miles where the battle of Culebra was being most fiercely fought. The powers that be—or that were—did not encourage this method of observation. They preferred to send visitors through this Death's Lane, this confusing network of busy tracks, in an observation car built for the purpose, or in one of the trim little motor cars built to run on the railroad tracks for the use of officials. From the fact that one of the latter bore the somewhat significant nickname "The Yellow Peril" and from stories of accidents which had occurred to occupants of these little scouts among the mighty engines of war, I am inclined to think that the journey on foot, if more wearisome, was not more perilous.

Put on then a suit of khaki with stout shoes and take the train for Culebra. That will be as good a spot as any to descend into the Cut, and we will find there some airy rows of perpendicular ladders connecting the various levels up and down which an agile monkey, or Col. Gaillard or any of his assistants, can run with ease, but which we descend with infinite caution and some measure of nervous apprehension. Probably the first sound that will greet your ears above the general clatter, when you have attained the floor of the Canal will be a stentorian

THE TRACK SHIFTER IN ACTION

cry of "Look out, there! Look out"! You will hear that warning hail many a time and oft in the forenoon's walk we are about to take. I don't know of any spot where Edward Everett Hale's motto, "Look Out and Not In; Look Up and Not Down; Look Forward and Not Back" needs editing more than at Culebra. The wise man looked all those ways and then some. For trains are bearing down upon you from all directions and so close are the tracks and so numerous the switches that it is impossible to tell the zone of safety except by observing the trains themselves. If your gaze is too intently fixed on one point a warning cry may call your attention to the arm of a steam shovel above

Photo by Underwood & Underwood

A LIDGERWOOD UNLOADER AT WORK

your head with a five-ton boulder insecurely balanced, or a big, black Jamaican a few yards ahead perfunctorily waving a red flag in token that a "dobe" blast is to be fired. A "dobe" blast is regarded with contempt by the fellows who explode a few tons of dynamite at a time and demolish a whole hillside, but the "dobes" throw fifty to one hundred pound stones about in a reckless way that compels unprofessional respect. They tell a story on the Zone of a negro who, not thinking himself in range, was sitting on a box of dynamite calmly smoking a cigarette. A heavy stone dropped squarely on his head killing him instantly, but was sufficiently deflected by the hardness of the Ethiopian skull to miss the box on which the victim sat.

ONE OF THE COLONEL'S TROUBLES

This shovel was overwhelmed by a slide. The accident is not uncommon

Had it been otherwise the neighboring landscape and its population would have been materially changed.

It is no wonder that we have trains to dodge during the course of our stroll. There are at the moment of our visit 115 locomotives and 2000 cars in service in the Cut. About 160 loaded trains go out daily, and, of course about 160 return empty. Three hundred and twenty trains in the eight-hour day, with two hours' intermission at noon, means almost one train a minute speeding through a right of way 300 feet wide and much cluttered up with shovels, drills and other machinery. In March, 1911, the record month, these trains handled 1,728,748 cubic yards of material, carrying all to the dumps which average 12 miles distant, the farthest one being

Photo by Underwood & Underwood

THE SLICED-OFF HILL AT ANCON

Photo by S. H. Elliott

A LOCK-CHAMBER FROM ABOVE

33 miles. The lay mind does not at first think of it, but it is a fact that it was no easy task to select spots for all this refuse in a territory only 436 square miles in area, of which 164 square miles is covered by Gatun Lake and much of the rest is higher than the Cut and therefore unsuited for dumps. The amount of material disposed of would create new land worth untold millions could it have been dumped along the lake front of Chicago, or in the Hackensack meadows near New York.

To load these busy trains there were in the Cut in its busiest days 43 steam shovels mainly of the type that would take five cubic yards of material at a bite. One load for each of these shovels weighed 8.7 tons of rock, 6.7 tons of earth, or 8.03 tons of the "run of the Cut"—the mixed candy of the Culebra shop. March 11, 1911, was the record day for work on the Central Division of which the Cut is the largest component part. That day 333 loaded trains were run out and as many in, and 51 steam shovels and 2 cranes with orange peel buckets excavated 127,742 tons of material. It was no day for nervous tourists to go sightseeing in the Cut.

Let us watch one of the steam shovels at work. You will notice first that it re-quires two railroad tracks for its operation—the one on which it stands and one by the side on which are the flat cars it is to load. If the material in which it is to work is clay or sand, the shovel track is run close to the side of the hill to be cut away; otherwise the blasters will have preceded it and a great pile of broken rock lies by the side of the track or covering it before the shovel. Perched on a seat which revolves with the swinging arm a man guides the great steel jaws to the point of excavation. A tug at one lever and the jaws begin to bite into the clay, or root around in the rock pile until the toothed scoops have filled the great shovel that, closed, is rather bigger than a boarding house hall bedroom. A tug at another

WHEN THE OBISPO BROKE IN

lever and they close. A third lever causes the arm to swing until it comes to a stop above the flat car, then with a roar and a clatter the whole load is dumped. Perhaps then the trouble is just beginning. Once in a while a boulder of irregular shape rolls about threatening to fall to the ground. With almost human intelligence the great

trained elephants pile teak lumber, pushing with tusk and pulling with trunk until the beams lie level and parallel to an inch. But marvelous as is the delicacy with which the unwieldy animals perform their work, it is outdone by the miraculous ingenuity with which the inventive mind of man has adapted these monsters of steel to their appointed

Photo by Underwood & Underwood

UNGAINLY MONSTERS OF STEEL WORKING WITH HUMAN SKILL

rigid arm of the shovel follows it, checking it as it approaches the edge of the car, pushing it back, buttressing it with other stones, so that when the train gets under way it may by no chance fall off. Sometimes you see all this done from a point at which the directing man is invisible and the effect is uncanny.

Travelers in Burmah are fond of telling how the

task. We shall see on the Zone many mechanical marvels, but to my mind the sight of a man, seated placidly in a comfortable chair, and with a touch on levers making a twenty foot steel arm, with a pair of scoops each as big as a hogshead at the end, feel up and down a bit of land until it comes upon a boulder weighing five tons, then pick it up, deposit it on a flat car, and block it around with smaller

THE CULEBRA CUT

Dazzling colors combined with its colossal proportions make this man-made gash in nature's eternal hills a magnificent spectacle.
Its fullest glory will soon be dimmed, for the tropic jungle will cover its brilliant hues with a robe of green.

BUILDING AN UPPER TIER OF LOCKS

a great while they deposit the six-ton load of a shovel on top of some laborer's head. Incidents of this sort are wearing on their nerves and also upon the physique of the individual upon whom the burden has been laid. On several occasions I timed steam shovels working in the Cut on various sorts of material and found the period occupied in getting a load, depositing it on the car and getting back into position for another bite to be a fraction less than two minutes. According to my observations from five to eight shovel loads filled a car. The car once filled, a big negro wig-wagged the tidings to the engineer who pulled the train ahead the length of one car. The Jamaica negro wig-wagging is always a pleasing spectacle. He seems to enjoy a job as flagman which gives from five to fifteen minutes of calm reflection to each one minute of wagging. Far be it from me to question the industry of these sable Britons by whom the Canal is being built. Their worth in any place, except that of waiters at the Tivoli Hotel, must be conceded. But their specialty is undoubt-

stones to hold it firm—this spectacle I think will rank with any as an illustration of mechanical genius. It is a pity old Archimedes, who professed himself able to move the world with a lever if he could only find a place for his fulcrum, could not sit a while in the chair of an Isthmian steam shoveler. These men earn from $210 to $240 a month and are the aristocracy of the mechanical force in a society where everybody is frankly graded according to his earnings. They say their work is exceedingly hard upon the nerves, a statement which I can readily credit after watching them at it. Once in

TRAVELING CRANES THAT BEAR THE BRUNT OF BURDEN CARRYING

edly wig-wag-
ging.

If we climb up-
on one of the emp-
ty flat cars we
will see that upon
the floor of the
whole train, usu-
ally made up of
about 20 cars, is
stretched a stout
cable attached to
a heavy iron
wedge like a snow
plow which, while
the train is load-
ing, is on the end
car. Hinged
sheets of steel fall
into place be-
tween the cars,
making the train
floor continuous

EXCAVATING WITH A MONITOR AS CALIFORNIANS DIG GOLD

from end to end. If we should accompany the train
to the dump—say at the great fill at Balboa about
twelve miles from the Cut—we shall find that when it

THE FLOOR OF A LOCK

has reached its assigned position a curious looking car
on which is an engine which revolves a huge drum,
or bull wheel, is attached in place of the locomotive.
The end of the steel cable buried under hundreds of
tons of rock and dirt is fastened to the bull wheel,
the latter begins to revolve and the steel plow begins to travel along the train thrusting the load off
to one side. One side of the flat cars is built up
and the plow is so constructed that the load is
thrown to the other side only. It takes from 7 to
15 minutes to unload a train by this device which is
known as the Lidgerwood Unloader.

Now it is apparent that after a certain number of
trains have thus been unloaded the side of the
track on which the load falls, unless it be a very
deep ravine, will presently be so filled up that no
more loads can be dumped there. To smooth out
this mound of dirt along the track another type of
snow plow is used, one stretching out a rigid steel
arm ten or twelve feet from the side of the locomotive which pushes it into the mass of débris. This
is called a spreader and as may well be imagined requires prodigious power. The dump heap thus
spread, and somewhat leveled by hand labor, becomes a base for another track.

In the early days of the work this business of shifting tracks required the services of hundreds of men. But it grew so steadily under the needs of the service—they say the Panama Railway runs sideways as well as lengthwise—that the mechanical genius of American engineers was called into play to meet the situation. Wherefore behold the track-shifter, an engine operating a long crane which picks up the track, ties, rails and all, and swings it to one side three feet or more according to the elasticity of the track. It takes nine men to operate a track shifter, and it does the work which took 500 men pursuing the old method of pulling spikes, shifting ties and rails separately and spiking the rails down again. It is estimated that by this device the government was saved several million dollars, to say nothing of an enormous amount of time. While the Panama Railroad is only 47 miles long it has laid almost 450 miles of rails, and these are con-

tinually being taken up and shifted, particularly those laid on the bed of the Canal in Culebra Cut. It is perfectly clear that to keep the steam shovels within reaching distance of the walls they are to dig away, the track on which they operate and the track on which their attendant dirt trains run must be shifted laterally every two or three days.

Looking up from the floor of the Canal one had in those days of rushing construction a prospect at once gigantic, brilliant and awe inspiring. Between Gold Hill and Contractors Hill the space open to the sky is half a mile wide and the two peaks tower toward the sky 534 feet to the one side and 410 on the other. We see again dimly through the smoke of the struggling locomotives and the fumes of exploding dynamite the prismatic color of the stripped sides of the hill, though on the higher altitudes untouched by recent work and unscarred by slides the tropical green has already covered all traces of

Photo by Underwood & Underwood

A STEAM SHOVEL IN OPERATION

BIRD'S EYE VIEW OF THE MIRAFLORES LOCKS

man's mutilations. In time, of course, all this coloring will disappear and the ships will steam along betwixt two towering walls of living green.

One's attention, however, when in the Cut is held mainly by its industrial rather than by its scenic features. For the latter the view from above, already described, is incalculably the better. But down here in the depths your mind is gripped by the signs of human activity on every side. Everything that a machine can do is being done by machinery, yet there are 6000 men working in this narrow way, men white and black and of every intermediate and indeterminate shade. Men who talk in Spanish, French, the gibberish of the Jamaican, in Hindoo, in Chinese. One thinks it a pity that Col. Goethals and his chief lieutenants could not have been at the Tower of Babel, for in that event that aspiring enterprise would never have been halted by so commonplace an obstacle as the confusion of tongues.

To us as we plod along all seems to be conducted with terrific energy, but without any recognizable plan. As a matter of fact all is being

directed in accordance with an iron-clad system. That train, the last cars of which are being loaded, on the second level must be out of the Cut and on the main line at a fixed hour or there will be a tie-up of the empties coming back from the distant dumps. That row of holes must be drilled by five o'clock, for the blast must be fired as soon as the Cut is emptied of workers. The very tourists on the observation car going through the Cut must be chary of their questions, for that track is needed now for a train of material. If they are puzzled by something they see, it will all be explained to them later by the guide in his lecture illustrated by the working model at the Tivoli Hotel.

So trudging through the Cut we pass under a slender foot bridge suspended across the Canal from towers of steel framework. The bridge was erected by the French and will have to come down when the procession of ships begins the passage of the Canal. Originally its towers were of wood, but a man idly ascending one thought it sounded hollow beneath his tread and, on examination, found the interior

THE ROCK-BREAK THAT ADMITTED THE BAS OBISPO

had been hollowed out by termite ants leaving a mere shell which might give way under any unaccustomed strain. This is a pleasant habit of these insects and sometimes produces rather ludicrous results when a heavy individual encounters a chair that has engaged their attention.

The activity and industry of the ant are of course proverbial in every clime, but it seems to me that in the Isthmus particularly he appears to put the sluggard to shame. As you make your way through the jungle you will now and again come upon miniature roads, only about four inches wide it is true, but vastly smoother and better cleaned of vegetation than the paths which the Panamanians dignify with the name of roads. Along these highways trudges an endless army of ants, those going homeward bearing burdens of leaves which, when buried in their subterranean homes, produce fungi on which the insects live. Out on the savanna you will occasionally find a curious mound of hard dirt, sometimes standing taller than a man and rising abruptly from the plain. It is an ant's nest built about a shrub or small tree, which usually dies off so that no branches protrude in any direction. A large one represents long years of the work of the tiny insects. Col. Goethals has made a great working machine of the Canal organization but

A TERMITE ANT'S NEST
The ants' work kills the tree

he can teach the ants nothing so far as patient and continuous industry is concerned.

We come in due time to the upper entrance of the Pedro Miguel lock. Here the precipitous sides of the Canal have vanished, and the walls of the lock have in fact to be built up above the adjacent land. This is the end of the Central Division— the end of the Culebra Cut. The 8.8 miles we have left behind us have been the scene, perhaps, of the most wonderful exercise of human ingenuity, skill and determination ever manifested in any equal space in the world—and I won't even except Wall Street, where ingenuity and skill in cutting things down are matter of daily observation. But nowhere else has man locked with nature in so desperate a combat. More spectacular engineering is perhaps to be seen on some of the railroads through our own Sierras or on the trans-Andean lines. Such dams as the Roosevelt or the Shoshone of our irrigation service are more im-

Photo by H. Pittier. Courtesy National Geographic Magazine
AN ANT'S NEST ON THE SAVANNA

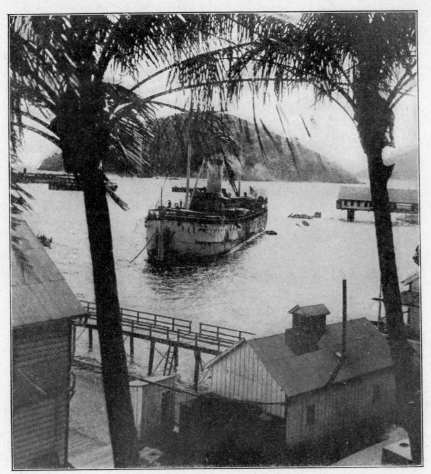

DEEP SEA DREDGE AT BALBOA

largely for the purpose of taking care of this water, though it also served to reduce somewhat the amount of dry excavation on the Canal. One advantage which both the Gatun and Miraflores lakes have for the sailor, that does not at first occur to the landsman, is that being filled with fresh water, as also is the main body of the Canal, they will cleanse the bottoms of the ships passing through of barnacles and other marine growths. This is a notable benefit to ships engaged in tropical trade, for in those latitudes their bottoms become befouled in a way that seriously interferes with their steaming capacity.

The name Pedro Miguel is given to this lock because the French began operations there on the feast day of St. Peter Michael, whose name in Spanish is applied to the spot. An omniscient gentleman on the train once assured me that the name came from a Spanish hermit who long lived on the spot in the odor of sanctity—and divers other odors if the haunts of the hermits I have visited elsewhere were any criterion.

pressive than the squat, immovable ridge at Gatun. But the engineers who planned the campaign against the Cordilleras at Culebra had to meet and overcome more novel obstacles, had to wrestle with a problem more appalling in magnitude than any that ever confronted men of their profession in any other land or time.

As no link in a chain is of less importance than any other link, so the Pacific Division of the Panama Canal is of equal importance with the other two. It has not, however, equally spectacular features. Its locks at Pedro Miguel and at Miraflores are merely replicas of the Gatun locks with different drops, and separated into one step of two parallel locks at the former point, and two steps, with four locks in pairs at Miraflores. Between the two locks is an artificial lake about 54 2-3 feet above sea level and about a mile and a half long. The lake is artificial, supplied partly by small rivers that flow into it and partly by the water that comes down from the operation of the locks above. In fact it was created

PROPORTIONS OF THE LOCKS

A six story building would stand in the lock-chamber. Size of conduits indicated by small sketches of wagon and locomotive.

Errors of fact, however, are common on the zone. They still laugh about a congressman who, on Gatun dam, struck an attitude and exclaimed with feeling—"At last then I stand in the far-famed Culebra Cut"! which spot was a trifle more than thirty miles away.

From the lower lock at Miraflores the canal describes a practically straight course to the Pacific Ocean at Balboa, about 4½ miles. The channel is continued out to sea about four miles further. All the conditions of the Pacific and Oriental trade give assurance that at Balboa will grow the greatest of all purely tropical ports. To it the commerce of the whole Pacific coast of North America, and of South America as far south at least as Lima, will irresistibly flow. To it will also come the trade of Japan, Northern China and the Philippines, seeking the shortest route to Europe or to our own Atlantic coast. It is true that much of this trade will pass by, but the ships will enter the Canal after long voyages in need of coal and in many cases of refitting. The government has anticipated this need by providing for a monster dry dock, able to accommodate the 1000 foot ships yet to be built, and establishing repair shops fit to build ships as well as to repair them. In 1913, however, when this trip through the Canal under construction was made, little sign of this coming greatness was apparent. The old dock of the Pacific Mail and a terminal pier of the Panama Railroad afforded sufficient dockage for the steamships of which eight or ten a week cleared or arrived. The chief signs of the grandeur yet to come were the never-ceasing dirt trains rumbling down from Culebra Cut and discharging their loads into the sea in a great fan shaped "fill" that will afford building sites for all the edifices of the future Balboa, however great it may become. Looking oceanward you see the three conical islands on which the United States is already erecting its fortifications.

Here then the Canal ends. Begun in the ooze of Colon it is finished in the basaltic rock of Balboa. To carry it through its fifty miles the greatest forces of nature have been utilized when possible; fought and overcome when not. It has enlisted genius, devotion and sacrifice, and has inflicted sickness, wounds and death. We can figure the work in millions of dollars, or of cubic yards, but to estimate the cost in life and health from the time the French began until the day the Americans ended is a task for the future historian, not the present-day chronicler.

THE GREAT FILL AT BALBOA WHERE THE CULEBRA SPOIL IS DUMPED

CHAPTER XIII

THE CITY OF PANAMA.

FOR an American not too much spoiled with foreign travel the city of Panama is a most entertaining stopping place for a week or more. In what its charm consists it is hard to say. Foreign it is, of course, a complete change from anything within the borders, or for that matter close to the bounds of the United States. But it is not so thorough a specimen of Latin-American city building as Cartagena, its neighbor. Its architecture is admittedly commonplace, the Cathedral itself being interesting mainly because of its antiquity—and it would be modern in old Spain. The Latin gaiety of its people breaks out in merry riot at carnival time, but it is equally riotous in every town of Central America. Withal there is a something about Panama that has an abiding novelty. Perhaps it is the tang of the tropics added to the flavor of antiquity. Anyhow the tourist who abides in the intensely modern and purely United States hotel, the Tivoli, has but to give a dime to a Panama hackman to be transported into an atmosphere as foreign as though he had suddenly been wafted to Madrid.

PANAMA BAY FROM ANCON HILL

Latter-day tourists complain that the sanitary efforts of the Isthmian Commission have robbed Panama of something of its picturesqueness. They deplore the loss of the streets that were too sticky for the passage of Venetian gondolas, but entirely too liquid for ordinary means of locomotion. They grieve over the disappearance of the public roulette wheels and the monotonous cry of the numbers at keno. They complain that the population has taken to the practice of wearing an inordinate quantity of clothes instead of being content with barely enough to pique curiosity concerning the few charms concealed. But though the city has been remarkably purified there is still enough of physical dirt apparent to displease the most fastidious, and quite sufficient moral uncleanliness if one seeks for it is like other towns.

SANTA ANA PLAZA

The fence is now removed.   During the French days this Plaza was the scene of much gaiety and still shows French influence

The entrance by railway to Panama is not prepossessing, but for that matter I know of few cities in which it is. Rome and Genoa perhaps excel in offering a fine front to the visitor. But in Panama when you emerge from the station after a journey clear across the continent, which has taken you about three hours, you are confronted by a sort of ragged triangular plaza. In the distance on a hill to your right is set the Tivoli Hotel looking cool and inviting with its broad piazzas and dress of green and white.

To your left is a new native hotel, the International, as different from the Tivoli as imaginable, built of rubble masonry covered with concrete stucco, with rooms twice as high as those of the usual American building. It looks cool too, in a way, and its most striking feature is a pleasingly commodious bar, with wide open unscreened doors on the level of the sidewalk. The Tivoli Hotel, being owned and managed by the United States government, has no bar. This statement is made in no spirit of invidious comparison, but merely as a matter of helpful information to the arriving traveler undecided which hotel to choose.

The plaza is filled with Panama cabs —small open victorias, drawn by stunted wiry horses like our cow ponies and driven by Panama negroes who either do not speak English, or, in many cases, pretend not to in order to save themselves the trouble of explaining any of the sights to their fares. There is none of the bustle that attends the arrival of a train in an American city. No raucous cries of "Keb, sir? Keb"! no ingratiating

Photo by Underwood & Underwood
PANAMA FROM THE SEA WALL; CATHEDRAL TOWERS IN DISTANCE

tuting a new engagement involving an additional dime. Tourists who jovially drew up to the curbstone to greet acquaintances met *en route* several times in a half-hour's ride are said to have been mulcted of a surprising number of dimes, but in justice to the Panama hackman—who really doesn't have the air of rioting in ill-gotten wealth— I must say that I never encountered an instance of this overcharge.

Your first introduction to the beauty of Panama architecture comes from a building that fronts you as you leave your train. Three sto-

eagerness to seize upon your baggage, no ready proffer of willingness to take you anywhere. If the Panama cabby shows any interest at all in getting a fare out of an arriving crowd it seems to be in evading the one who beckons him, and trying to capture someone else. One reason perhaps for the lethargy of these sable jehus is that the government has robbed their calling of its sporting feature by fixing their fare at ten cents to any place in town. Opportunity to rob a fare is almost wholly denied them, hence their dejected air as compared with the alert piratical demeanor of the buccaneers who kidnap passengers at the railway stations of our own enlightened land. The only way the Panama driver can get the best of the passenger is by construing each stop as the end of a trip, and the order to drive on as consti-

ries high it has the massive strength of a confectioner's creations, and is tastefully colored a sickly green, relieved by stripes of salmon pink, with occasional interludes of garnet and old gold. The fact that it houses a saloon, the proportions of which would be generous on the Bowery or South Clark Street, does not explain this brilliant color scheme. It is merely the expression of the local color sense, and is quite likely to be employed to lend distinction to a convent school or a fashionable club indiscriminately.

From the Railway Plaza—originality has not yet furnished a more attractive name—the Avenida Centrale stretches away in a generally southerly direction to the seawall at the city's end. What Broadway is to New York, the Corso to Rome, or Main Street to Podunk, this street is to Panama. It is narrow and in time will be exceedingly crowded, for the rails of a trolley line are laid on one side, and some time in the leisurely Panamanian future the cars will run through the old town and so on out to Balboa where the Americans are building the great docks at the entrance to the Canal. Just now however it is chiefly crowded with the light open carriages which toward eventide carry up and down the thoroughfare olive-complex-

THE PANAMA WATER FRONT

ioned gentlemen who look smilingly at the balconies on either side whence fair ones—of varying degrees of fairness with a tendency toward the rich shade of mahogany—look down approvingly.

Panama is an old city, as American cities run, for it was founded in 1673 when the Bishop marked with a cross the place for the Cathedral. The Bishop still plays a notable part in the life of the town, for it is to his palace in Cathedral Plaza that you repair Sunday mornings to hear the lucky number in the lottery announced. This curious partnership between the church and the great gambling game does not seem to shock or even perplex the Panamanians, and as the State turns over to the church a very considerable percentage of the lottery's profits it is perhaps only fair for the Bishop to be thus hospitable. If you jeer a well-informed Panamanian on the relations of his church to the lottery he counters by asking suavely about the filthy tenement houses owned by Old Trinity in New York. As a vested right under the Colombian government the lottery will continue until 1918, then expire under the clause in the Panama constitution which prohibits gambling. Drawings are held each Sunday. Ten thousand tickets are issued at a price of $2.50 each, though the custom is to buy one-fifth of a ticket at a time. The capital prize is $7500 with lesser prizes of various sums down to one dollar. The Americans on the Zone buy eagerly, but I could

THE BULL RING; BULL FIGHTS ARE NOW PROHIBITED

THE LOTTERY OFFICE IN THE BISHOP'S PALACE

not learn of any one who had captured a considerable prize. One official who systematically set aside $5 a week for tickets told me that, after four years' playing, he was several hundred dollars ahead "beside the fun".

Though old historically, Panama is modern architecturally. It was repeatedly swept by fires even before the era of overfumigation by the Canal builders. Five fires considerable enough to be called "great" are recorded. Most of the churches have been burned at least once and the façade of the Cathedral was overthrown by an earthquake. The San Domingo Church, the Church and Convent of San Francisco, and the Jesuit Church still stand in ruins. In Italy or England these ruins would be cared for, clothed by pious, or perhaps practical, hands with a certain sort of dignity. Not so in Panama. The San Domingo Church, much visited by

tourists because of its curious flat arch, long housed a cobbler's bench and a booth for curios. Now its owner is utilizing such portions of the ruin as are still stable as part of a tenement house he is building. When reproached for thus obliterating an historic relic he blandly offered to leave it in its former state, provided he were paid a rental equal to that the tenement would bring in. There being no society for the preservation of historic places in Panama his offer went unheeded, and the church is fast being built into the walls of a flat-house. As for the Church of the Jesuits its floor is gone, and cows and horses are stabled in the sanctuary of its apse.

The streets of Panama look older than they really are. The more substantial buildings are of rubble masonry faced with cement which quickly takes on an appearance of age. Avenida Centrale is lined for all but a quarter of a mile of its length with shops, over which as a rule the merchant's family lives—for the Panamanians, like other Latins, have not yet acquired the New York idea that it is vulgar to live over your own place of business but perfectly proper to live two miles or more away over someone else's drug store, grocery, stationery store, or what

SAN DOMINGO CHURCH AND THE FLAT ARCH

not. There might be an essay written on the precise sort of a business place above which it is correct for an American to live. Of course the nature of the entrance counts, and much propriety is saved if it be on the side front thus genteelly concealing from guests that there are any shops in the building at all. These considerations however are not important in Panama, and many of the best apartments are reached through dismal doors and up winding stairways which seldom show signs of any squeamishness on the part of the domestics, or intrusive activity by the sanitary officers.

THE PRESIDENT'S HOUSE; A FINE TYPE OF PANAMA RESIDENCE

Often, however, the apartments reached by such uninviting gateways are charming. The rooms are always big, equivalent each to about three rooms of our typical city flat. Great French windows open to the floor, and give upon broad verandas, from which the life of the street below may be observed—incidentally letting in the street noises which are many and varied. The tendency is to the minimum of furniture, and that light, so as to admit easy shifting to the breeziest spots. To our northern eyes the adjective "bare" would generally apply to these homes, but their furnishings are adapted to the climate and to the habits of people living largely out of doors. Rents are high for a town of 35,000 people. A five-room flat in a fairly good neighborhood will rent for from $60 to $75 gold a month, and as the construction is of the simplest and the landlord furnishes neither heat nor janitor service, it seems a heavy return on the capital invested.

It seemed to me, as the result of questioning and observation rather than by any personal experience, that living expenses in Panama City must be high, and good living according to our North American ideas impossible. What the visitor finds in the homes of the people on the Canal Zone offers no guide to the conditions existing in the native town. For the Zone dwellers have the commissary to buy from, and that draws from all the markets of the world, and is particularly efficient in buying meats, which it gets from our own Beef Trust and sells for about half of what the market man in Chicago or New York exacts. But the native Panamanian has no such source of supply. His meats are mainly native animals fresh killed, and if you have a taste for sanguinary sights you may see at early dawn every morning numbers of cattle and hogs slaughtered in a trim and cleanly open air abattoir which the Panamanians owe to the Canal authorities. However the climate tends to encourage a

Photo by F. A. Gause

CHIRIQUI CATTLE AT THE ABATTOIR

Photo by Gause

THE FISH MARKET

of San Miguel and from the land of the San Blas Indians. Great sailors these latter, veritable vikings of the tropics, driving their cayucas through shrieking gales when the ocean steamers find it prudent to stay in port.

Nature helps the primitive people of the jungle to bring their goods to the waiting purchasers. The breeze is constant, seldom growing to a gale, and the tide rising full 20 feet enables them to run their boats at high tide close to the market causeway, and when the tide retires land their products over the flats without the trouble of lighterage. True the bottom is of mud and stones, but the soles of the seamen are not tender, nor are they squeamish as to the nature of the soil on which they tread.

fish and vegetable diet, and the supplies of these staples are fairly good. The family buying is done at a central market which it is well worth the tourists' time to visit.

Every day is market day at Panama, but the crowded little open-air mart is seen at its best of a Saturday or Sunday in the early morning. All night long the native boats, mostly cayucas hewn out of a single log and often as much as 35 feet long, and with a schooner rig, have been drifting in, propelled by the never-failing trade wind. They come from the Bayano River country, from Chorrera, from Taboga and the Isles of Pearls, from the Bay

Photo by Gause

THE VEGETABLE MARKET

SAN BLAS BOATS AT THE MARKET PLACE

The market is open at dawn, and the buyers are there almost as soon as the sellers, for early rising is the rule in the tropics. Along the sidewalks, on the curbs, in the muddy roadway even, the diverse fruits and food products of the country are spread forth to tempt the robust appetites of those gathered about. Here is an Indian woman, the color of a cocoanut, and crinkled as to skin like a piece of Chinese crepe. Before her is spread out her stock, diverse and in some items curious. Green peppers, tomatoes a little larger than a small plum,

THE MARKET ON THE CURB

pit about the size of a peach-stone; the sapodilla, a plum colored fruit with a mushy interior, which when cut transversely shows a star-like marking and is sometimes called the star apple. It is eaten with a spoon and is palatable. The mamei, however, like the mango, requires a specially trained taste.

While puzzling over the native fruits a sudden clamor attracts us to a different part of the market. There drama is in full enactment. The market place is at the edge of the bay and up the water steps three exultant fishermen have dragged a tuna about five feet long, weighing perhaps 175 pounds. It is not a particularly large fish of the species, but its captors are highly exultant and one, with the

a cheese made of goat's milk and packed to about the consistency of Brie; a few yams, peas, limes and a papaya or two are the more familiar edibles. Something shaped like a banana and wrapped in corn husks arouses my curiosity.

"What is it"? "Five cents". "No, no! I mean what is it? What's it made of"? "Fi centavo"!

In despair over my lack of Indo-Spanish patois, I buy it and find a little native sugar, very moist and very dark, made up like a sausage, or a tamale in corn husks. Other mysterious objects turn out to be ginseng, which appeals to the resident Chinese; the mamei, a curious pulpy fruit the size of a large peach, with a skin like chamois and a fleshly looking

CAYUCAS ON MARKET DAY

WHERE THE FLIES GET BUSY

inborn instinct of the Latin-American to insult a captive or a fallen foe, stands on the poor tuna's head and strikes an attitude as one who invites admiration and applause. Perhaps our camera tempted him, but our inclination was to kick the brute, rather than to perpetuate his pose, for the poor fish was still living. It had been caught in a net, so its captors informed us. On our own Florida and California coasts the tunas give rare sport with a rod and line.

Like most people of a low order of intelligence the lower class native of Panama is without the slightest sense of humanity to dumb animals. He does not seem to be intentionally cruel—indeed he is too indolent to exert himself unless something is to

PANAMA FROM THE BAY; ANCON HILL IN THE BACKGROUND

be gained. But he never lets any consideration for the sufferings of an animal affect his method of treating it. The iguana, ugliest of lizards, which he eats with avidity, is one of his chief victims. This animal is usually taken alive by hunters in order that he may undergo a preliminary fattening process before being committed to the pot. In captivity his condition is not pleasant to contemplate. Here at the market are eight or ten, living, palpitating, looking out on the strange world with eyes of wistful misery. Their short legs are roughly twisted so as to cross above their backs, and the sharp claws on one foot are thrust through the fleshy part of the other so as to hold them together without other fastening. A five-foot iguana is fully three feet tail, and of that caudal yard at least two feet of its tapering length is useless for food, so the native calmly chops it off with his machete, exposing the mutilated but living animal for sale.

To our northern eyes there is probably no animal except a serpent more repulsive than the iguana. He is not only a lizard, but a peculiarly hideous one—horned, spined, mottled and warty like a toad. But loathsome as he is, the wanton, thoughtless

tortures inflicted upon him by the marketmen invest him with the pathetic dignity which martyrs bear.

Fish is apparently the great staple of the Panama market, as beseems a place which is practically an island and the very name of which signifies "many fishes". Yet at the time I was there the variety exposed for sale was not great. The corbina, apparently about as staple and certain a crop as our northern cod, the red snapper, mullet and a flat fish resembling our fresh water sunfish, were all that were exhibited. There were a few West Indian lobsters too, about as large as our average sized lobsters, but without claws, having antennae, perhaps 18 inches long, instead. Shrimps and small molluscs were plentifully displayed. As to meats the market was neither varied nor pleasing. If the assiduous attentions of flies produce any effect on raw meats prejudicial to human health, the Panama market offers rich field for some extension of the sanitary powers of Col. Gorgas.

In one notable respect this Panama market differs from most open air affairs of the sort. The vendors make no personal effort to sell their goods. There is no appeal to passing buyers, no crying of wares,

AVENIDA B. PANAMA CITY

Most of the streets in Panama end at the water side as the city is built upon a narrow promontory. The effect
of the blue water and sky closing the end of the narrow street of parti-colored houses is picturesque.

no "ballyhoo," to employ the language of Coney Island. What chatter there is is chiefly among the buyers; the sellers sit silent by their wares and are more apt to receive a prospective customer sulkily than with alert eagerness. Indeed the prevalent condition of the Panamanian, so far as observable on the streets, seems to be a chronic case of sulks. Doubtless amongst his own kind he can be a merry dog, but in the presence of the despised "gringo" his demeanor is one of apathy, or contemptuous indifference. Perhaps what he was doing to the tuna and the iguana the day of our visit to the market was only what he would like to be doing to the northern invaders of his nondescript market place.

If you view the subject fairly the Panamanian in the street is somewhat entitled to his view of the American invasion. Why should he be particularly pleased over the independence of Panama and the digging of the Canal? He got none of the ten million dollars, or of the $250,000 annual payment.

That went to his superiors who planned the "revolution" and told him about it when it was all over. The influx of Americans brought him no particular prosperity, unless he drove a hack. They lived in Commission houses and bought all their goods in their own commissary. It was true they cleaned up his town, but he was used to the dirt and the fumes of fumigation made him sneeze. Doubtless there was no more yellow fever, but he was immune to that anyway.

But way down in the bottom of his heart the real unexpressed reason for the dislike of the mass of Panamanians for our people is their resentment at our hardly concealed contempt for them. Toward the more prosperous Panamanian of social station this contempt is less manifested, and he accordingly shows less of the dislike for Americans that is too evident among the masses of the people. But as for the casual clerk or mechanic we Americans call him "spiggotty" with frank contempt for his undersize, his uneducation and above all for his

POTTERY VENDORS NEAR THE PANAMA CITY MARKET

large proportion of negro blood. And the lower class Panamanian smarting under the contemptuous epithet retorts by calling the North Americans "gringoes" and hating them with a deep, malevolent rancour that needs only a fit occasion to blaze forth in riot and in massacre.

"Spiggotty", which has not yet found its way into the dictionaries, is derived from the salutation of hackmen seeking a fare— "speaka-da-English". Our fellow countrymen with a lofty and it must be admitted a rather provincial scorn for foreign peoples—for your average citizen of the United States thinks himself as superior to the rest of the world as the citizen of New York holds himself above the rest of the United States —are not careful to limit its application to Panamanians of the hackdriving class. From his lofty pinnacle of superiority he brands them all, from the market woman with a stock of half a dozen bananas and a handful of mangoes to the banker or the merchant whose children are being educated in Europe like their father as "spiggotties". Whereat they writhe and curse the Yankees.

"Gringo" is in the dictionaries. It is applied to pure whites of whatever nation other than Spanish or Portuguese who happen to be sojourning in Spanish-American lands. The Century Dictionary rather inadequately defines it thus: "Among Spanish Americans an Englishman or an Anglo-American; a term of contempt. Probably from Greico, a Greek". The dictionary derivation is not wholly satisfactory. Another one, based wholly on tradition, is to the effect that during the war with Mexico our soldiers were much given to singing a song, "Green Grow the Grasses Oh"! whence the term "Gringoes" applied by the Mexicans. The etymology of international slang can never be an exact science, but perhaps this will serve.

Whatever the derivation, whatever the dictionary definitions, the two words "spiggotty" and "gringo" stand for racial antagonism, contempt and aversion on the part of the more northern people; malice and suppressed wrath on that of the Spanish-Americans.

You will find this feeling outcropping in every social plane in the Republic of Panama. It is, however, noticeably less prevalent among the more educated classes. Into the ten mile wide Canal Zone the Americans have poured millions upon millions of money and will continue to do so for a long time to come.

Photo by Underwood & Underwood

FROM A PANAMA BALCONY

In the narrow streets the broad balconies bring neighbors close together of this money necessarily finds its way into the hands of the Panamanians. The housing and commissary system adopted by the Commission have deprived the merchants and landowners of Colon of their richest pickings, but nevertheless the amount of good American money that has fallen to their lot is a golden stream greater than that which flowed over the old Royal Road in its most crowded days. Few small towns will show so many automobiles as Panama and they have all been bought since the American invasion.

Nevertheless the Americans are hated. They are hated for the commissary system. The French took no such step to protect their workers from the rapacity of Panama and Colon shopkeepers, and they are still talking of the time of the French richness. They hate us because we cleaned their towns and are keeping them clean—not perhaps because they actually prefer the old filth and fatalities, but because their correction implies that they were not altogether perfect before we came. For the strongest quality of the Panamanian is his pride, and it is precisely that sentiment which we North Americans have either wantonly or necessarily outraged.

Without pretension to intimate acquaintance with Panamanian home life I may state confidently that this attitude toward the Yankees is practically uni-

THEIR FIRST COMMUNION

Panama is a Roman Catholic City with picturesque church processions

versal. The ordinary demeanor of the native when accosted is sulky, even insolent. The shop-keeper, unless he be a Chinese, as most of the better ones are, makes a sale as if he were indifferent to your patronage, and throws you the finished bundle as though he were tossing a bone to a dog. One Sunday morning, viewing the lottery drawing at the Archbishop's palace, I saw a well-dressed Panamanian, apparently of the better class, roused to such wrath by a polite request that he remove his hat to give a lady a better view, that one might have thought the best blood of all Castile had been enraged by some deadly insult.

This smoldering wrath is ever ready to break out; the brutal savagery which manifests itself in the recurrent revolutions of Spanish-America is ever present in Panama. On the Fourth of July, 1912, the Americans resident on the Zone held patriotic exercises at Ancon. After the speeches and the lunch a number of the United States marines wandered into the City of Panama and, after the unfortunate fashion of their kind, sought out that red-lighted district of infamy which the Panama authorities have thoughtfully segregated in a space between the public hospital and the cemeteries. The men were unarmed, but in uniform. Naturally their holiday began by visits to a number of Panamanian gin mills

MARRIAGE IS AN AFFAIR OF SOME POMP

THE MANLY ART IN THE TROPICS

American authorities. At Ancon, separated from Panama City only by an imaginary boundary line, the Zone police were mustered for service in case of need, and at Camp Otis, an hour away by rail, the 10th Infantry, U. S. A., was drawn up under arms, and trains made ready to bring the troops to the riotous city at command. But the order never came, though the 10th officers and men alike were eager for it. It could come only through the American minister, and he was silent, believing that the occasion did not warrant the employment of the troops on the foreign soil of Panama. So the marines—or as many of them as their officers could gather up—were sent to their post, Camp Elliott, by train while those arrested by the Panamanians were taken to the Chiriqui Jail, or to the Panama hospitals. In jail the unarmed captives were beaten and tortured after the fashion of the average Latin-American when he has a foe, helpless in his power. The day ended with three American marines killed and many wounded;

where the liquid fuel for a fight was taken aboard. In due time the fight came. A Panama policeman intervened and was beaten for his pains. Other police came to his rescue. Somebody fired a shot and soon the police, running to their station, returned with magazine rifles and began pumping bullets into the unarmed marines. The latter for a time responded with stones, but the odds were too great and they broke and ran for the American territory of the Canal Zone. Meantime of course the noise of the fusillade had alarmed the

Photo by Underwood & Underwood

A GROUP OF NATIONAL POLICE

TABOGA, THE PLEASURE PLACE OF PANAMA

the Americans, soldiers and civilians, both gritting their teeth and eager to take possession of Panama; and the Panamanians, noisy, insolent, boastful, bragging of how they had whipped the "Yankee pigs" and daring the whole United States to attempt any punishment.

The United States seems to have supinely "taken the dare", as the boys would say, for though the affray and the murders occurred in July, 1912, nothing has yet been done. In answer to a formal query in April, 1913, the Department of State replied that the matter was "still the subject of diplomatic correspondence which it is hoped will have a satisfactory termination".

Americans on the Zone are depressed over the seeming lack of vigor on the part of the home government. They say that the apparent immunity enjoyed by the assailants of the marines has only enhanced the contemptuous hatred of the natives for the Americans. "Let them step on our side of the line", says the swashbuckling native with a chip on his shoulder, "and we'll show 'em". Among the Americans on the Zone there is almost universal regret that the troops were not marched into Panama on the day of the riot. Authority existed under the treaty with the Republic of Panama. The troops were ready. The lesson need not have been a severe one, but it was deserved and would have been lasting. Furthermore those best equipped to judge say that the event is only deferred, not averted. "Spiggotty" and "Gringo" will not continue long to make faces over an imaginary line without a clash.

Despite the feeling against the Americans, all classes of Panamanians must admit receiving a certain amount of advantage from the activities of the Canal builders. Moreover the $10,000,000 paid

over by the United States for the Canal Zone has not been squandered, nor has it been dissipated in graft. We are inclined to laugh because one of the first uses to which it was put was to build a

SANTA ANA CHURCH, 1764

THE PANAMA NATIONAL INSTITUTE

In the background is the Canal administration building and the residence of Col. Gorgas

government theater, which is opened scarce thirty days out of the year. But it is fair to take the Latin temperament into consideration. There is no Latin-American republic so impoverished as not to have a theater built by the public. The Republic of Panama, created overnight, found itself without any public buildings whatsoever, barring the jail. Obviously a national capitol was the first need and it was speedily supplied. If one wing was used to house a theater that was a matter for local consideration and not one for cold-blooded Yankees to jeer about. The Republic itself was a little theatrical, rather reminiscent of the papier-mâché creations of the stage carpenter, and might be expected to vanish like a transformation scene. At any rate with the money in hand the Panaman-

ians built a very creditable government building, including a National Theater, and an imposing building for the National Institute as well. They might have done worse. It showed that the revolution was more of a business affair than most Central-American enterprises of that sort. The average leader of so successful an enterprise would have concealed the greater part of the booty in a Paris bank account to his own order, and used the rest in building up an army for his own maintenance in power. Panama has her needed public buildings—let us wink at the theater—and $7,500,000 invested in New York against a time of need.

The three government buildings in the City of Panama are all creditable architecturally, and from a superficial standpoint structurally as well. Whenever you are shown a piece of government work in a Latin-American country your guide always whispers "graft"—as for that matter is the practice in New York as well. But Panama seems to have received the worth of its money. The Government Palace, which corresponds to our national capital, stands facing a little plaza open toward the sea. It is nearly square, 180 by 150 feet, surrounding a tasteful court or patio after the South American manner. Built of rubble masonry it is faced with white cement, and is of a singularly simple and effective architectural style for a Latin-American edifice.

THE NATIONAL PALACE AND THEATER

The building houses the Assembly Hall, the Government Theater and the public offices. The interior of the theater, which seats about 1000, is rather in the European than the North American style with a full tier of boxes, large foyers decorated with paintings by Panama artists, and all the appurtenances of a well-appointed opera house.

Next to the Government Palace the most ambitious public building in Panama is the home of

THE MUNICIPAL BUILDING

the National Institute, or University, which nestles at the foot of Ancon Hill. This is a group of seven buildings surrounding a central court. The Institute is designed in time to become a true university, but its accommodations are at present far in advance of its needs. Equipped with an excellent faculty it will for some time to come—it was opened only in 1911—suffer from a lack of pupils, because the public schools in the Republic are not yet fitted to equip pupils for a university course. The population of Panama is largely illiterate. The census in 1911 showed 60,491 children of school age, and only 18,607 enrolled in schools of all classes. Of those more than 16,000 were enrolled in the primary schools. The Government however is doing all it can to encourage education among the masses, and the National Institute will offer to all who fit themselves to enter its classes not only free tuition, but free board and lodging as well.

The third considerable public building in Panama is the Municipal Building which stands at one corner of the Cathedral Plaza. It contains, beside the council chamber and usual offices, the Columbus Library of about 2500 books, including many rare volumes on the ancient history of the Isthmian land and its people.

To return however to the physical aspects of the City of Panama. It is recorded of a certain King of Spain that when certain bills for the fortification of Panama City were presented to him he gazed

SALIENT ANGLE OF LANDWARD WALL

into vacancy with the rapt eyes of one seeing visions.

"Methinks I behold those walls from here", quoth he to the suppliant treasurer, "they must be so prodigious"!

Indeed what remains of the walls of Panama is impressive to American eyes that, accustomed to the peace and newness of our own towns, always rejoice in seeing the relics of the time when every city was a walled camp. Ruins and the remnants of by-gone days of battle are now and will become increasingly objects of human interest. For in the centuries to come our present edifices of iron sheathed with slabs of stone or brick will disintegrate into rust and clay, while as for the scenes of our most glorious battles they remain even today as barely discernible lines of earthworks. Gone is the day of turreted castles, frowning walls, bastions, ravelins and donjon keeps.

It is little wonder that even the remnants of Panama's wall are impressive. The new city was decreed by the Queen of Spain in 1672, or about a year after Morgan had despoiled and destroyed Old Panama. The site was chosen largely because of the opportunity it afforded for defense, and the good Bishop had scarcely selected the site for the Cathedral when the military officials began staking out the line of the walls.

Though almost 250 years have since passed a great part of these fortifications is still intact, and the plan of the whole is still easily traceable amid the narrow streets of the crowded little city. Most notable of the sections still standing is the sea wall, sometimes called Las Bovedas, from which on the one hand one looks down on the inmates of the flowery little Chiriqui Prison, and on the other out to sea—past the shallow harbor with its army of pelicans, past the tossing little native fishing and market boats, past the long Balboa fill where the Canal builders have thrown a mountain into the sea and made a vast plain, and so on to the three little islands, rising craggy from the ocean where the Great Republic of the North is mounting the cannon that shall guard the entrance of the Canal from any invader. Very different from the old Spanish fort of the 17th century are these military works of the 20th and not nearly so picturesque. Such as they are must be left to the imagination, for the military authorities rigidly bar the camera from the post.

The original city stood on a peninsula, and three sides of this were bounded by the sea wall, rising from about high water mark to a height of from twenty to thirty feet. About half way between the present plazas of the Cathedral and Santa Ana the wall turned inward with a great frowning bastion at each corner and crossed the Isthmus. A moat was dug on its landward side, shutting off all communication with the mainland save over the draw-

BOYS SKATING ON SEA WALL

bridge and through the sally-port on the line of the Avenida Centrale. With drawbridge up and sally-port closed the old town was effectually shut off from attack by land, while its guns on the landward wall effectually commanded the broad plain

grassy, and broad enough for a tennis court full thirty feet above the level of the town. The construction was not unlike that of the center walls of the locks designed by the best American engineers. Two parallel walls of masonry were built, about

VAULTS IN THE PANAMA CEMETERY

The small sepulchres are rented for a specified time, usually three years. Unless the lease is then renewed the bones of the tenant are cast out into a common pile.

on which now stands the upper part of the town, and the declivities of Ancon Hill where now are the buildings of the Zone hospital and the Tivoli Hotel.

A good bit of construction and of military engineering was the wall of Panama—our own engineers on the Canal have done no better. Round the corner from La Mercedes Church a salient bastion crops out among fragile frame tenements and jerry-built structures. The angle is as sharp as though the storms of two and a half centuries had not broken over it. Climb it and you will find the top level,

forty to fifty feet apart and the space between filled in with dirt, packed solidly. On this part of the wall were no bomb proofs, chambers or dungeons. The guns were mounted *en barbette*, on the very top of the wall and discharged through embrasures in the parapet. Rather let it be said that they were to have been fired, for the new Panama was built after the plague of the pirates had passed and the bane of the buccaneers was abated. No foe ever assaulted the city from its landward side. In the frequent revolutions the contending parties were

RUINS OF SAN DOMINGO CHURCH

the great open café of the historic Hotel Centrale at one side has a distinctly foreign flavor. Here as one sits in the open listening to the native band and sipping a drink—softer, if one be wise, than that the natives thrive upon—and watches the native girls of every shade and in gayest dress driving or loitering past, one feels far from the bustling North American world, far from that snap and ginger and hustle on which Americans pride themselves. And then perhaps the music is suddenly punctuated by heavy dull "booms", like a distant cannonade, and one knows that only a few miles away dynamite is rending rock and man is grappling fiercely with nature.

already within the town and did their fighting in its streets, the old walls serving no more useful purpose than the ropes which define a prize ring. Only the sea-wall has heard the thunder of cannon in deadly conflict. There during the brief revolution which gave the United States the whip hand in Panama a Colombian gunboat did indeed make a pretense of shelling the city, but was driven away by machine guns mounted on the wall.

Within the walls, or the portion of the town the walls once surrounded, live the older families of native Panamanians, or those of foreign birth who have lived so long upon the Isthmus as to become identified with its life. The edifices along the streets are more substantial, the shops more dignified than in the newer quarter without. There are few, if any, frame structures and these evidently patched in where some fire has swept away more substantial predecessors. This part of Panama is reminiscent of many small towns of Spain or Portugal. The galleries nod at each other across streets too narrow to admit the burning sun, or to permit the passage of more than one vehicle at a time. The older churches, or their ruins, diversify the city streets, and the Cathedral Plaza in the very center with

Carnival occupies the four days preceding Ash Wednesday, the period known in all Catholic countries as the Mardi Gras. For years its gaiety has been preceded by a vigorous political contest for the high honor of being Queen of the Carnival, though it is said that in later years this rivalry has been less determined than of yore. At one time, however, it was contended for as strenuously as though the presidency of the republic was at stake and the two political parties—liberal and conservative—made it as much a stake of political activity as though the destiny of the State was involved. Happy the young woman who had a father able and willing to foot the bills, for no corrupt practices act intervened to save candidates from the wiles of the campaign grafter, or to guard the integrity of the voter from the insidious temptations of the man with a barrel.

It would be chivalric to say that the one issue in the campaign is the beauty of the respective candidates, but alas for a mercenary age! The sordid spirit of commercialism has crept in and the Panamanian papa must look upon the ambitions of his beauteous daughter as almost as expensive as a six cylinder automobile, a trip to Europe, or a yearning for a titled husband. But sometimes there are compensations. It is whispered that for one in retail trade in a large way it is no bad adver-

tisement to have a Carnival Queen for a daughter.

We have tried carnivals in various of our more cold-blooded American cities, but we cannot get

SOME CARNIVAL FLOATS
In the car shown in the upper right-hand corner is the Queen of the Carnival of 1913

THE ANCIENT CATHEDRAL

Its towers have looked down on carnival, revolution, revelry and riot

of ebony. The noise of innumerable horns and rattles rises to Heaven and reverberates in the narrow streets, while the bells jangle out of tune, as is their custom. Oh, those bells of Panama! Never were so many peals and chimes out of harmony. Stedman, who heard them only in an ordinary moment, not in their Mardi Gras madness, put them to verse thus:

"Loudly the cracked bells overhead
    Of San Francisco ding
With Santa Ana, La Merced,
    Felipe answering.
Banged all at once, and four times four
Morn, noon and night the more and more,
Clatter and clang with huge uproar,
    The bells of Panama".

Señoritas of sundry shades look down sweetly from the balconies, and shower confetti on gallant caballeros who stalk along as giant chanticleers, or strive to entangle in parti-colored tapes the lances of a gay party of toreadors. At night some of the women enmesh giant fireflies in their raven locks with flashing effect. King License rules supreme, and some of the horseplay even in the brightly lighted cafés of the Centrale and Metropolitan rather transcends the limits of coldly descriptive prose. The natives will tell you that the Cathedral Plaza is the center of propriety; the Plaza Santa Ana a trifle risqué. After observation and a return at daybreak from the carnival balls held at the Centrale and Metropolitan Hotels you can meditate at your leisure upon the precise significance of the word propriety in Panama at Mardi Gras.

The clause in the treaty which grants to the United States authority to maintain order in the

the spirit. Our floats are more artistic and expensive, our decorations are more lavish, but we sit and view the parade with detached calmness as though the revelers were hired clowns. In Panama everybody joins in the sport. The line of carriages around the park in the Plaza Centrale, thence by the Avenida to the Plaza Santa Ana and back is unbroken. The confetti falls like a January snow and the streets are ankle deep. Everyone is in mask and you can never tell whether the languishing eyes peering out upon you are set in a face of pearl or

THE POLICE STATION, PANAMA

If there is any regulation of the liquor traffic in Panama, it is not apparent to the casual observer. Nowhere does one see so much drinking, and nowhere that people drink at all is there less drunkenness. It is a curious fact that these two phenomena—wide-open drinking places and little drunkenness—are often found together. In Panama the saloons are legion, and I regret to say the biggest of them are run by Americans. No screens obstruct a full view of the interiors, and hardened tipplers flaunt their vice in the faces of all beholders. Perhaps the very publicity impels them to quit before they are hopelessly befuddled. Possibly the moist and somewhat debilitating climate permits the innocuous use of stimulants to a greater extent than would be possible in the North. Beside the absence of any scandalous open drunkenness there seems to be some significance in the fact that the records of the Zone hospitals show a surprisingly small number of deaths from diseases induced by chronic alcoholism. But the casual observer strolling on Avenida Centrale, or along the streets tributary to it, might be excused for thinking Panama one great grog shop. It is curious, too, that despite

Republic might very readily be stretched to include police power over Panama. This has not been done however and the city has its own police force, an exceedingly numerous one for a town of its size. Undoubtedly, however, diplomatic representations from the United States have caused the Panamanians to put their police regulations somewhat in accord with North American ideas. There are no more bull fights—"We never had very good bull-fights anyway", said a Panama gentleman plaintively acquiescing in this reform. Cock-fights however flourish and form, with the lottery drawing, the chief Sunday diversion. A pretty dismal spectacle it is, too, with two attenuated birds, often covered with blood and half sightless, striking fiercely at each other with long steel spurs, while a crowd of a hundred or so, blacks and whites, indiscriminately yell encouragement and shriek for bets from the surrounding arena. The betting in fact is the real support of the game. The Jamaicans particularly have their favorite cocks and will wager a week's pay on their favorites and all of their wives' laundry earnings they can lay hands upon as well. One or two gamecocks tethered by the leg are as common a sight about a Jamaican's hut as "houn' dawgs" around a Missouri cabin.

CHURCH OF OUR LADY OF MERCY (LA MERCED)

YOUNG AMERICA ON PANAMA BEACH

merchants, who are the chief retail dealers in the tropics, compel respect. They live cleanly, are capable business men, show none of the sloth and indifference of the natives, and seem to prosper everywhere. The Chinese market gardens in the outskirts of Panama are a positive relief for the neatness of their trim rows of timely plants. The Panamanian eats yams and grumbles that the soil will grow nothing else; the Chinaman makes it produce practically all the vegetables that grow in our northern gardens.

the Latin character of the populace the taste for light wines, in which some see the hope of national temperance, does not seem general. Whisky, brandy and rum are the regular tipples. On a still remembered night in Panama, before the American invasion, the Centrale Hotel bar was made free to all. No drinks were served to the thirsty, but to all who appeared a bottle was given and the line marched past for some hours. Yet, even at that, there was no considerable drunkenness observed. Apparently for the Panamanians drink is not a hopeless evil, but to the soldiers and marines of the United States stationed on the Isthmus and denied the rational social life of a well-regulated canteen the open doors of the saloons of Panama are as the open doors to a hotter spot. Their more strenuous temperaments will not stand the stimulant which leaves a Panamanian as stolid as before. The fatal riot of July 4, 1912, is one illustration of what Panama saloon hospitality may do with the men who wear the khaki.

Shopping in Panama is a decidedly cosmopolitan enterprise. The shopkeeper of whom I bought a Panama hat, made in Ecuador, did business under a Spanish name, was in fact a Genoese and when he found I could speak neither Spanish nor Italian coaxed me up to his price in French. Most of the retail prices are of so elastic a sort that when you have beaten them down two-thirds you retire with your package perfectly confident that they would have stood another cut. Nevertheless the Chinese

Avenida Centrale ends its arterial course at the sea wall of the city, or at least at that part of the sea wall which is the best preserved and retains most of its old-time dignity. It is here something like the Battery at Charleston, S. C., though the houses fringing it are not of a like stateliness, and the aristocracy of the quarter is somewhat tempered by the fact that here, too, is the city prison. Into the courtyards of this calaboose you can gaze from sundry little sentry boxes, the little sentries in which seem ever ready to step out to let the tourist step in and afterward pose for his camera, with rifle, fixed bayonet and an even more fixed expression. The

READY TO CONTROL THE PACIFIC

greater part of one of the prison yards is given over to flower beds, and though sunken some twenty feet or more below the crest of the wall, is thoughtfully provided with such half-way stations in the way of lean-to sheds, ladders and water butts that there seems to be no reason why any prisoner should stay in who wants to get out. But perhaps they don't often yearn for liberty. A wire fence cuts off the woman's section of the jail and the several native women I observed flirting assiduously with desperate male malefactors from whom they were separated only by this fence, seemed content with their lot, and evidently helped to cultivate like resignation in the breasts of their dark adorers. A white-clad guard, machete at side and heavy pistol at belt, walks among them jingling a heavy bunch of keys authoritatively but offering no interruption to their tender interludes.

On the other side of the row of frame quarters by which the prison yard is bisected you can see at the normal hours the prisoners taking their meals at a long table in the open air. Over the parapet of the sea wall above, an equally long row of tourists is generally leveling cameras, and sometimes exchanging lively badinage with some criminal who objects to figuring in this amateur rogues' gallery. To the casual spectator it all savors of opera bouffe, but there are stories a-plenty that the Panama jail has had its share of brutal cruelty as have most places wherein men are locked away from sight and subject to the whims of others not so very much their superiors. Once the Chiriqui Prison was a fortress, the bank of quarters for the prisoners formed the barracks, and the deep archways under the sea wall were dungeons oft populated by political prisoners. Miasma, damp and the brutality of jailers have many a time brought to occupants of those dungeons their final discharge, and a patch of wall near by, with the bricks significantly chipped, is pointed out as the place where others have been from time to time stood up in front of a firing squad at too short a range for misses. The Latin-American lust for blood has had its manifestations in Panama, and the old prison has doubtless housed its share of martyrs.

But one thinks little of the grimmer history of the Chiriqui Prison, looking down upon the bright flower beds, and the gay quadroon girls flirting with some desperate character who is perhaps "in" for a too liberal indulgence in rum last pay day. Indeed

THE FLOWERY CHIRIQUI PRISON

Where native women prisoners may flirt without interruption with male malefactors, separated only by a wire fence

Photo by Underwood & Underwood

THE MARKET FOR SHELL FISH

The black spots on the roof are vultures, the official scavengers

the guard wards off more sanguinary reminiscences by telling you that they used to hold bull baitings— a milder form of bull-fight—in the yard that the captives in the dungeons might witness the sport, and perhaps envy the bull, *quien sabe?*

The present town of Panama does not impress one with the air of being the scene of dark crimes of covetousness, lust and hate. Its police system, viewed superficially, is effective and most of the malefactors in the Chiriqui Jail are there for trivial offenses only. One crime of a few years ago however bids fair to become historic. One of the banks in the town was well known to be the repository of

the funds needed for the payroll of the Canal force. It was the policy of the Commission to pay off as much as possible in gold and silver, and to a very great extent in coins of comparatively small denomination in order to keep it on the Zone. The money paid out on pay drafts comes swiftly back through the Commissary to the banks which accordingly accumulate a very considerable stock of ready cash as a subsequent pay day approaches. Now the banks of Panama do not seem to even the casual observer as strongholds, and probably to the professional cracksman they are positive invitations to enterprise. Accordingly, three men, only one of whom had any criminal record or was in any sense an habitué of the underworld, set about breaking into one of the principal banks. They laid their plans with deliberation and conducted their operations with due regard for their personal comfort. Their plan was to tunnel into the bank from an adjoining building, in which they set up a bogus contracting business to account for the odds and ends of machinery and implements they had about. The tunnel being dark they strung electric lights in it. Being hot, under that tropic air, they installed electric fans. All the comforts of a burglar's home were there.

From a strictly professional standpoint they made not a single blunder. Their one error—almost a fatal one—was in not being good churchmen. For they had planned to enter the bank late on a Saturday night. Tuesday was to be pay day and on Monday the full amount of the pay roll would be drawn out. But Saturday night it would all be there —several hundred thousand dollars—and they would have all day Sunday to pack it securely and make their getaway. Midnight, then, saw them creeping run-away child Panama, and no extradition treaty could have been appealed to by the Panamanians against their despoilers. As it was they quarreled over the booty. One of the three was killed; the other two were arrested for the murder, but soon went free. Their complete immunity from prosecution calls attention to the fact that a few hours' trip in a motor boat will take any one guilty of crime in Panama to a land where he will be wholly free from punishment.

Churches in Panama, or the ruins of them, are

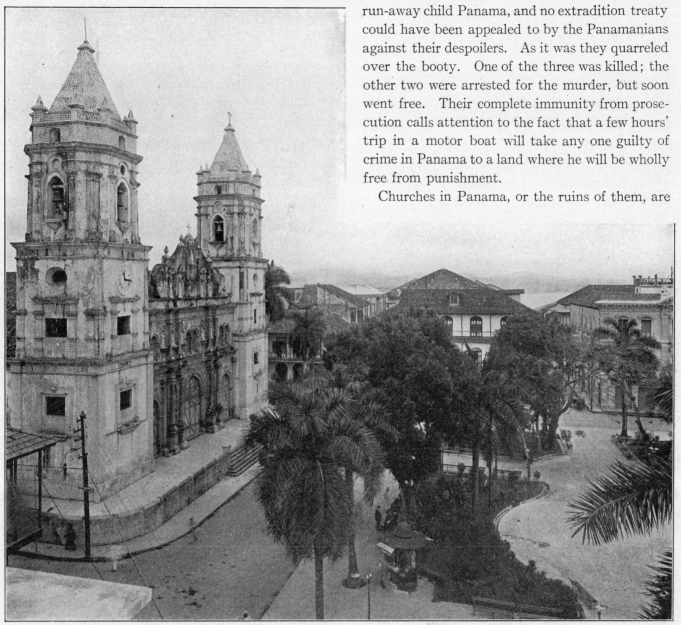

THE CATHEDRAL AND PLAZA

into the bank. The safe yielded readily to their assaults, but it disgorged only a beggarly $30,000 or so. What could be the trouble? Just then the knowledge dawned on the disappointed bandits that Monday was a Saint's day, the bank would be closed, therefore the prudent Zone paymaster had drawn his funds on Saturday. The joke was on the cracksmen.

With the comparatively few thousands they had accumulated the disappointed outlaws took a motor boat and made for Colombia. Had they secured the loot they expected they would have been made welcome there, for Colombia does not recognize her

many, and while not beautiful are interesting. Everybody goes to see the famous flat arch of the San Domingo Church, and its disappearance will be a sore blow to guides and post-card dealers. Aside from its curious architectural quality the arch derives interest from a legend of its construction by a pious monk. Twice it fell before the mortar had time to set. The third time its designer brought a stool and sat himself down below the heavy keystone. "If it falls", he said, "I go with it". But that time the arch stood firm, and it has withstood the assaults of centuries to come at last to the ignoble end of incorporation in a tenement house.

IN A PANAMA PARK

The arch, which certainly looks unstable, is often pointed to as an evidence of the slight peril on the Isthmus from earthquake shocks. Such convulsions of nature are indeed not unknown but are usually feeble. That great shock that overthrew San Francisco was not even registered by the seismograph on the Canal zone.

Practically all the churches are of the same plan—two towers at the front corners with the façade built between. The towers of the Cathedral rise high above the roof and the tapering steeples are covered with slabs of mother-of-pearl, which make a brave spectacle from the bay when the rosy rays of the setting sun play upon them. Within all the churches are poor and barren of ornament. They have been stripped of their funds by various authorities beginning with Spain itself, one of the Spanish generals in the revolutionary days having seized all the available funds to pay for transportation for his army. Perhaps the church resented this, for in later days it voluntarily contributed largely out of its remaining treasure to the revolutionary cause. Later still its gold and silver ornaments and altar pieces were confiscated by some faction temporarily in power. Indeed the church has been the football of politics, always entangled with the State and thus far suffering in prestige and pocket by the association.

The Cathedral owes its completion to a negro

SALVATION ARMY IN PANAMA

bishop, the son of a charcoal burner who had determined that his boy should rise to higher station. By hard study the lad secured admittance to the priesthood and ultimately rose to be Bishop of Panama, the first native to fill that post. Out of his own salary he paid much of the cost of building the great church, the corner-stone of which had been laid when the city was founded, and by his zeal in soliciting funds secured its completion.

A systematic tour of the churches of Panama is well worth the visitor's time. More that is curious will be found than there is of the beautiful, and to the former class I am inclined to consign a much begrimed painting in the Cathedral which tradition declares to be a Murillo. Perhaps more interesting than the Cathedral is the Church of San Francisco, in the Plaza Bolivar. The present structure dates back only to 1785, two former edifices on the same site having been burned. The ruins of the beautiful cloister of the Franciscan convent adjoin it, but are concealed from view by an unsightly board fence which the tourist, not having a guide, will not think of passing through. The ruins, however, are well worth seeing.

Clubs share with churches in the social life of Panama. Perhaps indeed they rather outshine the latter. At any rate such buildings as the Union Club and the University Club, both of which abut upon the bay would be a credit to a city twice the

COSTUME DE RIGUEUR FOR FEBRUARY

size. The former club, as its name implies, was intended to be a meeting place where liberals and conservatives could lay aside political differences in social unity. However, politics in Panama, as in all places where there are not real vital issues dividing the parties, breeds bitter personal feeling and the Union Club is said to be far from being the home of political unity. It has, however, an excellent building, with a spacious ball-room, a swimming tank and a magnificent view of Panama Bay with its picturesque islands. The University Club is more an American club than a Panamanian, and it no longer observes the restriction as to membership which its name would imply. It too has a spacious ball-room and is a social center for the Zone dwellers who form the major part of its membership.

The Cathedral Plaza is socially the center of town, though geographically the old French Plaza of Santa Ana is more near the center. Directly opposite the Cathedral is the Hotel Centrale, built after the Spanish fashion, with four stories around a central court. In the blither days of the French régime this court was the scene of a revelry to which the daily death roll formed a grim contrast. However the occasional gaiety of the Centrale Patio

did not end with the French. Even in the prosaic Yankee days of the last carnival the intervention of the police was necessary to prevent a gentleman from being wholly denuded, and displayed to the revelers in nature's garb as a specimen of the superior products of Panama.

On a nearby corner of the Plaza is the old French administration building, afterward occupied by the Isthmian Canal Commission. In 1905 it was a central point of infection for the yellow-fever epidemic, and though repeatedly fumigated was finally abandoned by the American engineers who moved their headquarters out to Culebra.

Life in Panama City is mainly outdoor life, in the dry season at any rate, and even in the wet season the Panamanians move about in the open like a lot of damp and discontented flies. The almost continuous line of balconies shields the sidewalks from the rain, and nobody in Panama is too busy to stop a half hour or so at street crossings for the downpour to lessen. Sunday nights the band of the Republic plays in the Plaza, and there all the people of the town congregate to listen to the music, promenade and chat. It is the scene of that curious Latin-American courtship which consists of following the adored one with

Photo by Underwood & Underwood

BUST OF LIEUT. NAPOLEON B. WYSE

This bust stands on the sea wall. The picture shows it guarded by a United States soldier and a Panama policeman appealing eyes, but never by any possibility speaking to her. The procession of girls and women is worth watching, whether the eyes be adoring or not, and the costumes have a sort of strangeness befitting the scene. The practice has grown up of leaving the outer walk for the negro and negroid people, the inner paths being kept for the whites—but as the walks merge into each other so too do the

ON PANAMA'S BATHING BEACH

colors. If one wearies of the moving crowds without, a step will bring him into the patio of the Hotel Centrale where an excellent orchestra plays, and a gathering chiefly native sips tropical drinks and disposes of the political issues of the day with much oratory and gesticulation.

As you make your way back to the hotel at night — if it is after eleven, the driver will lawfully charge you twenty cents—you will vainly try to recall any North American town of 40,000 people which can present so many objects of interests to the visitor,

lent as Wall Street after dark. But in a more sequestered section of the town, where the public hospital looks down significantly on the spectacle from one side, and the cemeteries show sinister on the other, revelry goes on apace until the cool dawn arises. There the clatter of pianolas which have felt the climate sorely mingles with the clink of glasses in cantinas that never close, and the laughter of lips to which, in public at least, laughter is a professional necessity. Under the red lights at midnight Panama shows its worst. Men of varied voyages, familiar with the slums of Singapore and the purlieus of Paris declare that this little city of a hybrid civilization outdoes them in all that makes up the fevered life of the underworld. Scarcely a minute's walk away is the American town, quiet and restful under the tropic moon, its winding streets well guarded by the Zone police, its houses wrapped in vines and fragrant with flowers all dark in the

Photo by Underwood & Underwood

QUARANTINE STATION AT PACIFIC ENTRANCE TO CANAL

and a spectacle of social life so varied, so cosmopolitan and so pleasing.

The night life of the streets is as a rule placid, however, rather than boisterous, nor is Panama an "all night town". The rule of the tropics is "early to rise" in any event and as a result those parts of the city which the visitor sees usually quiet down by midnight and presently thereafter the regions about the Cathedral Plaza are as quiet and somno-

hours of repose. But in the congested tangle of concrete houses between the hospitals and the cemetery madness and mirth reign, brains reel with the fumes of the strange drinks of the tropics, and life is worth a passing pleasure—nothing more. Men of many lands have cursed the Chagres fever and the jungle's ills, but the pest place of Panama has been subjected to no purging process with all the efforts of the United States to banish evil from the Isthmus.

CHAPTER XIV

THE SANITATION OF THE ZONE

THE seal of the Canal Zone shows a galleon under full sail passing between the towering banks of the Culebra Cut, with the motto, "The land divided; the world united". Sometimes as I trudged about the streets of Colon or Panama, or over the hills and through the jungle in the Zone, I have thought a more significant coat-of-arms might be made up of a garbage can rampant and a gigantic mosquito mordant—for verily by the collection and careful covering of filth and the slaughter of the pestilential mosquito all the work done on the Zone has been made possible. As for the motto how would this do—"A clean country and a salubrious strait"?

It is the universal opinion of those familiar with the Canal work that if we had approached the task with the lack of sanitary knowledge from which the French suffered we should have failed as they did. No evil known to man inspires such dread as yellow fever. Leprosy, in the individual, does indeed, although well-informed people know that it is not readily communicated and never becomes epidemic. Cholera did strike the heart of man with cold dread, but more than one generation has passed since cholera was an evil to be reckoned with in civilized countries. Yellow fever is now to be classed with it as an epidemic disease, the spread of which can be absolutely and unerringly controlled.

The demonstrated fact that yellow fever is transmitted only by the bite of a *stegomyia* mosquito which has already bitten, and been infected by, a human being sick of the fever has become one of the commonplaces of sanitary science. Yet that knowledge dates back comparatively few years, and

COL. W. C. GORGAS

The man who changed the Isthmus from a pest-hole to a spot as fit for human habitation as any place on the globe

253

Photo by Underwood & Underwood

WHAT COL. GORGAS HAD TO CORRECT

prise became apparent, rivalry for the prime honor grew up between the followers of the two chief figures, Col. Goethals and Col. Gorgas. That either of these gentlemen shared in this feeling is not asserted, but their friends divided the Isthmus into two hostile camps. Rivalry of this sort was unfortunate and needless. In the words of Admiral Schley after the battle of Santiago: "There was glory enough for all". But the result was to decry and to depreciate the work of Col. Gorgas in making the Isthmus habitable. As a matter of fact no historian will for one moment hesitate to state that only by that work was it made possible to dig the Canal at all. Col. Goethals himself in his moments of deepest doubt as to the

was not available to mankind at the time the French began their struggle with tropical nature. Over the honor of first discovering the fact of the malignant part played by the mosquito there has been some conflict, but credit is generally given to Dr. Donald Ross, a Scotchman in the Indian Civil Service. His investigations however were greatly extended and practical effect given to them by surgeons in the United States Army engaged in the work of eliminating pestilence from Havana. To Majors Walter Reed, Jesse W. Lazear and Carroll the chief credit is due for testing, proving and applying the theory in Havana. Lazear bravely gave up his life to the experiment, baring his arm to the bite of a mosquito, and dying afterward of yellow fever in terrible agony.

The fact of this earlier application of the mosquito theory does not in the slightest degree detract from the great honor due to Col. W. C. Gorgas for his work in changing the Isthmus of Panama from a pest-hole into a spot as fit for human habitation as any spot on the globe. Unfortunately, as the impending success of the Canal enter-

size of the appropriations for sanitation purposes would hardly question that statement. That some other man than Gorgas might have done the work with the experience of the French and the discovery of the malignant quality of the mosquito to guide him is undoubtedly true. That some other man than Goethals might have dug the Canal with the experience of two earlier engineers, as well as of the French to serve as warnings, is equally true. But these two finished the work and to each pertains the glory for his part.

ADMINISTRATION BUILDING, HOUSING THE SANITARY DEPARTMENT

Col. Gorgas first visited the Isthmus in 1904. In a little pamphlet which I have before me he then described simply the essence of the problem he had to meet. He found camped on a hill, perfectly drained and supplied with good water, 450 marines—who of course were men of exceptionally good physique, robust and vigorous. Yet in four months 170 out of the 450 were infected with malaria, and Col. Gorgas said, "if these men were our laborers, working daily in Culebra Cut, exposed to the sun and weather, many of these cases would

is partial to malaria—which had already bitten an infected negro. The result was the spread of the infection among the marines. As Col. Gorgas put it, "The condition is very much the same as if these four or five hundred natives had the smallpox and our marines had never been vaccinated". To correct this condition he proposed, "to take this village, put it under a systematic scheme of inspection, whereby we will be able to control all water barrels and deposits of water, so that no mosquitoes

DREDGING A COLON STREET

So near tide level is the surface of Colon that the dredges made canals in the public streets

be severe in type and at the end of the year we would be approaching the mortality of the French". The cause for the infection was apparent. Though the marines' camp was clean and sanitary there was at the foot of the hill, on which it was perched, a village of 400 or 500 Jamaica negroes. Examination of the people showed that all suffered from chronic malaria. The marine strolling in the village would be bitten by a mosquito—the *anopheles* which

will be allowed to breed, look after its street cleaning and disposal of night soil, etc., so as to get it in good sanitary condition, then have the population examined and recorded, so that we will have on a card a short history of each individual and keep track of them in this way. Those suffering from malaria will be put under treatment, and watched as long as the malarial parasite is found in the blood. I hope, in this way, to decrease to the smallest

THE WAR ON MOSQUITOES. I.
The men are oiling the surface of the streams to kill the larvae

an average force of 10,200 men employed, lost in nine years 22,189 men. We with an average force of 33,000 lost less than 4000 in about an equal period.

When Col. Gorgas came to the Isthmus the two towns Panama and Colon were well fitted to be breeding places for pestilence. Neither had sewers nor any drainage system. The streets of Panama were paved after a fashion with cobblestones and lined with gutters through which the liquid refuse of the town trickled slowly or stood still to fester and grow putrescent under the glowing rays of the tropic sun. Colon had no pavement whatsoever. Neither town had waterworks and the people gathered and stored rainwater in cisterns and pottery jars which afforded fine

limit the number of *anopheles*, the malarial-bearing mosquito, and, at the same time, to gradually eliminate the human being as a source of infection, so that at the end of a year it will be entirely safe for an unacclimated man to live in this village".

Being appointed Chief Sanitary Officer Col. Gorgas put this plan into effect not only in that village but in every part of the Canal Zone, particular attention being given to the cities of Panama and Colon. In these cities the visitor will be impressed with the comparative cleanliness of the streets and sidewalks and the covering of all garbage receptacles. No other Central American city shows so cleanly a front. Screening, however, is little in evidence. How great the mortality had been under the French it is impossible to tell. Their statistics related almost wholly to deaths in their hospitals and very largely to white patients. Men who died out on the line, natives who worked a day or two and went back to their villages to die were left unrecorded. In the hospitals it was recorded that between 1881 and 1889, 5618 employees died. The contractors were charged a dollar a day for every man sent to the hospitals, so it may be conjectured that not all were sent who should have been. Col. Gorgas estimates the average death rate at about 240 per 1000 annually. The American general death rate began with a maximum of 49.94 per 1000 sinking to 21.18, at or about which point it has remained for several years. Among employees alone our death rate was 7.50 per 1000. The French with

THE WAR ON MOSQUITOES. II.
Burning the grass that affords cover

PANAMA BAY FROM ANCON HOSPITAL

There are few more beautiful spots in the world than the grounds of Ancon Hospital. French taste selected the site, a French nun set out the first trees and shrubs, and nature has completed a charming picture.

breeding places for the mosquito. As a matter of fact, the whole Isthmus, not the towns alone, furnishes plenty of homes for the mosquito. With a rainy season lasting throughout eight months in the year much of the soil is waterlogged. The stagnant back waters of small streams; pools left by the rains; the footprints of cows and other animals filled up with rain water quickly breed the wrigglers that ultimately become mosquitoes. Mr. A. H. Jennings, the entomologist of the Commission, has identified 125 varieties of the mosquito, of which, however, the *anopheles* and the *stegomyia* are the ones peculiarly obnoxious to man. The others are merely the common or summer resort variety of mosquito with a fondness for ankles and the back of one's hand, which can be observed any time on Long Island or in New Jersey without the expense of a trip to Panama. A careful study of literary authorities indicates to me that at this point in the description of the mosquito plague on the Isthmus it is proper to indulge in humorous reflections upon the fact that the bite of the female only is dangerous. But, given the fact, the humorous applications seem so obvious that the reader may be trusted to draw them for himself—it would be idle to say "herself", for the women will not see anything humorous about it at all.

The fight then against disease on the Isthmus resolved itself largely into a war of extermination upon the two noxious varieties of mosquitoes. It involved first a cleaning up, paving and draining of the two towns. Curiously enough bad smells are not necessarily unhygienic, but they betoken the existence of matter that breeds disease germs, and flies and other insects distribute those germs where they will do the most harm. Colon and Panama therefore were paved and provided with sewage systems, while somewhat stringent ordinances checked the pleasant Panama practice of emptying all slops from the front gallery into the street. It is fair to the Panamanians to note that in the end they will pay for the vigorous cleaning and refurbishing of their towns by the Americans. Our sanitary forces did the work and did it well, by virtue of the clause in the treaty which grants the United States authority to prosecute such work in the two cities and collect from

THE WAR ON MOSQUITOES. III.
Spraying the brooks with larvacide

Photo by Underwood & Underwood

THE WAR ON MOSQUITOES. IV.
Cutting down brush which will later be burned thus destroying mosquito covert

SANITARY WORK IN A VILLAGE

The scene is in the outskirts of Culebra, now a model of cleanliness

fever anyway, and to some extent from malaria as well, so to their minds the whole thing was an imposition by which the Americans alone would profit. If the gringoes weren't able to live in Panama without smoking people out of house and home, they had better stay away was the generally expressed public opinion of Panama.

Here the peculiar personality of Col. Gorgas came into play. Had that gentleman not been a great health officer he would have made a no-

the householder its cost by means of water and sewage rates.

This work was completed in 1908 and the final report of the Division of Municipal Engineering which conducted it showed that nearly $6,000,000 had been expended, of which about $2,250,000 was for pavements, sewers and waterworks in the two cities, and about $3,500,000 for work in the Canal Zone. Nearly a million more was subsequently expended in the towns.

The first thing to do with the towns was to fumigate them. The Panamanians did not like this. Neither would we or any other people for that matter, for the process of fumigating necessarily interrupts the routine of life, invades domestic privacy, inevitably causes some loss by the discoloring of fabrics, interrupts trade in the case of stores and is in general an infernal nuisance. That much any people will say against wholesale fumigation. But to the Panamanians it was peculiarly offensive because they were immune from yellow

table diplomat, particularly in these new days when tact and charm of manner are considered more essential to an American diplomat than dollars. He went among the people of the two towns, argued, jollied and cajoled them until a work which it was thought might have to be accomplished at the point of the bayonet was finished with but little friction. The bayonet was always in the background, however, for the treaty gives the United States unqualified authority to enforce its sanitary ordinances in the cities of Colon and Panama. We can send a regiment if necessary to compel a man to keep his yard clean—which is perhaps more than we could do in some benighted towns of our own United States.

The tone of the man in the street toward these American innovations is partly surly, partly jocular. In Panama he will show you a very considerable section of the town which is not yet fully rebuilt and insist that the fire which started it was caused by the "fool fumigators". There is some difference of opinion as to the origin of this blaze, and the matter of damages is, as I write, in the hands of arbitrators, but the native opinion is solidly against the fumigating torch bearers. On the subject of the extermination of mosquitoes the native is always humorous. He will describe to you Col. Gorgas's trained bloodhounds and Old Sleuths tracking the criminal *stegomyia* to his lair; the corps of bearers of machetes and chloroform who follow to put an end to the malevolent mosquito's days; the scientist with the high-powered microscope who examines the remains and, if he finds the deceased carried germs, the wide search made for individuals whom he may have bitten that they may be segregated and put under proper treatment.

In reality there is a certain humor in this scientific bug hunting. You are at afternoon tea with a hostess in one of the charming tropical houses which the Commission supplies to its workers. The eyes of your hostess suddenly become fixed in a terrified gaze.

"Goodness gracious"! she exclaims, "look there"!

"What? where"? you cry, bounding from your

Photo by Dr. Orenstein
THE MOSQUITO CHLOROFORMER AT WORK
Once subdued by chloroform the mosquito is removed for analysis

seat in excitement. Perhaps a blast has just boomed on the circumambient air and you have visions of a fifty-pound rock about to fly through the drawing-room window. Life on the Zone abounds in such incidents.

"There"! dramatically. "That mosquito"!

"I'll swat it", you cry valorously, remembering the slogan of "Swat the Fly" which breaks forth recurrently in our newspapers every spring, though they are quite calm and unperturbed about the places which breed flies faster than they can be swatted.

"Goodness, no. I must telephone the department".

Speechless with amazement you wonder if the police or fire department is to be called out to cope with this mosquito. In due time there appears an official equipped with an electric flash-light, a phial and a small bottle of chloroform. The malefactor—no, the suspect, for the *anopheles malefactor* does no evil despite his sinister name—is mercifully chloroformed and deposited in the phial for a later post mortem. With his flash-light the inspector

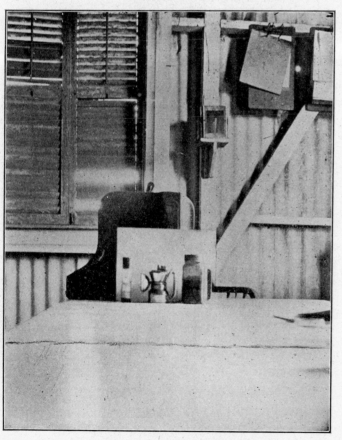

THE MOSQUITO CHLOROFORMER'S OUTFIT
Used in tracking the criminal *stegomyia* to his lair

ANCON HOSPITAL AS RECEIVED FROM THE FRENCH

the deceased, who was buried as speedily as possible, but the Sanitary Department did care about the source of his malady. Looking up his haunts it was discovered that he was much seen in company with an Italian. Thereupon all the Italians in town were interrogated; one declared he had seen the dead man in company with the man who tended bar at the theater. This worthy citizen was sought out and was discovered hiding away in a secluded lodging sick with yellow fever. Whereupon the theater was promptly fumigated as the center of infection.

Clearing up and keeping clean the two centers of population was, however, the least of the work of sanitation. The whole Isthmus was a breeding place for the mosquitoes. Obviously every foot of it could not be drained clear of pools and rivulets, but the preventive campaign of the sanitation men covered scores of square miles adjacent to villages and the Canal bed, and was marvelously effective in reducing the number of mosquitoes. Away from the towns the campaign was chiefly against the malarial mosquito—the *anophelinæ*. The yellow fever mosquito, the *stegomyia*, is a town-bred insect coming from cisterns, water pitchers, tin cans, fountains in the parks, water-filled pans used to keep ants from the legs of furniture and the like. It is even said to breed in the holy-water fonts of the multitudinous churches of Panama, and the sanitary officials secured the co-operation of the church authorities in having those receptacles kept fresh. The malarial mosquito however breeds in streams, marshes and pools and will travel sometimes

examines all the dark places of the house to seek for possible accomplices, and having learned that nobody has been bitten takes himself off.

It does seem a ridiculous amount of fuss about a mosquito, doesn't it? But since that sort of thing has been done on the Zone death carts no longer make their dismal rounds for the night's quota of the dead, and the ravages of malaria are no longer so general or so deadly as they were.

Nowadays there are no cases of yellow fever developing on the Zone, but in the earlier days when one did occur the sanitary officials set out to find the cause of infection. When the French seek to detect a criminal they follow the maxim "*Cherchez la femme*" (Look for the woman). When pursuing the yellow-fever germ to its source the Panama inspectors look for the *stegomyia* mosquito that bit the victim—which is a little reminiscent of hunting for a needle in a haystack.

A drunken man picked up on the street in Panama was taken to the hospital and there died of yellow fever. He was a stranger but his hotel was looked up and proved to be a native house occupied only by immunes, so that he could not have been infected there. Nobody seemed to care particularly about a mile and a half from his birth-place looking for trouble.

As you ride in a train across the Isthmus you will often see far from any human habitation a blackened barrel on a board crossing some little brook a few inches wide. If you have time to look carefully you will see that the edges of the gully through which the brook runs have been swept clear of grass by scythe or fire or both, and that the banks of the rivulet are blackened as though by a tar-brush while the water itself is covered by a black and greasy film.

This is one of the outposts of the army of health. Of them there are several hundred, perhaps thousands, scattered through the Zone. The barrel is filled with a certain fluid combination of oil and divers chemicals called larvacide. Day and night with monotonous regularity it falls drop by drop into the rivulet, spreads over its surface and is deposited on the pebbles on the banks. The mosquito larvæ below must come to the surface to breathe. There they meet with the noxious fluid and at the first breath are slain. Automatically this one barrel makes that stream a charnel house for mosquito larvæ. But up and down throughout the land go men with cans of the oil on their backs and sprinklers in their hands seeking for pools and stagnant puddles which they spray with the larvacide. So between the war on the larva at its breeding point and the system of screening off all residences, offices and eating places the malarial infection has been greatly reduced. It has not been

THE CANAL COMMISSION HOSPITAL AT COLON BUILT BY THE FRENCH

FRENCH VILLAGE OF EMPIRE AFTER CLEANING UP BY AMERICANS

ten suffer from occasional headaches, anemia or slight fever. These are the people most dangerous from the standpoint of the sanitarian. It is in the blood of these individuals that the malaria-causing parasite has attained the form in which, if taken by a female *anopheline*, it devel-

eradicated by any manner of means. The Panama cocktail (quinine) is still served with meals. In one year 2307.66 pounds of the drug were served out. But if not wholly obliterated the ailment has been greatly checked. Dr. A. J. Orenstein, of the Department of Sanitation, says in summing up the results of the policy:

"The campaign against malaria was inaugurated on the following plan: (1) Treatment with adequate doses of quinine (about 30 grains a day for adults) of all cases of malaria. First, because this treatment is curative; and, second, because unless so treated, each case of malaria constitutes a focus from which malaria spreads. In malarial regions there are many persons who have what is often spoken of as chronic malaria. Such individuals frequently do not suffer any serious inconvenience. They more of-

ops within this mosquito into the form capable of causing malaria in the individual whom the *anopheline* may bite a week or so thereafter. (2) Protecting dwelling with copper wire gauze against the ingress of mosquitoes. All houses occupied by Ameri-

THE BAY OF TABOGA FROM THE SANITARIUM

THE LITTLE PANGO BOATS COME TO MEET YOU

per cent of the working force per month in 1911, and the death from malaria among employees from 233 in 1906 to 47 in 1911".

"The malaria sick rate for 1906, if continued to 1911, would give, on the basis of the number of employees in 1911, about 40,000 cases of malaria sick in the hospitals for the year, or a loss in labor of about 200,000 days of work. The total number of employees sick in hospitals with malaria in 1911 was 8946—or a loss of 44,730 days of work. A gain of about 155,000 days was, therefore, made. Placing the loss to the Government for each day's labor,

cans and most of the others are screened. (3) Catching and killing mosquitoes within the dwellings. This is done by negro "mosquito catchers", and is of great value in preventing malaria where other prophylactic measures cannot be inaugurated. (4) Destroying the breeding places of *anophelinœ* by filling, draining, and training the banks of streams. (5) Destroying the *anophelinœ* in the larval and pupal stages by oiling the water in which they are found, or applying a special larva poison to this water. (6) Clearing the rank vegetation

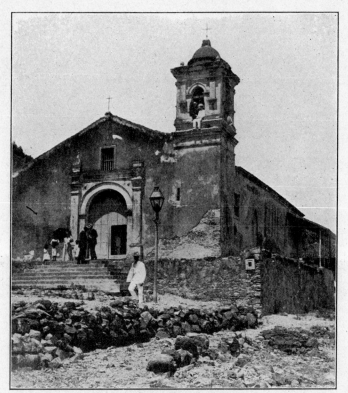

OLD CHURCH AT TABOGA
The square box on the corner of the wall contains the mummied head of a favorite priest

plus treatment, at the rather low figure of $3 per man, the gain in this one item of saving more than offset the cost of sanitation proper. These figures do not include malarial cases treated in the dispensaries and in homes. Among this class of patients the gain has undoubtedly been proportionate to the gain in hospital cases, and in addition it must not be forgotten that malaria is a disease that undermines a man's health insidiously and lowers his working efficiency to an extent not approached by any disease with the

in the immediate vicinity of dwellings and settlements, so as to destroy the shelter for such mosquitoes as may find their way to the vicinity of the houses; to hasten evaporation and the drying of small water collections and marshy places; to expose to view small breeding places and to remove the temptation to throw water containers into the vegetation.

"These measures, conscientiously and painstakingly carried out, resulted in reducing the number of malaria cases treated in the hospitals from 6.83 per cent of the working force per month in 1906 to 1.53

THE RIO GRANDE RESERVOIR

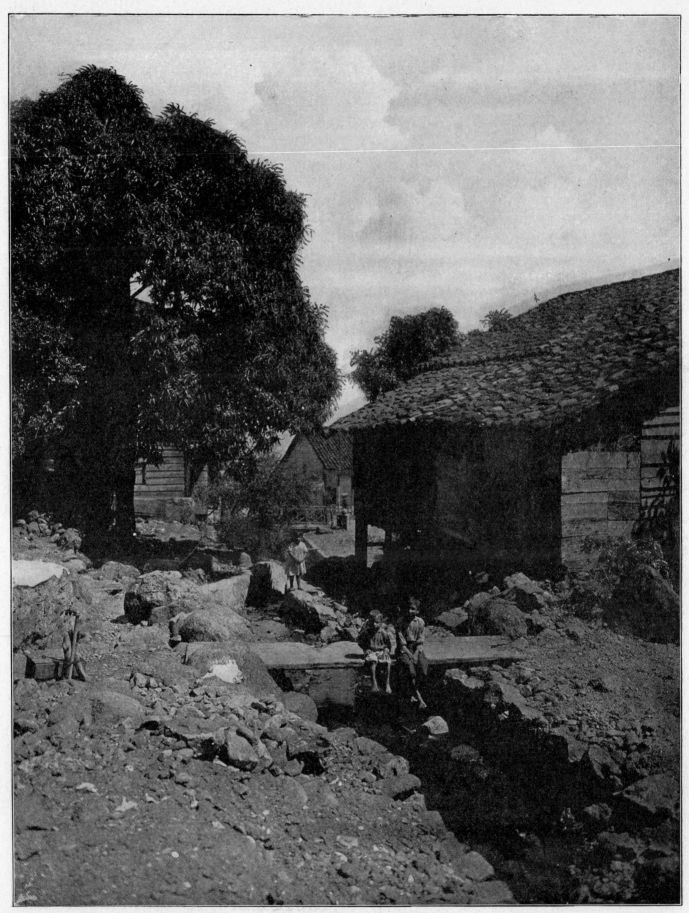

IN PICTURESQUE TABOGA

264

possible exception of hook-worm. The less malaria the fewer inefficient workers in an organization".

Of course the screening system was vital to any successful effort to control and check the transmission of fever germs by insects. But the early struggles of Col. Gorgas to get enough wire netting to properly protect the labor quarters were pathetic. "Why doesn't he screen in the whole Isthmus and let it go at that"? inquired one Congressman who thought it was all intended to put a few more frills on houses for already highly paid workers. The screening has indeed cost a pretty penny for only the best copper wire will stand the test of the climate. At first there was reluctance on the part of disbursing officers to meet the heavy requirements of Col. Gorgas. But the yellow-fever epidemic of 1905 stopped all that. Thereafter the screening was regarded as much of an integral part of a house as its shingling.

The efforts that were put forth to make the Canal Zone a liveable spot have not been relaxed in keeping it so. A glance at the report of the Chief Sanitary Officer for any year shows something of his continued activity. You find records of houses fumigated for beriberi, diphtheria, malaria, leprosy, and a dozen other evils. The number of rats killed is gravely enumerated—during the year 1911 for example there were nearly 13,000. It may be noted in passing that the rats distribute fleas and fleas carry the germs of the bubonic plague, hence the slaughter. Incidentally guests of the native hotels in Panama City say that the destruction was far from complete.

Two large hospitals are maintained by the Canal

Commission at Colon and at Ancon, together with smaller ones for emergency cases at Culebra and other points along the line. The two principal hospitals will be kept open after the completion of the Canal, but not of course to their full capacity.

IN THE GROUNDS OF ANCON HOSPITAL

Ancon alone has accommodations for more than 1500 patients, and when the army of labor has left the Zone there can be no possible demand for so great an infirmary. Both of these hospitals were inherited from the French, and the one at Colon has been left much in the condition they delivered it in, save for needed repairs and alterations. Its capacity has not been materially increased. The Ancon Hospital however has become one of the

THE SANITARIUM AT TABOGA INHERITED FROM THE FRENCH

upon by Col. Gorgas. Some of the doctors think that possibly it has been a wee bit overdone. Some of the folks along the Zone look on a brief space spent in the hospital as a pleasant interlude in an otherwise monotonous life. As they have thirty days' sick leave with pay every year they are quite prone to turn to the pleasant slopes of Ancon Hill, with a week at the charming sanitarium on Taboga Island as a fitting close— a sort of café parfait to top off the feast. Surgery even seems to have lost its terrors there. "Why, they even bring their friends to be operated on", said one of the surgeons laughingly when talking of the popularity of the hospital among the Zone dwellers.

Charity cases have numbered as many as 66,000 a year and the records show that during the period of greatest activity on the Zone as many as 70 different nationalities were ministered to. The question of color was often an embarrassing one. The gradations of shades between pure white to darkest African is so exceedingly delicate in Panama that there is always difficulty in determining whether the subject under consideration belongs to the "gold" or the "silver" class, for the words black and white

great institutions of its kind in the world. The French gave us a few buildings with over 300 patients sheltered in tents. The Americans developed this place until now more than fifty buildings are ranged along the side of Ancon Hill. When the French first established the hospital they installed as nurses a number of sisters of St. Vincent with Sister Rouleau as Sister Superior. The gentle sisters soon died. The yellow fever carried them off with heart-rending rapidity. Sister Marie however left a monument which will keep her fair fame alive for many years yet to come. She was a great lover of plants, and the luxuriance of the tropical foliage was to her a never-ending charm. To her early efforts is due the beauty of the grounds of the Ancon Hospital, where one looks between the stately trunks of the fronded royal palms past a hillside blazing with hibiscus, and cooled with the rustling of leaves of feather palms and plantains to where the blue Pacific lies smooth beneath the glowing tropic sun. Beside the beauty of its surroundings the hospital is eminently practical in its plan. The many separate buildings permit the segregation of cases, and the most complete and scientific ventilation.

Making the hospital attractive was one of the points insisted

A FETE DAY AT TABOGA

are tactfully avoided in the Zone in their reference to complexions. "This is my plan", said Col. Mason in charge of the hospital. "On certain days the patients are allowed visitors. When the color of the inmate is problematical, as is usually the case with women, I ask if she wants her husband to visit her. If she does and he proves to be a negro, she goes into the colored ward. If she still insists that she is white, she can go into the white ward, but must dispense with his visits".

FEATHER PALM AT ANCON

Under our treaty the Zone sanitary department takes charge of the insane of Colon and Panama, and a very considerable share of the grounds at Ancon is divided off with barbed wire for their use. The number of patients runs well into the hundreds, with very few Americans. Most are Jamaica negroes and the hospital authorities say that they are mentally unbalanced by the rush and excitement of life on the Zone. I never happened to see a Jamaica negro excited unless it happened to be a Tivoli Hotel waiter confronted with the awful responsibility of an extra guest at table. Then the excitement took the form of deep melancholy, exaggerated lethargy, and signs of suicidal mania in every facial expression.

Beside the hospital service the sanitary department maintains dispensaries at several points on the line, where necessary drugs are provided for patients in the Commission Service free. Patent medicines are frowned upon, and such as are purveyed must be bought through the Commissary. Medical service is free to employees and their families. All doctors practicing on the Zone are on the gold payroll for wages ranging from $1800 to $7000 a year. I could not find upon inquiry that the fact that they were not dependent upon the patient for payment made the doctors less alert or sympathetic. At least no complaints to that effect were current.

To my mind the most notable effect upon the life of the Zone of this system of free medical attendance was that it added one more to the many in-

TABOGA FROM THE BATHING BEACH

ducements to matrimony. Infantile colic and measles are shorn of much of their terror to the young parent when no doctor's bill attends them. Incidentally, too, the benevolent administration looks after the teeth of the employees as a part of its care of their general health. One effect of this is to impress the visitor with the remarkable number of incisors gleaming with fresh gold visible where Zone folk are gathered together.

The annual vacations of the workers during the

from more temperate climes. Every employee was given 42 days' vacation with full pay, but he had to quit the Zone for some country which would afford a beneficial climatic change. Of course most went back to the United States, being encouraged thereto by a special rate on the steamship of $30— the regular rate being $75. But beside this vacation each employee was entitled to 30 days' sick leave. It was not an exceedingly difficult task to conjure up enough symptoms to persuade a friendly physician to issue a sick order. The favorite method of enjoying this respite from work was to spend as little of the time as possible at Ancon, and the rest at the sanitarium on the Island of Taboga.

That garden spot in the Bay of Panama where the French left the sanitarium building we now use is worth a brief description. You go thither in a small steamboat from Balboa or Panama and after about three hours' steaming a flock of little white boats, each with a single oarsman, puts out from the shore to meet you like a flock of gulls as you drop anchor in a bay of truly Mediterranean hue. To the traveled visitor the scene is irresistibly reminiscent of some little port of Southern Italy, and the reminder is all the more vivid when one gets ashore and finds the narrow ways betwixt the elbowing houses quite Neapolitan for dirt and ill odor. But from the sea one looks upon a towering hill, bare toward its summit, closely covered lower down by mango, wild fig, and ceiba trees, bordered just above the red roofs of the little town by a fringe of the graceful cocoanut palms. Then come the houses, row below row, until they descend to the

TABOGA IS FURTHERMORE THE CONEY ISLAND OF PANAMA

construction period may properly be considered in connection with sanitation work on the Zone, for they were not permitted to be mere loafing time. The man who took a vacation was not allowed to stay on the Isthmus. If he tried to stay there Col. Goethals found it out in that omniscient fashion of his and it was a case of hike for a change of air or go back to work. For, notwithstanding the fact that Col. Gorgas pulled the teeth of the tropics with his sanitary devices and regulations, an uninterrupted residence in that climate does break down the stamina and enfeeble the energy of men curving beach where the fishing boats are drawn up out of reach of the tide which rises some 20 feet.

From the bay the village with its red-tiled roofs and yellow-white walls looks substantial, a bit like Villefranche, the port of Nice, but this impression is speedily dispelled when one lands in one of the boats, propelled by the oarsman standing and facing the bow — a fashion seldom seen save in Italian waters. For seen near at hand the houses are discovered to be of the flimsiest frame construction, save for a few clustering about the little church and sharing with it a general decrepitude and down-at-the-heels air that makes us think they have seen better days. As indeed they have and worse days too, for Taboga once shared in the prosperity of the early Spanish rule, and enjoyed the honor of having entertained for a few weeks Sir Henry Morgan, that murderous pirate, whom England made a baronet and a colonial governor by way of reward for his exploits in piracy and rapine. Taboga must have treated the buccaneer well, for not only did he forbear to sack the town, but so deep was the devotion paid by him and his men to certain tuns of excellent wine there discovered that they let a

Spanish galleon, deep-laden with gold and silver, slip through their fingers rather than interrupt their drinking bout.

Tradition has it that the galleon was sunk nearby to save it and its cargo from the pirates, and treasure seekers have been hunting it ever since with the luck that ordinarily attends aspirants for dead men's gold.

Just now the wine and wassail of Taboga is limited to about six grog shops, which seems an over-supply for the handful of fishermen who inhabit its tumble-down hovels. Each bar, too, has its billiard table and one is reminded of Mark Twain's islands in the South Sea where the people earned an honest living by taking in each other's washing. One wonders if the sole industry of the Tabogans is playing billiards. There is indeed little to support the town save fishing, and that, if one may judge from specimens carried through the lanes, must be good. Some of the boats at anchor or drawn up on the beach attest to some prosperity amongst them that go down to the sea in ships. One that I saw rigged with a fore-and-aft sail and a jigger was hewn out of a single log like a river cayuca and had a beam

BURDEN BEARERS ON THE SAVANNA

HOTEL AT BOUQUETTE, CHIRIQUI
The only point in Panama at which Canal employees may spend their vacations

exceeding four feet. Before many of the houses were lines hung with long strips of fish hanging out to dry, for it is a curious property of this atmosphere that despite its humidity it will cure animal tissues, both fish and flesh, quickly and without taint.

Agriculture in Taboga is limited to the culture of the pineapple, and the local variety is so highly esteemed in the Panama markets that some measure of prosperity might attend upon the Tabogans would they but undertake the raising of pines systematically and extensively. But not they. Their town was founded in 1549 when, at the instance of Las Casas, the King of Spain gave freedom to all Indian slaves. Taboga was set apart as a residence for a certain part of these freedmen. Now what did the freedom from slavery mean but freedom from work? This view was probably held in the 16th century and certainly obtains in Taboga today, having been enhanced no doubt by the lib-

eral mixture of negro blood with that of the native Indians. If the pineapples grow without too much attention well and good. They will be sold and the grog shops will know that real money has come into town. But as for seriously extending the business—well, that is a thing to think of for a long, long time and the thought has not yet ripened. It is a wonder that the Chinese who hold the retail trade of the island and who are painstaking gardeners have not taken up this industry.

We may laugh at the easy-going Tabogan if we will, but I do not think that anyone will come out of his church without a certain respect for his real religious sentiment. 'Tis but a little church, of stuccoed rubble, fallen badly into decay, flanked by a square tower holding two bells, and penetrated by so winding and narrow a stair that one ascending it may feel as a corkscrew penetrating a cork.

A BIT OF ANCON HOSPITAL GROUNDS

But within it shows signs of a reverent affection by its flock not common in Latin-American churches. We may laugh a little at the altar decorations which are certainly not costly and may be a little tawdry, but they show evidences of patient work on the part of the women, and contributions by the men from the slender gains permitted them by the harsh land and the reluctant sea. About the walls hang memorial tablets, not richly sculptured indeed, but showing a pious desire on the part of bygone generations to have the virtue of their loved ones commemorated within hallowed walls. Standing in a side aisle was an effigy of Christ, of human size, bearing the cross up the hill of Gethsemane. The figure stood on a sort of platform, surrounded by six quaint lanterns of panes of glass set in leaded frames of a design seen in the street lamps of the earlier Spanish cities. The platform was on poles for bearers, after the fashion of a sedan chair, and we learned from one who, more fortunate than we, had been there to see, that in Holy Week there is a sort of Passion Play—rude and elementary it is true, but bringing to the surface all the religious emotionalism of the simple people. The village is crowded with the faithful from afar, who make light of any lack of shelter in that kindly tropic air. The Taboga young men dress as Roman soldiers, the village maidens take their parts in the simple pageant. The floats, such as the one we saw, are borne up and down the village streets which no horse could ever tread, and the church is crowded

NURSES' QUARTERS AT ANCON

with devotional worshipers until Easter comes with the joyous tidings of the Resurrection.

As to the part of Taboga in the economy of the Canal work, we have there a sanitarium inherited from the French, and used as a place of convalescence for almost recovered patients from the hospitals of the Zone. After breathing the clear, soft air, glancing at the comfortable quarters and enjoying to the fullest a lunch costing fifty cents that would put Broadway's best to the test, and make the expensive Tivoli dining-room seem unappetizing in comparison, we could well understand why every employee with thirty days' sick leave to his credit gets just such a slight ailment as needs a rest at Taboga for its cure.

Near Taboga is the leper hospital and the steamer stops for a moment to send ashore supplies in a small boat. Always there are about 75 victims of this dread and incurable disease there, mostly Panamanians with some West India negroes. A native of North America with the disease is practically unknown. The affliction is horrible enough in itself, but some cause operating for ages back has caused mankind to regard it with more fear than the facts justify. It is not readily

THE CHIEF INDUSTRY OF THE NATIVES IS FISHING

communicable to healthy persons, even personal contact with a leper not necessarily causing infection unless there be some scratch or wound on the person of the healthy individual into which the virus may enter. Visitors to the Isthmus, who find interest in the spectacle of hopeless human suffering, frequently visit the colony without marked precautions and with no reported case of infection.

To what extent the sanitation system so painstakingly built up by Col. Gorgas and his associates will be continued after the seal "complete" shall be stamped upon the Canal work, and the workers scattered to all parts of the land, is not now determined. Panama and Colon will, of course, be kept up to their present standards, but whether the war against the malarial mosquito will be pursued in the jungle as it is today when the health of 40,000 human beings is dependent upon it is another question. The plan of the army authorities is to abandon the Zone to nature—which presumably includes the *anopheles*. Whether that plan shall prevail or whether the United States shall maintain it as an object lesson in government, including sanitation, is a matter yet to be determined. In a hearing before a congressional committee in 1913 Col. Gorgas estimated the cost for a system of permanent sanitation for the Zone, including the quarantine, at $90,000 a year. As his total esti-mates for the years 1913–14 amounted to $524,000, this is indicative of a very decided abandonment of activity in sanitary work.

At all times during his campaign against the forces of fever and infection Col. Gorgas has had to meet the opposition charge of extravagance and the waste of money. It has been flippantly asserted that it cost him $5 to kill a mosquito—of course an utterly baseless assertion, but one which is readily met by the truth that the bite of a single infected mosquito has more than once cost a life worth many thousand times five dollars. To fix precisely the cost of bringing the Zone to its present state of healthfulness is impossible, because the activities of the sanitary department comprehended many functions in addition to the actual work of sanitation. Col. Gorgas figures that the average expenses of sanitation during the whole construction period were about $365,000 a year and he points out that for the same period Chicago spent $600,000 without any quarantine or mosquito work. The total expenditures for sanitation when the Canal is finished will have amounted to less than one per cent of the cost of that great public work and without this sanitation the Canal could never have been built. That simple statement of fact seems sufficiently to cover the contribution of Col. Gorgas to the work, and to measure the credit he deserves for its completion.

THE LEPER SETTLEMENT ON PANAMA BAY

CHAPTER XV

THE REPUBLIC OF PANAMA

THE Republic of Panama has an area of from 30,000 to 35,000 square miles, roughly approximating that of the state of Indiana. No complete survey of the country has ever been made and there is pending now a boundary dispute with Costa Rica in which the United States is arbitrator. The only other boundary, not formed by the sea, is that at which Panama and Colombia join. But Colombia says there is no boundary at all, but that Panama is one of her provinces in a state of rebellion. So the real size and bounds of the Republic must be set down as somewhat indeterminate.

The circumstances under which Panama became an independent nation have been set forth in an earlier chapter. It is safe to say that with the heavy investment made by the United States in the Canal Zone, on the strength of a treaty with the infant republic, the sovereignty of Panama will be forever maintained against all comers—except the United States itself. There are political philosophers who think that the Isthmus state may yet be the southern boundary of the Great Republic of the North. For the present however Uncle Sam is quite content with the Canal Zone and a certain amount of diplomatic influence over the government of Panama.

Panama is divided into five provinces, Bocas del

THE GORGE OF SALAMANCA

NATIVE FAMILY IN CHORRERA

Toro, Cocle, Colon, Chiriqui, Los Santos, Panama and Veragua. Its total population by the census of 1911 was 386,749, a trifle more than the District of Columbia which has about one five-thousandth of its area, and almost precisely the same population as Montana which has less than half its size. So it is clearly not over-populated. Of its population 51,323 are set down by its own census takers as white, 191,933 as mestizo, or a cross between white and Indian, 48,967 as negro; 2313 Mongol, and 14,128 Indian. The census takers estimated that other Indians, living in barbarism remote from civilization and unapproachable by the enumerators, numbered 36,138.

All these figures have to be qualified somewhat. The mestizos are theoretically a cross between whites and Indians, but the negro blood is very generally present. It is doubtful, too, whether those classed as white are not often of mixed blood.

A singularly large proportion of the population lives in the towns. In 12 towns, exceeding 7000 inhabitants each, are more than 150,000 people. More than one-third of the people therefore are town dwellers, which is to say they are unproductive citizens. Meanwhile more than five-eighths of the arable land in the country is not under cultivation.

The five chief towns of Panama with their population in 1911 are:

Panama	37,505
Colon	17,748
David	15,059
Santiago	13,081
Bocas del Toro	9,759

Of these towns David is the capital of the Chiriqui province, the portion of the republic in which cattle growing and agriculture have been most developed. Bocas del Toro is a banana port, dependent upon that nutritious fruit for its very existence, and the center of the business of the United Fruit Company in Panama. At present the former town is reached by a 300 mile water trip from Panama City; the latter by boat from Colon. The government has under way plans for a railroad from Panama to David which give every indication of being consummated.

The soil of the Republic differs widely in its varying sections, from the rich vegetable loam of the lowlands along the Atlantic Coast, the outcome of years of falling leaves and twigs from the trees to the swamp below, to the high dry lands of the savannas and the hillsides of the Chiriqui province. All are undeniably fertile, that is demonstrated by the rapid and rank growth of the jungle. But opinions differ as to the extent to which they are available for useful agriculture. Some

hold that the jungle soil is so rich that the plants run to wood and leaves to the exclusion of fruits. Others declare that on the hillsides the heavy rains of the rainy seasons wash away the surface soil leaving only the harsh and arid substratum. This

THE HOTEL AT DAVID

theory seems to be overthrown by the fact that it is rare to see a hillside in all Panama not covered with dense vegetation. A fact that is well worth bearing in mind is that there has never been a systematic and scientific effort to utilize any part of the soil of Panama for productive purposes that has not been a success. The United Fruit Company in its plantations about Bocas del Toro has developed a fruitful province and created a prosperous town. In the province of Cocle a German company has set out about 75,000 cacao trees, 50,000 coffee bushes and 25,000 rubber trees, all of which have made good progress.

The obstacles in the path of the fuller development of the national resources of Panama have sprung wholly from the nature of its population. The Indian is, of course, not primarily an agriculturist, not a devel-

A STREET IN PENENOME

VIEW OF BOCAS DEL TORO

oper of the possibilities of the land he inhabits. The Spanish infusion brought to the native population no qualities of energy, of well-directed effort, of the laborious determination to build up a new and thriving commonwealth. Spanish ideals run directly counter to those involved in empire building. Such energy, such determination as built up our great northwest and is building in British Columbia the greatest agricultural empire in the world, despite seven months annually of drifting snow and frozen ground, would make of the Panama savannas and valleys the garden spot of the world. That will never be accomplished by the present agrarian population, but it is incredible that with population absorbing and overrunning the available agricultural lands of other zones, the tropics should long be left dormant in control of a lethargic and indolent people.

Benjamin Kidd, in his stimulative book. "Social Evolution", says on this subject:

"With the filling up to the full limit of the remaining territories suitable for European occupation, and the growing pressure of population therein, it may be expected that the inexpediency of allowing a great extent of territory in the richest region of the globe—that comprised within the tropics—to remain undeveloped, with its resources running largely to waste under the management of races of low social efficiency, will be brought home with ever-growing force to the minds of the Western (Northern) peoples. The day is probably not far distant when, with the advance science is making, we shall recognize that it is in the tropics and not in the temperate zones we have the greatest food-producing and material-producing regions of the earth; that the natural highways of commerce in the world are those which run north and south; and that we have the highest possible interest in the proper development and efficient administration of the tropical regions, and in an exchange of products therewith on a far larger scale than has yet been attempted or imagined. . . . It will probably be made clear, and that at no distant date, that the last thing our civilization is likely to permanently

Photo by Critchlow

VISTA ON THE RIO GRANDE

Photo by Underwood & Underwood

AT THE CATTLE PORT OF AGUADULCE

This is one of the chief shipping points for the cattle ranches of Chiriqui. The industry is one little developed

tolerate is the wasting of the resources of the richest regions of the earth through lack of the elementary qualities of social efficiency in the races possessing them".

Some of the modern psychologists who are so expert in solving the riddles of human consciousness that they hardly hesitate to approach the supreme problem of life after death may perhaps determine whether the indolence of the Panamanian is racial, climatic, or merely bred of consciousness that he does not have to work hard in order to get all the comforts of which he has knowledge. The life-story of an imaginary couple will serve as the short and simple annals of tens of thousands of Panama's poor:

Miguel lived on the banks of the Chagres River, about half way between Cruces and Alhajuela. To him Cruces was a city. Were there not at least thirty huts of bamboo and clay thatched with palmetto like the one in which he lived? Was there not a church of sawn boards, with an altar to which

THE ROYAL ROAD NEAR PANAMA

a priest came twice a month to say mass, and a school where a gringo taught the children strange things in the hated English tongue? Where he lived there was no other hut within two or three hours poling up the river, but down at Cruces the houses were so close together you could almost reach one while sitting in the shade of another. At home after dark you only heard the cry of the whippoorwill, or occasionally the wail of a tiger cat in the jungle, but at Cruces there was always the loud talk of the men in the cantina, and a tom-tom dance at least once a week, when everybody sat up till dawn dancing to the beat of the drums and drinking the good rum that made them all so jolly.

But greater than Cruces was the Yankee town of Matachin down on the banks of the river where the crazy Americans said there was going to be a lake that some day would cover all the country, and drown out Cruces and even his father's house. They were paying all the natives along the river for their lands that would be sunken, and the people were taking the pesos gladly and spending them gaily. They did not trouble to move away. Many years ago the French too said there would be a lake, but it never came and the French suddenly disappeared. The Americans would vanish the same way, and a good thing, too, for their thunderous noises where they were working frightened away all the good game, and you could hardly find an iguana, or a wild hog in a day's hunting.

Once a week Miguel's father went down to market at Matachin, and sometimes the boy went along. The long, narrow cayuca was loaded with oranges, bananas and yams, all covered with big banana leaves, and with Miguel in the bow and his father in the stern the voyage commenced. Going down stream was easy enough, and the canoists plied their paddles idly, trusting chiefly to the current to carry them along. But coming back would be the real work, then they would have to bend to their poles and push savagely to force the boat along. At places they would have to get overboard and fairly carry the boat through the swift, shallow rapids. But Miguel welcomed the work for it showed him the wonders of Matachin, where great iron machines rushed along like horses,

THE MEETING PLACE OF THE CAYUCAS

drawing long trains of cars; where more people worked with shovels tending queer machines than there were in ten towns like Cruces; where folk gave pesos for bananas and gave cloth, powder and shot, things to eat in cans, and rum in big bottles for the pesos again. It was an exciting place this Matachin and made Miguel understand what the gringoes meant when they talked about New York, Chicago and other cities like it.

When he grew older Miguel worked awhile for the men who were digging away all this dirt, and earned enough to buy himself a machete and a gun and a few ornaments for a girl named Maria who lived in another hut near the river. But what was the use of working in that mad way—picking up your shovel when a whistle blew and toiling away until it blew again, with a boss always scolding at you and ready with a kick if you tried to take a little siesta. The pesos once a week were good, that was true. If you worked long enough you might get enough to buy one of those boxes that made music, but *quien sabe?* It might get broken anyway, and the iguanas in the jungle, the fish in the river and the yams and bananas in the clearing needed no silver to come to his table. Besides he was preparing to become a man of family. Maria was quite willing, and so one day they strolled off together hand in hand to a clearing Miguel had made with his machete on the river bank. With that same useful tool he cut some wooden posts, set them erect in the ground and covered them with a heavy thatch of palmetto leaves impervious to sun or rain. The sides of the shelter were left open during the first months of wedded life. Later perhaps, when they had time they would go to Cruces at the period of the priest's regular visit and get regularly married. When the rainy season came on and walls were as necessary as a roof against the driving rain, they would build a little better. When that time came he would set ten stout uprights of bamboo in the ground in the shape of an oblong, and across the tops would fasten six cross pieces of girders with withes of vine well soaked to make them pliable. This would make the frame of the first floor of his house. The walls he would make by weaving reeds, or young bamboo stalks in and out betwixt the posts until a fairly tight basketwork filled the space. This was then plastered outside with clay. The dirt, which in time would be stamped down hard, formed the floor. For his second story a tent-shaped frame of lighter bamboo tightly tied together was fastened to the posts, and cane was tied to each of the rafters as we nail laths to scantling. Thus a strong peaked roof, about eight feet high from the second floor to the ridgepole was constructed, and thatched with palm leaves. Its angle being exceedingly steep it sheds water in the fierce tropic rain storms. The floor of the second story is made of bamboo poles laid transversely, and covered heavily with rushes and palmetto. This is used only as the family sleeping apartment, and to give access to it Miguel takes an 8-inch bamboo and cuts notches in it, into which the prehensile toes of his family

BANANA MARKET AT MATACHIN

IN THE CHIRIQUI COUNTRY

of the family and a phonograph, of a make usually discarded at home. But when Miguel and Maria start out on the journey of life a machete, a gun and the good will of their neighbors who will lend them yams until their own planting begins to yield forms a quite sufficient capital on which to establish their family. Wherefore, why work?

It is beyond doubt to the ease with which life can be sustained, and the torpidity of the native imagination which depicts no joys to spur one on to effort that the unwillingness of the native to do systematic work is due. And from this difficulty in

may fit as they clamber up to the land of Nod. Furniture to the chamber floor there is none. The family herd together like so many squirrels, and with the bamboo climbing pole drawn up there is no danger of intrusion by the beasts of the field.

In the typical Indian hut there is no furniture on the ground floor other than a rough hewn bench, a few pieces of pottery and gourds, iron cooking vessels and what they call a kitchen, which is in fact a large flat box with raised edges, about eight square feet in surface and about as high from the floor as a table. This is filled with sand and slabs of stone. In it a little fire is built of wood or charcoal, the stones laid about the fire support the pots and pans and cooking goes on as gaily as in any modern electric kitchen. The contrivance sounds primitive, but I have eaten a number of excellent meals cooked on just such an apparatus.

Now it will be noticed that in all this habitation, sufficient for the needs of an Indian, there is nothing except the iron pots and possibly some pottery for which money was needed, and there are thousands of families living in just this fashion in Panama today. True, luxury approaches in its insidious fashion and here and there you will see a $1.25 white iron bed on the main floor, real chairs, canned goods on the shelves and—final evidence of Indian prosperity!—a crayon portrait of the head

BANANA PLANT; NOTE SIZE OF MAN

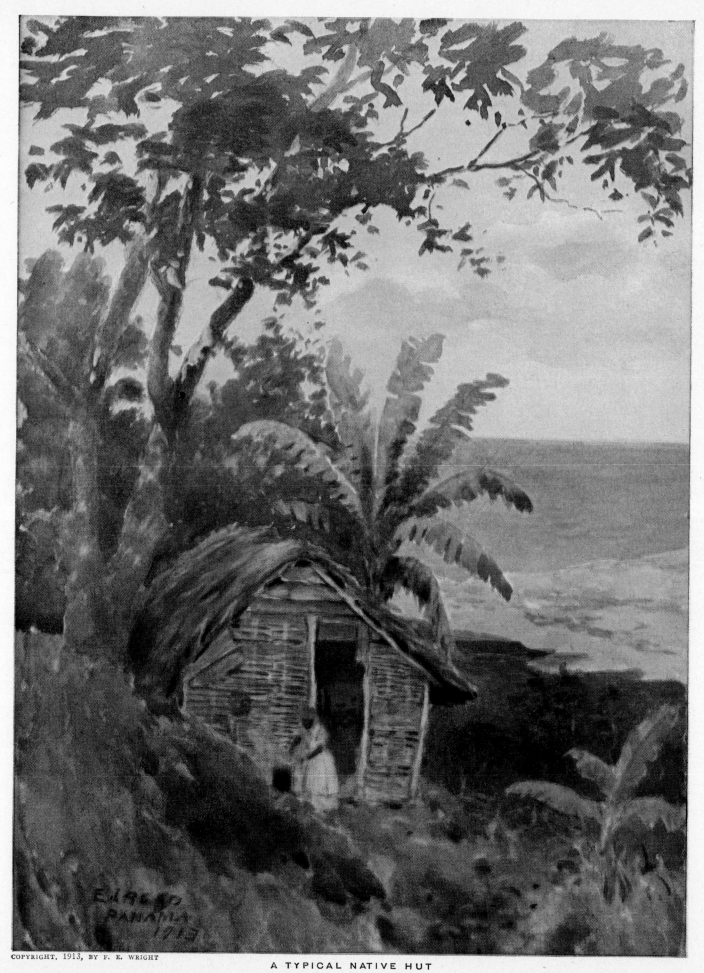

A TYPICAL NATIVE HUT

While native architecture is not stately it is artistic in that it harmonizes with its natural surroundings and is
eminently adapted to the needs of the people who inhabit the huts.

getting labor follows the fact
that not one quarter of the
natural resources of Panama
are developed. Whether the
labor problem will be solved
by the distribution throughout the republic of the Caribbean blacks who have worked
so well on the Zone is yet to
be seen. It may be possible
that because of this the fertile
lands of Panama, or the savannas so admirably fitted for
grazing, can only be utilized
by great corporations who will
do things on so great a scale
as to justify the importation

A NATIVE LIVING ROOM AND STAIRWAY
By pulling up the bamboo ladder, or turning it, communication with the upper floor is closed

of labor. Today the man who should take up a
large tract of land in the Chiriqui country with a
view to tilling it would be risking disaster because
of the uncertainty of the labor supply.

Another obstacle in the way of foreign settlement
of Panama has been the uncertainty of land titles.
Early surveyors seem to have been in the habit of
noting as the identification marks of their lines such
volatile objects as a blackbird in a tree, or such perishable ones as an ant hill or a decaying stump.
Facilities for recording titles also have been ill arranged. One of the first tasks of the new Republic
was to take up this matter and it has been reduced
to fairly systematic form. The Republic is offering

for sale great quantities of public lands long held as
commons by various municipalities. Much of this
land lies along the line of the railroad from Panama
to David, and is of varying grades suitable for grazing, forestry or agriculture. A fixed price of 50
cents per hectare is charged, a hectare being practically 2½ acres. The government has gone quite
efficiently into the task of disposing of these lands,
and pamphlets explanatory of methods of securing
titles, terms, etc., can be obtained by addressing the
Administrator-General at Panama. The Pan-American Union, of Washington, D. C., has issued a
pamphlet giving a summary in English of the Panamanian law bearing upon the subject.

With the lack of labor, and the
uncertainty of land titles, the final
impediment to the general development of the interior of Panama is to
be found in the lack of roads. It is
not that the roads are bad—that is
the case in many of our own common-
wealths. But in a great part of
Panama there are literally no roads
at all. Trails, choked by the jungle
and so washed by the rains that they
are merely lanes floored with boulders,
are the rule. The heavy ox-cart is
the only vehicle that will stand the
going, and our light American farm
wagons would be speedily racked to
pieces. In the Canal Zone the Com-

CONSTRUCTION OF ROOF OF A NATIVE HOUSE
The photograph is taken looking directly upward from the ground floor

mission has built some of the best roads in the world, utilizing the labor of employees convicted of minor offenses. Stimulated by this example the Panama government has built one excellent road from the chief city across the savannas to Old Panama and thence onward into the interior. It is hoped that the spectacle of the admirable roads in the Zone will encourage the authorities of the Republic to go into road building on a large scale in their own country. In no other way can its possibilities be realized. At present the rivers afford the surest highways and land abutting them brings higher prices.

David, the largest interior town of Panama, is the central point of the cattle industry. All around it are woods, or jungles, plentifully interspersed with broad prairies, or llanos, covered with grass, and on which no trees grow save here and there a wild fig or a ceibo. Cattle graze on the llanos, sleek reddish beasts with spreading horns like our Texas cattle. There are no huge herds as on our western ranges. Droves of from ten to twenty are about the average among the small owners who rely on the public range for subsistence. The grass is not sufficiently nutritious to bring the cattle up to market form, so the small owners sell to the owners of big ranches who maintain potreros, or fattening ground sown with better grasses. A range fed steer will fetch $15 to $18, and after six or eight months on the potrero it will bring $30 to $35 from the cattle shipper at David. Since the cost of feeding a beeve for that period is only about one dollar, and as the demand is fairly steady the profit of the ranchman is a good one. But like all other industries in Panama, this one is pursued in only a retail way. The market is great enough to enrich ranchmen who would go into the business on a large scale, but for some reason none do.

Passing from llano to llano the road cuts through the forest which towers dense and impenetrable on

RUBBER PLANTATION NEAR COCLE

The planter's original hut in the foreground. The board cabin with corugated iron roof shows prosperity

BOLIVAR PARK AT BOCAS DEL TORO

A FORD NEAR ANTON

either side, broken only here and there by small clearings made by some native with the indispensable machete. These in the main are less than four acres. The average Panamanian farmer will never incur the scriptural curse laid upon them that lay field unto field. He farms just enough for his daily needs, no more. The ambition that leads our northern farmer to always covet the lands on the other side of his boundary fence does not operate in Panama. One reason is, of course, the aggressiveness of the jungle. Stubborn to clear away, it is determined in its efforts to regain the land from which it has been ousted. Such a thing as allowing a field to lie fallow for two or three years is unknown in Panama. There would be no field visible for the new jungle growth.

Agriculture therefore is conducted in a small way only, except for the great corporations that have just begun the exploitation of Panama. Whether the country affords a hopeful field for the individual settler is at least doubtful. Its climate is excellent. The days are warm but never scorchingly hot as are customary in Washington and frequent in New York. The nights are cool. From December to May a steady trade wind blows over the Isthmus from north to south, carrying away the clouds so that there is no rain. In this dry season the fruits mature, so that it corresponds to the northern summer; on the other hand such vegetation as sheds its leaves, or dies down annually, does so at this season, giving it a seeming correspondence to the northern winter. In a temperature sense there is neither summer nor winter, and the variation of the thermometer is within narrow limits. The highest temperature in years at Culebra, a typical inland point, was 96 degrees; the lowest 61.

The list of natural products of the Isthmus is impressive in its length and variety, but for most of them even the home demand is not met or supplied by the production. Only where some stimulating force from the outside has intervened, like the United Fruit Company with the banana, has production been brought up to anything like its possibility. In the Chiriqui country you can see sugar cane fields that

OLD BANANA TREES

people to the square mile, nine-tenths of the land is unbroken and Panama imports fruit from Jamaica, sugar from Cuba and tobacco and food stuffs from the United States.

The fruits of Panama are the orange, which grows wild and for the proper cultivation of which no effort has been made, which is equally the case with the lemon and the lime; the banana, which plays so large a part in the economic development of the country that I shall treat of it at length later; the pineapple, cultivated in a haphazard way, still attains so high an order of excellence that Taboga pines are the standard for lusciousness; the mango, which grows in clusters so dense that the very trees bend under their weight, but for which as yet little market has been found, as they require an acquired taste; the mamei, hard to ship and difficult to eat because of its construction but withal a toothsome fruit; the paypaya, a melon not unlike our cantaloupe which has the eccentricity of growing on trees; the sapodillo, a fruit of excellent flavor tasting not unlike a ripe persimmon, but containing no pit. With cultivation all of these fruits could be grown in great quantities in all parts of the Republic, but to give them any economic importance some special arrangement for their regular and speedy marketing would have to be made, as with the banana, most of them being by nature extremely perishable.

have gone on producing practically without attention for fifteen seasons. Cornfields have been worked for half a century without fertilizing or rotation of crops. The soil there is volcanic detritus washed down during past ages from the mountainsides, and lies from six to twenty feet thick. It will grow anything that needs no frost, but the province supports less than four

PINEAPPLES IN THE FIELD

Northern companies are finding some profit in exploiting such natural resources of Panama as are available in their wild state. Of these the most promising is rubber, the tree being found in practically every part of the country. One

COUNTRY HOUSE OF A CACAO PLANTER AT CHORIA
This industry is in its infancy in Panama, but promises to be a considerable resource

concern, the Boston-Panama Company, has an estate approximating 400 square miles on which are about 100,000 wild rubber trees, and which is being further developed by the planting of bananas, pineapples, cocoanuts and other tropical fruits.

Coffee, sugar and cacao are raised on the Isthmus, but of the two former not enough to supply the local demand. The development of the cacao industry to large proportions seems probable, as several foreign corporations are experimenting on a considerable scale. Cocoanuts are easily grown along both coasts of the Isthmus. A new grove takes about five years to come into bearing, costing an average of about three dollars a tree. Once established the trees bring in a revenue of about one dollar each at present prices and, as the demand for Panama cocoanuts is steady, the industry seems to offer attractive possibilities. The groves must be near the coast, as the cocoanut tree needs salt air to reach its best estate. Given the right atmospheric conditions they will thrive where no other plant will take root. Growing at the edge of the sea, water transportation is easy.

There is still much land available for cocoanut planting, though but little of it is government land. Both coasts are fit for this industry, unlike the banana industry, which thrives only on the Atlantic shore. Panama is outside of the hurricane belt, which gives an added advantage to the cocoanut planter. Elsewhere in the Caribbean the trees suffer severely from the high winds.

The lumber of Panama will in time come to be

WAITING FOR THE BOAT

STARTED FOR MARKET

one of its richest assets. In the dense forests hardwoods of a dozen varieties or more are to be found, but as yet the cost of getting it out is prohibitive in most sections. Only those forests adjacent to streams are economically valuable and such activity as is shown is mainly along the Bayano, Chucunaque, and Tuyra Rivers. The list of woods is almost interminable. The prospectus of one of the companies with an extended territory on the Bayano River notes eighteen varieties of timber, commercially valuable on its territory. Among those the names of which are unfamiliar are the espavé (sometimes spelled espevé), the cocobolo, the espinosa cedar, the zoro and the sangre. All are hard woods serviceable in cabinet making. The espavé is as hard as mahogany and of similar color and marking. The trees will run four to five feet thick at the stump with saw timber 60 to 70 feet in length. Espinosa trees are of the cedar type, growing to enormous size, frequently exceeding 16 feet in circumference. The cocobolo is a hard wood, but without the beauty to fit it for cabinet work. The sangre derives its name from its red sap which exudes from a gash like blood. It takes a high polish, and is in its general characteristics not unlike our cherry.

For the casual tourist the lumber district most easy of access is that along the Bayano River reached by a motor boat or steam launch in a few hours from Panama. The trip is frequently made by pleasure seekers, for perhaps nowhere in the world is the beauty of a phosphorescent sea at night so marvelously shown, and few places easily found by man show such a horde of alligators or crocodiles, as are seen in Crocodile Creek, one of the affluents of the Bayano. This river, which empties into the Gulf of Panama, is in its lower reaches a tide-water stream and perhaps because of the mingling of the salt and the fresh the water is densely filled with the microscopic infusoria which at night blaze forth in coldly phosphorescent gleams suggestive of the sparkling of a spray of diamonds. Put your hand into the stream, lift it and let the water trickle through your fingers. Every drop gleams and glistens as it falls with a radiance comparable with nothing in nature unless it be the great fire-flies of the tropics. Even diamonds have to pass through the hands of the cutter before they will blaze with any such effulgence as the trickling waters of this tropical stream. One who has passed a night upon it may well feel that he has lived with one of the world's marvels, and can but wonder at the matter-of-fact manner in which the natives go about their tasks unmoved by the contact with so much shining glory.

There is always controversy on the Isthmus over the question whether the gigantic saurians of Crocodile Creek are in fact crocodiles or alligators. Wheth-

LOADING CATTLE AT AGUADULCE

er expert scientific opinion has ever been called upon to settle the problem I do not know, but I rather suspect that crocodile was determined upon because it gave to the name of Crocodile Creek in which they are so plentifully found "apt alliteration's art-

DOLEGA IN THE CHIRIQUI PROVINCE

ful aid" to make it picturesque. Whatever the precise zoological classification given to the huge lizards may be is likely to be relatively unimportant

MAHOGANY TREES WITH ORCHIDS

before long, because the greatest joy of every tourist is found in killing them. The fascination which slaughter possesses for men is always hard to understand, but just what gives the killing of alligators its peculiar zest I could never understand. The beasts are slow, torpid and do not afford a peculiarly difficult test of marksmanship, even though the vulnerable part of their bodies is small. They are timid and will not fight for their lives. There is nothing of the sporting proposition in pursuing them that is to be found in hunting the tiger or the grizzly. They are practically harmless, and in the Bayano region wholly so, as there are no domestic animals upon which they can prey. It is true their teeth and skins have a certain value in the market, but it is not for these the tourist kills them. Most of those slain for "sport" sink instantly and cannot be recovered.

However if you visit Crocodile Creek with a typical party you will be given a very fair imitation of a lively skirmish in actual war. From every part of the deck, from the roof of the cabin, and from the pilot house shots ring out from repeating rifles in a fierce desire to kill. The Emersonian doctrine of compensation is often given illustration by the killing of one of the hunters in the eagerness to get at the quarry. In fact that is one of the commonest accidents of the tourist season in Panama.

Crocodile Creek is a deep, sluggish black stream, almost arched over by the boughs of the thick forest along the shores. Here and there the jungle is broken by a broad shelving beach on which the ungainly beasts love to sun themselves, and to which the females resort to deposit their eggs. At the sound of a voice or a paddle in the stream the awkward brutes take to the water in terror, for there

BAYANO CEDAR, EIGHT FEET DIAMETER

are few animals more timid than they. When in the water the crocodile floats lazily, displaying only three small bumps above the surface—the nostrils and the horny protruberances above the eyes. Once the pool in which they float is disturbed they sink to the bottom and lurk there for hours. Alligator hunting for business purposes is not as yet generally pursued on the Isthmus, though one hunter and trapper is said to have secured as many as 60,000 in a year. But as the demand for the skins, and to a lesser degree for the teeth, of the animals is a constant one, it is probable that with the aid of the tourists they will be exterminated there as thoroughly as they have been in the settled parts of Florida. While on

THE CACAO TREE

the subject of slaughter and the extermination of game it may be noted that the Canal Commission has already established very stringent game laws on the Zone, particularly for the protection of plumed birds like the egret, and it is seriously proposed to make of that part of Gatun Lake within the Zone a refuge for birds in which no shooting shall be permitted. Such action would stop mere wanton slaughter from the decks of passing steamers, and in the end would greatly enhance the beauty and interest of the trip

STREET IN DAVID

through the lake which would be fairly alive with birds and other animal life.

The Bayano River region beside being the center of such lumbering activities as the Zone knows at present is the section in which are found the curious vegetable ivory nuts which, though growing wild, have become one of the principal products of Panama. Only a few years ago they were looked upon merely as curiosities but are now a useful new material. They are gathered by the natives and sold to dealers in Panama

IN THE BANANA COUNTRY

289

who ship them north to be made into buttons and other articles of general use. Nobody has yet experimented with the cultivation of the tree, and there is reason to believe that with cultivation larger nuts could be obtained, and, by planting, considerable groves established. The trees grow well in every part of the Darien, and the demand, with the rapid diminution in the supply of real ivory, should be a growing one.

Indeed, the more one studies Panama and its resources the more one is convinced that all that is necessary to make the country a rich and prosperous one, or at any rate to cause it to create riches and prosperity for investors, is the application of capital, labor and systematic management to the resources it already possesses. In its 400 years of Spanish and mestizo control these three factors have been continuously lacking. There are men in Panama, of native birth and of Spanish origin, who have undertaken to develop certain of the land's resources and have moderately enriched themselves. But the most striking evidence of the

success to be obtained from attacking the industrial problem in Panama systematically and in a big way is that furnished by the operations of the United Fruit Company, the biggest business fact in the tropics.

Panama is, of course, only one link in the colossal chain of the operations of this company in the tropics. The rapidly increasing prosperity of many of the Central Republics is due largely to the sweeping scope of the United Fruit Company, and its impress is in evidence all along the north coast of South America and throughout the West Indies. Its interests in Jamaica are enormous. Cuba put Jamaica off the sugar map, but the United Fruit Company came to her rescue with an offer to purchase all the bananas her planters could furnish, and Jamaica now leads the American tropics with 17,000,000 bunches annually, of which the United Fruit Company obtains nearly half, the balance being handled by its competitors. The company also owns the famous Titchfield Hotel of Port Antonio, and operates the Myrtle Bank Hotel of Kingston. In Cuba the company owns

MARKET PLACE AT ANCON

FRUIT COMPANY STEAMER AT WHARF

United Fruit Company made gardens of the low Caribbean coast lands and created from the virgin wilderness such ports as Barrios, Cortez, Limon and Bocos del Toro.

This Yankee enterprise has erected and maintains at its own expense many of the lighthouses which serve its own great fleet and the ships of all the world. It has dredged new channels and marked them with buoys. It has installed along the Central and South American coasts a wireless telegraph service of the highest power and efficiency. It has constructed hundreds of miles of public roads, maintains public schools, and in other ways renders at its own expense the services which are presumed to fall on governments. The American financiers associated with it are now pushing to completion the Pan-American railroad which soon will connect New

60,000 acres of sugar plantations and its two great sugar mills will this year add to the world's product an

UNITED FRUIT COMPANY TRAIN

This narrow guage railroad carries no freight except bananas. Nearly 1000 miles of such road are maintained

amount with a market value in excess of $10,000,000. Its scores of white steamships, amazingly well contrived and fitted for tropical service, constitute one of the pleasantest features of travel on these sunlit seas.

The United Fruit Company is by far the greatest agricultural enterprise the world has ever known. Its fruit plantations constitute a farm half a mile wide and more than seven hundred miles long. All of its farm lands exceed in area the 1332 square miles which constitute the sovereign State of Rhode Island. On these farms are more than 25,000 head of live stock. This agricultural empire is traversed by nearly 1000 miles of railroad. To carry the fruits from the plantations to the seaports there are employed 100 locomotives and 3000 freight cars. An army of nearly 40,000 men is employed in this new and mammoth industry. The republics of Central America were inland nations before the

York with Panama by an all-rail route, and thus realize what once was esteemed an impractical dream.

SANITARY OFFICE, BOCAS DEL TORO

A PILE OF REJECTED BANANAS

The fruit is thrown out by the company's inspectors for scarcely visible flaws

prosperity of this section on a firm basis. Lands that a few years ago were miasmatic swamps are now improved and planted with bananas. Over 4,000,000 bunches were exported from this plantation in 1911, and 35,000 acres are under cultivation there. A narrow gauge railway carries bananas exclusively. The great white steamships sail almost daily carrying away little except bananas. The money spent over the counters of the stores in Bocas del Toro comes from natives who have no way of getting money except by raising bananas and selling them, mostly to the United Fruit Company. It has its competitors, but it invented

But it is the United Fruit Company's activities in Panama only that are pertinent to this book. They demonstrate strikingly how readily one natural opportunity afforded by this land responded to the call of systematic effort, and there are a dozen products beside the banana which might thus be exploited.

On the Atlantic coast, only a night's sail from Colon, is the port of Bocos del Toro (The Mouths of the Bull), a town of about 9000 inhabitants, built and largely maintained by the banana trade. Here is the largest and most beautiful natural harbor in the American tropics, and here some day will be established a winter resort to which will flock people from all parts of the world. Almirante Bay and the Chiriqui Lagoon extend thirty or forty miles, dotted with thousands of islands decked with tropical verdure, and flanked to the north and west by superb mountain ranges with peaks of from seven to ten thousand feet in height.

The towns of Bocas del Toro and Almirante are maintained almost entirely by the banana trade. Other companies than the United Fruit raise and buy bananas here, but it was the initiative of the leading company which by systematic work put the

A PERFECT BUNCH OF BANANAS

the business and has brought it to its highest development. At this Panama town, and for that matter in the other territories it controls, the company has established and enforces the sanitary reforms which Col. Gorgas applied so effectively in Colon and Panama. Its officials proudly claim that they were the pioneers in inventing and applying the methods which have conquered tropical diseases. At Bocas del Toro the company maintains a hospital which lacks nothing of the equipment of the Ancon Hospital, though of course not so large. It has successfully adopted the commissary system established on the Canal Zone. Labor has always been the troublesome factor in industrial enterprises in Central America. The Fruit Company has joined with the Isthmian Commission in the systematic endeavor to keep labor contented and therefore efficient.

THE BAY OF BOCAS

This harbor of the chief banana port of Panama would accommodate a navy

To my mind the United Fruit Company, next to the Panama Canal, is the great phenomenon of the Caribbean world today. Some day some one with knowledge will write a book about it as men have written the history of the British East India Company, or the Worshipful Company of Hudson Bay Adventurers, for this distinctly American enterprise has accomplished a creative work so wonderful and so romantic as to entitle it to equal literary consideration. Its coöperation with the Republic of Panama and the manner in which it has followed the plans formulated by the Isthmian Commission entitles it to attention in a book treating of Panama.

The banana business is the great trade of the tropics, and one that cannot be reduced in volume by new competition, as cane sugar was checked by beet sugar. But it is a business which requires special machinery of distribution for its success. From the time the banana is picked until it is in the stomach of the ultimate consumer should not exceed three weeks.

THE ASTOR YACHT
AT CRISTOBAL

Probably it will be the policy which any corporation attempting to do work on a large scale will be compelled to adopt.

BRINGING HOME THE CROCODILE

upon to absorb the cargoes of the ships as regularly as they arrive. From its budding near the Panama Canal to its finish in the alimentary canal of its final purchaser the banana has to be handled systematically and swiftly.

To establish this machinery the United Fruit Company has invested more than $190,000,000 in the tropics—doubtless the greatest investment next to the Panama Canal made in that Zone. How much of this is properly a Panama investment can hardly be told, since for example the Fruit Company's ships which ply to Colon and Bocas del Toro call at other banana ports as well. These ships are peculiarly attractive in design and in their clothing of snowy white, and I do not think there is any American who, seeing them in a Caribbean port, fails to resent the sight of the British flag flying at the stern. His discontent is not allayed when he learns that the company has in all more than 100 ships of various sizes, and

The fruit must be picked green, as, if allowed to ripen on the trees, it splits open and the tropical insects infect it. This same condition, by the way, affects all tropical fruits. All must be gathered while still unripe. The nearest wholesale market for bananas is New Orleans, five days' steaming. New York is seven days away. That means that once landed the fruit must be distributed to commission houses and agents all over the United States with the utmost expedition lest it spoil in transit. There can be no holding it in storage, cold or otherwise, for a stronger demand or a higher market. This means that the corporation must deal with agents who can be relied

A MORNING'S SHOOTING

nearly all of British registry. The transfer of that fleet alone to American registry would be a notable and most desirable step.

From officials of the company I learned that they would welcome the opportunity to transfer their ships to American registry, except for certain requirements of the navigation laws which make such a change hazardous. Practically all the ownership of the ships is vested in Americans and to fly the British flag is to them an offensive necessity. Chief among the objections is the clause which would give the United States authority to seize the vessels in time of war. It is quite evident that this power might be employed to the complete destruction of the Fruit Company's trade; in fact to its practical extinction as a business concern. A like power existing in England or Germany would not be of equal menace to any single company flying the flag of that nation, for there the government's needs could be fully supplied by a proper apportionment of requisitions for ships among the many companies. But with the exceedingly restricted merchant marine of the United

Photo by Carl Hayden

THE END OF THE CROCODILE

States the danger of the enforcement of this right would be an ever-present menace. It is for this reason that the Fruit Company steamers fly the British flag, and the American in Colon may see, as I did one day, nine great ocean ships in the port with only one flying the stars and stripes. The opening of the canal will not wholly remedy this.

In all respects save the registry of its ships, however, the Fruit Company is a thoroughly American concern and to its operations in the Caribbean is due much of the good feeling toward the United States which is observable there. In 1912 it carried 1,113,741 tons of freight, of which 359,686 was general freight, carried for the public

ON CROCODILE CREEK

Each spot looking like a leaf on the water is the nose of a submerged saurian

ABOVE THE CLOUDS, CHIRIQUI VOLCANO

trade along the Caribbean, both are matters of common knowledge.

The banana thrives best in rich soil covered with alluvial deposits and in a climate of great humidity where the temperature never falls below 75 degrees Fahrenheit. Once established the plantation needs little attention, the plant being self-propagat-

in addition to company freight. This is a notable public service, profitable no doubt but vital to the interests of the American tropics. It owns or holds under leases 852,650 acres, and in 1912 carried to the United States about 25,000,000 bunches of bananas, and 16,000,000 bunches to Great Britain and the Continent. Viewed from the standpoint of the consumer its work certainly has operated to cheapen bananas and to place them on sale at points where they were never before seen. The banana has not participated in the high cost of living nor has one company monopolized the market, for the trade statistics show 17,000,000 bunches of bananas imported by rival companies in 1912. As for its stimulation of the business of the ports of New Orleans, Galveston and Mobile, and its revivifying of

ing from suckers which shoot off from the "mat," the tangled roots of the mother plant. It begins to bear fruit at the age of ten or eleven months, and with the maturing of one bunch of fruit the parent plant is at once cut down so that the strength of the soil may go into the suckers that succeed it. Per-

THE CHIRIQUI VOLCANO

haps the most technical work of the cultivator is to select the suckers so that the plantation will not bring all its fruit to maturity in one season, but rather yield a regular succession of crops, month after month. It was interesting to learn from a representative of the United Fruit Company at Bocas del Toro, that the banana has its dull season —not in production but in the demand for it which falls off heavily in winter, though one would suppose that summer, when our own fruits are in the market, would be the period of its eclipse.

While most of the fruit gathered in the

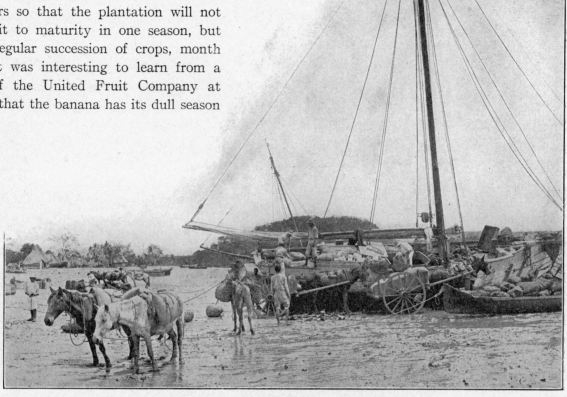

NATIVE MARKET BOAT AT CHORRERA

neighborhood of Bocas del Toro is grown on land owned and tilled by the Company, there are hundreds of small individual growers with plantations of from half an acre to fifty acres or even more. All fruit is delivered along the railway lines, and the larger growers have tramways, the cars drawn by oxen or mules, to carry their fruit to the stipulated point. Notice is given the growers of the date on which the fruit will be called for, and within twelve to eighteen hours after it has been cut it is in the hold of the vessel. It is subjected to a rigid inspection at the docks, and the flaws for which whole bunches are rejected would often be quite undiscernible to the ordinary observer.

The banana is one of the few fruits which are free from insect pests, being protected by its thick, bitter skin. If allowed to ripen in the open, however, it speedily falls a prey to a multitude of egg-laying insects. The tree itself is not so immune. Lately a small rodent, something like the gopher

IN BOUQUETTE VALLEY, THE MOST FERTILE PART OF CHIRIQUI

COFFEE PLANT AT BOUQUETTE

Baron Humboldt is said to have first called the attention of civilized people to the food value of the banana, but it was one of the founders of the United Fruit Company, a New England sea captain trading to Colon, who first introduced it to the general market in the United States. For a time he carried home a few bunches in the cabin of his schooner for his family and friends, but, finding a certain demand for the fruit, later began to import it systematically. From this casual start the United Fruit Company and its hustling competitors have grown. The whole business is the development of a few decade's and people still young can remember when bananas were sold, each wrapped in tissue paper, for five or ten cents, while today ten or fifteen cents a dozen is a fair price. The fruit can be prepared in a multitude of fashions, particularly the coarser varieties of plantains, and the Fruit Company has compiled a banana cook book but has taken little pains to circulate it, the demand for the fruit being at times still in excess of the supply. There seems every indication that the demand is constant and new banana territory is being steadily developed.

Several companies share with the United Fruit Company the Panama market. The methods of gathering and marketing the crop employed by all are practically the same, but the United Fruit Company is used as an illustration here because its business is the largest and because it has so closely followed the Isthmian Canal Commission in its welfare work.

The banana country lies close to the ocean and of our American states, has discovered that banana roots are good to eat. From time immemorial he lived in the jungle, burrowing and nibbling the roots of the plants there, but in an unlucky moment for the fruit companies he discovered that tunneling in soil that had been worked was easier and the roots of the cultivated banana more succulent than his normal diet. Therefore a large importation of scientists from Europe and the United States to find some way of eradicating the industrious pest that has attacked the chief industry of the tropics at the root, so to speak.

DRYING THE COFFEE BEANS

DRYING CLOTHS FOR COFFEE
Where the planter has no regular drying floor, cloths are spread on which the berries are exposed

takes thirty hours. When the government railroad is built, about which there is some slight doubt, the whole country will be opened and should be quickly settled. The road in all probability will be continued to Bocas del Toro on the Atlantic coast.

While the cattle business of the Chiriqui region is its chief mainstay, it is far from being developed to its natural extent. The Commissary officials of the Canal organization tried to interest cattle growers to the extent of raising enough beef for the need of the Canal workers, but failed. Practically all of the meat thus used is furnished by the so-called "Beef Trust" of the United States. It is believed that there are not more than 50,000 head of cattle all told in Panama. I was told on the Isthmus that agents of a large Chicago firm had traveled through Chiriqui

mainly on the Atlantic side of the Isthmus. The lumber industry nestles close to the rivers, mainly in the Bayano region. Cocoanuts need the beaches and the sea breezes. Native rubber is found in every part of the Republic, though at present it is collected mainly in the Darien, which is true also of vegetable ivory. The only gold which is mined on a large scale is taken from the neighborhood of the Tuyra River in the Darien. But for products requiring cultivation like cacao and coffee the high lands in the Chiriqui province offer the best opportunity.

David is really the center of this territory. It is a typical Central American town of about 15,000 people, with a plaza, a cathedral, a hotel and all the appurtenances of metropolitan life in Panama. The place is attractive in its way, with its streets of white-walled, red-tiled dwellings, with blue or green doors and shutters. It seems to have grown with some steadiness, for though the Panama census for 1912 gave it 15,000 inhabitants, travelers like Mr. Forbes Lindsay and Albert Edwards, who visited it only a year or two earlier, gave it only from 5000 to 8000 people. Its growth, however, is natural and healthy, for the country round it is developing rapidly. You reach David now by boats of the Pacific Mail and the National Navigation Company from Panama. The quickest trip

Photo by Underwood & Underwood

BREADFRUIT TREE

PRIMITIVE SUGAR MILL

ing industry which should be profitable in Panama if a heavy protective tariff could make it so. But not even enough of the fragrant berries are grown to supply home needs, and the industry is as yet largely prosecuted in an unsystematic and haphazard manner. It is claimed that sample shipments of coffee brought high prices in New York, but as yet not enough is grown to permit exportation. Cacao, which thrives, is grown chiefly by English and German planters, but as yet in a small

with a view to establishing a packing house there, but reported that the supply of cattle was inadequate for even the smallest establishment. Yet the country is admirably adapted for cattle raising.

The climate of this region is equable, both as to temperature and humidity. Epidemic diseases are practically unknown among either men or beasts. Should irrigation in future seem needful to agriculture the multitude of streams furnish an ample water supply and innumerable sites for reservoirs.

Westward from David the face of the country rises gently until you come to the Caldera Valley which lies at the foot of the Chiriqui Peak, an extinct volcano perhaps 8000 feet high. Nowhere in Panama do the mountains rise very high, though the range is clearly a connection of the Cordilleras of North and South America. The Chiriqui Peak has not in the memory of man been in eruption, but the traces of its volcanic character are unmistakable. Its crater is a circular plain about half a mile in diameter surrounded by a densely wooded precipitous ridge. As the ascent is continued the woods give way to grass and rocks. While there is a distinct timber line, no snow line is attained. At the foot of the mountain is El Bouquette, much esteemed by the Panamanians as a health resort. Thither go Canal workers who, not being permitted to remain on the Zone during their vacations, wish to avoid the long voyage to North American ports.

This neighborhood is the center of the coffee-grow-

CHIRIQUI NATIVES IN AN OX-CART

way only. Cotton, tobacco and fiber plants also grow readily in this region but are little cultivated.

A curious industry of the Chiriqui country, now nearly abandoned, was the collection of gold ornaments which the Guaymi Indians formerly buried with their dead. These images sometimes in human form, more often in that of a fish, sometimes like frogs

THE CATTLE RANGE NEAR DAVID
In Chiriqui province there is much of this open savanna or prairie land bordered by thick jungle

and alligators, jointed and flexible, were at one time found in great quantities and formed a conspicuous feature of the Panama curiosity shops. In seeking these the hunters walked back and forth over the grounds known to be Indian burial places, tapping the ground with rods. When the earth gave forth a hollow sound the spade was resorted to, and usually a grave was uncovered. Jars which had contained wine and food were usually found in the graves, which were in fact subterranean tombs care-fully built with flat stones. The diggers tell of finding skulls perfectly preserved apparently but which crumbled to pieces at a touch. Evidently the burial places which can be identified through local tradition have been nearly exhausted, for the ancient trinkets cannot longer be readily found in the Panama shops.

Another Panamanian product which the tourists buy eagerly but which is rapidly becoming rare is the pearl. In the Gulf of Panama are a group of islands which have been known as Las Islas des Perlas— the Pearl Islands. This archipelago is about thirty miles long, with sixteen big islands and a quantity of small ones, and lies about sixty miles south of Panama City. Balboa saw them from the shore and intended to visit them but never did. Pizarro stopped there on his way to Peru and plundered them to his heart's content. Otherwise their history has been uneventful. Saboga on the island of the same name is a beautiful little tropical village of about 300 huts, on

PROCLAIMING A LAW AT DAVID
There being a dearth of newspapers and readers, new laws are promulgated by being read aloud

DESPOILING OLD GUAYMI GRAVES

a high bluff bordering a bay that affords excellent anchorage. Whales are plentiful in these waters and Pacific whalers are often seen in port. San Miguel, the largest town of the archipelago, is on Rey Island and has about 1000 inhabitants. The tower of its old church is thickly inlaid with glistening, pearly shell.

The pearl fisheries have been overworked for years, perhaps centuries, and begin to show signs of being exhausted. Nevertheless the tourist who takes the trip to the islands from the City of Panama will find himself beset by children as he lands offering seed pearls in quantities. Occasionally real bargains may be had from "beach combers" not only at Rey Island, but even at Taboga, where I knew an American visitor to pick up for eleven dollars three pearls valued at ten or twelve times as much when shown in the United States. There are stories of lucky finds among divers that vie with the tales of nuggets among gold prospectors. Once a native boy diving for sport in one of the channels near Naos Island brought up an oyster in which was a black pearl that was sold in Panama for $3000. The report does not say how much of this the boy got, but as the pearl was afterward sold in Paris for $12,000 it is quite evident that the share of the middleman, of whom political economists just now talk so much, was heavy. The Panama pearls are sometimes of beautiful colors, green, pale blue and a delicate pink. On the Chiriqui coast a year or two ago a pearl weighing about forty-two carats, about the size and shape of a partridge egg, greenish black at the base and shading to a steel gray at the tip, was found. It was sold in Paris for $5000.

It is a curious fact that the use of mussels from our western rivers is one cause for the decadence of the Panama pearl industry. For years the actual expense of maintaining these fisheries was met by the sale of the shell for use in making buttons and mother-of-pearl ornaments. The pearls represented the profit of the enterprise, which was always therefore more or less of a gamble—but a game in which it was impossible to lose, though the winnings might be great or small according to luck. Now that the demand for pearl oyster shells has fallen off, owing to the competition of mussels, the chances in the game are rather against the player and the sport languishes.

The authorities of the Republic are making some effort to establish a system of industrial schools which may lead to the fuller utilization of the natural resources of the country. Every tourist who visits the Isthmus is immediately taught by one who has been there a day or two longer than he that Panama hats are not made in Panama. This seems to be,

A DAY'S SHOOTING, GAME MOSTLY MONKEYS

the most precious information that anyone on the Zone has to impart. Most of the hats there sold are indeed made in Ecuador and the name "Panama" was first attached to them years ago, because their chief market was found in Panama City, whence they were distributed to more northern countries. The palm of which they are made however grows generally in Panama and the government has established in the Chiriqui province a school in which native boys are taught the art of hat making. In the National Institute at Panama City there is also a government trades school where boys are given a three years' course in the elements of the carpenters' and machinists' trades. Indeed the rulers of the Republic, which was so abruptly created, deserve great credit for the steps they are taking for the creation of a general system of public education, both literary and practical. The school system is not yet on a par with that of states of longer existence, nor will it in all probability ever quite conform to more northern ideas of an educational establishment. For example, the National Institute is closed to girls, who for their higher education are limited to the schools maintained by the church. A normal school, however, in which girls are prepared for teaching in the primary grades is maintained with about 125 students. The school system of Panama must be regarded merely as a nucleus from which a larger organism may grow. Yet when

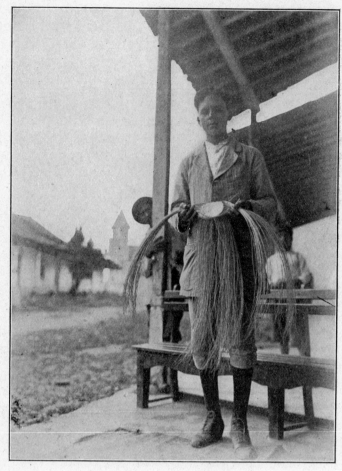

BEGINNING A PANAMA HAT

one recalls the state of society which has resulted from revolutions in other Central American states, one is impelled to a certain admiration for the promptitude with which the men who erected the Republic of Panama gave thought to the educational needs of people. They were suddenly put in authority over an infant state which had no debt, but, on the contrary, possessed a capital of $10,000,000 equivalent to about $30 for every man, woman and child of its population. Instead of creating an army, buying a navy and thus wasting the money on mere militarism which appeals so strongly to the Latin-American mind, they organ-

THE GOVERNMENT SCHOOL OF HAT MAKING

COFFEE PLANTATION AT BOUQUETTE

of its neighbors. Its monetary system affords one illustration. The highest coin of the land is the peso, a piece the size of our silver dollar but circulating at a value of fifty cents. If a man should want to pay a debt of $500 he would have to deliver 1000 pesos unless he was possessed of a bank account and could settle by check. No paper money is issued. "Who would take paper money issued by a Central American republic"? Ask the knowing ones scornfully when you inquire about this seeming lack in the monetary system. Yet the Republic of Panama is the most solvent of nations, having no national debt and with money in bank.

Probably the one obstacle to the progress of the Republic to greatness is the one common to all tropical countries on which Benjamin Kidd laid an unerring finger when he referred to the unwisdom of

ized a civil government, equipped it with the necessary buildings, established a university and laid the foundation of a national system of education.

The thoughtful traveler will concede to the Republic of Panama great natural resources and a most happy entrance to the family of nations. It is the especial protégé of the United States

WORK OF INDIAN STUDENTS IN THE NATIONAL INSTITUTE

longer permitting the riches of the tropics to "remain undeveloped with resources running to waste under the management of races of low social efficiency". The Panamanian authorities are making apparently sincere

and under the watchful care of its patron will be free from the apprehension of misuse, revolution or invasion from without which has kept other Central American governments in a constant state of unrest. About the international morality of the proceedings which created the relations now existing between the United States and Panama perhaps the least said the better. But even if we reprobate the sale of Joseph by his brethren, in the scripture story, we must at least admit that he did better in Egypt than in his father's house and that the protection and favor of the mighty Pharaoh was of the highest advantage to him, and in time to his unnatural brethren as well.

At present the Republic suffers not only from its own checkered past, but from the varied failings

endeavors to attract new settlers of greater efficiency. In proportion to the success that attends the efforts the future of Panama will be bright.

THE CRATER OF THE CHIRIQUI VOLCANO

VENDOR OF FRUIT AND POTTERY

Like all tropical towns Panama displays interesting bits of outdoor life in its street markets and vendors. The
sidewalks are the true shops and almost the homes of the people.

CHAPTER XVI

THE INDIANS OF PANAMA

WHILE that portion of the Panama territory that lies along the border of Colombia known as the Darien is rather ill-defined as to area and to boundaries, it is known to be rich in timber and is believed to possess gold mines of great richness. But it is practically impenetrable by the white man. Through this country Balboa led his force on his expedition to the unknown Pacific, and was followed by the bloodthirsty Pedrarias who bred up in the Indians a hatred of the white man that has grown as the ages passed. No expedition can enter this region even today except as an armed force ready to fight for the right of passage. In 1786 the Spaniards sought to subdue the territory, built forts on both the Atlantic and Pacific coasts and established a line of trading posts connecting them. But the effort failed. The posts were abandoned. Today the white man who tries to enter the Darien does so at the risk of his life.

In 1854 a navy exploring expedition of twenty-seven men, under command of Lieutenant Isaac C. Strain, entered the jungle of the Darien at Caledonia Bay, on the Atlantic side, the site of Patterson's ill-fated colony. They purposed crossing the Isthmus and making a survey for a canal route, as an English adventurer not long before had asserted—falsely as it proved—that he had discovered a route by which a canal could be built with but three or four miles of cutting. The party carried ten days' provisions and forty rounds of ball cartridge per man. They expected to have to traverse about forty or fifty miles, for which the supply of provisions seemed

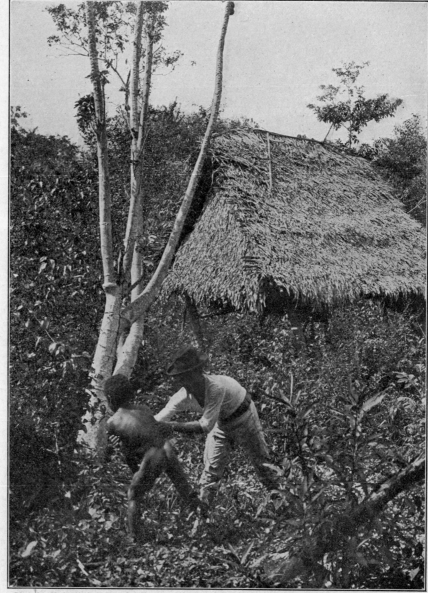

TRAPPING AN ABORIGINE
In houses and clothing the Darien Indians are decidedly primitive

NATIVE VILLAGE ON PANAMA BAY

are getting quite particular. Something of an epicure, eh'? With these words he quietly devoured the head himself."

Nine of the twenty-seven men who entered the Darien with Strain died. When the leader returned with the relief party they were found, like Greely at Camp Starvation, unable to move and slowly dying. Those who retained life never fully regained strength. Every condition which brought such frightful disaster upon the Strain party

wholly adequate. But when they had cut their way through the jungle, waded through swamps and climbed hills until their muscles were exhausted and their clothing torn to tatters, they found themselves lost in the very interior of the Isthmus with all their food gone. Diaries kept by members of the party show that they lived in constant terror of the Indians. But no attack was made upon them. The inhabitants contented themselves with disappearing before the white men's advance, sweeping their huts and fields clear of any sort of food. The jungle not its people fought the invaders. For food they had mainly nuts with a few birds and the diet disturbed their stomachs, caused sores and loosened their teeth. The bite of a certain insect deposited under the skin a kind of larva, or worm, which grew to the length of an inch and caused the most frightful torments. Despairing of getting his full party out alive, after they had been twenty-three days fighting with the jungle, Strain took three men and pushed ahead to secure and send back relief. It was thirty-nine days before the men left behind saw him again.

Death came fast to those in the jungle. The agonies they suffered from starvation, exposure and insect pests baffle description. "Truxton in casting his eyes on the ground saw a toad", wrote the historian. "Instantly snatching it up, he bit off the head and, spitting it away, devoured the body. Maury looked at him a moment, and then picked up the rejected head, saying, 'Well, Truxton, you

exists in the Darien today. The Indians are as hostile, the trails as faintly outlined, the jungle as dense, the insects as savage. Only along the banks of the rivers has civilization made some little headway, but the richest gold field twenty miles back in the interior is as safe from civilized workings as though it were walled in with steel and guarded by dragons. Every speculative man you meet in Panama will assure you that the gold is there but all agree that conditions must be radically changed before it can be gotten out unless a regiment and a subsistence train shall follow the miners.

The authorities of Panama estimate that there are about 36,000 tribal Indians, that is to say aborigines,

A RIVER LANDING PLACE

still holding their tribal organizations and acknowledging fealty to no other government now in the Isthmus. The estimate is of course largely guesswork, for few of the wild Indians leave the jungle and fewer still of the census enumerators enter it. Most of these Indians live in the mountains of the provinces of Bocas del Toro, Chiriqui and Veragua, or in the Darien. Their tribes are many and the sources of information concerning them but few. The most accessible and complete record of the various tribes is in a pamphlet issued by the Smithsonian Institution, and now obtainable only through public libraries, as the edition for distribution has been exhausted. The author, Miss Eleanor Yorke Bell, beside studies made at first hand has diligently examined the authorities on the subject and has presented the only considerable treatise on the subject of which I have knowledge.

Of life among the more civilized natives she says:

"The natives of the Isthmus in general, even in the larger towns, live together without any marriage ceremony, separating at will and dividing the

Photo by Underwood & Underwood

ON THE RIO GRANDE

children. As there is little or no personal property, this is accomplished amicably as a rule, though should disputes arise the alcalde of the district is appealed to, who settles the matter. This informal system is always stoutly defended by the women, even more than by the men, for, as among all people low in the scale of civilization, it is generally held that the women receive better treatment when not bound and therefore free to depart at any time. Recently an effort has been made to bring more of the inhabitants under the marriage laws, with rather amusing results in many instances. The majority of the population is nominally Catholic, but the teachings of the church are only vaguely understood, and its practices consist in the adoration of a few battered images of saints whose particular degree of sanctity is not even guessed at and who, when their owners are displeased with them, receive rather harsh treatment, as these people have usually no real

THE FALLS AT CHORRERA

OLD SPANISH CHURCH, CHORRERA

water, cutting the wood, making the fire, cooking the food, etc., ending in a burst of song symbolizing the joys of the new prepared feast. In an extremely crude form it reminds one of the old opera ballets and seems to be a composite of the original African and the ancient Spanish, which is very probably the case.

"The Orientals of the Isthmus deserve a word in passing. They are chiefly Chinese coolies and form a large part of the small merchant class. Others, in the hill districts, cultivate large truck gardens, bringing their produce swinging over the shoulders on poles to the city markets. Their houses and grounds are very attractive, built of reed or bamboo in the eastern fashion and marked everywhere by extreme neatness, contrasting so strikingly with the homes and surroundings of their negro neighbors. Many cultivate fields of cane or rice as well, and amidst the silvery greens, stretching for some distance, the quaint blue figures of the workmen in their huge hats make a charming picture. Through the rubber sections Chinese

idea of Christianity beyond a few distorted and superstitious beliefs. After the widespread surveys of the French engineers, a sincere effort was made to re-Christianize the inhabitants of the towns in Darien as well as elsewhere, for, until this time, nothing had been done toward their spiritual welfare since the days of the early Jesuits. In the last thirty years spasmodic efforts have been made to reach the people with little result, and, excepting at Penonome, David, and Santiago, there are few churches where services are held outside of Panama and the towns along the railroad.

"The chief amusements of the Isthmian are gambling, cock-fighting, and dancing, the latter assisted by the music of the tom-tom and by dried beans rattled in a calabash. After feasts or burials, when much bad rum and whisky is consumed, the hilarity keeps up all night and can be heard for miles, increased by the incessant howls of the cur dogs lying under every shack. Seldom does an opportunity come to the stranger to witness the really characteristic dances, as the natives do not care to perform before them, though a little money will sometimes work wonders. Occasionally, their dancing is really remarkably interesting, when a large amount of pantomime enters into it and they develop the story of some primitive action, as, for instance, the drawing of the

THE CHURCH AT ANTON

'middlemen' are of late frequently found buying that valuable commodity for their fellow countrymen in Panama City, who are now doing quite a large business in rubber. These people live much as in their native land, seldom learning more than a few words of Spanish (except those living in the towns), and they form a very substantial and good element of the population".

To enumerate even by names the aboriginal tribes would be tedious and unavailing. Among the more notable are the Doracho-Changuina, of Chiriqui, light of color, believing that the Great Spirit lived in the volcano of Chiriqui, and occasionally showing their displeasure with him by shooting arrows at the mountain. The Guaymies, of whom perhaps 6000 are left, are the tribe that buried with their dead the curious golden images that were once plentiful in the bazaars of Panama, but are now hard to find. They have a pleasant

inhabiting the Darien. All were, and some are, believed still to be cannibals. Eleven lesser tribes are grouped under this general name. As a rule

NATIVE VILLAGE AT CAPERA

they are small and muscular. Most of them have abandoned their ancient gaudy dress, and so far as they are clothed at all wear ordinary cotton clothing. Painting the face and body is still practiced. The dead often are swung in hammocks from trees and supplied with fresh provisions until the cords rot and the body falls to the ground. Then the spirit's journey to the promised land is held to be ended and provisions are no longer needed. Sorcery and soothsaying are much in vogue, and the sorcerers who correspond to the medicine men of our North American Indians will sometimes shut themselves up in a small hut shrieking, beating tom-toms and imitating the cries of wild animals. When they emerge in a sort of self-hypnotized state they are held to be peculiarly fit for prophesying.

All the Indians drink heavily, and the white man's rum is to some extent displacing the native drink of chica. This is manufactured by the women, usually the old ones, who sit in a circle chewing yam roots or cassava and expectorating

THE PEARL ISLAND VILLAGE OF SABOGA

practice of putting a calabash of water and some plantains by a man they think dying and leaving him to his fate, usually in some lonesome part of the jungle. The Cunas or Caribs are the tribes the saliva into a large bowl in the center. This ferments and is made the basis of a highly intoxicating drink. Curiously enough the same drink is similarly made in far-away Samoa. The dutiful wives after thus manufacturing the material upon which their spouses get drunk complete their service by swinging their hammocks, sprinkling them with cold water and fanning them as they lie in a stupor. Smoking is another social custom, but the cigars are mere hollow rolls of tobacco and the lighted end is held in the mouth. Among some of the tribes in Comagre the bodies of the caciques, or chief men, were preserved after death by surrounding them with a ring of fire built at a sufficient distance to gradually dry the body until skin and bone alone remained.

The Indians with whom the visitor to Panama most frequently comes into contact are those of the San Blas or Manzanillo country. These Indians hover curiously about the bounds of civilization, and approach without actually crossing them. They are fishermen and sailors, and many of their young men ship on the vessels touching at Colon, and, after visiting the chief seaports of the United States, and even of France and England, are swallowed up again in their tribe without affecting its customs to any appreciable degree. If in their wanderings they gain new ideas or new desires they are not apparent. The man who silently offers you fish, fruits or vegetables from his cayuca on the beach at Colon may have trod the docks at Havre

Photo by H. Pittier   *Courtesy National Geographic Magazine*
A CHOCO INDIAN IN FULL COSTUME
His cuffs are silver; his head adorned with flowers

or Liverpool, the levee at New Orleans or wandered along South Street in New York. Not a word of that can you coax from him. Even in proffering his wares he does so with the fewest possible words, and an air of lofty indifference. Uncas of the Leather-Stocking Tales was no more silent and self-possessed a red-skin than he.

In physiognomy the San Blas Indians are heavy of feature and stocky of frame. Their color is dark olive, with no trace of the negro apparent, for it has been their unceasing study for centuries to retain their racial purity. Their features are regular and pleasing and, among the children particularly, a high order of beauty is often found. To get a glimpse of their women is almost impossible, and a photograph of one is practically unknown. If overtaken on the water, to which they often resort in their cayucas, the women will wrap their clothing about their faces, rather heedless of what other portions of their bodies may be exposed, and make all speed for the shore. These women paint their faces in glaring colors, wear nose rings, and always blacken their teeth on being married. Among them more pains is taken with clothing than among most of the savage Indians, many of their garments being made of a sort of appliqué work in gaudy colors, with figures, often in representation of the human form, cut out and inset in the garment.

So determined are the men of this tribe to maintain its blood untarnished by any admixture whatsoever, that they long made it an invariable rule to expel every white man from their territory at nightfall. Of late years there has been a very slight relaxation of this severity. Dr. Henri Pittier of the United States Department of Agriculture, one of the best-equipped scientific explorers in the tropics, several of whose photographs elucidate this volume, has lived much among the San Blas and the Cuna-Cuna Indians and won their friendship.

It was the ancestors of these Indians who made welcome Patterson and his luckless Scotchmen, and in the 200 years that have elasped they have clung to the tradition of friendship for the Briton and hatred for the Spaniard. Dr. Pittier reports having found that Queen Victoria occupied in their villages the position of a patron saint, and that they refused to believe his assertion that she was dead. His account of the attitude of these Indians toward outsiders, recently printed in the National Geographic Magazine, is an authoritative statement on the subject:

"The often circulated reports of the difficulty of penetrating into the territory of the Cuna-Cuna are true only in part", he says. "The backwoods aborigines, in the valleys of the Bayano and Chucunaque rivers, have nourished to this day their hatred for all strangers, especially those of Spanish blood. That feeling is not a reasoned one: it is the instinctive distrust of the savage for the un-

SOME SAN BLAS GIRLS
The dresses are covered with elaborate designs in appliqué work

known or inexplicable, intensified in this particular case by the tradition of a long series of wrongs at the hands of the hated Spaniards.

"So they feel that isolation is their best policy,

and it would not be safe for anybody to penetrate into their forests without a strong escort and continual watchfulness. Many instances of murders, some confirmed and others only suspected, are on record, and even the natives of the San Blas coast are not a little afraid of their brothers of the mountains.

"Of late, however, conditions seem to have bettered, owing to a more frequent intercourse with the surrounding settlements. A negro of La Palma, at the mouth of the Tuyra River, told me of his crossing, some time ago, from the latter place to Chepo, through the Chucunaque and Bayano territories, gathering rubber as he went along with his party. At the headwaters of the Canaza River he and his companions were held up by the 'bravos', who contented themselves with taking away the rubber and part of the equipment

Photo by H. Pittier   Courtesy of National Geographic Magazine
CHIEF DON CARLOS OF THE CHOCOES AND HIS SON

and then let their prisoners go with the warning not to come again.

"The narrative of that expedition was supplemented by the reflection of an old man among the hearers that twenty years ago none of the party would have come out alive.

"Among the San Blas Indians, who are at a far higher level of civilization, the exclusion of aliens is the result of well-founded political reasons. Their respected traditions are a long record of proud independence; they have maintained the purity of their race and enjoyed freely for hundreds of years every inch of their territory. They feel that the day the negro or the white man acquires a foothold in their midst these privileges will become a thing of the past. This is why, without undue hostility to strangers, they discourage their incursions.

Courtesy of National Geographic Magazine

THE VILLAGE OF PLAYON GRAND, EIGHTY-FIVE MILES EAST OF THE CANAL
The houses are about 150 x 50 feet and each shelters 16 to 20 families. The members of each family herd together in a single room

Photo by H. Pittier   Courtesy Nat'l Geographic Magazine
SAN BLAS WOMAN IN DAILY GARB

"Their means of persuasion are adjusted to the importance of the intruder. They do not hesitate to shoot at any negro of the nearby settlements poaching on their cocoanuts or other products; the trader or any occasional visitor is very seldom allowed to stay ashore at night; the adventurers who try to go prospecting into Indian territory are invariably caught and shipped back to the next Panamanian port".

Among the men of the San Blas tribe the land held by their people is regarded as a sacred trust, bequeathed to them by their ancestors and to be handed down by them to the remotest posterity. During the early days of the Canal project it was desired to dig sand from a beach in the San Blas country. A small United States man-of-war was sent thither to broach the subject to the Indians, and the Captain held parley with the chief. After hearing the plea and all the arguments and promises with which it was strengthened the old Indian courteously refused the privilege:

"He who made this land", said he, "made it for Cuna-Cuna who live no longer, for those who are here today and also for the ones to come. So it is not ours only and we could not sell it".

To this decision the tribe adhered, and the wishes of the aborigines have been respected. It has been the policy of the United States to avoid any

Photo by H. Pittier Courtesy Nat'l Geographic Magazine
A GIRL OF THE CHOCO TRIBE

Photo by H. Pittier   Courtesy National Geographic Magazine
DAUGHTER OF CHIEF DON CARLOS
This young girl is merry, plump and fond of finger rings

possibility of giving offense to the native population of the Isthmus, and even a request from the chief that the war vessel that brought the negotiator on his fruitless errand should leave was acceded to. It is quite unlikely, however, that the Indians will be able to maintain their isolation much longer. Already there are signs of its breaking down. While I was in Panama they sent a request that a missionary, a woman it is true, who had been much among them, should come and live with them permanently. They also expressed a desire that she should bring her melodeon, thus giving new illustration to the poetic adage, "Music hath charms to soothe the savage breast". Perhaps the phonograph may in time prove the open sesame to many savage bosoms. Among this people it is the women who cling most

NATIVE BRIDGE OVER THE CALDERA RIVER

grove or an orange tree planted and cared for, becomes a positive possession handed down to descendants of the owner through the female line. Perhaps one reason for keeping the women so shut off from the world is that they are the real owners of all individual property. Ownership does not, however, attach to trees or plants growing wild; they are as much communal as the land. So the vegetable ivory, balata and cocoanuts which form the marketable products are gathered by whomsoever may take the trouble. Land that has been tilled belongs to the one who improved it. If he let it lapse into wilderness it reverts to the community. The San Blas Indians have the essence of the single tax theory without the tax.

They have a hazily defined religious system, and have curiously reversed the position held by their priests or sorcerers. These influential persons are not representatives of the spirit of good, but of the bad spirit. Very logically the San Blas savages hold that any one may represent the good spirit by being himself good, and that the unsupported prayers of such a one are sure to be heard. But to reach the devil, to induce that malicious practitioner of evil to rest from his persecutions and to abandon the pursuit of the unfortunate, it is desirable to have as intermediary some one who possesses his confidence and high regard. Hence the strong position of the sorcerers in the villages. The people defer to them on the principle that it is well to make friends with "the Mammon of Unrighteousness".

Polygamy is permitted among these Indians, but little practiced. Even the chiefs whose high estate gives them the right to more than one wife seldom avail themselves of the privilege. The women, as in most primitive tribes, are the hewers of wood and drawers of water. Dress is rather a more serious matter with them than among some of the other Indians, the Chocoes for example. They wear as a rule blouses and two skirts, where other denizens of the Darien dispense with clothing above the waist altogether. Their hair is usually kept short. The nose ring is looked upon as indispensable, and other ornaments of both gold and silver are worn by both sexes. Americans who have had much to do with the Indians of the Darien always comment on the extreme reticence shown by them in speaking of their golden ornaments, or the spot whence they

tenaciously to the primitive customs, as might be expected, since they have been so assiduously guarded against the wiles of the world. But Catholic missionaries have made some headway in the country, and at Narganá schools for girls have been opened under auspices of the church. It is probably due to the feminine influence that the San Blas men return so unfailingly to primitive customs after the voyages that have made them familiar with civilization. If the women yield to the desire for novelty the splendid isolation of the San Blas will not long endure. Perhaps that would be unfortunate, for all other primitive peoples who have surrendered to the wiles of the white men have suffered and disappeared.

In their present state the San Blas are relatively rich. All the land belongs to all the people—that is why the old chief declined to sell the sandy beach. There is a sort of private property in improvements. A banana plantation, a cocoanut were obtained. It is as though vague traditions had kept alive the story of the pestilence of fire and sword which ravaged their land when the Spaniards swept over it in search of the yellow metal. Gold is in the Darien in plenty. Everybody knows that, and the one or two mines near the rivers now being worked afford sufficient proof that the region is auriferous. But no Indian will tell of the existence of these mines, nor will any guide a white man to the spot where it is rumored gold is to be found. Seemingly ineradicably fixed in the inner consciousness of the Indian is the conviction that the white man's lust for the yellow metal is the greatest menace that confronts the well-being of himself and his people.

The San Blas are decidedly a town-dwelling tribe. They seem to hate solitude and even today, in their comparatively reduced state, build villages of a size that make understandable Balboa's records of the size and state of the chief with whom he first fought, and then made friends. At Nargana are two large islands, fairly covered with spacious houses about 150 feet long by 50 broad. The ridge pole of the palm-thatched roof is 30 to 40 feet from the ground. A long corridor runs through the house longitudinally, and on either side the space is divided by upright posts into square compartments, each of which is supposed to house an entire family. The side walls are made of wattled reeds caked with clay. One of these houses holds from sixteen to twenty families, and the edifices are packed so closely together as to leave scarce room between for a razorback hog to browse. The people within must be packed about as closely and the precise parental relationship sustained to each other by the various members of the family would be an interesting study.

The Choco Indians are one of the smaller and least known tribes of the Darien. Prof. Pittier—who may without disrespect be described as the most seasoned "tropical tramp" of all Central America—described them so vividly that extracts from his article in the National Geographic Magazine will be of interest:

"Never, in our twenty-five years of tropical experience, have we met with such a sun-loving, bright and trusting people, living nearest to nature and ignoring the most elementary wiles of so-called civilization. They are several hundred in number

Photo by H. Pittier Courtesy National Geographic Magazine

GUAYMI INDIAN MAN
Note the tattoed marking of face and the negroid lips

and their dwellings are scattered along the meandrous Sambu and its main reaches, always at short distance, but never near enough to each other to form real villages. Like their houses, their small plantations are close to the river, but mostly far enough to escape the eye of the casual passer-by.

"Dugouts drawn up on the beach and a narrow trail breaking the reed wall at the edge of the bank are the only visible signs of human presence, except at the morning hours and near sunset, when a crowd of women and children will be seen playing in the water, and the men, armed with their bows and long harpooned arrows, scrutinizing the deeper places for fish or looking for iguanas and crabs hidden in the holes of the banks.

"Physically the Chocoes are a fine and healthy race. They are tall, as compared with the Cuna-Cuna, well proportioned, and with a graceful bearing. The men have wiry limbs and faces that are at once kind and energetic, while as a rule the girls are plump, fat, and full of mischief. The grown women preserve their good looks and attractiveness much longer than is generally the case in primitive peoples, in which their sex bears the heaviest share of every day's work.

"Both males and females have unusually fine white teeth, which they sometimes dye black by chewing the shoots of one of the numerous wild peppers growing in the forests. The skin is of a rich olive-brown color and, as usual, a little lighter in women and children. Though all go almost naked, they look fairer than the San Blas Cunas, and some of the women would compare advantageously in this respect with certain Mediterranean types of the white race.

"The hair is left by all to grow to its natural length, except in a few cases, in which the men have it cropped at the neck. It is coarse and not jet black, as reported of most Indians, but with a reddish hue, which is better noticed when the sun is playing through the thick mass.

"In young children it decidedly turns at times to a blond color, the only difference from the Caucasian hair being the pronounced coarseness of the former. As there are no white people living within a radius of fifty miles, but only negroes, mulattoes and zambos, this peculiarity cannot be explained by miscegenation, and may therefore be considered as a racial feature of the Choco tribe.

"In men the every-day dress consists of a scanty clout, made of a strip of red calico about one foot broad and five feet long. This clout is passed in front and back of the body over a string tied around the hips, the forward extremity being left longer and flowing like an apron. On feast days the string is replaced by a broad band of white beads. Around the neck and chest they wear thick cords of the same beads and on their wrists broad silver cuffs. Hats are not used; the hair is usually tied with a red ribbon and often adorned with the bright flowers of the forest.

Photo by H. Pittier   Courtesy National Geographic Magazine

INDIAN GIRL OF THE DARIEN

"The female outfit is not less simple, consisting of a piece of calico less than three feet wide and about nine feet long, wrapped around the lower part of the body and reaching a little below the knees. This is all, except that the neck is more or less loaded with beads or silver coins. But for this the women display less coquetry than the men, which may be because they feel sufficiently adorned with their mere natural charms. Fondness for cheap rings is, however, common to both sexes, and little children often wear earrings or pendants.

"The scantiness of the clothing is remedied very effectually by face and body painting, in which black and red colors are used, the first exclusively for daily wear. At times men and women are painted black from the waist down; at other times it is the whole body or only the hands and feet, etc., all according to the day's fashion, as was explained by one of our guides. For feast days the paintings are an elaborate and artistic affair, consisting of elegantly drawn lines and patterns—red and black or simply black—which clothe the body as effectually as any costly dress.

"From the above one might conclude that cleanliness and modesty are not the rule among the Chocos. As a matter of fact, the first thing they do in the morning is to jump into the near-by river, and these ablutions are repeated several times in the course of the day.

"The kitchen utensils are always thoroughly washed before using, and, contrary to our former experience, their simple dishes, prepared mostly in our presence, looked almost always inviting. During our stay among these good people nothing was noticed that would hurt the most delicate sense of decency.

"The Chocoes seem to be exclusively monogamist, and both parents surround their babies with tender care, being mindful, however, to prepare them early for the hard and struggling life ahead of them. Small bows and arrows, dexterously handled by tiny hands, are the favorite toys of the boys, while the girls spend more time in the water playing with miniature dugouts, washing, and swimming. The only dolls seen among them were imported ones, and they seemed to be as much in favor among grown women as among children. These latter go naked until they are about five years old, when the girls receive a large handkerchief to be used as a 'paruma', or skirt, and the boys a strip of some old maternal dress for an 'antia' or clout.

"The Chocoes are very industrious. During the dry spells their life, of course, is an out-of-door one, planting and watching their crops, hunting, fishing and canoeing. But when the heavy rains come they stay at home, weaving baskets of all kinds—a work in which the women are proficient—making ropes and hammocks, carving dishes, mortars, stools, and other objects out of tree trunks".

In the country which will be traversed by the Panama-David Railroad are found the Guaymies, the only primitive people living in large numbers outside the Darien. There are about 5000 of them, living for the most part in the valley of Mirando which lies high up in the Cordilleras, and in a region cut off from the plains. Here they have successfully defended their independence against the assaults of both whites and blacks. To remain in their country without consent of the Great Chief is practically impossible, for they are savage fighters and in earlier days it was rare to see a man whose body was not covered with scars. It is apparent that in some ways progress has destroyed their industries and made the people less rather than more civilized, for they now buy cloth, arms, tools, and utensils which they were once able to make. At one time they were much under the

Photo by H. Pittier   Courtesy National Geographic Magazine
CHOCO INDIAN OF SAMBU VALLEY
Silver beads about his neck and leg.   Face painted in glaring colors

influence of the Catholic missionaries, but of late mission work has languished in wild Panama and perhaps the chief relic of that earlier religious influence is the fact that the women go clothed in a single garment. This simple raiment, not needed for warmth, seems to be prized, for if caught in a rainstorm the women will quickly strip off their clothing, wrap it in a large banana or palm leaf that it may not get wet, and continue their work, or their play, in nature's garb.

It is said, too, that when strangers are not near clothes are never thought of. The men follow a like custom, and invariably when pursuing a quarry strip off their trousers, tying their shirts about their loins. Trousers seem to impede their movements, and if a lone traveler in Chiriqui comes on a row of blue cotton trousers tied to the bushes he may be sure that a band of Guaymies is somewhere in the neighborhood pursuing an ant bear or a deer.

As a rule these Indians—men or women—are not pleasing to the eye. The lips are thick, the nose flat and broad, the hair coarse and always jet black. Yet the children are not infrequently really beautiful. Any traveler in Panama who forsakes the beaten track up and down the Canal Zone will be impressed by the wide extent to which beauty is found among the children, whatever their race or combination of races. But the charm soon fades. It is seldom that one sees a mature woman who is attractive to Caucasian eyes. Among the women of the Guaymies face painting is practiced only on great occasions, black, red and white being the usual colors. The men go painted at all times, the invariable pattern being a sort of inverted V, with the apex between the eyes, and the two arms extending to points, half an inch or so from the corners of the mouth. The lips are colored to make them seem thicker than normal, and heavy shadows are painted in under the eyes.

Among some tribes the wealth of a man is reckoned by the number of his cattle; among the Guaymies by the number of his wives. For this reason, perhaps, the attainment of marriageable age is an occasion of much festivity for children of both sexes. The boy is exposed to tests of his manly and war-like qualities, and, in company with his fellows of equal age, is taken by the wisemen of the tribe into the solitude of the forest that by performing tasks assigned to him he may prove himself a man. There, too, they learn from the elders, who go masked and crowned with wreaths, the traditions of their tribes told in rude chants like the Norse sagas. Until this ceremony has been fulfilled the youth has no name whatsoever. After it he is named and celebrates his first birthday.

The ceremonies in which the girls play the chief part are less elaborate, but one would think rather painful, since they include the breaking of a front tooth in sign that they are ready for marriage. They marry young and mothers at twelve years are not uncommon.

Once a year the Guaymies have a great tribal feast—"balceria" the Spaniards call it. Word is sent to all outlying huts and villages by a mystic symbol of knotted rags, which is also tied to the branches of the trees along the more frequented trails. On the appointed day several hundred will gather on the banks of some river in which a general bath is taken, with much frolicking and horseplay. Then the women employ several hours in painting

PANAMANIAN FATHER AND CHILD

the men with red and blue colors, following the figures still to be seen on the old pottery, after which the men garb themselves uncouthly in bark or in pelts like children "dressing up" for a frolic. At night is a curious ceremonial dance and game called balsa, in which the Indians strike each other with heavy sticks, and are knocked down amid the pile of broken boughs. The music—if it could be so called—the incantations of the wisemen, the frenzy of the dancers, all combine to produce a sort of self-hypnotism, during which the Indians feel no pain from injuries which a day later often prove to be very serious.

There are a multitude of distinct Indian tribes on the Isthmus, each with its own tribal government, its distinctive customs and its allotted territory, though boundaries are, of course, exceedingly vague and the territories overlap. The Smithsonian pamphlet enumerates 21 such tribes in the Darien region alone. But there seems to be among them no such condition of continual tribal warfare as existed between our North American Indians as long as they survived in any considerable numbers the aggressions of the white settlers. It is true that the historian of Balboa's expedition records that the great leader was besought by chieftains to assist them in their affrays with rival tribes, and made more than one alliance by giving such assistance. But the later atrocities perpetrated by the Spaniards seem to have had the effect of uniting the Indians in a tacit peaceful bond against the whites. Picturesque and graphic as are the writings of men like Esquemelin, the Fray d'Acosta and Wafer, who saw the Indians in the days of their earliest experience with the sort of civilization that Pedrarias and Pizarro brought to their villages, they do not bear more convincing evidence of the savagery of the invaders, than is afforded by the sullen aloofness with which the Darien Indians of today regard white men of any race. More than the third and fourth generation have passed away but the sins of the Spaniards are still recalled among a people who have no written records whatsoever, and the memory or tradition causes them to withhold their friendship from the remotest descendants of the historic oppressors.

There seems to have been no written language, nor even any system of hieroglyphics among the tribes of Panama, a fact that places them far below our North American Indians in the scale of mental development. On the other hand in weaving and in fashioning articles for domestic use they were in advance of the North American aborigines. Their

Photo by H. Pittier
Courtesy National Geographic Magazine

CHOCO INDIAN IN EVERY-DAY
DRESS

domestic architecture was more substantial, and they were less nomadic, the latter fact being probably due to the slight encouragement given to wandering by the jungle. The great houses of the San Blas Indians in their villages recall the "Long houses" of the Iroquois as described by Parkman.

Thus far what we call civilization has dealt less harshly with the Indians of the Isthmus than with our own. They have at least survived it and kept a great part of their territory for their own. The

"squaw-man" who figures so largely in our own southwestern Indian country is unknown there. Unquestionably during the feverish days of the Spaniards, hunt for gold the tribes were frightfully thinned out, and even today sections of the country which writers of Balboa's time describe as thickly populated are desert and untenanted. Yet much land is still held by its aboriginal owners, and unless the operation of the Canal shall turn American settlement that way will continue so to be held. The Panamanian has not the energy to dislodge the Indians nor to till their lands if he should possess them.

Many studies of the Panama Indians as a body, or of isolated tribes, have been made by explorers or scientists, and mainly by French or Spanish students. The Smithsonian Institution catalogues forty-seven publications dealing with the subject. But there is an immense mine of anthropological information yet to be worked in the Isthmus. It is not to be acquired readily or without heavy expenditure of energy, patience and money. A thoroughly scientific exploring expedition to unravel the riddle of the Darien, to count and describe the Indian tribes of the Isthmus, and to record and authenticate traditions dating back to the Spanish days, would be well worth the while of a geographical society, a university or some patron of exploring enterprises.

CHAPTER XVII

SOCIAL LIFE ON THE CANAL ZONE

FROM ocean to ocean the territory which is called the Canal Zone is about forty-three miles long, ten miles wide and contains about 436 square miles, about ninety-five of which are under the waters of the Canal, and Miraflores and Gatun Lakes. It is bounded on the north by the Caribbean Sea, on the south by the Pacific Ocean, and on the east and west by the Republic of Panama. It traverses the narrowest part of Panama, the waist so to speak, and has been taken out of that body politic by the diplomatic surgeons as neatly as though it had been an obnoxious vermiform appendix. Its territory does not terminate at low water-mark, but extends three marine miles out to sea, and, as I write, a question of jurisdiction has arisen between the two Republics—hardly twin Republics—of Panama and the United States concerning jurisdiction over three malefactors captured by the Zone police in a motor boat out at sea. It may be noted in passing that Panama is properly tenacious of its rights and dignity, and that cases of conflicting jurisdiction are continually arising when any offender has only to foot it a mile or two to be out of the territory in which his offense was committed. The police officials of the Zone affect to think that the Panama authorities are inclined to deal lightly with native offenders who commit robbery or murder on the Zone and then stroll across the line to be arrested in their native State.

There was a quarrel on while I was on the Zone over the custody of a Panamanian who killed his wife, with attendant circumstances of peculiar

A SQUAD OF CANAL ZONE POLICE OFFICERS

brutality, and then balked the vengeance of the Zone criminal authorities by getting himself arrested in Panama. "We want to show these fellows", remarked a high police official of the Zone, "that if they do murder in our territory we are going to do the hanging". That seemed a laudable purpose— that is if hanging is ever laudable—but the Panama officials are quite as determined to keep the wheels of their criminal law moving. The proprietors of machines like to see them run—which is one of the reasons why too many battleships are not good for a nation.

VINE-CLAD FAMILY QUARTERS

To return, however, to the statistics of the Zone. Its population is shifting, of course, and varies somewhat in its size according to the extent to which labor is in demand. The completion of a part of the work occasionally reduces the force. In January, 1912, the total population of the Zone, according to the official census, was 62,810; at the same time, by the same authority, there were employed by the Canal Commission and the Panama Railroad 36,600 men. These figures emphasize the fact that the working force on the Zone is made up mainly of unmarried men, for a working population of 36,600 would, under the conditions existing in the ordinary American community, give a popula-

QUARTERS OF A BACHELOR TEACHER

tion of well over 100,000. Though statistics are not on hand, and would probably be impossible to compile among the foreign laborers, it is probable that not more than one man in four on the Zone is married.

From this situation it results that the average maiden who visits the Zone for a brief holiday goes rushing home to get her trousseau ready before some young engineer's next annual vacation shall give him time to go like a young Lochinvar in search of his bride. Indeed, the life of the Zone for many reasons has been singularly conducive to matrimony, and as a game preserve for the exciting sport of husband-hunting, it has been unexcelled.

Perhaps it may be as well to turn aside from the orderly and informative discussion of the statistics of the Zone to expand a little further here upon the remarkable matrimonial phenomena it presented in its halcyon days—for it must be remembered that even as I am writing, that society, which I found so hospitable and so admirable, has begun to disintegrate. Marriage, it must be admitted, is a somewhat cosmopolitan passion. It attacks spiggotty and gringo alike. In an earlier chapter I have described how the low cost of living enabled Miguel of the Chagres country to set up a home of his own. Let us consider how the benevolent arrangements made by the Isthmian Canal Commission impelled a typical American boy to the same step.

A PRIMITIVE SUGAR MILL

Probably it was more a desire for experience and adventure than any idea of increased financial returns that led young Jack Maxon to seek a job in engineering on the Canal. Graduated from the engineering department of a State university, with two years or so of active experience in the field, Jack was a fair type of young American—clean, wholesome, healthy, technically trained, ambitious for his future but quite solicitous about the pleasures of the present, as becomes a youth of twenty-three.

The job he obtained seemed at the outset quite ideal. In the States he could earn about $225 a month. The day he took his number on the Canal Zone he began to draw $250 a month. And that $250 was quite as good as $300 at home. To begin with he had no room-rent to pay, but was assigned comfortable if not elegant quarters, which he shared

cated in the States for seventy-five cents, but I prefer to quote that statement rather than to make it on my own authority. By taking two meals a day and making the third of fruit, or a sandwich at a Y. M. C. A. clubhouse, he would cut his restaurant charges to $18 a month; the whole three meals would come to $27.80, so however voracious his appetite Bachelor Jack's charges for food are light and for shelter nothing. Clothing troubles him little; his working clothes of khaki, and several suits of white cotton duck will cost him less than one woolen suit such as he must have "up home". All seasons are alike on the Zone, and there is no need of various types of hats, overcoats and underwear.

All in all Bachelor Jack thinks he has come in for a good thing. Moreover, he gets a vacation of forty-two days on pay, a sick leave of thirty days on pay — and the sanitarium on the Island of Taboga being a very pleasant resort few fail to have slight ailments requiring precisely thirty days' rest— and nine holidays also with pay. All in all Jack is neither overworked nor underpaid. His letters to his chums at home tell no stories of adversity but rather indi-

MAIN STREET AT GORGONA

with one other man, carefully screened and protected from all insects by netting, lighted by electricity, with a shower-bath handy and all janitor or chambermaid service free. Instead of a boarding-house table or a cheap city restaurant, he took his meals at a Commission hotel at a charge of thirty cents a meal. People say that the fare could not be dupli-

cate that he is enjoying exceedingly good times. With reasonable care he will have ample means for really lavish expenditures on his vacation. Indeed it would require rather unreasonable effort to spend an engineer's salary on the zone unless it went in riotous living in Panama City or Colon.

But a vision of better things opens before him—is always spread out before his enraptured vision. His friend who came down a year or two before him and who is earning only a little bit more money sets a standard of living which arouses new ambitions in Jack's mind. His friend is married. Instead of one room shared with one or more tired engineers subject to grouches, he has a four-room apartment with bath—really a five-room flat, for the broad sheltered balconies shaded by vines form the real living room. Instead of eating at the crowded, noisy hotels, he has his quiet dining-room, and menus dictated by individual taste instead of by the mechanical methods of a Chief of Subsistence. Practically everything that can be done for the house-

IN THE LOBBY OF A Y.M.C.A. CLUB

hold by official hands is done free by the Commission—free rent, free light, free janitor service, free distilled water, free fuel for cooking—the climate saves that bugbear of married life at home, the annual coal bill. Moreover the flat or house comes to its tenant freely furnished. The smallest equipment supplied consists of a range, two kitchen chairs, a double bed, a mosquito bar, two pillows, a chiffonier, a double dresser, a double mattress, a dining table, six dining chairs, a sideboard, a bed-room mat, two center tables and three wicker porch chairs. This equipment is for the moderately paid employees who live in four-family quarters. The outfit is made more comprehensive as salaries increase.

Housekeepers must buy their own tableware, bedclothes, light furniture and bric-à-brac. But here again the paternal Commission comes to the

rescue, for these purchases, and all others needful for utility, comfort or beauty, are made at the Commissary stores, where goods are sold practically at cost. Moreover, there is no protective tariff collected on imported goods and it would take another article to relate the rhapsodies of the Zone women over the prices at which they can buy Boulton tableware, Irish linen, Swiss and Scandinavian delicatessen, and French products of all sorts. And finally, to round out the privileges of married life on the Zone, medical service is free and little Tommy's slightest ill may be prescribed for without fear of the doctor's bill—though, indeed, the children you see romping in the pleasant places do not look as though they ever needed a prescription or a pill.

So Jack looks from his bachelor quarters over toward Married Row and it looks good to him. His amusements are but limited and his life does verge on the monotonous. His only place of recreation is the Y. M. C. A., which, while filling the want admirably week days, is a bit solemn Sundays—his only day off. The only theaters on the Zone are at Colon and Panama, and those are in the main only exhibitions of "movies." Moreover, the Panama Railroad has thoughtfully arranged its schedule

STREET SCENE IN CULEBRA

so that no Zone employee can go to the theater save on Saturday or Sunday night without staying out all night. As Jack smokes in his half a room (perhaps only a quarter) or wrangles with his roommate for place at the table lighted by one electric light his mind naturally turns toward the comforts enjoyed by his married friends, and he sees himself greeted on his return from toil in the jungle or the "Cut" by a cool, trim divinity in white, instead of by a lumbering giant in muddy khaki, as weary, hungry and grouchy as he.

Were he at home prudence would compel the consideration of cost. Here the paternal Commission puts a premium on matrimony. Very often, so often, indeed, that it is almost the rule, Jack returns from his first vacation home with a wife, or else coming alone is followed by the girl, and all goes merry as a marriage bell. But the time comes when Jack, a bachelor no longer, but a husband and perhaps a father, must leave the Isthmus. That time must come for all of them when the work is done. Enough, however, have already gone home to tell sad tales of the difficulty of readjusting themselves to normal conditions. Down comes the salary at least twenty-five per cent, up go living expenses at least thirty per cent. Nothing at home is free—coal, light, rent, and medical service least of all. Where Jack used to be lordly, he must be parsimonious; where he once bought untaxed in the markets of the world, he must buy in the most expensive of all market places, the United States. He absolutely cannot maintain at home the standard of life he adopted here, and the change with the endless little economies and pettinesses it entails gets on the nerves of both husband and wife. To start life thriftily and learn to be free-handed as prosperity increases is the natural line of development and does not mar happiness. But to be forced to pinch after a long period of lavishness is wearing. Back to the Zone come so many stories of romances begun by the Canal and ended in the divorce courts that one wonders if the paternalism of the Commission has been good for those who enjoyed it.

But it has been good for the supreme purpose of digging the Canal and that was the one end sought.

Let me return from this excursion into the domain of matrimonial philosophy and take up once again the account of the population of the Zone and its characteristics. It must be remembered that a very large part of the unskilled labor on the Canal is done by negroes from Jamaica and Barbadoes. But not all of it. The cleavage was not so distinct that the skilled labor could be classed as white, and the unskilled black, for among the latter were many Spaniards, Portuguese, Italians and the peoples of Southwestern Europe. The brilliant idea occurred to someone in the early days of the American campaign that as the West Indians, Panamanians and

YOUNG AMERICA AT PLAY

Photo by Underwood & Underwood
HINDOO MERCHANTS AT A ZONE TOWN

Latin-Americans generally were accustomed to do their monetary thinking in terms of silver all day labor might be put on the silver pay roll; the more highly paid workers on a gold pay roll. Thenceforward the metal line rather than the color line was drawn. The latter indeed would have been difficult as the Latin-American peoples never drew it very definitely in their marital relations, with the result that a sort of twilight zone made any very positive differentiation between whites and blacks practically impossible. So despite Bobby Burns' historic dictum—

"the gowd is but the guinea's stamp
    The man's the man for a' that",

on the Zone the man is silver or gold according to the nature of his work and the size of his wages. Of gold employees there were in 1913, 5362, of silver 31,298, so it is easy to see which pay roll bore the names of the aristocracy.

Practically all of the gold force are Americans. It is for them, in the main, that the cool, dark green houses with white trimmings, and all carefully screened in, are built. For them the buyers of the Commissary ransack the markets of the world, buying only the best. For them the Hotel Tivoli at Ancon and the Washington Hotel at Colon were built, though it is true that tourist trade rather than the patronage of the Canal workers supports them. For them are eighteen hotels, so-called—really only eating houses—scattered along the line, serving excellent meals for thirty cents each. Indeed, most of the features of Isthmian life which catch the eye of the tourist and make him think existence there quite ideal are planned to make the place attractive

enough to keep the gold employees on the job. To him that hath shall be given, and it required greater inducements to anchor to a desk in Panama the man capable of earning a good salary at home than it did to hold the negro from Jamaica or Martinique, or the Spaniard or Italian steady to his job.

In endeavoring to make things pleasant and easy for the gold employee the Isthmian Commission has made so many provisions for his comfort that many timid souls at home raised the cry of "socialism" and professed to discern in the system perfected by Col. Goethals the entering wedge that would split

THE NATIVE MILLS GRIND SLOWLY

in pieces the ancient system of free competition and the contract system for public work. While I was on the Zone a very distinguished financier of New York, a banker of the modern type with fingers in a host of industrial enterprises, delivered himself of this interesting forecast of the results of the education in collectivism which the United States government is giving to some thousands of men upon the Isthmus:

"The big thing is the spirit of paternalism, of modern socialism, of governmental parenthood, if you will, which is being engendered and nursed to full strength by Federal control of the Canal. This is no idle dream, and within five years, yes, within three years, it will begin to be felt in the United States.

"Quietly large corporations are studying this feature of the unloading of the skilled, highly in-telligent Canal workers on the industries of the United States. There are thousands of trained employees of the Panama Canal Commission—which is to say of the United States government. When these well paid, lightly worked, well and cheaply fed men return to their native land they will form a powerful addition to the Socialist party.

"These workmen will take up tasks for private corporations. They will find lower salaries, longer hours and a greatly increased cost of living. The conveniences and amusements which they have found either free or very cheap in the Canal Zone will be beyond the reach of many of them, and they are going to chafe under the changed conditions.

"They will compare private or corporate owner-ship with government control as manifested in the

COMMISSION ROAD NEAR EMPIRE

Canal works, and the comparison will inevitably result to the detriment of the methods followed in the United States. This will be in no sense an array of capital against labor. It will be a psychological and political movement for the betterment of the conditions of the trained worker irrespective of party or class or union affiliations. That is one reason that it will be so powerful.

"These men will be engaged in industries subject to strikes and other industrial and sociological disturbances. They will give their fellow workmen, who have always been employed in the United States, a new and logical idea of the value of government ownership and its advantages to

THE FIRE FORCE OF CRISTOBAL

the workingman as shown on the Canal Zone.

"Around them will gather the socialists, the union men who think for themselves and all other upper class workingmen. Do not mistake my meaning. This will be no Coxey's army movement, no gathering of the riffraff of failures seeking to rob the toiler of his gains or the investor of his dollars, but earnest men, whose weapon will not be the torch and the dynamite bomb, but the ballot. By their votes and the enormous following they can rally to their standard they will force the government to take over the public utilities, if not all the large corporations, of the country. They will force the adoption of government standards of work, wages and cost of living as exemplified in the work on the Canal.

In other words the influx of workers will lead directly to paternalism".

Let us, however, consider this bogy of socialism fairly. Before proceeding to a more detailed account of the manner of life upon the Canal Zone let me outline hastily the conditions which regarded superficially seem socialistic, and with a line or two show why they are not so at all.

Our Uncle Sam owns and manages a line of steamships plying between New York and Panama, carrying both passengers and freight and competing successfully with several lines of foreign-built ships. The largest vessels are of ten thousand tons and would rank well with the lesser transatlantic liners. On them Congressmen and Panama Zone officials are carried free, while employees of the Isthmian Canal Commission get an exceedingly low rate for themselves and their families. The government also owns and conducts the Panama Railroad, which crosses in less than three hours from the Atlantic to the Pacific, while the privately owned railroads of the United States take about seven days to pass from one ocean to the other. This sounds like a mighty good argument for government ownership and it is not much more fallacious than some others drawn from Isthmian conditions. The President of the Panama Railroad is Col. George W. Goethals. The government caught him young, educated him at its excellent West Point school, paying him a salary while he was learning to be useful, and has been employing and paying him ever since. Like a citizen of the ideal Co-operative Commonwealth he has never had to worry about a job. The State has always employed him and paid him. While he has done his work better than others of equal rank, he has only recently begun to draw any more pay than other colonels. Sounds very socialistic, doesn't it? And he seems to make a very good railroad president too, though the shuffling of shares in Wall Street had nothing to do with his appointment, and he hasn't got a director on his board interlocked with J. P. Morgan & Co., or the City National Bank.

The government which runs this railroad and steamship line doesn't confine its activity to big things. It will wash a shirt for one of its Canal employees at about half the price that John Chinaman doing business nearby would charge, press his clothing, or it will send a man into your home—if you live in the Zone—to chloroform any stray mosquitoes lurking there and convey them away in a bottle. It will house in an electric-lighted, wire-screened tenement, a Jamaica negro who at home lived in a basket-work shack, plastered with mud and thatched with palmetto leaves. It is very democratic too, this government, for it won't issue to Mrs. Highflyer more than three wicker arm-chairs, even if she does entertain every day, while her neighbor Mrs. Domus who gets just exactly as many never entertains at all. It can be just too mean for anything, like socialism, which we are so often told "puts everybody on a dead level."

The dream of the late Edward Bellamy is given actuality on the Zone where we find a great central authority, buying everything imaginable in all the markets of the world, at the moment when prices are lowest —an authority big enough to snap its fingers at any trust—and selling again without profit to the ultimate consumers. There are no trust profits, no middleman's profits included in prices of things bought at the Commissary stores. There are eighteen such stores in the Zone. The total business of the Commissary stores amounts to about $6,000,000 annually. Everything is sold at prices materially less than it can be bought in the United States, yet the department

ORCHIDS ON GOV. THATCHER'S PORCH

shows an actual profit, which is at once put back into the business. A Zone housewife told me that a steak for her family that would cost at least ninety cents in her home in Brooklyn cost her forty here. Shoddy or merely "cheap" goods are not carried and the United States pure food law is strictly observed. That terrible problem of the "higher cost of living" hardly presents itself to Zone dwellers except purchasers of purely native products; those, thanks to the tourists, have doubled in price several times in the last five years. But articles purveyed by Uncle Sam are furnished to his nephews and nieces here for about one-third less than the luckless ones must pay who are sticking to the old homestead instead of faring forth to the tropics.

I have already enumerated the valuable privileges, like free quarters, light, furniture, medical service, etc., supplied to the Zone worker without charge. If all these apparent gratuities were accompanied by a rate of pay lower than that in force for like occupations in the States it might be fair to say, as one of the most careful writers on Isthmian topics says, "these form part of the contract the employee makes with the government, and are just as much part of his pay as his monthly salary". But that pay averages twenty-five per cent higher than at home. The things enumerated are looked upon by those who receive them as gratuities, and rightly so. They are, in fact, extra inducements offered by Uncle Sam to persuade men to come and work on his Canal and to keep them happy and contented while doing so.

Now the chief material argument for the socialistic state, the co-operative commonwealth, is that it will secure for every citizen comfort and contentment, so far as contentment is possible to restless human minds; that it will abolish at a stroke monopoly and privilege, purge society of parasites, add to the efficiency of labor and proportionately increase its rewards. All of which is measurably accomplished on the Canal Zone and the less cautious socialists—the well-grounded ones see the difference —are excusable for hailing the government there as an evidence of the practicability of socialism.

But it isn't—at least not quite. The incarnation of the difference between this and socialism is Col. George W. Goethals. Nobody on the Zone had

Photo by H. Pittier   Courtesy National Geographic Magazine

THE CATASETUM SCURRA

A curiously shaped orchid rediscovered by Mrs. H. H. Rousseau

part in electing Goethals; nobody can say him nay, or abate or hinder in any degree his complete personal control of all that is done here. This is not the co-operative commonwealth we long have sought. Rather is it like the commonwealth of old with Oliver Cromwell as Lord Protector—and at that Goethals has no parliament to purge.

This is a benevolent despotism, the sort of government that philosophers agree would be ideal if the benevolence of the despot could only be assured invariably and eternally. The Czar of Russia could do what is being done down there were he vested with Goethals' intolerance of bureaucracies, red-tape, parasites, grafters, disobedience and delay. But Goethals is equally intolerant of opposition, argument, even advice from below. His is the military method of personal command and personal

Photo by Underwood & Underwood

MARRIED QUARTERS AT COROZAL

No. The organization of the Zone has been purely military, not socialistic. It was created for a purpose and it will vanish when that purpose has been attained. Admirably adapted to its end it had many elements of charm to those living under it. The Zone villages, even those like Culebra and Gorgona which are to be abandoned, were beautiful in appearance, delightful in social refinement. Culebra with its winding streets, bordered by tropical shrubbery in which nestled the cool and commodious houses of the engineers and higher employees, leading up to the hill crested by the residence of the Colonel

responsibility. I don't believe he is over-fond even of the council of war. In a socialistic community, where every man had a voice in the government, he would last only long enough for a new election to be called. Though his popularity there is universal, it would not withstand the attacks of demagogues were there field for demagogy.

But what has been done, and is still doing, on the Zone is not socialistic, because it is done from the top, by the orders of an autocrat, instead of by an act of a town meeting. One might as well say that the patience, prudence, attention to detail, insistence on proper sanitation which enabled Japan's great General Nogi to keep his army in the field with the minimum loss from preventable sickness was all socialistic. Col. Goethals commanded an army. The Isthmus was the enemy. The army must be fed and clothed, hence the Commissary. Its communications must be kept open, hence the steamship line and the railroad. The soldiers must be housed, and as it became early apparent that the siege was to be a long one the camps were built of timber instead of tents. There is nothing new about that. Back in the fifteenth century Queen Isabella, concluding that it would take a long time to starve the Moors out of Granada, kept her soldiers busy building a city of stone and mortar before the walls of the beleaguered town. Culebra has been a more stubborn fortress than was ever Granada.

FIGHTING THE INDUSTRIOUS ANT

—of course there were five colonels on the Commission, but only one "The Colonel"—Culebra was a delight to the visitor and must have been a joy to the resident.

Try to figure to yourself the home of a young engineer as I saw it. The house is two storeys with a pent-house roof, painted dark green, with the window frames, door casings and posts of the broad verandas, by which it is nearly surrounded, done in shining white. Between the posts is wire

netting and behind is a piazza probably twelve feet wide which in that climate is as good as a room for living, eating or sleeping purposes. The main body of the house is oblong, about fifty feet long by thirty to forty feet deep. A living-room and dining-room fill the entire front. The hall, instead of running from the front to the back of the house, as is customary with us, runs across the house, back

FOLIAGE ON THE ZONE

of these two rooms. It is in no sense an entry, though it has a door opening from the garden, but separates the living-rooms from the kitchen and other working rooms. The stairway ascends from this hall to the second floor where two large bed-rooms fill the front of the house, a big bath-room, a bed-room and the dry-room being in the rear. About that last apartment let me go into some detail. The climate of the Zone is always rather humid, and in the rainy season you can wring water out of everything that can absorb it. So in each house is a room kept tightly closed with two electric lights in it burning day and night. Therein are kept all clothes, shoes, etc., not in actual use, and the combined heat and light keep damp and mold out of the goods thus stored. Mold is one of the chief pests of the Panama housekeeper. You will see few books in even the most tastefully furnished houses, because the mold attacks their bindings. Every piano has an electric light inserted within its case and kept burning constantly to dispel the damp. By way of quieting the alarm of readers it may be mentioned again that electric light is furnished free to Isthmian Commission employees. "We always laugh", said a hostess one night, as she looked back at my darkened room in her house from the walk outside, "at the care people from the States take to turn out the lights. We enjoy being extravagant and let them burn all day if we feel like it".

In such a house there is no plaster. From within you see the entire frame of the house—uprights, joists, stanchions, floor beams, all—and the interior is painted as a rule precisely like the exterior without the white trimming. You don't notice this at first. Then it fascinates you. You think it amusing and improper to see a house's underpinning so indecently exposed. All that we cover with laths, plaster, calcimine and wall paper is here naked to the eye. Only a skin of half-inch lumber intervenes between you and the outer world, or the people in the next room. You notice the windows look strange. There is no sash. To a house of the sort I am de-

scribing four or six glass windows are allotted to be put in the orifices the housekeeper may select. The other windows are unclosed except at night, when you may, if you wish, swing heavy board shutters across them.

A house of the type I have described is known as Type 10, and is assigned to employees drawing from $300 to $400 a month. Those getting from $200 to $300 a month are assigned either to quarters in a two-family house, or to a small cottage of six or seven rooms, though, as the supply of the latter is limited, they are greatly prized. Employees drawing less than $200 a month have four-room flats in buildings accommodating four families. Those who receive more than $400 a month are given large houses of a type distinguished by spaciousness and artistic design.

When you come to analyze it such houses are only large shacks, and yet their proportions and coloring, coupled with their obvious fitness for the climate, make them, when tastefully furnished and decorated, thoroughly artistic homes. For these homes the Commission furnishes all the bare essentials. With mechanical precision it furnishes the number of tables, chairs, beds and dressers which the Commission in its sovereign wisdom has decided to be proper for a gentleman of the station in life to which that house is fitted. For the merely æsthetic the Commission cares nothing, though it is fair to say

THE CHIEF COMMISSARY AT CRISTOBAL

WHAT THE SLIDE DID TO THE RAILROAD
The pernicious activity of slides occasionally creates this novel condition in railroad construction

that the furniture it supplies, though commonplace, is not in bad taste. But for decoration the Zone dwellers must go down into their own pockets and to a greater or less degree all do so. The authorities have not gone to the extent of prohibiting this rivalry as at West Point and Annapolis where the cadets are not permitted to decorate their rooms lest inequality and mortification result. But in Panama the climate enforces such a prohibition to some extent. Luxury there would be positive discomfort. Costly rugs and hangings, richly upholstered furniture are out of place. Air space is the greatest luxury, and a room cluttered with objects of priceless art would be scarcely habitable.

Within their limitations, however, the hostesses of the Zone have made their homes thoroughly charming. The visitor was, I think, most impressed by those who frankly used the trimmings of the tropics for their chief decorations. The orchid-lined porches of Mrs. M. H. Thatcher, wife of the civil commissioner, or Mrs. H. H. Rousseau, wife of the naval representative on the Commission, were a veritable fairyland when the swift tropic night had fallen and the colored lights began to glow among the rustling palms and delicately tinted orchids. No more beautiful apartment could possibly be imagined.

Housekeeping is vastly simplified by the Commissary. When there is but one place to shop, and only one quality of goods to select from—namely the best, for that is all the Commissary carries—the shopping tasks of the housekeeper are reduced to a minimum. Nevertheless they grumble—perhaps because women like to shop, more probably because this situation creates a dull and monotonous sameness amongst the families. "What's the good of giving a dinner party", asked a hostess plaintively,

NOT FROM JAMAICA BUT THE Y. M. C. A.

This comparative cheapness in prices is, of course, due to the elimination of the middlemen, the buying by the commissary in large quantities and the disregard of profit as an element in the business. There is but one step between the Beef Trust, or other manufacturers, and the ultimate consumers on the Zone. The one intermediary is the Commissary. It buys in such quantities that it can be sure of the lowest prices. It buys in markets 3,000 miles or more away from its stores, but it gets the lowest freight rates and an all-water carriage from New York. Finally it pays no rent and seeks no profit, hence its prices should be the lowest. Here is a selection from the printed list issued in April, 1913, from which any house-keeper can judge of Zone prices:

"when your guests all know exactly what everything on your table costs, and they can guess just what you are going to serve? They say, 'I wish she'd bought lamb at the Commissary, it costs just the same as turkey'. Or 'the Commissary had new asparagus today. Wonder why she took cauliflower'? They get the Commissary list just as I do and know exactly to what I am limited, as we can only buy at the Commissary. There is no chance for the little surprises that make an interesting dinner party".

That is perhaps a trifle disquieting to the adventurous housekeeper, but, except for the purpose of entertaining, the Commissary must be a great boon. Its selection of household necessities is sufficiently varied to meet every need; the quality the best and its prices are uniformly lower than in the United States.

A BACHELOR'S QUARTERS

Veal Cutlets, per pound................. 17c
Lamb Chops, per pound............... 24c
Corned Beef, No. 1.................... 14c
Sirloin Steak, per pound.............. 19c
Halibut, fresh, per pound.............. 15c
Chickens, fancy roasting, 5½ pounds each $1.25
Ducks, blackhead, pair................. 60c
Pork, salt, family..................... 14c
Eggs, fresh, dozen.................... 25c
Butter, creamery, special............... 41c
American Cheese, per pound........... 22c
Celery, per head..................... 11c
Cabbage, per pound.................. 3c
Onions, per pound.................... 3c
Potatoes, white, per pound............ 3c
Turnips, per pound................... 3c
Grapefruit, each..................... 4c
Oranges, Jamaica, per dozen........... 12c

THE GRAPE FRUIT OF PANAMA

If, however, the Commissary system reduces life to something of a general uniformity and destroys shopping as a subject of conversation, the ladies of the Zone still have the eternal servant problem of which to talk. De Amicis, the travel writer, said that servants formed the one universal topic for conversation and that he bid a hasty farewell to his mother in Naples after a monologue on the sins of servants, only to find, at his first dinner in Amsterdam, whither he had traveled with all possible speed, that the same topic engrossed the mind of his hostess there. In Panama the matter is somewhat simplified by the fact that only one type of servant is obtainable, namely the Jamaica negress.

It is complicated by the complete lack of intelligence offices. If a housekeeper wants a maid she asks her friends to spread the tidings to their servants, and then waits, supine, until the treasure comes to the door. Servants out of employment seek it by trudging from house to house and from village to village. Once hired they do what they have to do and no more. Among them is none of the spirit of loyalty which makes the "old Southern mammy" a figure in our fiction, nor any of the energy which in the Northern States Bridget contributes to household life—though, indeed, Bridget is disappearing from domestic service before the flood of Scandinavians and Germans.

The only wail I heard on the Isthmus about the increasing cost of living had to do with the wages of servants. "In the earlier days", said one of my hostesses reminiscently, "it was possible to get servants for very low wages. They were accustomed to doing little and getting little, as in Jamaica and other West Indian islands, where many servants are employed by

THE TIVOLI HOTEL

one family, each with a particular 'line'. People say that in Panama City servants can still be found who will work for $5 silver ($2.50) per month, and that Americans have spoiled them by paying too much. But I think they have developed a capacity for work and management equal to that of servants in the States and deserve their increased wages. I pay $15, gold, a month to my one capable servant. Occasionally you will find one who will work for $10, but many get $20 if they are good cooks and help with baby. Probably $12 to $15 is an average price.

"These Jamaica servants speak very English English—you can't call it Cockney, for they don't drop their h's, but it differs greatly from our American English. They are very fond of big words, which they usually use incorrectly, especially the men. A Commissary salesman, to whom I sent a note asking for five pounds of salt meat, sent back

the child who carried it to 'ask her mother to differentiate', meaning what kind of salt meat. A cook asked me once 'the potatoes to crush, ma'am'? meaning to ask if they were to be mashed. Another after seizing time to air a blanket between showers reported exultantly, 'the rain did let it sun, mum'. And always when they wish to know if you want hot water they inquire, 'the water to hot, mum'?

"Their names are usually elaborate. Celeste, Geraldine, Katherine, Eugenie, are some that I recall. My own maid is Susannah, which reminds me—without reflecting on this particular one—that as a class they are hopelessly unmoral, though extremely religious withal. I have known them to be clean and efficient, but as a rule they are quite the reverse. Some are woefully ignorant of modern utensils. One for example, being new to kitchen ranges, built a fire in the oven on the first day of her service. Another, having been carefully in-

PURE PANAMA, PURE INDIAN AND ALL BETWEEN

E.J.READ
PANAMA

OLD LANDING AT TABOGA

The concrete walls leading from the beach up to the level of the street were built as a memorial of the successful revolution of 1905.

structed always to take a visitor's card on a tray, neglected the trim salver provided for that purpose and extended to the astonished caller a huge lacquered tin tray used for carrying dishes from the kitchen.

"I'll never forget", concluded my hostess between smiles and sorrow, "how I felt when I saw that lonesome little card reposing on the broad black and battered expanse of that nasty old tray"!

Social life on the Zone is rather complex. At the apex, of course, are the Commissioners and their families. The presence of an Envoy Extraordinary and Minister Plenipotentiary of the United States in Panama City adds another factor to the always vexed question of precedence, while the maintenance of a military post with a full regiment, and a marine camp with a battalion does not help to simplify matters. Social affiliations among those not in the Commission or the Army set are based with primitive simplicity upon the

Y. M. C. A. CLUB AT GATUN
These clubs are the true centers of the social life of the zone

amount of the husband's earnings. One advantage of this system is that it is based upon perfectly accurate information, for everybody on the Zone works for the Commission and the payrolls are periodically published. But it jars the ingenuous outsider to have a woman, apparently without a trace of snobbery, remark casually of another, "well, we don't see much of her. Her husband is in the $2000 class you know".

Social life is further complicated by the fact that the people of the Zone came from all parts of the United States, with a few from Europe. They have no common home associations. When the settlement of the Zone first began the women were dismally lonely, and the Commission called in a professional organizer of women's clubs to get them together. Clubs were organized from Ancon to Cristobal and federated with Mrs. Goethals for President and Mrs. Gorgas for Vice-President. Culebra entertained Gorgona with tea and Tolstoi, and Empire challenged Corozal to an interchange of views on eugenics over the

Photo by Underwood & Underwood

INTERIOR OF GATUN Y. M. C. A. CLUB

MARINE POST AT CAMP ELLIOTT
A force of about 500 marines will be kept permanently on the Zone

coffee cups and wafers. In a recent number of *The Canal Record*, the official paper of the Zone, I find nearly a page given over to an account of the activities of the women's societies and church work. It appears that there were in April, 1913, twenty-five societies of various sorts existing among the women on the Zone. The Canal Zone Federation of Women's Clubs had five subsidiary clubs with a membership of fifty-eight. There were twelve church organizations with a membership of 239. Nearly 290 women were enrolled in auxiliaries to men's organizations. But these organizations were rapidly breaking up even then and the completion of the Canal will witness their general disintegration. They served their purpose. Only a mind that could mix the ideal with the practical could have foreseen that discussions of the Baconian Cipher, or the philosophy of Nietzsche might have a bearing on the job of digging a canal, but whoever conceived the idea was right.

The same clear foresight that led the Commission to encourage the establishment of women's clubs caused the installation of the Y. M. C. A. on the Isthmus, where it has become perhaps the dominating social force. With a host of young bachelors employed far away from home there was need of social meeting places other than the saloons of Panama and Colon. Many schemes were suggested before it was determined to turn over the whole organization of social clubs to the governing body of the Y. M. C. A. There were at the period of the greatest activity on the Zone seven Y. M. C. A. clubs located at Cristobal, Gatun, Porto Bello,

TOURISTS IN THE CULEBRA CUT

Gorgona, Empire, Culebra and Corozal. The buildings are spacious, and, as shown by the illustrations, of pleasing architectural style. On the first floor are a lobby, reading-room and library, pool and billiard room, bowling alley, a business-like bar which serves only soft drinks, a quick lunch counter, and in some cases a barber shop and baths. On the second floor is always a large assembly-room used for entertainments and dances. This matter of dancing was at first embarrassing to the Y. M. C. A., for at home this organization does not encourage the dreamy mazes of the waltz, and I am quite sure frowns disapprovingly on the swaying tango and terrible turkey trot. But conditions on the Isthmus were different and though the organization does not itself give dances, it permits the use of its halls by other clubs which do. The halls also are used for moving picture shows, concerts and lectures. The Superintendent of Club Houses, Mr. A. B. Dickson, acts as a sort of impresario, but the task of filling dates with desirable attractions is rather a complicated one 2000 miles away from the lyceum bureaus of New York.

The service of the Y. M. C. A. is not gratuitous. Members pay an annual fee of $10 each. This, however, does not wholly meet the cost of maintenance and the deficit is taken care of by the Commission, which built the club houses at the outset.

That the service of the organization is useful is shown by the fact that Col. Goethals has recommended the erection of a concrete club house to cost $52,500 in the permanent town of Balboa.

Social intercourse on the Zone is further impeded by the fact that the few thousand "gold" employees are scattered over a strip of territory 43 miles long traversed by a railroad which runs but three passenger trains daily in each direction. Dances are held on alternate Saturday nights at the Tivoli and Washington Hotels and guests cross from the Atlantic to the Pacific or vice-versa to attend them, but on these nights a special train takes the merrymakers home. If, however, a lady living at Culebra desires to have guests from Cristobal to dinner, she must keep them all night, while a popular bachelor with half a dozen dinner or party calls to make needs about three uninterrupted days to cover his list.

Church work, too, has been fostered by the Commission. Twenty-six of the churches are owned by it, and all but two are on land it owns. In 1912 there were forty churches on the Zone—seven Roman Catholic, thirteen Episcopal, seven Baptist, two Wesleyan and eight undenominational. Fifteen chaplains are maintained by the government, apportioned among the denominations in proportion to their numbers. Much good work is done by the

Photo by Underwood & Underwood

LOBBY IN TIVOLI HOTEL

churches, but one scarcely feels that the church spirit is as strong as it would be among the same group of people in the States. The changed order of life, due to the need of deferring to tropical conditions, has something to do with this. The stroll home from church at midday is not so pleasant a Sunday function under a glaring tropical sun. Moreover no one town can support churches of every denomination, and the railroad is at least impartial in that it does not encourage one to go down the line to church any more than to a dance or the theater.

Even as I write the disintegration of this society has begun. On the tables of the Zone dwellers you find books about South America or Alaska —the widely separated points at which opportunity for engineering activity seems to be most promising. Alaska particularly was at the time engaging the speculative thought of the young engineers in view of the discussion in Congress of the advisability of building two government railroads in that territory.

Photo by Underwood & Underwood
ALTAR IN GATUN CATHOLIC CHURCH

The preparation of moving thither the Canal organization was highly pleasing to the younger men who seemed to think that working over glacial moraines and running lines over snow fields would form a pleasing sequel to several years in the tropical jungles and swamps. You will see on the Isthmus bronzed and swarthy men who are pointed out to you as "T T's" which is to say tropical tramps who served first in the Philippines. Just what appellation will be given those who go from the tropics to the arctic is yet to be discovered. In the *Canal Record* I read of the final dissolution of the Federation of Women's Clubs. Stories of the ambitions of individual commissioners for new employment are appearing in the public prints. Only the pernicious activity of the slides at Culebra and Cucaracha can much longer delay the dissolution of the social life that has so pleasingly flourished under the benevolent despotism of Col. Goethals.

CHAPTER XVIII

LABOR AND THE GOVERNMENT OF THE ZONE

BY its provision for the comfort of the unmarried employees the Isthmian Commission has justified the allegation that it systematically encourages matrimony among the men. The bachelor employee upon the gold roll is housed in large barracks which rarely afford him a room to himself, but ordinarily force upon him one, two or even three "chums." The intimacies of chumming are delightful when sought, but apt to be irksome when involuntary. The bachelor quarters house from twelve to sixty men, and are wholly made up of sleeping rooms. The broad screened verandas constitute the only living room or social hall. If that does not serve the young bachelor's purpose he has the Y. M. C. A. which is quite as public. In fact, unless he be one of the few favored with a room to himself, he must wander off, like a misanthrope, into the heart of the jungle to meditate in solitude. As hard outdoor work does not make for misanthropy most of them wander off to the church and get married.

The unmarried employees take their meals in what are called Commission Hotels, though these are hotels only in the sense of being great eating houses. Here men and women on the gold roll are served, for there are bachelor girls on the Zone and at these hotels special veranda tables are reserved for them and for such men as retain enough of the frills of civilization as to prefer wearing their coats at their meals. Meals for employees cost thirty cents each, or fifty cents for non-employees. There is some divergence of judgment concerning the excellence of this food. Col. Roosevelt, while on the Isthmus, evaded his guides, dashed into a Commission hotel and devoured a thirty-cent meal, pronouncing it bully and declaring it unapproachable by any Broadway meal at $1.00. The Colonel sincerely believed that his approach was unheralded, but they do say on the Zone that his descent was "tipped off" like a raid in the "Tenderloin," and that a meal costing the contractors many times thirty cents was set before him.

Undoubtedly one who should order the same variety of dishes in a city restaurant in the States would have to pay more than fifty cents, although there are country hotels in which equal variety and excellence for the price are not unattainable. A typical dinner menu includes soup, two kinds of meat, four kinds of vegetables, hot rolls or light bread, a salad, tea, coffee, or cocoa and for dessert pie or ice cream. The Isthmian appetite for ice

LA BOCA FROM THE CITY

341

cream is a truly tropical wonder.   In the early days of the work the novice on the Isthmus was likely to mistake an open bowl of quinine on the table for pul-

AT LOS ANGOSTURAS
Some Panama rivers flow through dales like those of the Wisconsin

verized sugar, but this has very generally disappeared.

No money changes hands at the Commission hotels, unless the diner happens to be a non-employee. Meals are paid for by coupons from books purchased at the Commissary. By omitting the luncheon, and filling its place with a little fruit, or a sandwich, the Canal employee can make his food cost only $18 a month. He has no lodging to pay; clothes are the cheapest imaginable, for there are no seasons to provide for, nor any rotations of fashions to be observed; theaters are practically non-existent and away from Panama City temptation to riotous living are slight. The Zone worker is the most solvent individual in all industry and ought to close up a four or five years' service with a comfortable nest egg.

The economy and comfort of life on the Canal

Zone are mainly due to the Commissary system which has grown up under the American régime. This is part of the Subsistence Department, which is divided into two branches,—hotel and commissary. The hotel department not only runs the Commission hotels already described, but the two large hotels patronized by tourists —the Tivoli at Ancon and the Washington at Colon. Though a special rate is made at these two hotels for employees, their prices are still too high for them to be patronized by any except the most highly paid workers. Even the pleasure seeker on the Isthmus is likely to regard their rates as rather exorbitant.

Their prices, however, are essentially those of the native Panamanian hotels in the city, and in cleanliness they are vastly superior. The visitor to Panama, however, who seeks local color or native food need not expect to find either at the Tivoli.   That is a typical resort hotel which might have been moved

THE WATER FRONT AT COLON
Cocoanut palms are picturesque but beware of the falling nuts

down to the Isthmus from the Jersey beaches or Saratoga Springs. Its only local color resides in its Jamaica waiters, and as I am assured that they are no less a trial to the managers than to the

NEGRO QUARTERS AT CRISTOBAL
The Jamaica negroes frequently elect to live in the shacks rather than the commission barracks

guests, criticism would be perhaps ungenerous. As for native fruits and food, you must go away from the hotel to seek them. An infrequent papaya appears on the menu, but for the mamei, mango, sapodilla and other fruits, the guests at the time of my visit sought the native fruit stores.

After all, however, the two big hotels are the least of the tasks imposed on the Subsistence Department. The string of Commission hotels, 18 in all, serve about 200,000 meals monthly. There are also 17 messes for European laborers who pay 40 cents per ration of three meals a day. Sixteen kitchens serve the West India laborers who get three meals for 27 cents. About 100,000 meals of this sort are served monthly. Receipts and expendi-

tures for the line hotels, messes and kitchens are very nicely adjusted. The Official Handbook puts receipts at about $105,000 a month; expenditures, $104,500. The Tivoli Hotel earns a profit, but the Washington Hotel, being newly built, had not at the time of publication of this book made a financial report.

As I have noted, the hotels are not open to all sorts and conditions of men. Those which I have described are established for the use of gold employees only. Different methods had to be adopted in providing lodging and eating places for the more than 30,000 silver employees, most of whom belong to the unskilled labor class. About 25,000 of the silver employees are West Indians, mainly from

Photo by Underwood & Underwood
LABOR TRAIN AT ANCON

coming. But few Japanese laborers are enrolled, which is the more strange when the part they took in railroad building in the Pacific northwest is remembered.

In all forty nationalities and eighty-five geographical subdivisions were noted in the census of 1912. Greenland is missing, but if we amend the hymn to "From Iceland's icy mountains to India's coral strands", it will fit the situation. When work was busiest the West Indian laborers were paid 10 cents an hour, for an eight-hour day, except in the case of those doing special work who got 16 and 20 cents. The next higher type of manual labor, largely composed of Spaniards, drew 20 cents. Artisans received from 16 to 44 cents an hour. In figuring the cost of work it was the custom of the engineers to reckon the West Indian labor as only 33 per cent as efficient as American labor. That is to say, $3 paid to a Jamaican produced no greater results than $1 paid to an American. Reckoned by results therefore, the prices paid for native labor were high.

Jamaica or the Barbados, though some French are found. A very few Chinese are employed. In 1906 Engineer Stevens advertised for 2500 Chinese coolies, and planned to take 15,000 if they offered themselves, but there was no considerable response. Perhaps the story of the unhappy Chinamen who destroyed themselves during the French régime rather than live on the Isthmus may have been told in the Flowery Kingdom and deterred others from

Quarters and a Commissary service were of course provided for the silver employees. Their quarters were as a rule huge barracks, though many of the natives and West Indians spurn the free quarters provided by the Commission and make their homes in shacks of their own. This is particularly the case with those who are married, or living in the free unions not uncommon among the Jamaica negroes. The visitor who saw first the trim and really attractive houses and bachelor quarters assigned to the gold employees could hardly avoid a certain revulsion of opinion as to the sweetness and light of Isthmian life when he wandered into the negro quarters across the railroad in front of the Tivoli Hotel at Ancon, or in some of the back streets

NEGRO SLEEPING QUARTERS
All extra clothing etc., is piled on shelf above. The floor is flushed daily

of Empire or Gorgona. The best kept barracks for silver employees were at Cristobal, but even there the restlessness and independence of the Jamaicans were so great that many moved across into the frame rookeries of the native town of Colon.

In the crowded negro quarters one evidence of the activities of the sanitation department was largely missing. No attempt was made to screen all the barracks and shacks that housed the workers. But the self-closing garbage can, the oil-sprinkled gutters, the clean pavement and all the other evidences of the activities of Col. Gorgas' men were there. Perhaps the feature of the barracks which most puzzled and amused visitors to the Zone were the kitchens. Imagine a frame building 300 feet long by 75 feet wide, three stories high with railed balconies at every story. Perched on the rails of the balustrades, at intervals of 20 feet, and usually facing a door leading into the building are boxes of corrugated iron about 3 feet high, the top sloping upward like one side of a roof and the inner side open. These are the kitchens—one to each family. Within is room for a smoldering fire of soft coal, or charcoal, and a few pots and frying pans. Here the family meal is prepared, or heated up if, as is usually the case, the ingredients are obtained at the Commissary kitchen.

The reader may notice that the gold employees are supplied with food at a fixed price per meal; the silver employees at so much per ration of three meals. The reason for this is that it was early discovered that the laborers were apt to economize by irregularity in eating— seldom taking more than two meals a day and often limiting themselves to one, making that one of such prodigious proportions as to unfit them for work for some hours, after which they went unfed until too weak to work properly. As the Commission lost by this practice at both ends, the evil was corrected by

Photo by Underwood & Underwood

A WORKMEN'S SLEEPING CAR

making the laborers pay for three meals, whether they ate them or not—and naturally they did. It is a matter of record that the quality of the work improved notably after this expedient was adopted.

The gold messes are principally for the foreign laborers, Italians, Spaniards and Portuguese, and pains are taken to give them food of the sort they are accustomed to at home. Spaghetti is consumed by the ton, as well as rice, garlic, lentils and other vegetables sought by the people of southern Europe.

Photo by Underwood & Underwood

A WORKMEN'S DINING CAR

OLD FRENCH BUCKET DREDGES

Some of these dredges are still in use for wet dredging

and Italian laborers were accustomed to have wine with their meals and were not contented without it. But at the later date the end of the work was in sight. There was no longer need to secure contented labor at the expense of violating a national statute. Hence the imposition of a stern prohibition law.

That system of regulating the sale of liquor on the Canal Zone is brimful of anomalies and inconsistencies, but fairly well characterized by a robust common sense. There is no liquor sold or served at the Commissary hotels or kitchens, with the result that the Spanish and Italian laborers to some extent refuse to patronize either, but get their meals at some cantina where the wine of their country can be had. There is no bar at the Hotel Tivoli. That tavern being owned by the United States government and in a government reservation the law is nominally obeyed. But

In 1909 the Commission reported with satisfaction that "the rations at the messes for European laborers have been increased, among the additions being wine three time a week instead of twice a week". This record of accomplishment suggests some account of the way in which the problem of the liquor traffic was handled on the Zone during the most active period of construction work and prior to the order abolishing all liquor selling. The problem was a difficult one, for the Zone was in effect a government reservation, and under a general law of Congress the sale of liquor on such reservations is prohibited. But on this reservation there were at divers times from 34 to 63 licensed saloons. July 1, 1913, all licenses were canceled and the Zone went "dry". The earlier latitude granted to liquor sellers was excused by the necessities of the case. The Spanish

OLD FRENCH BRIDGE AT BAS OBISPO

as the tastes of men are not fixed by law, and only imperfectly regulated by it, you will find the tables of this hospitable inn plentifully dotted by comfortable looking bottles. According to report the hotel authorities "send out" to some mysterious spot for these supplies as ordered, but I never happened to see the messenger of Bacchus on his errand and rather suspect that the hotel cellar contains the cheering spring. At any rate the United States as a hotel-keeper does not encourage liquor drinking at a bar, though it does not absolutely prohibit it at table.

The saloons of the Zone, viewed superficially, seemed to be conducted for the convenience and comfort of

Photo by Underwood & Underwood

BAS OBISPO AS THE FRENCH LEFT IT

the day laboring class—the silver employees— mainly. The police regulations made any particular attractiveness other than that supplied by their stock in trade quite impossible. They could not have chairs or tables—"perpendicular drinking" was the rigid rule. They could not have cozy corners, snuggeries, or screens—all drinking must be done at the bar and in full view of the passers-by. Perhaps these rules discouraged the saloonkeepers from any attempt to attract the better class of custom. At any rate the glitter of mirrors and of cut glass was notably absent and the sheen of mahogany was more apparent in the complexions of the patrons than on the woodwork of the bar. They were frankly rough, frontier whisky shops, places that cater to men who want drink rather than companionship, and who when tired of standing at the bar can get out. Accordingly most of the saloons were in

THE RELAXATION OF PAY DAY

CONVICTS BUILDING A COMMISSION ROAD
The excellence of these roads should be an object lesson to Central America

the day laborer quarters, and it was seldom indeed that a "gold employee" or salaried man above the grade of day laborer was seen in one. The saloons paid a high license tax which was appropriated to the schools of the Zone, and they were shut sharp at eleven o'clock because, as the chief of police explained, "we want all the laborers fit and hearty for work when the morning whistle blows".

That is the keynote of all law and rule on the Zone—to keep the employees fit for work. If morals and sobriety are advanced why so much the better, but they are only by-products of the machine which is set to grind out so many units of human labor per working day.

Unhappily all the safeguards made and provided on the Zone are missing in the code by which the saloons of Colon and Panama are regulated—if a wide-open policy is to be described as regulation. These two towns at the two ends of the Panama

Railroad are, one or the other, within an hour's ride of any village on the line. Their saloons are many, varied and largely disreputable. The more sequestered ones have attached to them the evils which commonly hang about low drinking places, and the doors swing hospitably open to the resident of the Zone, whether he be a Canal worker or a soldier or marine from one of the camps.

The uniformed men are more in evidence than they ought to be—more than they would be if an erratic and uninformed public sentiment at home had not led Congress to close the army canteens in which the soldier could have his beer or light wine amid orderly surroundings. If the good ladies of the W. C. T. U. who hold the abolition of the army canteen one of their triumphs could see the surroundings into which the enlisted man is driven, and know the sort of stuff he is led to drink, they might doubt the wisdom of their perfected work. But as one after another Secretaries of War and Generals of the Army have unavailingly pleaded for a return to the canteen system, it is unlikely that facts presented by a mere writer will have any effect on the narrow illiberality which prompted the Congressional action.

It is a curious fact that in the tropics where one would expect to find cooling rather than heating beverages as a rule the demand is chiefly for the "hard stuff." The walls of the saloons, the floors of the cantinas, or native drinking places, are covered with bottles or barrels of whisky, rum, brandy and gin. Only in places frequented by the Spanish and Italians are the lighter wines often seen. The Jamaica negro is devoted to the rum of his country,

and one sees him continually in the most unexpected places producing a quart bottle from some mysterious hiding place in his scanty clothing, and benevolently treating his crowd. In excess—and that is what he aims at—it makes him quarrelsome and a very fair share of the 7000 annual arrests on the Zone are due to the fortuitous combination of the two chief products of Jamaica—rum and the black. It is doubtful, however, whether the Jamaican could be kept to his work without his tipple, and it was for that reason that the unusual expedient of permitting liquor selling on a government reservation was adopted.

The Commissary branch of the Subsistence Department is a colossal business run by the govern-

CONSTRUCTION WORK SHOWING CONCRETE CARRIERS AND MOULDS
The buckets containing concrete are controlled from a station in the steel scaffolding—run out, stopped and emptied at the proper point

HOW THE NATIVES GATHER COCOANUTS

foie gras you can get every article of use or luxury at the Commissary. At least you can in theory, in fact the statement needs toning down a little, for you will hear plenty of grumbling on the Zone about the scanty satisfaction derived from shopping in "that old Commissary."

All the same its activites are amazing. It launders linen at prices that make the tourist who has to pay the charges of the Tivoli Laundry envy the employees their privileges. It bakes bread, cake and pies for the whole 65,000 of the working population, and does it with such nice calculation that there is never an overstock and the bread is always fresh. Everything of course is done by machinery. Kneading dough for bread and mixing cement and gravel to make concrete are merely co-ordinate tasks in the process of building the Canal and both are performed in the way to get the best results in the least time. Everything is done by wholesale, Hamburger steak is much liked on the Isthmus, so the Commissary has a neat machine which makes 500 pounds of it in a batch. That reminds me, of a hostess who preferred to make her own Hamburger steak, and so told her Jamaica cook to mince up a piece of beef. Being disquieted by the noise of chopping, she returned to the kitchen to find the cook diligently performing the appointed task with a hatchet.

ment for the good of the dwellers on the Zone. It gathers together from the ends of the earth everything needful for these pampered wards of Uncle Sam, and sells its stock practically at cost price. From pins to pianos, from pigs-knuckles to pâté de

In the icy depths of the cold storage plant at Cristobal, where the temperature hovers around 14 degrees, while it is averaging 96 outside, you walk through long avenues of dressed beef, broad pergolas hung with frozen chicken, ducks and game, sunken

LOOKING DOWN MIRAFLORES LOCKS

gardens of cabbage, carrots, cauliflower and other vegetable provender. You come to a spot where a light flashes fitfully from an orifice which is presently closed as a man bows his head before it. He straightens up, the light flashes and is again blotted out. You find, on closer approach, two men testing eggs by peering through them at an electric light. Betwixt them they gaze thus into the very soul of this germ of life 30,000 times a day, for thus many eggs do they handle. Yet the odds are that neither has read the answer to the riddle, "did the first hen lay the first egg, or the first egg hatch the first chicken?" Unless relieved by some such philosophical problem to occupy the mind one might think the egg tester's job would savor of monotony.

Out of the railroad yards at Cristobal at 3.45 every morning starts the Commissary train, usually of 21 cars, 11 of which are refrigerated. Its business is to deliver to all the consumers along the 47 miles of Canal villages and camps the supplies for the day. Nineteen stores, and as many kitchens, messes and hotels, must be supplied. Ice must be delivered to each household by eight in the morning. Ice is one of the things that the employees do not get free, but though nature has no share in making it, they get it cheaper than our own people, for whom nature manufactures it gratis and a few men monopolize the supply.

If one is fond of big figures the records of the Commissary Department furnish them. The bakery for example puts forth over 6,000,000 loaves of bread, 651,844 rolls and 114,134 pounds of cake annually. Panama is a clean country. Every tourist exclaims at the multitudinous companies of native women perpetually washing at the river's brink and in the

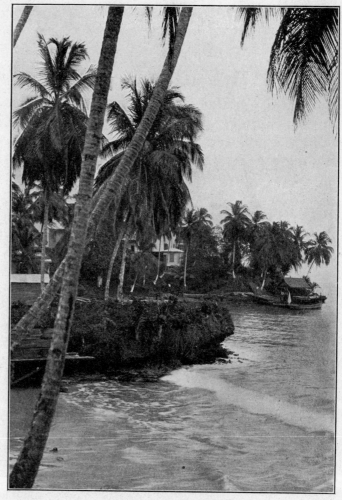

HOSPITAL AT BOCAS

interior I never saw a native hut without quantities of wash spread out to dry. But the Commissary laundry beats native industry with a record in one year of 3,581,923 pieces laundered—and it isn't much of a climate for "biled" shirts and starched collars either. There is a really enterprising proposition under consideration for the retention of this laundry. A ship going west would land all its laundry work at Cristobal and by the time it had made the passage of the Canal—10 hours—all would be delivered clean at Balboa via the railroad. East bound ships would send their laundry from Balboa by rail.

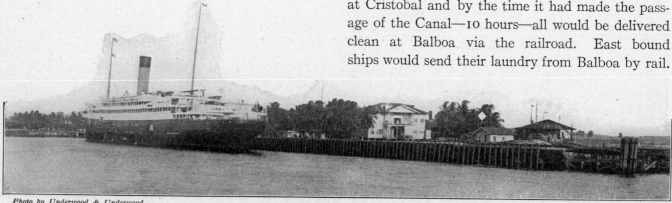

Photo by Underwood & Underwood

NEW AMERICAN DOCKS AT CRISTOBAL

It is an amazing climate for ice cream, however, and the Commissary supplied 110,208 gallons of that. Some other annual figures that help to complete the picture of mere size are butter, 429,267 pounds; eggs, 792,043 dozen; poultry, 560,000 pounds; flour, 320,491 pounds.

As I said before, the population of the Zone,

OX METHOD OF TRANSPORTATION

those days perhaps eggs and ice cream did not figure in the Commissariat, and we have no statistics as to poultry, though the poet laureate of Sherman's army referred feelingly to "how the turkeys gobbled that our Commissaries found."

The Commissary is not wholly popular. Native shop keepers, of course, are against

fed mainly through the Commissary, numbers about 65,000. When one reads of the quantity of food needed one wonders at the skill and energy that must have been employed in our Civil War to keep armies of 300,000 and more in the field. However, in it. For a time Zone employees were permitted to use their books of coupons for purchases in native stores, the storekeepers afterwards exchanging them for cash at the Commissary. This practice for some reason has been ruled out, and the native stores lost a certain amount of trade by the ruling. Nor are the natives the only discontented ones.

Americans in Panama, not in the employ of the Isthmian Canal Commission, are inclined to grumble because

ROAD MAKING BY CONVICTS

they are not permitted to make purchases at the Commissary. That, however, was a matter of serious agreement between the United States and the Republic of Panama. When the United States first announced its purpose of taking over the Zone and building the Canal, there was joy among the business folks of Panama and Colon. They saw fat pickings in purveying the necessities of life for a new population of considerable size. Visions of the return of the flush times of the French engaged their imaginations. All these pleasurable anticipations were doused under the wet blanket of the Commissary into which goes the major part of the spending money of the employees. But there are Americans on the Zone, other than employees and their families, and these by a solemn international compact are handed over to the Panamanian mercies. To buy at the Commissary you must have a coupon book, and without an employee's number

COCOANUT PALMS NEAR ANCON

all very well, but lacks in those superfluities for which every one yearns. The two governments, by the way, which protected the Panama merchants against American competition also protected a handful of Panamanians in their clutch upon certain municipal monopolies. With the completion of its power house at Gatun the Canal Commission will have a great volume of power to sell or waste. Wasted it will have to be, for a group of capitalists control the light and power company in Panama City, and the United States has agreed not to compete with them.

Salaries on the Zone during the period of the "big job" were much higher than in the States, but it is probable that upon reorganization they will be materially reduced for those who remain in permanent service—of these Col. Goethals reckons that there will be for the Canal alone about 2700.

ENTRANCE TO BOUQUETTE VALLEY

and brass check no coupon book will be forthcoming. Of course many evade the rule by borrowing a book from a friend, but after one has thus evaded the provisions of a treaty, one usually finds there is nothing special to buy after all. My own opinion is that for the necessities of life the Commissary is

If the Panama Railroad organization should be kept up to its present strength there will be in all about 7700 men employed. This is altogether unlikely however. The railroad will no longer have the construction work and débris of the Canal to carry, and the ships will take much of its commercial business away. During the construction period the wages paid were as follows:

Col. Goethals	$21,000	
Other Commissioners, each	14,000	
Clerks	$ 75 to $250	monthly
Foremen	75 " 275	"
Engineers	225 " 600	"
Draftsmen	100. " 250	"
Master mechanics	225 " 275	"
Physicians	150 " 300	"
Teachers	60 " 110	"
Policemen	80 " 107.50	"

The minimum wage of a gold employee is $75 a month; the maximum, except in the case of heads of departments, $600. The hourly pay in some sample trades was, blacksmith, 30 to 75 cents; bricklayers, 65 cents; carpenters, 32 to 65 cents; iron workers, 44 to 70 cents; painters, 32 to 65 cents; plumbers, 32 to 75 cents. In the higher paid trades steam engineers earned $75 to $200 a month; locomotive engineers from $125 to $210, and steam shovel engineers $210 to $240.

Some of the hourly rates are said to be nearly double those paid in the United States, and the workers had the added advantages of free quarters

Photo by Underwood & Underwood
OPENING THE COCOANUT
The natives cut open the green nuts with swift cuts of their heavy machetes. A miss would cost a finger

and the other perquisites of employment heretofore described.

The Canal Zone is not a democracy. It has no constitution so far as its residents are concerned. There are no elections and no elected officers. Naturally, however, it must needs have a government, though the individual will of Col. Goethals has sufficient authority to override that government if he chooses to exert it. But for the orderly discharge of public business there exists the Department of Civil Administration with Commissioner Maurice H. Thatcher as its chief during the last year of the constructive work.

NATIVE RELIGIOUS PROCESSION AT CHORRERA
The figure of the Savior is faintly shown behind the central crucifix, riding on a mule

RICE STACKED FOR DRYING

000 were sold annually and the money order business during the active years exceeded $5,000,000 annually, most of which represented the savings of the workers.

The Zone police force compels admiration. It is not spectacular, but is eminently business-like and with the heterogeneous population with which it has to deal it has no doubt been busy. At the outset President Roosevelt sent down to command it an old time Rough Rider comrade of his. In late years a regular army officer has been Chief of Police. At that period it was a problem. Not only was the population rough and of mixed antecedents, but many foreign nations were looking on the Isthmus as an excellent dumping place for their criminals and other undesirable citizens. It was not quite Botany Bay, but bade fair to rival that unsavory penal colony. Closer scrutiny of applicants for employment checked that tendency, and a vigorous enforcement of the criminal law together with the application of the power to deport undesirables soon reduced the population to order.

In the early days crimes of violence were common. If one carried money it was wise to carry a gun as well. Organized bandits used to tear up the railroad tracks and wantonly destroy property for no reason

Gov. Thatcher was appointed in 1909 and brought his department to a high state of efficiency. This department has supervision over the posts, revenues and customs, the police and fire departments, the Division of Public Works, and schools, churches and the judiciary.

There were, during the period of greatest activity, 17 post offices on the Zone. The stamps used are Panama stamps, purchased from the Republic at 40 per cent of their face value and with the words "Canal Zone" printed across their face. Stamps to the amount of about $80,-

BULLOCK CART IN CHORRERA

save to satisfy a grudge against the Commission. But the organization of the police force stopped it all. In the cities of Colon and Panama is little or no public gambling, and the brood of outlaws that follow the goddess chance are not to be found there. On the Zone is no gambling at all. Even private poker games, if they become habitual, are broken up by quiet warningsfrom the police. It isn't that there is any great moral aversion to poker, but men who sit up all night with cards and chips are not good at the drawing board or with a transit the next day. Everything on the Zone, from the food in the Commissary to the moral code, is designed with

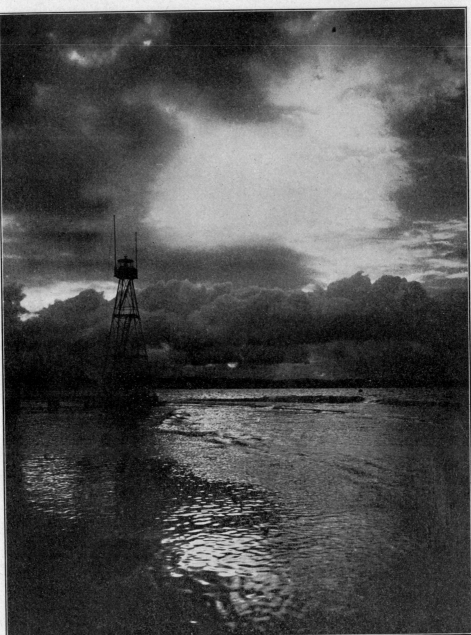

SUN SETTING IN THE ATLANTIC AT LIGHTHOUSE POINT

332 policemen, two inspectors and a chief. Of the policemen 90 were negroes, all of whom had been in the West India constabulary or in West Indian regiments of the British army. The white policemen had all served in the United States army, navy or marine corps. The men are garbed in khaki, and look more like cavalrymen than police officers—indeed a stalwart, well-set-up body of a high order of intelligence and excellent carriage. Arrests are numerous, yet not more so than in an American city of 65,000 people. Of about 150 convicts nearly all are black and these are employed in the construction of roads within the Zone. The work of the police is

an eye single to its effect on the working capacity of the men. It is a fortunate thing that bad morals do not as a rule conduce to industrial efficiency, else I shudder at what Col. Goethals might be tempted to do to the Decalogue.

The police force in its latter days was in the command of a regular army officer. In 1913 it numbered greatly expedited by the celerity of practice in the courts. That Anglo-Saxon fetish, trial by jury, is religiously observed, but the juries are of three men instead of twelve and are held strictly to the consideration of questions of fact alone. There is a full equipment of civil and criminal courts with an appellate division, but no appeal lies to the courts of the United States. There do not seem to be many lawyers in the Zone, hence there is little litigation—or perhaps because there is little litigation there are few lawyers. It is always a mooted question whether lawyers are the cause or the effect of litigation, the bane or the antidote.

Children thrive on the Canal Zone. Nearly every visitor who has had the time to go into the residence sections of Culebra, Gorgona and other large Canal villages has exclaimed at the number of children visible and their uniform good health. Naturally therefore a school system has grown up of which Americans, who lead the world in public education, may well be proud. Three thousand pupils are enrolled, and besides a superintendent and general officials, eighty teachers attend to their education. The school buildings are planned and

The children like their elders come in for the beneficence of the Commission. Free books, free stationery, free medical treatment and free transportation are provided for all. Prof. Frank A. Gause, superintendent of the Zone schools, is an Indianian and has taken a justifiable pride in developing the school system there so that it shall be on a par with the school of like grades in "the States." He declares that so far as the colored schools are concerned they are of a higher degree of excellence than those in our more northern communities. Native and West Indian children attend the schools of this class, in which the teachers are colored men who have graduated in the best West Indian colleges and who have had ample teaching experience in West Indian schools.

The curriculum of the Zone schools covers all the grades up to the eighth, that is the primary

THE FRUITFUL MANGO TREE

equipped according to the most approved requirements for school hygiene, and are especially adapted to the tropics—which means that the rooms are open to the air on at least two sides, and that wide aisles and spaces between the desks give every child at least twice the air space he would have had in a northern school.

and grammar school grades, and a well-conducted high school as well. Pupils have been prepared for Harvard, Wellesley, Vassar and the University of Chicago. The white schools are all taught by American teachers, each of whom must have had four years' high school training, two years in either a university or a normal school and two years of

COMPLETED CANAL NEAR GATUN

dency among Americans on the Zone to decry the soil as unfit for any profitable agriculture. A very excellent report on "The Agricultural Possibilities of the Canal Zone", issued by the Department of Agriculture, should effectually still this sort of talk. To the mere superficial observer it seems incredible that a soil which produces such a wealth of useless vegetation should be unable to produce anything useful, and the scientists of the Department of Agriculture have shown that that paradoxical condition does not exist. Practically all our northern vegetables and many of our most desirable fruits can be raised on the Zone according to this report, and it goes on to say:

"Opportunities for establishing paying dairy herds appear good, . . . there is unquestionably a good opening for raising both pork and poultry. Small

practical teaching experience. These requirements are obviously higher than those of the average American city school system. Prof. Gause declares that politics and the recommendation of politicians have no share in the administration of the Zone schools, though the efforts of Washington statesmen to place their relatives on the payroll have been frequent and persistent.

For the native and West Indian children a course in horticulture is given and school gardens established in which radishes, beans, peas, okra, papayas, bananas, turnips, cabbages, lettuce, tomatoes, and yams are cultivated. It is worth noting that considerable success has been achieved with products of the temperate zone, though especial care was needed for their cultivation. One garden of three-quarters of an acre produced vegetables worth $350. There is a ten-

TRAVELLING CRANES AT MIRAFLORES

farming, including the production of vegetables and choice tropical fruits, such as the avocado, mango, papaya, pineapple, orange, guava, anona, etc., can be carried on profitably with the application of intensive methods, coupled with proper care in the selection of crop varieties and soil. The supply of pineapples, avocados, and papayas is very much below the demand, notwithstanding the fact that these fruits are

PACIFIC FLATS LEFT BY RECEDING TIDE
The fall is 18 feet and the receding tide leaves more than a mile thus bare

apparently well adapted to a considerable portion of the Zone. With the introduction of varieties of mangos better than the seedling types now grown this fruit could be made very much more popular with the northern population. As an evidence of the good opportunities for the production of choice fruits not only to supply local demand, but for export trade, the Island of Taboga in Panama may be cited. Here upon very steep slopes, including much extremely stony land, large quantities of delightfully flavored pineapples are grown for shipment. The mango and avocada (aguacate) are also shipped from this small island with profit".

Consideration of the agricultural and industrial possibilities of the Canal Zone is made desirable, indeed imperative, by the proposition of the military authorities to abandon the whole territory to the jungle—to expel from it every human being not employed by the Canal Commission or the Panama Railroad, or not having business of some sort in connection with those organizations. This was not in con-

THE REVIEW AT ONE OF THE ROOSEVELT RECEPTIONS

A WHALER AT PEARL ISLAND

templation in the early days of the Zone. It was planned to invite settlement, though retaining the actual ownership of the land to the United States. By way of encouraging such settlement the Isthmian Commission was authorized to lease to settlers farms not exceeding 50 hectares (125 acres) each, at an annual rental of $3 a hectare. This was not particularly attractive and the proposition was made less so by limiting the period of leases to twenty-five years. Moreover the limitation on the size of the individual farm made cattle farming quite impossible, and even ordinary farming doubtful, for in 50 hectares the actual area of good farming land is likely to be small. Although criticism of these provisions was current, in 1913 nothing was done for their correction because of the vigor with which the military authorities urged the entire depopulation of the Zone.

That proposition has not yet come before the American people. It has not even been debated in Congress, but at the moment of the publication of this book the Commission is proceeding calmly with its arrangements, as though the program were definitely fixed. The argument advanced by Col. Goethals and other military experts is that the Canal is primarily a military work. That the Canal Zone exists only because of and for the Canal, and should be so governed as to protect the dams and locks from any treacherous assault is admitted. The advocates of the depopulation program insist that with a residence on the Zone refused to any save those employed by the Commission and subject to its daily control, with the land grown up once

more into an impenetrable jungle so that access to the Canal can be had only through its two ends, or by the Panama Railroad—both easily guarded— the Canal will be safe from the dynamiter hired by some hostile government.

It may be so, but there is another side to the question. The Canal Zone is an outpost of a high civilization in the tropics. It affords object lessons to the neighboring republics of Central America in architecture, sanitation, road building, education, civil government and indeed all the practical arts that go to make a State comfortable and prosperous. Without intention to offend any of the neighboring States it may fairly be said that the Zone, if maintained according to its present standards, should exercise an influence for good on all of them. It is the little leaven that may leaven the whole lump.

That it can be maintained with its present population is of course impossible. When the employment, furnished by the construction of the Canal is finished, the army of engineers and laborers will disintegrate and scatter to other fields of industry. This process is already begun. Our government in

AN OLD WELL AT CHIRIQUI

securing labor from the West India islands assumed the task of returning the laborers to their homes at the expiration of their term of service and this is now being done, though not so rapidly as would have been the case except for the persistent activity of the slides at Culebra. It has been suggested that gifts of land, instead of passage money home, would be acceptable to these laborers, not merely West Indians, but Europeans as well. Thrown open to settlement under proper conditions the Zone would no doubt attract a certain class of agriculturists from the States.

Undoubtedly there will be a field for skilled agricultural endeavor there. As I have already noted Col. Goethals estimates the necessary force for the operation of the Canal at 2700. For the operation of the Panama Railroad in 1913 five thousand men were required but with the cessation of Canal work this number would be largely reduced. Probably 6000 men would constitute the working force of both Canal and railroad. A working force of that number would create a population of about 15,000. There is further the military force to be

CHOLO GIRLS AT THE STREAM

considered. Col. Goethals strenuously urged that 25,000 men be kept on the Isthmus permanently, but the opinion of Congress, toward the period of the opening of the Canal, seemed to be that about 7000 would be sufficient. In all probability the latter figure will be the smallest number of men that will go to make up the military establishment.

There is every reason to believe that at Balboa particularly the shipping interests will create a large and prosperous town, while already the cities of Panama and Colon, geographically part of the Zone, though politically independent, have a population of at least 60,000.

When the Canal is once in operation there will be from 75,000 to 100,000 people on the Zone and in the two native cities within it to furnish a market for the food products that can be raised on that fertile strip of land. Today the vegetables of the temperate zone are brought 3000 miles to the Zone dwellers, sometimes in cold storage, but chiefly in cans. As for those who live in the Panama towns and are denied access to the Commissary, they get fresh vegetables only from the limited supply furnished by the few Chinese market gardens. According to the Department of Agriculture nearly all vegetables of the temperate clime and all tropical fruits can be grown on the Zone lands. This being the case it seems a flat affront to civilization and to the intelligent utilization of natural resources to permit these lands to revert to the jungle, and force our citizens and soldiers in these tropic lands to go without the health-giving

A GOOD YIELD OF COCOANUTS

vegetable food that could easily be raised in the outskirts of their towns and camps. Of the sufficiency of the market for the output of all the farms for which the Zone has space and arable soil there can be no doubt, for to the townspeople, the Canal operatives and the garrisons there will be added the ships which reach Colon or Balboa after long voyages and with larders empty of fresh green vegetables.

To the mind not wholly given over to militarism the idea that this region in which so admirable, so unparalleled a beginning of industrial development has been made should be now abandoned is intolerable. And it does not seem at all plausible that our locks and dams and spillways would be safer in a wilderness patrolled by perfunctory guards than they would be in a well-settled and thriving community every man in which would know that his prosperity was wholly dependent upon the peaceful and uninterrupted operation of the Canal.

Doubtless there will be some discussion before acquiescence is given to the military proposition that the Canal Zone—as large as the State of Indiana—shall be allowed to revert to jungle, be given over to the serpent, the sloth and the jaguar. That would be a sorry anti-climax to the work of Gorgas in banishing yellow fever and malaria, and of Goethals in showing how an industrial community could be organized, housed and fed.

Photo by Underwood & Underwood

SHIPPING AT BALBOA DOCKS

CHAPTER XIX

FORTIFICATIONS; TOLLS; COMMERCE AND QUARANTINE

WITH the completion of the Canal appeared many problems other than the engineering ones which had for so many years engrossed public attention. Some of these problems— like the question whether the Canal should be fortified or its neutrality guaranteed by international agreement—had reached a conclusion during the last year of the constructive work. But the question of Canal tolls, the future management of the Canal Zone and the broad speculation as to the general effect upon the trade of the world were still subjects of discussion.

That there should have been any serious opposition to the fortification of the Canal seems amazing, but the promptitude with which it died out seems to indicate that, while noisy, it had no very solid foundation in public sentiment. Indeed it was urged mainly by well-meaning theorists who condemn upon principle any addition to the already heavy burden which the need for the national defense has laid upon the shoulders of the people. That in theory they were right is

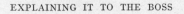

EXPLAINING IT TO THE BOSS

undeniable. Perhaps the greatest anomaly of the twentieth century is the proportions of our preparations for war contrasted with our oratorical protestations of a desire for peace. But the inconsistencies of the United States are trivial in comparison with those of other nations, and while the whole world is armed—nominally for defense, but in a way to encourage aggressions—it is wise that the United States put bolts on its front gate. And that in effect is what forts and coast defenses are. They are not aggressive, and cannot be a menace to any one—either to a foreign land, as a great navy might conceivably be, or to our people, as a great standing army might prove. The guns at Toro Point and Naos Island will never speak, save in ceremonial salute, unless some foreign foe menaces the Canal which the United States gives freely to the peaceful trade of the world. But if the menace should be presented, it will be well not for our nation alone, but for all the peoples of the earth, that we are prepared to defend the integrity of the strait of which man has dreamed for more than 400 years, and in the creation of which thousands of useful lives have been sacrificed.

Mistaken but well-meaning opponents of fortification have insisted that it was a violation of our pact with Great Britain, and a breach of international comity. This,

SPANISH MONASTERY AT PANAMA

however, is an error. True, in the Clayton-Bulwer treaty of 1850, both the United States and Great Britain expressly agreed not to fortify or assume any dominion over any part of Central America through which a canal might be dug. But that treaty was expressly abrogated by the Hay-Pauncefote treaty. In its first draft this latter treaty contained the anti-fortification clause and was rejected by the United States Senate for that very reason. In its second draft the treaty omitted the reference to fortifications and was ratified. Lord Lansdowne, one of the negotiators for the British government, explicitly said that he thoroughly understood the United States wished to reserve the right to fortify the Canal.

CHOCO INDIAN OF SANBU VALLEY

It was so clear that no question of treaty obligations was involved that the opponents of fortification early dropped that line of argument. The discussion of the treaty in the Senate silenced them. They fell back upon the question of expediency. "Why", they asked, "go to the expense of building and manning fortifications and maintaining a heavy garrison on the Zone? Why not, through international agreement, make it neutral and protect it from seizure or blockade in time of war? Look at Suez"!

This was more plausible. At first glance the questions seem answerable in only one way. But consideration weakens their force. There is a Latin copy-book maxim, *"Inter armas silent leges"*—"In time of war the law is silent". It is cynically correct. International agreements to maintain the integrity or neutrality of a territory last only until one of the parties to the agreement thinks it profitable to break it. It then becomes the business of all the other parties to enforce the pact, and it is usually shown that what is everybody's business is nobody's business. Consider a partial record:

The independence of Korea was guaranteed by four Great Powers in 1902. Inside of two years the Japanese Admiral Uriu violated the independence of the Korean port of Chemulpo by sinking two Russian cruisers in it, and shortly thereafter Japan practically annexed the country. None of the Powers that had "guaranteed" its independence protested.

Austria-Hungary in 1908 annexed Bosnia and Herzegovina, despite the fact that seven Powers, including Austria-Hungary herself, had fixed the sovereignty of those provinces in Turkey. The signatory powers grumbled a little, but that was all. Mr. W. E. Hall, recognized as the greatest living

THE RISING GENERATION

authority on international law, observes cynically, and truthfully, that "treaties are only permanently obeyed when they represent the continued wishes of the contracting parties".

Prussia once guaranteed the independence of Poland, and in two years took the leading part in blotting it off the roll of nations.

Illustrations of the failure of nations to observe the rights of neutrals are common. Turkey and Korea afford recent illustrations of nations that have entrusted their national integrity to international agreements. Nothing remains of Korea's nationality but a name, and the Allies are rapidly carving Turkey to bits while the Great Powers that guaranteed her integrity look on in amazed and impotent alarm. The United States itself has not been wholly without share in such high-handed proceedings. In the event of a general war

ANCON HILL, WHERE AMERICANS LIVE IN COMFORT

Panama Canal would be kept neutral just so long as our military and naval power could defend its neutrality and no longer.

Moreover, we do not want it neutral in a quarrel in which we are involved. The Canal is dug by our money and in our territory and is part of our line of defense. We do not propose to permit its passage by an enemy. That would be strict neutrality indeed, but it would make the Canal a weakness instead of a defense. Without it our Pacific Coast is practically safe from European aggression; our Atlantic coast protected by thousands of miles of ocean from any foe whose naval strength is in the Pacific. To throw open the Canal to our foes as well as to our friends would be like supplying the key to the bank vaults to the cracksmen as well as to the cashier.

The parallel with the Suez Canal strenuously urged by the advocates of neutrality does not hold. The waterway between the Mediterranean and the Red Sea was not dug as a government enterprise. It was a distinctly commercial enterprise, with its shares listed upon the exchanges and bought and sold in the open market. By the purchase of a majority of those shares the ownership of the Canal passed into the hands of the British government, but all the nations had joined in the international agreement to protect their individual rights before the British ownership was effected. Moreover, Great Britain is by no means content with the safeguards provided by the Constantinople convention, but has planted her great fortresses at Malta and at Aden, near the ends of the Canal, and maintains in the Mediterranean a naval force equal to that of any other two nations. The Caribbean is to be the American Mediterranean, and the visible and effective power of the United States in those waters must be equal, probably vastly superior, to that of England in Europe's great inland sea.

GATUN LAKE, SHOWING SMALL FLOATING ISLANDS

Nor does the existence of a powerful navy, even the material multiplication of our present naval force, obviate to any considerable degree the necessity for powerful forts at either end of the Canal. Our fleet cannot be anchored during the continuance of a war to any one fixed point. The navy is essentially an offensive force, its part in the defense of our country being best performed by keeping the enemy busy defending his own. Farragut said that the best defense against the attack of any enemy is the rapid fire of your own guns. Extend this principle and it appears that the best way to defend our own coasts is to menace those of the enemy. This principle was not applied in our recent war with Spain, but we had not the navy then, and diplomatic considerations further intervened to prevent our employing against Spain's sea coast cities such vessels as we had. Should we rely wholly on the navy to defend our Canal entrances a mere demonstration against those points would tie up a considerable portion of our floating force, while an enemy's main fleet might ravage our thickly populated sea coasts.

A SPECTACULAR BLAST

Discussion of this question, however, is largely academic, for the fortification of the Canal has been determined upon, and construction of the forts is well advanced. There is, however, some disquietude over a fear, expressed by the late Admiral Evans, that the topography at the Atlantic terminus of the Canal is such that fortifications, however great their strength, would not be sufficient to prevent the enemy holding a position so near the Canal's mouth as to be able to concentrate its fire on each ship as it emerged and thus destroy seriatim any fleet seeking to make the passage of the Canal. The criticism was a serious one. Even to the civilian mind the inequalities of a battle in which six or eight battleships can concentrate their broadside fire on a single ship navigating a narrow and tortuous channel and able to reply with her bow guns only are sufficiently obvious. Indeed the criticism was held of sufficient force to be referred to the General Board of the Navy, which, after due consideration, made a report of which the following quotations form the substance:

THE FIRST VIEW OF COLON

"The General Board believes that the proposed fortifications at the termini of the Isthmian Canal would be invaluable in assisting the transfer of a United States fleet from one ocean to the other through the Canal, in the face of an opposing fleet. The function of the fortifications in this particular is precisely the same at the Canal termini as it is at any fortified place from which a fleet may have to issue in the face of an enemy's fleet.

A PORCH AT CULEBRA

advantage over the ship gun which is universally recognized, and this advantage is increased if the former be mounted on disappearing carriages, as are the seacoast guns of the United States. The mere statement of these elementary facts is a sufficient proof of the value of seacoast guns to assist a fleet in passing out from behind them to engage a waiting hostile fleet outside, provided the shore guns are mounted in advance of, or abreast, the point where the ship channel joins the open sea. Even if somewhat retired from that point they would be useful, but to a less extent.

"Guns mounted on shore are on an unsinkable and steady platform, and they can be provided with unlimited protection and accurate range-finding devices. Guns mounted on board ship are on a sinkable, unsteady platform, their protection is limited, and range-finding devices on board ship have a very limited range of accuracy. The shore gun of equal power has thus a great

"At the Pacific terminus of the Canal there are outlying islands that afford sites for fortifications, the usefulness of which in assisting the egress of a fleet in the face of opposition is universally ad-

Photo by American Press Ass'n

AVENIDA CENTRALE, PANAMA, NEAR THE STATION

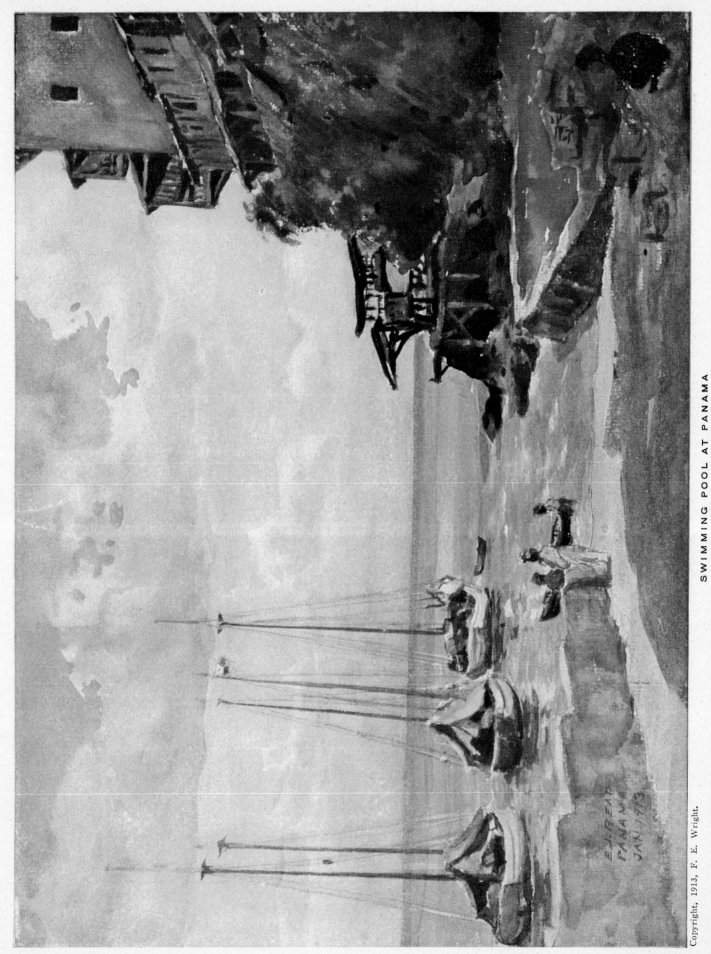

SWIMMING POOL AT PANAMA

Some say that before the days of the city water supply this pool held water for protection against fire. Nowadays it is chiefly used for the aquatic revels of the boys.

mitted, as far as the General Board knows; but there has been unfavorable criticism of the possibility of fortifications at the Atlantic end to serve this purpose. The General Board regards these criticisms as unfounded and believes, on the contrary, that the conditions at the Atlantic terminus of the Canal are unusually favorable for the emplacement of guns that would be of assistance to a fleet issuing in the face of hostile ships.

"On both sides of Limon Bay, in which the Canal terminates at the Atlantic end, there are excellent sites for forts, well advanced on outlying points. The line joining these sites is 3000 yards in front of the point where the Canal prism reaches a low-water depth sufficient for battleships, and Limon Bay from this point outward is wide enough for a formation of eight ships abreast. The outer end of the most advanced breakwater proposed is only 600 yards in front of the line joining the sites for the forts; and as long as ships remain behind the breakwater, it will afford them a considerable amount of protection from the enemy's fire, while they will themselves be

A MOUNTAIN RIVER IN CHIRIQUI

IN A CHIRIQUI TOWN

able to fire over it. In order to make his fire effective against the issuing ships the enemy must come within the effective fire of the fortifications. Under these circumstances it is impossible to deny the usefulness of fortifications in assisting the issue of a fleet against opposition. The conditions in this respect at the Atlantic end of the Canal are incomparably better than those existing at Sandy Hook, whose forts nobody would dream of dismantling".

Concerning the type of fortifications now building there is little to be said. The War Department is not as eager for publicity as are certain other departments of our federal administration. In November, 1912, Secretary of War Stimson made a formal statement of the general plan of defense. No change has been made in this plan, and it may be quoted as representing the general scheme as fixed upon by the War Department and authorized by Congress:

"The defenses to the Isthmus are divided into two general heads:

"1. A seacoast armament with submarine mines at the termini of the Canal, for protection against a sea attack and to secure a safe exit for our fleet in the face of a hostile fleet.

"2.   The construction of field works and a mobile force of troops to protect the locks and assure important utilities against an attack by land".

"The seacoast fortifications will include 16-inch, 14-inch and 6-inch rifles and 12-inch mortars. This armament will be of more powerful and effective types than that installed in any other locality in the world.   At the Atlantic end of the Canal the armament will be located on both sides of Limon Bay.

Panama Canal Zone of a mobile force consisting of three regiments of infantry, at a war strength of nearly 2000 men for each regiment, a squadron of cavalry, and a battalion of field artillery.   These latter fortifications and the mobile garrison are intended to repel any attacks that might be made by landing parties from an enemy's fleet against the locks and other important elements or accessories to the Canal.   As an attack of this character might

BITING THROUGH A SLIDE: FIVE CUBIC YARDS PER BITE

At the Pacific end the greater part of the armament will be located on several small islands, Flamenco, Perico and Naos, which lie abreast of the terminus. Submarine mines will complete the seacoast armament and will prevent actual entry into the Canal and harbors by hostile vessels.

"In addition to these fortifications, and the necessary coast artillery and garrison to man them, the defensive plans provide for the erection of field works, and for the maintenance at all times on the

be coincident with or even precede an actual declaration of war, it is necessary that a force of the strength above outlined should be maintained on the Canal Zone at all times.   This mobile garrison will furnish the necessary police force to protect the Zone and preserve order within its limits in time of peace.   Congress has made the initial appropriations for the construction of these fortifications, and they are now under construction.   A portion of the mobile garrison is also on the Isthmus, and the remainder will be sent there as soon as provision is made for its being housed".

It is to be noted that these plans contemplate only the garrisoning of the Isthmus in time of peace. The department has steadfastly refused, even in response to congressional inquiry, to make public its plans for action in war time. The only hint offered on the subject is the estimate of Col. Goethals that 25,000 men would be needed there in such a contingency and his urgency that such a garrison be maintained on the Zone at all times.

The most vulnerable point of the Canal is of course the locks. The destruction or interruption of the electrical machinery which operates the great gates would put the entire Canal out of commission. If in war time it should be vitally necessary to shift our Atlantic fleet to the Pacific, or vice versa, the enemy could effectively check that operation by a bomb dropped on the lock machinery at Gatun, Pedro Miguel or Miraflores. It is, however, the universal opinion of the military experts that this danger is guarded against to the utmost extent demanded by extraordinary prudence. Against the miraculous, such as the presence of an aeroplane with an operator so skilled as to drop bombs upon a target of less than 40 feet square, no defense could fully prevail. The lock gates themselves are necessarily exposed and an injury to them would as effectually put the lock out of commission as would the wrecking of the controlling machinery.

Col. Goethals has repeatedly declared his belief that the construction of the locks is sufficiently massive to withstand any ordinary assaults with explosives. No one man could carry and place secretly enough dynamite to wreck or even seriously impair the immediate usefulness of the locks. Even in time of peace they will be continually guarded and patroled, while in time of war they will naturally be protected from enemies on every side and even in the air above. The locks are not out of range of a fleet in Limon Bay and a very few 13-inch naval shells would put them out of commission. But for that very reason we are building forts at Toro Point and its neighborhood to keep hostile fleets out of Limon Bay, and the United States navy, which has usually given a good account of itself in time of war, will be further charged with this duty and will no doubt duly discharge it.

COMMISSARY BUILDING AND FRONT STREET, COLON

That the locks make the Canal more vulnerable than a sea-level canal would have been is doubtless true. The fact only adds to the argument in behalf of defending it by powerful forts and an adequate navy.

General Weaver, U. S. A., raised the only serious question as to the sufficiency of the defenses on the Pacific side in his testimony before the House Committeee on Appropriations:

"My views are entirely in harmony with those expressed by Col. Goethals. I think that the defenses are wholly adequate. The only question I have noted raised as to the adequacy of the defense has been as to whether guns would not be mounted by an enemy on Taboga Island, and as to whether an enemy's ships could not stand behind Taboga Island, and as to whether these land guns and naval guns could not from there control the water area in front of the Pacific terminus? The new type of mortars that the Ordnance Department is making for the fortifications at Panama will have a range of 20,000 yards. They will cover the water well over beyond Taboga Island, and have under fire all of Taboga Island and the water for a considerable distance beyond the outermost shore lines of Taboga Island. It is about 12,000 yards from the fortifications at the Canal terminus to Taboga Island. The mortars will reach 8000 yards beyond Taboga. The 16-inch gun on Perico will have a range of 20,000 yards. The 14-inch guns on Flamenco and Naos Islands will have ranges of 18,400 yards. The 6-inch guns on Naos Island and on the mainland have a range of 6000 yards, and are well placed to oppose any attempt at landing on the lands on which the fortifications are located.

"*Mr. Sherley.*—'So far you have spoken only of the Pacific side. Now, what have you to say about the defense on the Atlantic side'?

"*Gen. Weaver.*—'On the Atlantic side the defense is, in my opinion, equally adequate. At Fort Ran-

PEDRO MIGUEL LOCKS
The deep arched recesses are provided that the gates may fold flush with the walls

DETAIL CONSTRUCTION OF A LOCK
The great tube, later covered by concrete, carries the water for filling the chamber

dolph, on Margarita Island, there are eight mortars of the new type, two 14-inch guns and two 6-inch guns. That armament will protect the Margarita Island side of the entrance and it also controls the waters to the south. On the Toro Point side at Fort Sherman we have eight mortars, two 14-inch guns, and two 6-inch guns. There are in addition two 6-inch guns provided at Manzanillo Point, city of Colon. In my opinion this armament is entirely adequate for the defense of the Atlantic side' ".

It is apparent, therefore, that the unfortified Island of Taboga is the one questionable point in our Pacific line of defense. It is wholly probable that steps will be taken to erect such defenses as will make the seizure of this island impracticable to any enemy.

Plans for the landward defenses of the coast forts had not been determined upon at the time of publication of this book. Necessary no doubt from a

strictly military point of view, they seem to the civilian mind rather superfluous in view of the character of the countryside along the borders of the Zone. The general who would undertake to lead an army through the jungle would encounter a natural foe such as armed forces have never had to overcome, and his invading column would hardly emerge upon the Zone in fit condition to give battle to any considerable army of occupation.

However, should an enemy once effect a landing at any point within striking distance of Panama or Colon, say on the Chorrera coast, or at Nombre de Dios or Porto Bello, some defensive works would be needed to prevent their taking the coast forts in the rear. Such works are being planned and an extensive permanent camp is to be built at Miraflores, at which point the Canal can be readily crossed—there are to be no permanent bridges— and smaller posts at Margarita Island, Toro Point and Culebra Island. To man the actual seacoast forts there will be 12 companies of coast artillery of 109 men each; while distributed in the army camps will be, according to present estimates, three

Photo by H. Pittier   Courtesy National Geographic Magazine

A GROUP OF GUYAMI GIRLS

regiments of infantry, a squadron of cavalry and a battalion of field artillery, making in all rather more than 8000 men.

The probable influence of the Panama Canal on commerce, on trade routes, on the commercial supremacy of this or that country, on the development of hitherto dormant lands is a question that opens an endless variety of speculations. Discussion of it requires so broad a knowledge of international affairs as to be almost cosmic, a foresight so gifted as to be prophetic. A century from now the fullest results of the Canal's completion will not have been fully attained. This creation of a new waterway where a rocky barrier stood from the infinite past in the pathway of commerce will make great cities where hamlets now sit in somno-

lence, and perhaps reduce to insignificance some of the present considerable ports of the world.

Certain very common misbeliefs may be corrected with merely a word or two of explanation. Nothing is more common than to look upon all South America as a territory to be vastly benefited by the Canal, and brought by it nearer to our United States markets. A moment's thought will show the error of this belief. When we speak of South America we think first of all of the rich eastern coast, of the cities of Rio de Janeiro, Montevideo and Buenos Ayres. But it is not to this section that the greatest advantage will come from the Canal. Vessels from our Pacific coast can indeed carry the timber of Puget Sound, the fish of Alaska and the Columbia River, the fruits of California thither more cheaply than now, but that is but a slight fraction of their trade. Nor are Brazil and the Argentine participators in Oriental trade to any great extent, though the Canal may make them so. The western coast of South America is chiefly affected by the Canal, and that to a degree rigidly limited by the distance of the point considered from the Straits of Magellan, and the size of the Canal tolls imposed.

Nor will the Suez Canal be an abandoned waterway after our own cut at Panama is completed. It will, indeed, be not surprising to see the Suez Canal tonnage increase, for trade breeds trade, and the Panama Canal will be a stimulant as well as a competitor. To all of British India and Southern China the distance from Liverpool via Suez is less than via Panama, and to Melbourne, Sidney and other Australian ports the saving in distance via Panama is less than 2000 miles. The Suez Canal,

A ZONE SIGN OF CIVILIZATION

it is to be remembered, is owned by Great Britain and a very slight concession in rates will be all that is needed to keep British merchant vessels to their long accustomed routes. We have had a harder task in digging our Canal than the French had at Suez, but we need cherish no delusive idea that we are going to put the earlier waterway out of business.

The really great material advantage which the United States is to derive from this monumental national undertaking will come from the all-water connection between our own Atlantic and Pacific coasts. A ship going from New York to San Francisco via the Straits of Magellan traverses 14,000 miles of sea—some of it the very most turbulent of all King Neptune's tossing domain. By Panama the same ship will have but 5000 miles to cover. The amazing thing is that ships are going around the Horn, or at least through the Straits, but the high rates on transcontinental railroads make even that protracted voyage profitable. What the Canal will do to transcontinental rates is a matter that is giving some railroad managers deep concern. It was in fact a consideration which led to prolonged and obstinate opposition to the building of any canal at all. Water carriage between the two coasts has long been a bogey to the railroad managers. When coastwise steamships on the Atlantic and Pacific with the Panama Railroad for a connecting link offered some competition, the five transcontinental railways pooled together and, securing control of the Pacific Mail Steamship line operating between San Francisco and Panama, used it to cripple all competition. For a time there was danger that the methods then employed might be

adopted to destroy the usefulness of the Panama Canal, and it was to guard against this that Congress adopted the law denying the use of the Canal to vessels owned by railroad companies.

HIS MORNING TUB

At the time of its passage this law created much discussion. The reason for it was widely misunderstood. Its first effect was the canceling of several orders for ships placed by railroad companies with shipbuilders in anticipation of the Canal's opening, and the public naturally cried out against a measure which seemed to interpose an obstacle to the reappearance of the American flag on the high seas. But the law was bred of bitter experience. In bygone days it was discovered that both time and money could be saved on shipments from California to New York or other Atlantic seaports by sending them to Panama by water, across the Isthmus by rail, and then by water from Colon to their destina-

PART OF THE COMPLETED CANAL

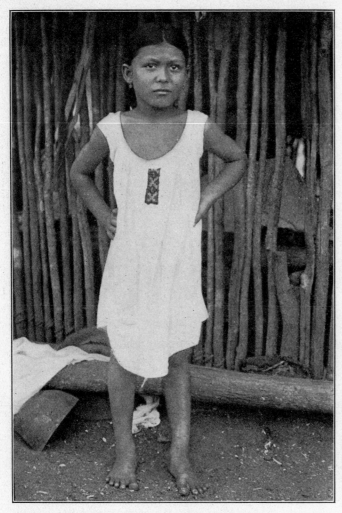

NATIVE GIRL, CHORRERA PROVINCE

docks on the plea that all their cargo space was disposed of. It was—to the railroads who afterward gathered up the rejected freight and shipped it east over their own lines at prices to suit themselves.

Taught wisdom by these tactics—against which they had unavailingly employed all the expedients of law and of coöperative competition—the shippers of California appealed to Congress to act wisely lest the Panama Canal as a waterway for all and a regulator of transcontinental freight rates be throttled by the railroads. They pointed out that the roads might in combination maintain one line of ships between New York and San Francisco which would make rates so low that no other line could meet them and live. Doubtless such a line would lose money, but the loss, divided among the conspiring roads, would be but a flea bite to each, and would be more than recouped by the higher rail rates they might charge. In response to this

tion. This route grew in favor until the transcontinental railroads intervened to check its further development. Getting control of the Pacific Mail line of steamers from San Francisco to Panama, they first put their rates so low as to drive all competing ships from the route. Of course they lost money, but the loss was apportioned among the companies forming the pool, and when the competing concerns had been ruined or driven out of business, the rates were put up again and the losses that had been incurred were speedily recouped. Once the complete monopoly on the Pacific had been secured, every effort was made to discourage shipments by that route. The ships passed Los Angeles, the greatest fruit port in the country, without a call, but touched at innumerable little mud villages in Central America so as to make the time of through shipments intolerable. They often sailed with half a cargo—refusing to take freight that lay at their

NATIVE BOY, CHORRERA PROVINCE

appeal Congress enacted the law denying railroads the right to maintain lines of water carriage on what would be normally competitive routes. The statute though planned primarily for the maintenance of the highest usefulness of the Panama Canal affects other routes, notably Long Island Sound. It is denounced by the railroads and has doubtless checked to some extent American shipbuilding, but it is nevertheless the only apparent weapon against a very real and harmful device in the railroads' efforts to maintain high rates.

The question of the tolls to be charged for passage through the Canal is one that has evoked a somewhat acrimonious discussion, the end of which is not yet. About the amount of the toll there was little dispute. It was determined by taking the cost of maintenance of the Canal, which is estimated at about $4,000,000 annually, and the interest on its cost, about $10,000,000 a year, and comparing the total with the

for the first year at 10,500,000 tons, with an increase at the end of the first decade of operation to 17,000,000, and at the end of the second decade to 27,000,000 tons. The annual expenses of the Canal, including interest, approximates $14,000,-

MAIN STREET, CHORRERA

000, and Congress has accordingly fixed the tolls at $1.20 a ton for freight and $1.50 per passenger. It is anticipated that these figures will cause a deficit in the first two or three years of operation, but that the growth of commerce through the Canal will speedily make it up.

In legislating upon the question of tolls Congress opened an international question which has been fiercely debated and which remains a subject of diplomatic negotiation between our State Department and the British Foreign Office. This was done by the section of the law which granted to American-built ships engaged in the coasting trade the right to

PARK AT DAVID

amount of tonnage which might reasonably be expected to pass through annually. Prof. Emory R. Johnson, the government expert upon whose figures are based all estimates concerning canal revenues, fixed the probable tonnage of the Canal

use the Canal without the payment of any tolls whatsoever. At the time of its appearance in Congress this proposition attracted little attention and evoked no discussion. It seemed to be a perfectly obvious and entirely justifiable employment of the Canal for the encouragement of American shipping. The United States had bought the territory through which the Canal extended and was paying every dollar of the cost of the great work. What could be more natural than that it should concede to American shipping owners, who had borne their share of the taxation which the cost of the Canal necessitated, the right of free passage through it?

The concession seemed the more obvious and proper because the privilege of free passage was limited to vessels in the coastwise trade. Under our navigation laws maritime trade between ports in the United States is confined to ships built in American shipyards. This regulation is clearly intended to confer upon the United States a monopoly of the building of coastwise ships, and the subsequent exemption of coastwise ships from Panama Canal tolls was a further benefaction to this monopoly. As a matter of fact, our coastwise trade was at the moment passing into monopolistic control, and the wisdom of making so prodigious a gift to a monopolistic combination might have justly been questioned. But the strictly business features of the Canal have always been decorated with more or less sentimental declamation about reëstablishing the American flag on the high seas, and it was to contribute to the latter desirable end that the tolls were to be remitted. It seemed to occur to no one that the ships thus favored were either owned by railroad com-

A PLACID BACK WATER IN CHIRIQUI

panies and used largely to stifle competition or by a somewhat notorious organizer of trusts whose ambition was to control water transportation from Maine to the Mexico border, and who was checked in the attainment of his aim by a sentence to the Federal penitentiary. It is not only in war time that the flag is waved most enthusiastically by men who only want the bounty that goes with it.

Nobody, however, at the time of the passage of the act regulating tolls thought it had any particular international significance. Its signature by the President was taken as a matter of course and it was not until some time afterward that the Ambassador of Great Britain presented his country's claim that the exemption clause was in violation of the Hay-Pauncefote treaty. The section of that treaty which it is claimed is violated reads thus:

"The Canal shall be free and open to the vessels of commerce and of war of all nations observing these rules on terms of entire equality, so that there shall be no discrimination against any such nation, or its citizens or subjects, in respect of the conditions or changes of traffic".

The outcry against the exemption clause soon became very vociferous. It is said to have been fomented largely by the Canadian railroads, or persons interested in them. They saw possible profit in running ships from Montreal or Quebec, to Vancouver or Victoria, touching at various United States ports en route. Such a voyage would not constitute a "coastwise passage" under our laws, and foreign vessels might engage in such traffic. But they saw that the exemption in tolls by which a United States vessel of 12,000 tons would escape canal tolls amounting to $15,000 would put them at a serious disadvantage. Hence they appealed to Great Britain and the protest followed. Too diplomatic to express the real reason for its protest,

sacrificed her coastwise register if she continued her voyage to Yokohama or Hong Kong.

American public men and the American press are radically divided on the question. A majority, perhaps, are inclined to thrust it aside with a mere declaration of our power in the matter. "We built the Canal and paid for it", they say, "and our ships have the same rights in it that they have in the

GATUN LAKE.   FLOATING ISLANDS MASSED AGAINST TRESTLE

the British government urges that the United States will very properly adjust its tolls to meet the needs of the Canal for revenue, and that if the coastwise shipping be exempted there will be a loss of some millions of dollars in revenue which will compel the imposition of higher tolls on other shipping. It is urged also on behalf of the protestants that the word "coastwise" is capable of various constructions and that a vessel plying between New York and Los Angeles might be held not to have

Hudson River or the canal at the Soo. Besides the British cannot engage in our coasting trade anyway, and what we do to help our coastwise ships concerns no one but us". Which seems a pretty fair and reasonable statement of the case until the opponents of the exemption clause put in their rejoinder. "Read the treaty", they say. "It is perfectly clear in its agreement that the United States will not do this thing it now proposes to do. Treaties are, by the Constitution, the supreme law of the land. To violate one is to violate our national honor. It would be disgraceful to let the word go out to all the world that the United States entered into sacred obligations by treaty and repudiated them the moment their fulfilment proved galling. The protected shipyards, the already subsidized coastwise steamship companies, are asking for more gratuities at the cost of our national honor. What is the use of reëstablishing on the high seas a flag which all peoples may point out as the emblem of a dishonorable state"?

So rests the argument. The advocates of the remission of tolls to the coastwise ships of the United States have the best of the position, since their contention is already enacted into law, but the opposing forces are vigorously urging the repeal of the law. Congress will of course be the final arbiter, and as the Canal cannot be opened to commerce before 1915 there is ample time for deliberation and just judgment. A phase of the problem which I do not recall having seen discussed arises out of the literal acceptance of the language of the treaty as bearing upon the use of the Canal in war time. It declares that the Canal "shall be free and open to the vessels of commerce and of war of all nations . . . on terms of entire equality", and while it goes on to prescribe the rules to be followed in war time it nowhere declares the right of the United States to debar to the warships of a hostile nation the privilege of passing through the Canal. Under the strictest construction of the language of the treaty the refusal of the United States to permit a German or a Japanese fleet to pass through, even though that nation was at war with us, would be a violation of the treaty which would justify English interference to enforce the opening of the Canal—which of course would be war. No such contingency could possibly arise, nor any such construction be put upon the language of the treaty by any reasonable and responsible party. Yet it

GUIDE WALL AT MIRAFLORES

This picture shows method of lock construction. The space within these two walls will be filled with dirt and cement. The ground on either side will be inundated, forming a small lake through which the Canal passes.

is scarcely a more forced construction than the one applied in order to make it appear that we may not free our own ships in purely domestic trade from canal tolls.

The fundamental principle controlling the amount of the tolls is to fix them at such a figure as to minimize the competition of Suez. Commerce proceeds by the cheapest route. Some slight advantage may accrue to the Panama route if the government can make such contracts with American mines as to be able to furnish coal at the Isthmus at a price materially less than is charged at Suez. The estimates, supplied by Prof. Johnson, of probable commerce have been based on a price for coal at Cristobal or Colon of $5 a ton and at Balboa of $5.50 a ton. At the time the prices for coal at Port Said on the Suez

POLING OVER THE SHALLOWS

Canal were from $6.20 to $6.32 a ton. This, plus cheaper tolls, will give Panama a great advantage over Suez.

The first immediate and direct profit accruing to the people of the United States from the Canal will come from the quick, short and cheap communication it will afford between the eastern and western coasts of the United States. People who think of passenger schedules when they speak of communication between distant cities will doubtless be surprised to learn that on freight, an average of two weeks will be saved by the Canal route between New York and San Francisco. The saving in money, even should the railroads materially reduce their present transcontinental rates, will be even more striking. Even now for many classes of freights there is a

THE SPILLWAY ALMOST COMPLETE.

The scaffolding will be removed and all towers built to height of those on left

SAN BLAS LUGGER IN PORT

At least one month's steaming will be saved by 12-knot vessels going through the Panama Canal over those making the voyage by way of the Straits of Magellan. A general idea of the saving in distance between points likely to be affected by the Canal is given by the table prepared by Hon. John Barrett, Director General of the Pan-American Union and published on page 384.

The Pacific coasts both of the United States and of South and Central America will be quickened into new life when the stream of commerce begins to flow through the new channel at Panama. It may be wise to lay emphasis at this point upon the fact that so far as industrial and commercial life on our own Pacific coast is concerned it needs little quickening, as the march to civic greatness of those communities has been unparalleled. But even that magnificent advance has been impeded and harassed by the difficulty of communication with the markets of the Atlantic coast. The struggles of the Pacific coast planters and lumbermen to break the bondage imposed upon them by the railroads have been fairly frantic, and their uniform failure pathetic. Perhaps the railroad managers have demanded no

profit in shipping by way of the Straits of Magellan— a distance of 13,135 miles. By Panama the distance between New York and San Francisco is but 5262 miles, a saving of 7873 miles or about the distance across the Atlantic and back. From New Orleans to San Francisco will be but 8868 miles. Today there is little or no water communication between the two cities and their tributary territory.

Photo by Brown Bros.

THE BEGINNING OF A SLIDE

The great crack has opened in the side of a road; note house in the distance about to go more than a rightful care for the interests of their stockholders warranted. This is no place to argue the railroad rate question. But from the shipper's point of view the demands have been so intolerable that every expedient for resisting them has been tried and failed. Even now there is profit to a corporation—and to the shippers that patronize it— in carrying goods from San Francisco to Hawaii, thence to Tehuantepec and across that Isthmus to the Gulf and thence again to New York in competition with the direct railroad lines. If freight can be thus handled profitably, with two changes from ship to car and vice versa, it is easy to see how vastly beneath the charges of the railroads will be the all-water route between New York and San Francisco. It is little exaggeration to say that for commercial purposes all the Pacific seaboard will be brought as near New York and European markets as Chicago is today. The forward impetus given by this to the commercial interests of the Pacific baffles computation.

But it is Latin America that has reason to look forward with the utmost avidity to the results that will follow the opening of the Canal. For the people of that little developed and still mysterious coast line reaching from the United States-Mexico boundary, as far south at least as Valparaiso, the United States has prepared a gift of in-

THE HAPPY CHILDREN OF THE ZONE

calculable richness. Our share in the benefit will come in increased trade, if our merchants seize upon the opportunity offered.

From Liverpool to Valparaiso today is 8747 miles and from New York 8380. But when the ships go through the Canal the English vessels will save little. For them the run will be reduced to 7207 miles, while from New York the distance will be cut to 4633. With such a handicap in their favor New York shippers should control the commerce of Pacific South America north of Valparaiso. Guayaquil, in Ecuador, will be but 2232 miles from New Orleans; it has been 10,631. Callao, with all Peru at its back, will be 3363 miles from New York, 2784 from New Orleans. In every instance the saving of distance by the Panama route is more to the advantage of the United States than of Great Britain. Today the lion's share of the commerce of the South American countries goes to England or to Germany.

North of the Canal

"MAKING THE DIRT FLY"

DISTANCE SAVED BY THE PANAMA CUTOFF

COMPARATIVE DISTANCES (IN NAUTICAL MILES) IN THE WORLD'S SEA TRAFFIC AND DIFFERENCE IN DISTANCES VIA PANAMA CANAL AND OTHER PRINCIPAL ROUTES

To	Via	From New York	New Orleans	Liverpool	Hamburg	Suez	Panama
Seattle	Magellan	13,953	14,369	14,320	14,701	15,397	......
	Panama	6,080	5,501	8,654	9,173	10,447	4,063
Distance	saved	**7,873**	**8,868**	**5,666**	**5,528**	**4,950**	......
San Francisco	Magellan	13,135	13,551	13,502	13,883	14,579	......
	Panama	5,262	4,683	7,836	8,355	9,629	3,245
Distance	saved	**7,873**	**8,868**	**5,666**	**5,528**	**4,950**	
Honolulu	Magellan	13,312	13,728	13,679	14,060	14,756	......
	Panama	6,702	6,123	9,276	9,795	11,069	4,685
Distance	saved	**6,610**	**7,605**	**4,403**	**4,265**	**3,687**	
Guayaquil	Magellan	10,215	10,631	10,582	10,963	11,659	......
	Panama	2,810	2,231	5,384	5,903	9,192	793
Distance	saved	**7,405**	**8,400**	**5,198**	**5,060**	**2,467**	
Callao	Magellan	9,613	10,029	9,980	10,361	11,057	......
	Panama	3,363	2,784	5,937	6,456	7,730	1,346
Distance	saved	**6,250**	**7,245**	**4,043**	**3,905**	**3,327**	
Valparaiso	Magellan	8,380	8,796	8,747	9,128	9,824	......
	Panama	4,633	4,054	7,207	7,726	9,000	2,616
Distance	saved	**3,747**	**4,742**	**1,540**	**1,402**	**824**	
Wellington	Magellan	11,344	11,760	......	13,353	9,694	......
	Suez			12,989			
	Panama	8,857	8,272	11,425	11,944	9,205	6,834
Distance	saved	**2,493**	**3,488**	**1,564**	**1,409**	**489**	
Melbourne	Cape Good Hope	13,162	14,095	......	11,845	8,186	......
	Suez			11,654			
	Panama	10,392	9,813	12,966	13,452	10,713	8,342
Distance	saved	**2,770**	**4,282**	**1,312**	**1,607**	**2,527**	
Manila	Suez	11,589	12,943	9,701	9,892	6,233	......
	Panama	11,548	10,969	14,122	14,608	11,869	9,370
Distance	saved	**41**	**1,974**	**4,421**	**4,716**	**5,636**	
Hongkong	Suez	11,673	13,031	9,785	9,976	6,317	......
	Panama	11,691	11,112	13,957	14,443	11,704	9,173
Distance	saved	**18**	**1,919**	**4,172**	**4,467**	**5,387**	
Yokohama	Suez	13,566	14,924	11,678	11,869	8,210	......
	Panama	9,798	9,219	12,372	13,858	11,119	7,660
Distance	saved	**3,768**	**5,705**	**694**	**1,989**	**2,909**	
Panama		2,017	1,438	4,591	5,110	6,387	......

See also map on page 385

are the Central American countries of Costa Rica, Nicaragua, Honduras, Salvador, Guatemala and Mexico. On their Gulf coasts harbors are infrequent and poor, but on the Pacific plentiful. Their territory is as yet little developed, but with few manufacturers of their own they offer a still undeveloped market for ours. In all, the twelve Latin-American countries bordering on the Pacific have an area of

to which the Canal will give the readiest access. Here other nations will profit equally with ours unless our merchants show a greater energy in the pursuit of foreign trade than they have of late years. Time was that the old shipping merchants of Boston, Philadelphia and New York asked odds of no man nor of any nation, but had their own ships plying in the waters of all the world, with

THE PANAMA CUT OFF

THIS MAP SHOULD BE STUDIED IN CONNECTION WITH THE TABLE OF COMPARATIVE DISTANCES ON PAGE 384

over 2,500,000 square miles, or about that of the United States exclusive of Alaska and its insular possessions. They have a population of 37,000,000 and their foreign trade is estimated at $740,000,000. In this trade the United States is at the present time a sharer to the extent of $277,000,000 or about 37 per cent. With the Canal in operation it is believed that the total commerce will be doubled and the share of the United States raised to 50 per cent.

However, it is the great Australasian and Asiatic markets, now scarcely touched about the outskirts,

captains who were at once navigators and traders—equally alert to avoid a typhoon and to secure a profitable cargo or charter. But that sort of foreign trade is now vanished with the adventurous spirits who pursued it. Unless conditions governing the American merchant marine materially change within the next two years—of which there seems today no likelihood—it will be England and Germany with their existing lines of ships that will chiefly benefit by the United States $400,000,000 gift to the commerce of the world.

Curiously enough New York, or for that matter

AN ERUPTION OF THE CANAL BED

The pressure of the adjoining hills has forced up the soil at its weakest point, namely the bed of the Canal, to a height of 18 feet,
as shown by the dotted line

any North Atlantic seaport of the United States, is in a sort a way station for ships from Europe to North Asiatic ports. In navigation the straight course is not always the shortest course, for the very simple reason that the equator is the longest way around the world. On account of the curvature of the earth's surface a vessel from Liverpool to Hamburg to the Panama Canal by following the great circle route can make New York a stopping-place by adding only one day's steaming to the voyage. On the other hand a vessel en route from Panama to Yokohama can touch at San Diego and San Francisco with only two days' extra steaming. These facts make for the advantage of the shipper by adding to the vigor of competition for cargoes, but they add to the fierceness of the rivalry which the American ship owner will have to meet and for which the kindly government prepares him by forcing him to buy his ships in the costliest market

and operate them in accordance with a hampering and extravagant system of navigation laws.

The ease however with which English or German ships en route to the Far East may touch at New York, Boston or Philadelphia will doubtless divert to Panama some of the traffic that would find a shorter through route via Suez. For example, from Liverpool to Melbourne is 1312 miles less via Suez than by way of Panama, while to Hongkong it is 694 miles less. Yet it is quite conceivable that the advantage of taking New York or other United States Atlantic ports on the way may secure some of this traffic for Panama.

The really striking saving in time and distance is shown by a comparison of the present distances between our Atlantic coast towns and Australasia and the Orient. Prof. Johnson has put this in two compact tables, which I quote from *The Scientific American:*

TABLE I.—DISTANCES AND TIME SAVED VIA THE PANAMA CANAL AS CONTRASTED WITH ROUTES VIA THE SUEZ CANAL, THE CAPE OF GOOD HOPE, AND THE STRAITS OF MAGELLAN BETWEEN THE ATLANTIC GULF SEABOARD OF THE UNITED STATES AND AUSTRALASIA

| To | FROM NEW YORK | | | | | | FROM NEW ORLEANS | | | | | | REMARKS |
| | Distance saved | Days saved for vessels of | | | | | Distance saved | Days saved for vessels of | | | | | |
		9 knots	10 knots	12 knots	14 knots	16 knots		9 knots	10 knots	12 knots	14 knots	16 knots	
Adelaide...	Miles 1,746	7.5	6.7	5.6	4.6	4.0	Miles 3,258	14.6	13.1	10.8	9.2	8.0	Difference between routes via Panama, Tahiti, Sydney, and Melbourne, and via St. Vincent and Cape of Good Hope.
Melbourne.	2,770	12.3	11.0	9.1	7.7	6.7	4,282	19.3	17.3	14.3	12.2	10.7	Difference between routes via Panama, Tahiti, and Sydney and via St. Vincent, Cape of Good Hope, and Adelaide.
Sydney....	3,932	17.7	15.8	13.1	11.2	9.7	5,444	24.6	22.2	18.4	15.7	13.7	Difference between routes via Panama and Tahiti, and via St. Vincent, Cape of Good Hope, Adelaide, and Melbourne.
Wellington	2,493	11.0	9.9	8.1	6.9	6.0	3,488	15.6	14.0	11.6	9.9	8.6	Difference between routes via Panama and Tahiti and via Straits of Magellan.

TABLE II.—DISTANCES AND DAYS SAVED BY THE PANAMA OR THE SUEZ CANAL BETWEEN THE ATLANTIC GULF SEABOARD OF THE UNITED STATES AND JAPAN, CHINA, THE PHILIPPINES, AND SINGAPORE

| To | Via | FROM NEW YORK | | | | | | FROM NEW ORLEANS | | | | | | REMARKS |
| | | Distance saved | Days saved for vessels of | | | | | Distance saved | Days saved for vessels of | | | | | |
			9 knots	10 knots	12 knots	14 knots	16 knots		9 knots	10 knots	12 knots	14 knots	16 knots	
Yokohama..	Panama.	Miles 3,768	16.9	15.2	12.6	10.7	9.3	Miles 5,705	25.9	23.3	19.3	16.5	14.4	Via San Francisco.
	Suez....	.....	....	....	....	....	....	.....	....	....	....	....	....	Via Colombo, Singapore, Hongkong and Shanghai.
Shanghai	Panama.	1,876	8.1	7.3	6.0	5.1	4.4	3,813	17.1	15.4	12.7	10.8	9.4	Via San Francisco and Yokohama.
	Suez....													Via Colombo, Singapore and Hongkong.
Hong-kong...	Panama.	.....	....	....	....	....	....	1,919	8.4	7.5	6.2	5.2	4.5	Via San Francisco. Yokohama and Shanghai.
	Suez....	18												Via Colombo and Singapore.
Manila..	Panama.	41	....	....	....	....	....	1,978	8.6	7.7	6.4	5.4	4.7	Via San Francisco and Yokohama.
	Suez....													Via Colombo and Singapore.
Singa-pore...	Panama.	.....												Via San Francisco and Yokohama.
	Suez....	2,484	11.0	9.8	8.4	6.9	5.9	547	2.0	1.7	1.4	1.1	0.9	Via Colombo.

So far as Asiatic traffic is concerned, there is almost sure to be some overlapping of routes. Conditions other than those of time and space will occasionally control shipmasters in the choice of a route. But so far as the trade of our Atlantic ports with Hongkong, the Philippines and points north and east thereof is concerned it will all go through Panama. So, too, with the vessels from English, French or German ports. If the contemplated economies offered by the price of coal and fuel oil at Balboa are effected, the inducements of this route will divert from Suez all European shipping bound for Asiatic ports north of India. A careful study of the Suez Canal shows that the trade of the United States with all foreign countries made up 33 per cent of the total traffic, and the commerce of Europe with the west coast of South America comprised 38 per cent. Col. Johnson compiled for the benefit of the Commission a table which showed the vessels which might advantageously have used the Canal in 1909 and 1910, and accompanied it with another giving his estimate of the amount of shipping that actually will use the Canal in 1915 and thereafter. As the expression of official opinion based upon the most careful research, these tables are here republished.

CLASSIFICATION OF ESTIMATED NET TONNAGE OF SHIPPING USING THE PANAMA CANAL IN 1915, 1920 AND 1925

	Average per annum during 1915 and 1916	1920	1925
Coast-to-coast American shipping..............	1,000,000	1,414,000	2,000,000
American shipping carrying foreign commerce of the United States...........	720,000	910,000	1,500,000
Foreign shipping carrying commerce of the United States and foreign countries.................	8,780,000	11,020,000	13,850,000
Total..............	10,500,000	13,344,000	17,000,000

CULEBRA CUT ON A HAZY DAY

NET TONNAGE OF VESSELS THAT MIGHT HAVE AD-
VANTAGEOUSLY USED A PANAMA CANAL
IN 1909–10.

	Total Entrances	Total Clearances	Total Entrances and Clearances
Europe with:			
Western South America.....	1,553,887	1,594,513	3,148,400
Western Central America and Pacific Mexico...........	80,788	118,714	199,502
Pacific United States, British Columbia, and Hawaii....	419,865	269,853	689,718
Pacific United States via Suez Canal.................	(1)	(1)	(1) 158,000
Oriental countries east of Singapore and Oceania....	618,704	555,881	1,174,585
Eastern United States coast with:			
Western South America, Pacific Mexico, and Hawaii..	309,909	166,686	467,595
Pacific Coast of United States (via Cape Horn)..........	117,147	55,508	172,655
Pacific Coast of United States and Hawaii (via American-Hawaiian S.S. Co.)........	181,713	181,713	363,426
Oriental countries east of Singapore and Oceania....	600,000	900,000	1,500,000
Pacific traffic:			
Pacific Coast..............	158,558	259,932	418,490
Atlantic Coast............	....	....	....
Eastern Canada with Alaska, Chile and Australia........	13,410	22,248	35,658
Total..................	4,044,981	4,125,048	8,328,029

NOTE.—(1) Reported by Suez Canal Company; hence the total is not separable into entrances and clearances at American ports.

After all, however, the most patient investigation of the past and the most careful and scientific calculations of the probabilities of the future may produce a wholly inaccurate result. The real effect of the Canal on the world's commerce may be something wholly different from what the experts expect. But we may proceed upon the well-established fact that no new route of swifter and cheaper transportation ever failed to create a great business, and to develop thriving communities along its route. This fact finds illustration in the building up of the suburbs and back country by the development of trolley lines, and, on a larger scale, the prodigious growth of our Pacific coast after the transcontinental railroads had fought their way to every corner of that empire still in the making. Much is uncertain about what the Panama Canal will do for the expansion of our trade and influence, but the one thing that is certain is that no sane man is likely to put the figures of increase and extension too high.

More and more the exports of the United States are taking the form of manufactured goods. The old times when we were the granary of the world are passing away and the moment is not far distant when we shall produce barely enough for our rapidly increasing population. British Columbia is taking

Photo by Brown Bros.

BIRD'S-EYE VIEW OF MIRAFLORES LOCK

At the upper end of the lock the guide wall extends into Miraflores lake; the lower end opens into the tide-water Canal.

up the task of feeding the world where we are dropping it. On the other hand, our manufacturing industry is progressing with giant strides and, while a few years ago our manufacturers were content with their rigidly protected home market, they are now reaching out for the markets of foreign lands. Figures just issued show that in 10 years our exports of manufactured goods have increased 70 per cent. The possibilities of the Asiatic market, which the Canal brings so much more closely to our doors, are almost incalculable. For cotton goods alone China and India will afford a market vastly exceeding any which is now open to our cotton mills, and if, as many hold, the Chinese shall themselves take up the manufacture of the fleecy staple they will have to turn to New England and Pennsylvania for their

HANDLING BROKEN ROCK

machinery and to our cotton belt of states for the material. The ships from Charleston, Savannah, New Orleans and Galveston, which so long steamed eastward with their cargoes of cotton, will in a few years turn their prows toward the setting sun. Indeed these southern ports should be among the first to feel the stimulating effect of the new markets. Southern tobacco, lumber, iron and coal will find a new outlet, and freight which has been going to Atlantic ports will go to the Gulf —the front door to the Canal.

How swiftly and efficiently American manufacturers and jobbers will seize upon the new conditions and avail themselves of this opening of new fields is yet to be determined. The enemies of a protective tariff are not the only ones who hold that it has had the

LOCK CONSTRUCTION SHOWING CONDUITS

result of dulling the keen spirit of adventurous enterprise for which our people were once noted. The absolute possession of a home market ever growing in size and into which no foreigner could enter with any hope of successful competition has naturally engaged at home the attention of our captains of industry. Bold and dashing spirits of the sort that one hundred years ago were covering

president or the head of a great manufacturing industry.

Whether the earlier spirit of world conquest will again spring up in the American mind so long content with the profits of its own national preserves is yet to be demonstrated. To what extent it has vanished any thoughtful traveler in foreign lands observes with a sigh. One sees evidences of its

TRAVELING CRANE HANDLING CONCRETE IN LOCK-BUILDING
These cranes are the striking feature of the Canal landscape, handling thousands of tons of concrete daily

the seas with Baltimore clippers and the output of the New England shipyards turned their attention half a century ago to the building of railroads and the development of our western frontier. When the middle-aged men of today were boys, the heroes of their story books ran away to sea and after incredible adventures came home in command of clipper ships trading to China. Today the same class of fiction starts the aspiring boy in as a brakeman or a mill hand and he emerges as a railroad

weakness at every foreign international exhibition, for the American section is generally the least impressive there. The opinion of our manufacturers is often that to show their products abroad is folly because foreign manufacturers will imitate them with cheaper materials and labor. In most foreign markets, in the cities of Europe, South America and the Orient the chief American products you see displayed are those manufactured by one of those combinations of capital we call a trust, and they are usually sold abroad at lower prices than at home. Typewriters, adding machines, sewing machines, shoes and the divers products of the protean Standard Oil Company seem to be the most vigorous representatives of American industrial activity abroad. Nevertheless the recent statistics show that our experts are on the up-grade, and evidences of growing interest in our export trade multiply daily.

That the Canal of itself will not make amends for indifference or lethargy on the part of our manufacturers goes without saying. The nation may supply them with the waterway, but it cannot compel them to use it, or even teach them how. Every American traveler in South America has groaned over the reports that come from every side concerning the fatuity with which our manufacturers permit themselves to be distanced in the race for the trade of those republics. Our consular reports are filled with suggestions from consuls, but the various associations of exporters are so busy passing platitudinous resolutions about the need of taking the consular service out of politics that they have no time to heed the really valuable suggestions offered. Our methods of packing goods, and our systems of credits, are repugnant to the South American needs and customs and the fact has been set forth in detail in innumerable consular reports without any response on the part of our exporters. The American attitude is "what is good enough at home is good enough abroad"—which is patriotic but not a good rule on which to attempt

MESTIZO GIRL OF CHORRERA

building up foreign trade. Incidentally sometimes what is good enough for a home market is often too good for a Latin-American one. The English and the Germans recognize this and govern themselves accordingly.

It is a far cry from digging a canal to the system of educating young men to represent a firm in foreign lands. Yet one finds in visiting South America, or for that matter Oriental cities, that a great deal of the rapid expansion of German trade is due to the systematic education of boys for business in foreign lands. The weakest part of the educational system of the United States is its indifference to foreign tongues, an indifference possibly quite natural because but few Americans have really any need for any language except their own. But the German representatives sent to South America are at home in the Spanish tongue, and care-

TIVOLI HOTEL FROM HOSPITAL GROUNDS

SANTA ANA PLAZA, PANAMA

This plaza was built up largely during the French régime and the open air cafés are relics of that period of pleasure.
It is the gayest of the town's rallying places.

fully schooled in the commercial needs and customs of the Latin-American countries before they reach them. They are backed, too, by a strong semi-official organization in their own country. They have in most of the principal South American towns German banks quite as interested as the salesmen themselves in the extension of German trade. It is reported that whenever paper involved in an American transaction with a South American buyer passes through a German bank in South America a report of the transaction is sent to some central German agency which tries to divert the next business of the same sort into German hands. I have no personal knowledge of such transactions, but the story is current in South America and it is quite in accord with the German's infinite capacity for taking pains with little things.

Foreign ships, no less than foreign banks and the excellence of foreign commercial schools, are and will continue to be a factor in the building up of foreign trade via the Canal. Just as the German banks report to their home commercial organizations the transactions of other countries in lands whose trade is sought, so foreign ships naturally work for the advantage of the country whose flag they fly. Surprising as it may seem to many, and dis-

HOW CORN IS GROUND

appointing as it must be to all, it is the unfortunate fact that within a year of the time set for opening the Panama Canal to commerce there is not the slightest evidence that that great work is going to have any influence whatsoever toward the creation of a United States fleet in foreign trade. England, Germany, Italy and Japan are all establishing new lines, the last three with the aid of heavy subsidies. But in April, 1913, a recognized authority on the American merchant marine published this statement: "So far as international commerce via Panama is concerned not one new keel is being laid in the United States and not one new ship has even been projected. The Panama Canal act of last August reversed our former policy and granted free American registry to foreign-built ships for international commerce through the Panama Canal or elsewhere. But this 'free-ship' policy has utterly failed. Not one foreign ship has hoisted the American flag, not one request for the flag has reached the Bureau of Navigation".

The reason for this is the archaic condition of our navigation laws. The first cost of a ship, even though somewhat greater when built in American yards, becomes a negligible factor in comparison with a law which makes every expense incurred in

THEY USED TO DO THIS IN NEW ENGLAND

operating it 10 to 20 per cent higher than like charges on foreign vessels. James J. Hill, the great railroad builder, who planned a line of steamships to the Orient and built the two greatest ships that ever came from an American yard, said once to the writer, "I can build ships in the United States as advantageously as on the Clyde and operate has been to deprive the sailor of the ships necessary to earn his livelihood.

However, coastwise shipping will be greatly stimulated by the Canal. In the midst of the lamentation about the disappearance of the American flag from the high seas it is gratifying to reflect that the merchant marine of the United States is really

Photo by Brown Bros.

PILE-DRIVER AND DREDGE AT BALBOA DOCK

them without a subsidy. But neither I nor any other man can maintain a line of American ships at a profit while the navigation laws put us at a disadvantage in competition with those of every other nation". Those mainly responsible for the enactment and maintenance of the navigation laws declare them to be essential to secure proper wages and treatment of the American sailor, but the effect the second in the world, though our share in international shipping is almost negligible. That we rank second as a whole is due to the phenomenal development of our shipping on the great lakes where with a season barely eight months long a shipping business is done that dwarfs the Mediterranean or the German Ocean into insignificance. This has built up a great shipbuilding business on the lakes, and steel ships are even now being built on the Detroit River to engage in Panama trade. There are not wanting those who hold that if the money which has been spent at Panama for the good of the whole world, had been expended in making a thirty-foot ship canal from Lake Erie to tide-water on the Hudson, the benefit to the people of the

Gulf and from the Lakes to the Atlantic. After Panama the nation is unlikely to be daunted by any canal-digging project. Having improved the ocean highway, the people will demand easier access to it. Already there is discussion of whether the railroads will help or hamstring the Canal. Cargoes for the ships have to be gathered in the interior. When delivered

Photo by Brown Bros.

GIANT CEMENT CARRIERS AT WORK

Placed in pairs on either side of a piece of work requiring concrete, these frames support cables in which swing cars carrying concrete and controlled by a workman in the elevated house shown

United States, and to American shipping would have been vastly greater.

Indeed one of the pathetic things in the history of commerce is the persistence with which enterprising Chicagoans, and other mid-westerners, have tried to establish all-water routes to the European markets. All such endeavors have failed, costing their projectors heavily. It will aid, however, if the success of the Panama Canal shall not reanimate the effort to secure deep-water channels from the Lakes to the

at the seaport of their destination they have to be distributed to interior markets. It is in the power of the railroads to make such charges for this service as would seriously impede the economic use of the Canal.

Among the great canals of the world that at Panama ranks easily first in point of cost, though in length it is outdone by many, and its place as a carrier of traffic is yet to be determined. There are now in operation nine artificial waterways which may properly be called ship canals, namely:

1.—The Suez Canal, begun in 1859 and completed in 1869.

2.—The Cronstadt and St. Petersburg Canal, begun in 1877 and completed in 1890.

3.—The Corinth Canal, begun in 1884 and completed in 1893.

4.—The Manchester Ship Canal, completed in 1893.

5.—The Kaiser Wilhelm Canal, connecting the Baltic and North Seas, completed in 1895.

6.—The Elbe and Trave Canal, connecting the North Sea and Baltic, opened in 1900.

7.—The Welland Canal, connecting Lake Erie with Lake Ontario.

8 and 9.—The two canals, United States and Canadian, respectively, connecting Lake Superior with Lake Huron.

The Suez Canal naturally suggests itself for comparison, though it falls far short in volume of traffic of either of the two canals at Sault Ste. Marie, between Lake Superior and Lake Huron. It is ninety miles long, or just about twice the length of the Panama, and about two-thirds of its length is dredged through shallow lakes. It is 31 feet deep as against Panama's 45, with a surface width of 420 feet, while the Panama Canal is from 300 to 1000 feet. The Suez Canal cost slightly under $100,000,-000 and pays dividends at the rate of 12 per cent. Lord Beaconsfield, who bought control of it for England in face of fierce opposition and was savagely denounced for wild-cat financiering, secured for the Empire not merely its strongest bond, but a highly profitable investment as well. The tolls now charged are about $2 a ton according to the United States net measurement.

TRACKS ASCENDING FROM LOWER TO UPPER LOCK
Doors giving access to service tunnels are shown at either side of the central ascent

Of the other canals enumerated some, like the Manchester and the Elbe and Trave Canals, are of purely local importance, while others, like the Kaiser Wilhelm (better known as the Kiel) Canal, are mainly for naval and military purposes. In volume of traffic the first of all canals in the world is the American canal at the "Soo", with the Canadian canal paralleling it a fair second. The volume of traffic passing through these waterways during the eight or nine months they are free from ice is incredible. In 1911 it approximated 40,000,000 tons and exceeded in volume Suez and all the other ship canals heretofore enumerated together. To the facilities for water carriage afforded by this and the neighboring Canadian canal is due much of the rapid growth and development of the country about the western end of Lake Superior. What countries will profit in the same way by the work at Panama? The Pacific coast, both of North and South America. Perhaps South America even more than our own land, for its present state admits of such development.

One problem opened by the Panama Canal which seldom suggests itself to the merely casual mind is the one involved in keeping it clear of the infectious and epidemic diseases for which Asiatic and tropical ports have a sinister reputation. The opening of the Suez Canal was followed by new danger from plague, cholera and yellow fever in Mediterranean countries. A like situation may arise at Panama.

Photo by Brown Bros.

COL. GOETHALS' HOUSE AT CULEBRA

As is fitting, "The Colonel's" house tops the highest hill in Culebra, looking down the cut

It is proposed, though I think not yet officially, to have passing vessels from infected ports inspected at the entrance to the Canal. If infection exists the ship can be fumigated during the passage through the Canal, which will take from ten to twelve hours, while the subsequent voyage to her home port, whether on our Atlantic coast or in Europe, will make any subsequent delay in quarantine needless. The plague is the disease most dreaded in civilized communities, which it only enters by being brought by ship from some Asiatic port in which it is prevalent. Its germs can be carried by rats as well as by human beings, and for this reason in some ports vessels from suspected ports are not allowed to come up to a dock lest the rodents slip ashore carrying the pestilence. Sometimes in such ports you will see a vessel's hawsers obstructed by large metal disks, past which no rat may slip if he tries the tight-rope route to the shore. The new contracts for wharves, docks and piers at all our Zone ports prescribe that they shall be rat-proof. Indeed the rodents are very much under the ban in Panama, and the annual slaughter by the Sanitary Department exceeds 12,000.

Preparations are being made to make Balboa a quarantine station of world-wide importance. The mere proximity of the date for opening the Canal has caused discussion of its effect upon the health of civilized nations. At Suez an International Board exists for the purpose of so guarding that gateway from the East that none of the pestilences for which the Orient has an ill-fame can slip through. No suggestion has been made of international control at nation alone. Despite this cheerful optimism of Europe, there has not yet been a very prompt acquiescence by Congress in the estimates presented by

ELECTRIC TOWING LOCOMOTIVES ON A LOCK

Panama. In fact such of the foreign articles as have come under my eye have been flattering to us as a nation, asserting, as they all do, that in sanitary science the United States is so far ahead that the quarantine service may be safely entrusted to this Col. Gorgas for the permanent housing and maintenance of the quarantine service. Since the United States is to give the Canal to the world, it should so equip the gift that it will not be a menace to the world's health.

CHAPTER XX

DIPLOMACY AND POLITICS OF THE CANAL

HAVING built the Panama Canal at a heavy cost of treasure and no light cost of life, having subdued to our will the greatest forces of nature and put a curb upon the malevolent powers of tropical miasma and infection, we are about to give the completed result to the whole world. It stands as a free gift, for never can any tolls that will be imposed make of it a commercial success. It was the failure to recognize this inevitable fact that made it impossible for the French to complete the task. It will be a national asset, not because of the income gathered at its two entrances, but because of the cheapening of freight rates between our two coasts and the consequent reduction of prices to our citizens. But this advantage will accrue to peoples who have not paid a dollar of taxation toward the construction of the Canal. There is absolutely no advantage which the Canal may present to the people of New England that will not be shared equally by the people of the Canadian provinces of Quebec and Ontario if they desire to avail themselves of the opportunity. Our gulf ports of Mobile, New Orleans and Galveston expect, and reasonably so, that the volume of their traffic will be greatly in-

creased by the opening of the Canal. But if Rio de Janeiro, Buenos Ayres and Montevideo have products they desire to ship to the Orient or to the western coast of their own continent of South America the Canal is open to them as freely as to our ships.

Having given to the world so great a benefaction, it will be the part of the international statesmen of the United States, the diplomatists, to see to it that the gift is not distorted, nor, through any act of ours, divided unequally among those sharing in it. Upon the diplomacy of the United States the opening of the Canal will impose many new burdens and responsibilities.

Scarcely any general European war involved more intricate and delicate questions of the reciprocal rights of nations than did the acquisition of the Suez Canal by Great Britain. Volumes have been

A CHURCH IN CHORRERA

399

A NATIVE KITCHEN

America, where that doctrine should be hailed as a bulwark of protection, it is looked upon askance. That feeling is largely due to the attitude of this country toward the Republic of Colombia at the time of the secession of Panama.

A problem of the highest importance to the credit of the United States in Latin America, which should be settled in accordance with principles of national honor and international equity, is the determination of what reparation we owe the Republic of Colombia for our part in the revolution which made Panama an independent state and gave us the Canal Zone.

written on the subject of the diplomacy of Suez. The Constantinople conference called for the discussion of that topic, and the specific delimitation of the authority of Great Britain and the rights of other maritime nations was one of the most notable gatherings in the history of diplomacy. The Panama waterway will bring new problems and intensify old ones for the consideration of our statesmen. The Monroe Doctrine is likely to come in for a very thorough testing and perhaps a new formulation. The precise scope of that doctrine has of late years become somewhat ill defined. Foreign nations say that the tendency of the United States is to extend its powers and ignore its responsibilities under this theory. In Latin

In an earlier chapter I have tried to tell, without bias, the story of that revolution and to leave to the readers' own judgment the question whether our part in it was that merely of an innocent bystander, a neutral looker-on, or whether we did not, by methods of indirection at least, make it impossible

NATIVE HOUSE IN PENOMENE

for Colombia to employ her own troops for the suppression of rebellion in her own territory. As President, and later as private citizen, Mr. Roosevelt was always exceedingly insistent that he had adhered to the strictest letter of the neutrality law—always that is except in that one impetuous speech in San Francisco, in which he blurted out the boast, "I took Panama and left Congress to debate about it afterward".

Mr. Roosevelt's protestations of innocence had, however, little effect upon his own friends and party associates, for early in the Taft administration the conviction became general among men in high station that reparation of some sort was due to Colombia for what was—to express it guardedly—our connivance at a conspiracy that cost that republic its richest province—cost it further a lump payment of $10,000,000 and an annual sum of $250,000 to eternity. The records of diplomacy are enmeshed in many concealing veils, but enough is known of the progress of the negotiations to reflect

A STREET IN CHORRERA

credit upon the diplomacy of Colombia. That country has neither threatened nor blustered—and the undeniable fact that the comparative power of Colombia and the United States would make threats and bluster ridiculous would not ordinarily deter a Latin-American President from shrieking shrill defiance at least for the benefit of his compatriots. Colombia has been persistent but not petulant. It has stated its case to two administrations and has wrung from both the confession that the United States in that revolution acted the part of an international bandit. Out of the recesses of the Department of State has leaked the information that the United States has made to Colombia a tentative offer of $10,000,000, but that it had been refused. But the offer itself was a complete confession on the part of the United States of its guilt in the transaction complained of. Naturally, Colombia declined the proffered conscience money. Panama received from the United States not merely $10,000,000, but will get $250,000 a year for an indefinite period. All this Colombia lost and her valuable province as well because the captain of a United States man-of-war would not let the Colombian

GIANT CACTI OFTEN USED FOR HEDGING

Planted close together, these cacti form a barrier impassible by animals colonels on that day of revolution use force to compel a railroad manager to carry their troops across the Isthmus. The grievance of the Colombians is a very real and seemingly just one.

We hear much of the national honor in reference to canal tolls but less of it in relation to this controversy with Colombia. Yet that controversy ought to be settled and settled justly. It is inconceivable, of course, that it should be determined by restoring the status as it existed before that day of opera-

President Roosevelt wrote the word Panama on the list of nations and moved on vastly pleased with the record.

The situation at the same time is one not to be lightly dealt with. The United States is none too popular at any point south of its own borders. It is at the one time hated and feared. The very Panamanians whom we invested with independence have no liking for us and the hatred of the Colombians for the nation that despoiled them is so general and

Photo by Brown Bros.

THE TOWN OF EMPIRE, SOON TO BE ABANDONED

bouffe revolution. Our investment in the Canal Zone, our duty to the world which awaits the opening of the Canal, and our loyalty to our partner in crime, Panama, alike make that impossible. The Republic of Panama is an acccomplished fact not to be obliterated even in the interest of precise justice. As the Persian poet put it:

"The moving finger writes, and having writ
   Moves on; nor all your piety nor wit,
Shall lure it back to cancel half a line,
   Nor all your tears wash out one word of it".

extreme that their rulers are entitled to the utmost credit for having observed all the courtesies of diplomacy in their efforts to secure some measure of reparation. The question presents itself, is it wise to leave such a hot-bed of hatred, of resentment perhaps justifiable, in the very midst of Latin America, just when we are hoping by our new Canal to extend and cement our commercial relations with them? Among the Latin Americans there is a very general feeling that our devotion to the Monroe Doctrine is indicative only of our purpose to protect our neighbors against any selfish aggressions except our own. It is of the very highest importance that this feeling be dissipated, and there is perhaps no more immediate way of beginning that task than by reaching such an agreement with Colombia as shall indicate to other South American governments our purpose of doing exact justice among our neighbors, be they great and powerful or small and weak.

With all the South American countries the commerce of the Canal will tend to bring us into closer

besides maintaining two nitrate plants in Chile does a prodigious business in explosives with the various states—and not mainly for military purposes only. The United States Steel Company has a vanadium mine in Peru where 3000 Americans are working. The equipment of street railways and electric-lighting plants in South American cities is almost wholly of American manufacture. Even without the systematic encouragement of their home government, American business men have begun to make

THE PANAMA RAILROAD BRIDGE AT GAMBOA

relations and to multiply the possibility of international dissension. Moreover, the growing interests of United States business men in those countries form national outposts on which we must ever keep a friendly eye. It is ridiculous to urge upon individuals the task of stimulating and extending our foreign trade if the government is to be wholly indifferent to their efforts. It is known that the great beef packers of Chicago have considerable plants in the Argentine; that a famous iron manufacturer of Pittsburgh has in Chile what is believed to be the largest iron mine in the world; that the Standard Oil Company has its agencies throughout the continent; and the Du Pont Powder Company

inroads upon German and English commercial power in South America, and the opening of the Canal will increase their activities. Today our Pacific coast is practically shut off from any interchange of commodities with Brazil and the Argentine; with the Canal open a direct waterway will undoubtedly stimulate a considerable trade. The more trade is stimulated, the more general travel becomes between nations, the less becomes the danger of war. There is no inconsistency in the statement that the Canal will become a powerful factor in the world's peace, even though it does necessitate the maintenance of a bigger navy and the erection of powerful forts for its defense in the improbable event of war.

A STREET IN CHORRERA

This is but one phase of the influence the Canal will exercise upon countries other than the United States. What it will do for the Latin-American countries immediately adjacent to Panama in the direction of leading them to establish improved sanitation systems, or to perfect those they now maintain, is beyond present estimate. Many such governments have had their representatives on the Zone to study the methods there in force, and while the present writer was there Col. Gorgas was besought to visit Guayaquil to give its rulers expert advice on the correction of the unsanitary state of that city. Members of the staff of Col. Gorgas are in demand as experts in all parts of the world. I know of one who in the last days of the Canal construction was sent by the German government to establish in some of the German South African provinces the methods that brought health to the Isthmus after the days of the futile French struggle with fever and malaria.

It is because of this influence upon foreign peoples, already apparent, that far-sighted people find intolerable the proposition to let the Canal Zone grow up into jungle and return to its original

state of savagery. It can and should be made an object lesson to the world. From every ship that makes the ten-hour passage of the Canal some passengers will go ashore for rest from the long voyage and to see what the Zone may have to show them. Are we content to have them see only the hovels of Colon and the languid streets of Panama—exhibits that give no idea of the force, the imagination, the idealism that gave being to the Canal? Today the Zone is a little bit of typical United States life set down in the tropics. So it might remain if due encouragement were given to industrious settlers. There is not so much land in the world that this need be wasted, nor have there been so many examples of the successful creation and continuance of such a community as the Zone has been as to justify its obliteration before the world has grasped its greatest significance.

There are not lacking those philosophers who hold that the first political effect of the Canal will be to force us to abandon that attitude of national isolation and aloofness prescribed in Washington's deprecation of "entangling alliances abroad". They hold that this latest and greatest addition to our reasons for solicitude about the control of the Pacific will compel us to seek the coöperation of other powers—or *another* power —to make that control

A PEARL ISLAND VILLAGE

complete. Perhaps the proposition is most frankly stated in this paragraph from Mr. Frank Fox's "Problems of the Pacific".

"The friendly coöperation between the United States and Great Britain would give to the Anglo-Saxon race the mastery of the world's greatest ocean, laying forever the fear of the Yellow Peril, securing for the world that its greatest readjustment of the balance of power shall be effected in peace, while rivalry between these two kindred nations may cause the gravest evils and possibly irreparable disasters".

This is no place to discuss this thesis, but even the most casual consideration shows how great a mutual interest the United States and Great Britain have in the Panama Canal and its safeguarding from any disturbing conditions in the Pacific. Until conditions change and the United States regains its place among the maritime nations of the world the bulk of the trade passing through the Canal will be in British ships. For New Zealand and all of the eastern part of British Australia the Panama route offers the most expeditious connection with Liverpool. Canada, too, is vitally interested in the Canal. By the employment of the system of Georgian Bay and St. Lawrence Canals, which the Dominion government has created, with a foresight far greater than our own, the wheat, even of the Winnipeg region, may be sent by water

DIAGRAM OF COMPARATIVE EXCAVATIONS BY THE FRENCH AND AMERICANS
IN CULEBRA CUT

BIRD'S-EYE VIEW OF THE PANAMA CANAL

NATIVE WOMAN, COCLE

promises no support to Japan in the event of the latter being the aggressor.

Any formal convention, however, any international agreement for the control of the Pacific which should leave Germany out, would be an incentive to trouble rather than a bright harbinger of peace. For no nation is making more active and intelligent preparations to reap to the fullest the advantages of the Canal than are the Germans. Their nation's great interests in Brazil, Argentine, and Chile, her colonizing activities in Asia, her Chinese port of Kiau-Chou, forcibly wrested from China, all impel her to take a lively interest in the Canal and the Pacific. The Kaiser would not look with any placid indifference upon such an Anglo-American agreement as has been urged, and as its ends can be, and probably

to Montreal and thence in sea-going ships to the further shore of the Pacific. Even though owned by the United States, the Canal will be a powerful tie to bind closer together the widely separated parts of the British Empire.

That being true it will further cement the spirit of friendliness between the United

RIVER VILLAGE IN CHIRIQUI

will be attained without formal pronouncement, any open diplomatic negotiations for such a convention would probably be unwise. Enough to say that while speculation concerning such an agreement is quite general among publicists today, no discussion of

States and Great Britain. It will accomplish it has yet engaged the attention of any statesmen. this without formal treaties or proclaimed alliance. The alliance will be tacit, resulting from the very logic of the situation. Great Britain cannot afford to be otherwise than friendly with the owner of the Canal—the little passing tiff over the question of tolls on coastwise shipping notwithstanding. It is idle to ask that the control of the Pacific be assured by an Anglo-American compact. More intelligent is it to assume that any effort to break down that control, which now virtually exists, would be met by action on the part of the two English-speaking nations quite as effective as though a treaty existed. This, too, despite the present Anglo-Japanese treaty which so disquiets our California citizens, but quite needlessly, in fact, because of that convention for it

THE PEARL ISLAND VILLAGE OF SABOGA

After considering the problem of what the Canal will be worth, let us reverse the ordinary process and figure out what it will cost. Exact statement is still impossible, for as this book is being printed the Canal is months away from being usable and probably two years short of completion if we reckon terminals and fortifications as part of the completed work.

In an earlier chapter I have set forth some of the estimates of its cost from the figure of $131,000,000 set by the volatile De Lesseps to the $375,000,000 of the better informed and more judicious Goethals. In June, 1913, however, we had at hand the official report of all expenditures to March, 1913, duly classified as follows:

It is worth noting that all this colossal expenditure of money has been made without any evidence of graft, and practically without charge of that all-pervading canker in American public work. During a long stay on the Isthmus, associating constantly with men in every grade of the Commission's service, I never heard a definite charge of illegal profits being taken by anyone concerned in the work. In certain publications dealing with the undertaking in its earlier days one will find assertions of underhanded collusion with contractors and of official raids upon the more select importations of the Commissary without due payment therefore. But even these charges were vague, resting only on hearsay, and

CLASSIFIED EXPENDITURES—ISTHMIAN CANAL COMMISSION

A statement of classified expenditures of the Isthmian Canal Commission to March 31, 1913, follows:

Periods	Department of Civil Administration	Department of Law	Department of Sanitation	Department of Construction and Engineering	General Items	Fortifications	Total
Total to June 30, 1909....	$3,427,090.29	....	$9,673,539.28	$69,622,561.42	$78,022,606.10	....	$160,745,797.09
Total—Fiscal Year, 1910...	709,351.37	....	1,803,040.95	26,300,167.05	2,863,088.83	....	31,675,648.20
Total—Fiscal Year, 1911...	755,079.44	....	1,717,792.62	27,477,776.19	3,097,959.72	....	33,048,607.97
Total—Fiscal Year, 1912...	820,398.57	24,729.16	1,620,391.12	28,897,738.10	2,819,926.53	1,212,881.66	35,396,065.14
July, 1912...............	63,913.12	1,448.53	123,803.64	2,649,246.61	200,970.55	104,126.92	3,143,509.37
August, 1912............	62,182.51	1,468.26	123,154.48	2,539,680.83	*98,054.61	111,402.55	2,739,834.02
September, 1912.........	59,201.01	1,207.82	120,385.70	2,285,979.89	77,003.53	127,168.25	2,670,946.20
October, 1912...........	64,383.37	2,033.75	137,574.61	2,473,280.76	83,523.30	129,736.37	2,890,532.16
November, 1912.........	62,200.12	1,892.14	119,031.66	2,420,085.77	75,779.01	300,016.33	2,979,005.03
December, 1912..........	58,987.96	1,462.18	115,819.26	2,871,977.03	120,946.61	118,152.57	3,287,345.61
January, 1913...........	57,699.58	1,469.59	114,562.04	2,825,872.06	6,463.72	119,272.77	3,125,339.76
February, 1913..........	56,586.06	1,649.00	127,324.80	3,784,370.51	123,034.12	314,994.96	4,407,959.45
March, 1913.............	58,761.03	1,899.22	105,891.08	2,712,218.10	7,706.70	131,940.75	3,003,003.48
Grand total..........	$6,255,834.43	$39,259.65	$15,902,311.24	$176,860,954.32	$87,385,540.71	$2,669,693.13	$289,113,593.48

*Denotes credit.

It will be observed that since the beginning of the fiscal year 1913, expenditures have averaged a trifle over $3,000,000 a month. This rate of expenditure may be expected to decrease somewhat during the eighteen months likely to elapse before the Canal, terminals and forts are completed. Probably if we allow $250,000 a month for this decrease we will be near the mark making the future expenditures average $2,750,000 monthly until January, 1915, making in all $57,750,000. Adding this to the Commission expenditures up to March 31, 1913, and adding further the $50,000,000 paid to the French stockholders and the Republic of Panama we reach the sum of $396,863,593—a reasonable estimate of the final cost of the great world enterprise; the measure in dollars and cents of the greatest gift ever made by a single nation to the world.

had to do with an administration which vanished six or more years ago. Today that chronic libeler "the man in the street" has nothing to say about graft in connection with Canal contracts, and "common notoriety", which usually upholds all sorts of scandalous imputations, and is cited to maintain various vague allegations, is decidedly on the side of official integrity at Panama.

This is not to say that the work has been conducted with an eye single to economy. It has not. That is to say it has not been conducted in accordance with the common idea of economy. All over the land contractors, apprehensive of the effect of the Panama example of government efficiency in public work, are telling how much more cheaply they could have dug the Panama Canal. Probably they could if they could have dug it at all. But the sort of

THE BROOK AT TABOGA

largest employer of labor in the land. It ought to be the best employer. On the Zone it has been the best employer, and has secured the best results. When government work is to be done hereafter it will not be let out to private contractors without hesitation and discussion. A consideration of the results obtained by the State of New York in its latest expenditure, by the methods of private contract, of the Erie Canal appropriation of $101,-000,000, will go far to show the superiority of the Panama system. In a recent interview the Secretary of the Navy, Josephus Daniels, declared it to be the policy of the Department to build battleships in navy yards so far as possible—a policy which the shipbuilding interests have steadily resisted in the past. It is not too much to infer that the success of the army in digging a canal encouraged the Secretary to show what the navy could do in building its own ships.

economy they are talking about was definitely abandoned when Col. Gorgas convinced the Commission that it was reckless extravagance to save $50,000 or so on wire screens and lose forty or fifty lives in a yellow-fever epidemic. The contractor's idea of economy was emphatically set aside when Col. Goethals determined that it was cheaper to pay engineers one-third more than the current rate at home, and make such arrangements for their comfort on the Zone that they would stay on the job, rather than to pay ordinary prices and have them leave in haste after a month or two of dissatisfied and half-hearted work.

From which it appears that a new definition of "economy" is needed in the application of the word to the Canal work.

Whatever may be the influence of the Canal on the position of the United States as a world power, its influence on the industrial life at home is likely to be all pervasive and revolutionary. The government is the

If the system and conditions of employment that have existed in Panama could be applied to public

ONE OF THE SMALLER SLIDES
This slide, near Bas Obispo, blocked the tracks for a week

service in all other parts of the United States, the condition of all labor, all industry, all professional service would be correspondingly improved. For with the most extensive employer setting the pace all others would have to keep step with it.

When the long account comes to be balanced we may find that the United States will owe quite as much to the Panama enterprise on the moral as on the material side. Of course it is going to increase our trade both foreign and domestic—that, as the

cities along the Atlantic coast. At the same time the output of our eastern steel mills and New England cotton and woolen factories will find a more expeditious and cheaper route to the builders and workers of the Pacific coast.

Incidentally the labors of the Interstate Commerce Commission are likely to be multiplied almost incalculably. For it must be accepted as a fact that free competition is no longer a complete regulator of freight rates whether by rail or by water. Any

GIANT STEAM MIXERS

These machines discharge the mixed concrete into the carriers, which electric locomotives drag to the cranes at the top of the lock shown in the distance

French say, goes without saying. It will cheapen the cost of building cottages in New York suburbs, because lumber will be brought from the forests of Oregon and Washington for half the freight cost now exacted. It will stimulate every manufacturing interest on the Pacific coast for coal from West Virginia will be laid down there at dollars per ton less than now. The men who catch and can salmon in the rushing waters of the Columbia, the men who raise and pack the luscious oranges of southern California will have a new and cheaper way of carrying their products to the eager markets of the great

one can charter a ship and send it through the Canal with the same rights and privileges that a long established line will enjoy. But not every independent ship can find dockage facilities at both ends of its voyage, although it is true that the enterprising cities of the Pacific coast are warding off monopoly by building municipal docks. Moreover, the owner of the independent ship will have his troubles in getting the railroads at either end to handle his cargoes and distribute them at such charges as will leave him any profit. Indeed the independent ship will be but little of a factor in fixing rates. That will be done by the regular lines. Normally there should be keen competition between the railroads and the steamships with a very marked drop in rates. But it will not be well to base too great hopes on this possibility. Transportation rates, even where there is nominally free competition, are not often based wholly on the cost of the service. What the traffic will bear is more often the chief factor in rate making. Because ships can carry freight from New York to San Francisco for three

less vigilance and probably necessitate a material extension of its authority.

In other than material ways the nation will largely profit. I think that the fact of the Canal's having been built by army engineers will go far toward correcting a certain hostility toward the army which is common in American thought. The Canal proves that the organization of the army, the education of its officers, is worth something in peace as well as in war. Of course this has been shown before in

MACHINERY WRECKED BY A SLIDE
This damage was wrought overnight. A new track must be built to extricate the less injured shovel

dollars a traffic-ton less than the railroads does not imply that they will do so. Nor does it ensure that railroad rates will drop spasmodically in a vain effort to keep all the business away from the ships. Rather is it probable that certain classes of freight like lumber, coal and ore will be left wholly to the ships, and some form of agreement as to the essentials of the general rate card will be arrived at. It is this agreement, which in some form or other is sure to come, that will engage the attention of the Interstate Commerce Commission, arouse its cease-

countless public works scattered over the land, but never hitherto in a fashion to command such attention and to compel such plaudits. There were five Colonels, besides "The Colonel," on the Commission which put the big job through, and I do not believe that the most shrinking civilian who visited the Isthmus on either business or pleasure found any ground to complain of militarism, or was overawed by any display of "fuss and feathers."

The Canal Zone was, of course, a rural community harboring about 65,000 people scattered along a railroad 47 miles long. Yet in the story of its government there is much that is instructive to the rulers of our American cities. Every head of the Department of Sanitation in an American city would profit by a study of Col. Gorgas's methods in dealing with the problems of dirt, sewage, and infection. Indeed many of the ideas he developed are already being adapted to the needs of North American municipalities. It is becoming quite evident that the scientific method of controlling insect pests by destroying their breeding places is the only efficient one. The larvacide man in the waste places, or the covered garbage can, and screened stable are not as melodramatic as newspaper shrieks of "Swat the Fly", but they accomplish more in the end.

The management of the Panama Railroad by and for the government affords an object lesson that will be cited when we come to open Alaska. Though over-capitalized in the time of its private ownership and operation the railroad under the direction of Col. Goethals has paid a substantial profit. Though rushed with the work incident to the Canal construction it has successfully dealt with its commercial business, and has offered in many ways a true example of successful railway management.

But to my mind more important than any other outcome of the Canal work, is its complete demonstration of the ability of the United States to do its own work for its own people, efficiently, successfully and honestly. That is an exhibit that will not down. The expenditure of fully $375,000,000 with no perceptible taint of graft is a victory in itself. There

Photo by Thompson

THE GREAT FALLS OF CHORRERA

are exceedingly few of our great railroad corporations that can show as clean a record, and the fact somewhat depreciates the hostility of some of their heads to the extension into their domain of the activities of the government. In urging this point no one can be blind to the fact that the Zone was governed and the Canal work directed by an autocrat. But the autocrat was directly subject to Congress and had to come to that body annually for his supplies of money. It was dug by the army, but no one now doubts that the navy could have done as well, and few will question that, with the Panama experience as a guide, a mixed commission of civilians and military and naval officers could efficiently direct any public work the nation might undertake.

wholly by the United States, it is to exist for the general good of all mankind, it should be, in the ages to come, the greatest glory attached to the American flag. In abolishing human slavery we only followed last in the train of all civilized nations.

A TWENTIETH CENTURY LINER LOCKING

The bulk of the world trade is done in ships of between 8,000 and 12,000 tons. A ship of the Olympic type would have 50 feet leeway at either fore and aft, nearly 10 feet on either beam in the lock at Gatun

So with the Panama Canal approaching completion we can see that its effects are to be manifold— domestic as well as foreign, moral as well as material, political as well as economic. If it be properly conducted in its completed state, managed and directed upon the broad principle that, though paid for

But in tearing away the most difficult barrier that nature has placed in the way of world-wide trade, acquaintance, friendship and peace, we have done a service to the cause of universal progress and civilization the worth of which the passage of time will never dim.

F